FIGHTING THE CURRENT

L. J. WEDE

ISBN:

978-1-965706-05-3 (Digital)

978-1-965706-03-9 (Paperback)

978-1-965706-04-6 (Hardcover)

CONTENT EXPECTATIONS

Certain scenes in this book may be upsetting for some readers. A non-exhaustive list of potentially upsetting content may be reviewed at https://ljwede.com/content-warnings/.

To my cat, Morticia, who made writing this a lot harder.

CONTENTS

AUTHOR'S NOTE

You guys didn't think I'd leave Sparks and Astrid hanging like
that, did you?

I may be cruel, but my maleficence only extends to killing off
beloved characters and crafting tear-wrenching scenarios for my
protagonists to live through.

In this novel, I really wanted to dig my teeth into the concept of
overwhelmingly strong emotions masquerading as other
feelings. There's a fine line between love and hate, between
passion and fury, between heartache and desperation.

How can you care about someone you despise so deeply? How
can you force yourself to work alongside a person who is
opposed to everything you stand for?

I won't spoil too much (all of the answers are in the next three
hundred or so pages), but let it be said, it's not easy. Even more
so when the two of them are fighting for their lives on the daily.

Here's to hoping that dinosaurs will come back to life.

— L. J. Wede

CHAPTER 1
ASTRID

Water. It has a spirituality. Water heals and revitalizes. Picture your mother's chicken noodle soup, or perhaps more relevant to my situation, your morning coffee. My family has always had a special connection to this element, so when the spirits gave me the power to control and influence water, it felt right.

My eyes scan the patrons of the cafe as I pull another shot of espresso. It's a busy day, a few more customers than I would normally expect this late in the afternoon, but it's nothing I can't handle. I reach out with my mind and take stock of the mugs scattered around the room. A few of them have gotten a bit cool, so I raise their temperature to a soothing warm.

That's what makes a coffee shop successful, being able to keep water at the perfect temperature. Not many people know this, but coffee beans need to be steeped at a certain temperature for a specific amount of time. Too many shops just boil water and dump it in! No passion, no precision, no care for the perfect beverage.

Not here, not at Brew for Two. I'm not messing around. Every blend is steeped at the optimum temperature to bring out the sultry flavors of the beverage, while tamping the bitter notes. Then, I make sure the drinks stay at the perfect drinking temperature so the guests can enjoy the coffee in their own time.

Of course... I do cheat a bit. Having powers does make this a lot easier. I can feel the ambient temperature of all of the liquids around me and correct them when necessary.

Technically, I don't even really need most of the machines around me – I could just heat the drinks myself – but people would find that very strange.

The bell on the door rings, drawing my attention away from the cappuccino in progress. Dolores, one of my regulars, walks in. She's a prickly lady with her hair in a tight gray bun, but deep inside there is a warm and caring person. Deep, deep inside. It was hard for her when Edmund, her former husband, passed away a few years ago, but she still stops by the cafe several times a week with the crossword tucked under her arm. That crossword is the most important thing in the world to her, so much so that she won't let anyone help. Anyone except... nevermind.

"Good afternoon, Dolores!" I greet, hoping my happiness is infectious. "Standard black coffee today?"

"That will be sufficient." Dolores nods neatly and pulls out her pocketbook. Exact change, as always. She leans to the side and peeks into the back room.

"Sasha is helping out today." A fake smile is plastered on my face. I know who she is looking for. It's been months, yet Dolores always checks. I've told Dolores that she's gone, no longer a member of the team, but she always responds the same way.

"Let me know when Anise comes in," Dolores curtly instructs.

"Perhaps I could help with your crossword?" I offer. Stop asking about her. Stop asking about her. Stop asking. "I'm happy to give it a shot."

"I'll wait." She straightens out her crisp jacket, a bit warm for today but you never know the weather in the spring. "I know she'll be back."

"Let me know if you change your mind." I force myself to look happy, but on the inside, I feel a crack in my mask. I quickly pour her black coffee and slide it across the counter. "Enjoy!"

Dolores takes the mug and strolls to her usual seat. I deliver the cappuccino to a college student working on some essay and make my way to the back, picking up empty cups as I go. Sasha is there, scrubbing dishes in soapy water. She moves to take the tray from me, but I wave her off.

"Do you mind manning the front for a minute?" I ask. "I'll take care of these dishes."

"You sure?" She tilts her head and looks at me. It's unusual, I know. Normally, you can't peel me away from the counter. But after an affirming nod, Sasha bops toward the front of the house.

I slump against the sink, my shoulders sagging as I try to keep my composure from slipping away. It's been months, but I still feel the stab when she crosses my mind.

Her red hair flying as she speeds down the street on her motorcycle.

Her smirk as she teases me for something stupid.

Her sinful grin as she lowers her head between my...

Fuck.

It's been a few years since I took up the crusade of the Water Weaver, using my powers to try and make the world around me a better place. When I first donned the mask, I promised myself that no matter what, I would never kill anyone. After all, would I be any better than the criminals I catch if I did? No, it wasn't something I would ever consider doing.

Until I did.

For her.

I still remember the biting cold of that December night. The knife glinting in the moonlight, inches from her stomach. The horror I felt knowing she was about to die. I didn't know what I was doing until I pulled the trigger. The growing patch of red on his torso. My panic when he dragged her overboard with him, into the inky black water.

I dove into the water after them, desperately searching for any sign of life. Finding her limp body was the scariest moment of my life. I pleaded with every god I could name that she would be okay as I used my powers to draw the water from her lungs.

I went back into the ocean, searching for the man I shot... but he was gone. And I couldn't forgive myself.

So I broke up with her. After all the lies, cover ups, deceit, I was done. I turned my back and walked across the sandy beach, leaving her alone by the shore.

I tell myself every day that I made the right choice.

But every day, I'm not convinced.

"The crowd's dying out," Sasha says. I jump, not realizing I wasn't alone anymore. "I can finish the rest of the shift by myself if you want to bounce."

"You sure?" I snap my shoulders back. "Wouldn't want to leave you hanging."

"I've got it." She smiles, and for a moment, I think she can see through my mask. No, there's nothing to see. Everything is fine. I'm fine.

"Okay then, I'm going to do boring owner's paperwork upstairs," I chuckle. "Give me a call if a wave comes in and you need another pair of hands."

Sasha shoos me off as I hang up my apron. I leave the shop and walk up the stairs to my apartment. It's still strange to me to have employees manning the shop on their own. I used to run the cafe entirely by myself. Anise would pop in and wash dishes when she didn't have a freelance contract that day, the customers all loved her. But then we broke up, and I decided I needed an extra set of hands. I hired a few part-timers, then a manager, and now I have a full roster of team members. I don't remember how long it took me to realize that I didn't need another pair of hands, I just missed hers.

But it is nice to be able to step away from the cafe. Go on vacations, take a day off, or just sit on my sofa and ruminate on the past. Business has been booming recently. Things must be going well, so then why do I feel like everything is wrong?

Mimi says that when it feels like the world is against you, it is time for a spiritual cleansing. Grandmas always know what is best, so I figure I should take a quick shower. I fill a sachet with rosemary, lavender, and sage, and tie it to the showerhead. Soon, the steam is carrying their scent through my apartment.

As the hot water flows down my body, I fight against the flashbacks streaking through my mind. Her body wash. Her hands. Water dripping down her curves. I dunk my head into the downpour, but I can't shake the sensation of her fingertips trailing down my back. Frustrated, I turn off the shower. With a single thought, I use my powers to dry off, directing the water down the drain.

I pull my hair into a high ponytail, tugging the ends to make it tight. It doesn't do any good for me to be moping in my self-pity. I broke up with her. It's over. I need to pull myself together.

I walk over to my closet and open the doors, ignoring the boxes of Anise's things. She never came back. She didn't bang on my door in the rain, begging for a second chance. She didn't ask for any of her clothes. I thought at least she'd come back for her viola, but I haven't seen her since that night on the beach.

Deep breath. Focus. I push my clothes aside and slide open the hidden panel in the back, revealing my Water Weaver costume and mask. The cobalt blue fabric glides over my skin, while the tulle overlay adds a subtle shimmer. I love the material that drapes across my torso, and how a second piece falls behind me as a skirt. It's so fluid as I move, it makes me feel lithe and graceful. My reflection catches my eye, and a wave of conviction courses through my body. My shoulders roll back, and I relax into a state of composure. I am no longer Astrid, I am now the Water Weaver.

$\dots$

The streets are quiet as the sun begins to set. There has been talk about new players in town, filling the void left after I killed the last crime boss. My informants say that it's a duo, focusing on illegal gambling and betting events. One of the pair is a man who comes from a long line of mafiosos. He went quiet after his entire family was wiped out by a rival gang, but for some reason, he's decided to reenter the game. Apparently, he also has a partner, but no one has any information on them. Nada. Zilch. Zero.

If you ask me, there's probably not a partner. Instead, the guy is running solo and using the elusive mystery of a second to gain more power. Typical scumbag behavior. However, I do make a point to do thorough recon before I make any moves and get the authorities involved, so here I am, loitering on a rooftop near a supposed casino location.

There's a rumble of thunder as raindrops start to fall. It doesn't bother me any, I simply use my powers to create an umbrella over where I'm sitting. The rain can actually be helpful – providing cover and distraction, preventing people from looking up, and also, supplying me with water. My powers can't create or destroy water, I can only move it and change its temperature. Unfortunately, I am quite useless in a dry area.

The sound of an engine echoes through the alley, and three motorcycles pull up in front of the establishment. I slink down the fire escape and crouch behind a dumpster.

Leading the pack is a strongly built man. It's clear that this is the one in charge. He pulls a razor blade out of his pocket and starts flipping it around his fingers as he strides to the door. On his left is another man, slightly smaller in stature, but could still handle his own. This second man appears to not be as well-rested as the first, with subtle bags under his eyes. On the right is...

Oh. Oh god.

It's her.

She pulls off her helmet and her fiery curls fall free, brushing the tops of her shoulders. She's cut her hair. It looks nice. She's wearing the same black bodysuit that she used to wear as "Sparks." It hugs her curves tighter than before, and I can tell she's been working out. She laughs as she pulls her cloth mask over the bottom half of her face. Though she raises her hood to cover her head, I can still see the glint in her eyes as she banters with the other two men.

She looks... happy.

I don't understand.

The one with the razor blade bangs on the door and a third man pops out. Typical greasy slimeball. He rubs his hands together before gesturing wildly at the man. I creep closer to hear their conversation.

"I know the payment is late, but it's not my fault," Slimeball says. "You don't understand what it's like working with Sammy."

"Don't blame Sammy for your own ineptitudes." Razor Blade steps closer to Slimeball. "He's never had a problem with any other contractors. Now, when can we expect payment? I'll give you a hint. The answer is tonight."

"Yes, sir," Slimeball stammers. "How do you prefer payment?"

"Bring the cash to the Lightning Bolt," the second man interjects as Razor Blade rubs the bridge of his nose. "Tell the bartender—"

I accidentally kick a rock that goes skidding across the road. Oh crap. Instinctively, I dive behind the cover of a building. I peek around to gauge whether the rock blew my cover. The three men are still deep in their conversation, unperturbed. But Anise, she's always been more observant than most. She steps away from the group, head on a swivel. I move behind the corner as she looks my way and I hear footsteps coming toward me.

Crap. Crap. Crap.

Out of the corner of my eye, I see a ladder with roof access. Good enough. I scurry up the rungs, my chest heaves as I flatten myself against the roof. This is not the game of hide and seek I want to be playing right now.

"Astrid?" I hear her voice call uncertainly from below. "Is that you?"

I close my eyes as if that would make me disappear.

"Astrid?" Her voice is quieter and hesitant, but she doesn't climb the ladder.

"Sparks!" I hear Razor Blade shout. "Time to go!"

"I'm going crazy," she mutters, and I hear her footsteps recede. I lay there until the sound of motorcycles fade in the distance.

Anise is the mystery partner. It makes sense, with her obsessive need to keep everything about herself a secret. Heck, that's practically why we broke up. I mean, she was a part of the gang called the Tributaries for who knows how long. Combine that with her own superpowers, she's a natural fit. I guess, I just never thought she would fully commit to a life of crime. What is she up to?

Oh, Anise. What have you done?

CHAPTER 2

SPARKS

I will never grow tired of riding a motorcycle. The rumble of the engine as you soar down the street, the wind ripping at your clothes, weaving through traffic at frankly unreasonable speeds. It's absolutely thrilling. When I'm off-duty, I rarely wear my helmet, but I need the extra layer of anonymity in my working clothes. But that just means I can drive faster, right? I'm sure Derek would disagree, but he loves to ride just as recklessly so he can't say shit.

The Lightning Bolt comes into view and our trio pulls into the attached parking garage. We find our reserved spots in the bottom level and turn off the engines. The fresh air invigorates me as I pull off my helmet and hang it on my handlebars. I run my fingers through my hair, hoping to counter the inevitable helmet head.

My mind wanders back to the rounds we just did. One of our gambling dens has been slow delivering the profits, so we had to shake them down a bit. They'll pay tonight. They always do. But something bothered me about the stop this time. I swear I heard something behind us, then the flash of blue. It's almost like...

"Sparks!" Derek snaps his fingers. "You there or do we need to send out a manhunt?"

"Huh?" I jolt back to the present moment. "Sorry, I'm with you. What did you say?"

Derek is my business partner and my closest confidante. We formed the syndicate a few months ago when the previous gang leader was killed. Well, gang leader and my abusive boyfriend of eight years. He was killed by my ex-girlfriend, Astrid. She moonlights as a morally-superior vigilante, the Water Weaver. That was... not a great day. Since then, Derek has become a surrogate older brother, helping me keep my head above water.

"I said that Oliver needs to go home to his family." He gestures toward Oliver who groggily rubs his eyes. "His youngest hasn't been sleeping, therefore he hasn't been sleeping. I'll go to the club tonight to ensure we receive payment in his stead. Want a drink?"

Oliver is the last member of what would be our "C-Suite." He's pretty much the accountant and HR rep for our gang. First rule of running a criminal organization, ensure everyone gets paid – including Uncle Sam. It's never a good idea to skimp on felons' salaries, and tax evasion tends to attract government scrutiny. It could be said that Oliver has the most important job of the three of us. As an added bonus, it's one of the least dangerous positions. While Oliver can hang with the rest of us, his wife appreciates getting him home in one piece to help with the children.

"I'll be right up," I answer. "Give me a minute to change."

I wave to Oliver before stepping onto the elevator. After scanning my thumbprint, it descends into the lower level of our compound. We had our base built beneath the club to provide cover for our operations. The club is an easy way to launder money and has people coming and going at odd hours. Plus, I like to dance. Seems like a natural fit to me.

The elevator doors open, and I step into the living area of the dormitory. Gray vinyl and white drywall cover the concrete foundations. Modest, yet comfortable, couches form a U facing the TV on the wall. The kitchen is always stocked with a basic pantry and whatever else Derek orders. Three hallways branch off from the common area.

The eastern hallway leads to the barracks – spare rooms built for the staff to use at will. Primarily used by those with overnight shifts who need a nap before driving home or those who are in-between residences. They mostly keep to themselves, except for occasional movie marathons and video game tournaments. One room is reserved for Oliver who will occasionally stay over when we need to have late-night strategy meetings and to use as his office, but the rest of the rooms rotate so frequently I don't catch the names of the inhabitants.

The northern hallway leads to our amenities. Armory, storage, med bay, gym – the basics. The gym is pretty neat. Full weight rack with a few exercise machines and treadmills, a court to be used for basketball or volleyball, and of course, a fighting ring. Derek and I spend a lot of time sparring together, partially for work-related skill development but also because sometimes, you just need to hit something. But anyway, standard apartment amenities I suppose.

The final hallway leads to only two rooms – leadership quarters. One for Derek, and one for me. Derek's the only family I have left, and vice versa, so we figured we might as well live on base full time. Instead of the small dorms in the eastern wing, we have much more spacious accommodations.

I punch in my keycode and swing open my door. My bike keys clatter into their dish on my entryway table as I step out of my boots. I nudge them into their slot on the shoe rack before walking down the three stairs into my den. The furnishings are masculine and plain, mostly because I just had Derek order duplicates of whatever he wanted. I wasn't exactly in the best headspace then to be picking out backsplash colors. Derek might have the same furniture, but he decorated his space. Pillows, art, knick-knacks. I have none of that, claiming to be a minimalist.

Derek has shown me paintings from practically every gallery in Boston, but I never come home with anything, much to his chagrin. He says that my room is too sterile, that it doesn't feel like a home. He's probably right. White walls, white rug, white couches. Dark floors, dark coffee table, dark shelves. Even the adjoining kitchen is a combination of white and slate. The only color is from the small collection of books on the bookshelf, even still, those are mostly muted. I'm not blind, I see how stale and lifeless my place is, but any vibrancy I add just feels like I'm in a room that belongs to someone else, like I'm living a lie.

I pour myself a handful of almonds before walking into my bedroom. I slide the lights up partly, keeping the room fairly dim. I set my almonds on the top of my dresser, not caring about the crumbs scattering about. Unzipping my bodysuit, I move toward the walk-in closet to find an empty hanger. My bodysuit collection has expanded over the past few months. They are all pretty much the same, black with silver aluminum thread woven through to provide a route for an electrical current. I've upgraded to include light body armor panels on the torso, curved to fit me perfectly while being undetectable. They won't stop a bullet, but they will deflect a punch.

Do you know what the best part of owning a club is? I get to go whenever I want. We also use it to provide cover for business meetings and such, like tonight. Due to this fun fact, an obscene amount of my closet is skimpy dresses and tops. I can't exactly fit in wearing sweatpants.

Tonight, I've picked out a loose tank dress covered in large silver sequins. It won't cover the long scar winding from my left palm up my forearm, but hey, getting struck by lightning is a cool conversation starter. Besides, guys tend to not look that far down. I buckle some ridiculously strappy black heels and then move to the bathroom to do my makeup. I pull out my only mirror from the vanity drawer and set it on the countertop. Looking into the tiny hand mirror, I can only see a small part of my face at a time. Eyelid. Swipe of glitter. Lips. Swipe of red. Cheek. Swipe of highlight. Swipe. Swipe. Swipe. And then I'm done. The mirror goes back in the drawer, and I don't have to confront my reflection for another day.

The elevator goes directly to the VIP section of the club. There's a booth that's perpetually reserved for management. Derek is already waiting for me when I arrive, wearing his standard black button-up and slacks. His sleeves are rolled up slightly, showing off the latest addition to his watch collection. A waitress catches my eye as I sit down, and moments later, a glass of whiskey appears before me. Ah, I love this place.

"Opening a club was the best decision we ever made." I close my eyes as I take my first sip, savoring the burn in my throat and the warmth in my stomach.

"I don't know," Derek teases, swirling the ice in his drink – also a whiskey. "I really enjoy the elevator music we picked."

I roll my eyes and recline in the booth. From the loft, we can see the entire dance floor and the main bar. The lights are dim so it's hard for people to see up. Derek is practically invisible in his all-back attire, however, the sequins of my dress sparkle in the faint light, casting a subtle glow over the rest of my body. While I do enjoy a good amount of anonymity in my job, I also love the attention of the longing boys below.

"You've got a few admirers tonight," Derek notices. "Any catch your eye?"

"Oh, you know how it is." I take another sip of my drink and toss my hair over my shoulder. "I'll see where the dancing takes me tonight, but of course, business first."

As if on cue, the skeezy man from earlier walks up to the bar holding a briefcase. He stands out in the club, wearing a ratty blazer despite the much too warm temperature. He is quickly intercepted and escorted upstairs to our table where he sits across from us. Derek pulls out his iconic razor blade. It's a brilliant instrument of intimidation — both a weapon and a genuine fidget tool.

"It's all here." The man slides the case across the table. "My apologies for the delay."

"Sparks, give it a once over," Derek commands nonchalantly, asserting his dominance over the table.

This dynamic has been carefully crafted. While Derek and I are in reality equal partners, this faux division of authority serves several purposes. One, it allows me to maintain a level of anonymity. No one knows who his partner is, it couldn't possibly be the eye candy in the dress, could it? Idiots. Two, my subservience implicitly serves as an example for the poor fuck across the table. He unknowingly follows my lead, and lets Derek stay in control of the group. Rather genius if you ask me.

I flip open the briefcase and leaf through a few of the bundles of bills. I don't remember how much is supposed to be in here, and I don't really care. If he has the balls to stiff us to our faces, we'll just have to have an additional conversation. One that he won't enjoy nearly as much. I shut the briefcase and give Derek a disinterested nod. One of the security members takes the case for processing and accounting. I recline in the booth, ready for Derek to wrap this up.

"See, all there." The creep from across the table waves his hand. "A little steep, but worth it for the pleasure of doing business with such a pretty face."

My eyes flick up to meet his, except he's looking much lower. The nerve of this prick. It's one thing for payment to be late. It happens. A single warning is usually enough to ensure it doesn't continue. But this asshole is so brazen to come into my club and treat this meeting with such flippancy? No. This isn't happening.

"I think you could use a lesson in respect," I say casually, examining my cuticles. "Stand."

"What?" He huffs. "Learn to take a joke, sugartits."

Heads whip to face him, and I swear I heard one of the guards gasp. For the first time, the man across the table squirms as he realizes that was perhaps not the wisest thing to say. Derek clasps his fingers behind his head and chuckles, excited to watch the show unfold.

"Perhaps you didn't hear me." The only sign of my anger is the glare in my eyes. "Stand."

Before he can move, a duo of guards grab his shoulders and a third yanks his chair out from under him. His face pales as he stands, shaking in front of the table. I reach up and grab my glass, admiring the small amount of amber liquid left in the glass.

"Kneel," I command.

I stare at the swirling whiskey. The third guard whips out a baton and drives it into the back of the prick's knees. He cries out as he falls to the ground, arms suspended above him by the other two guards. I slowly sip the last of my drink before standing, drawing out every second with deliberate and concise movements.

I hold my empty glass out as a waitress takes it away. My hand stays in the air, waiting patiently until a new drink is placed in it. I take a sip of the whiskey, allowing the liquid to burn my throat in the way I love so much.

"Derek, do you think that there should be a one-time increase on next month's payment? Maybe five percent?" I look at him over my shoulder as I take a second sip.

"Works for me." Derek plays along. "Thanks for the idea."

I set down the glass and then turn toward the simpering man cowering on the ground. I place a finger under his chin and direct his gaze to meet mine. He nods frantically.

"Five percent!" He exclaims. "Brilliant!"

I lean in close, and just for a moment allow him to see the rage behind my calm facade.

"Not bad for a pretty face, huh?" Venom drips from my words, whispered just loud enough for him to hear. I snap back into character and face Derek, gesturing vaguely at the kneeling man. "I'm bored. Can you finish up here?"

"My pleasure." Derek smirks, rising from his seat.

I don't stick around to see what happens next, I'm already walking down the staircase toward the thumping bass and strobing lights. That's another reason why we chose to open a club instead of a restaurant or other money laundering classics. Electricity. The flashing lights and blasting speakers require obscene amounts of energy to function. While it's rough on the utility bill, it provides me with an extra layer of protection.

See, ever since Synergy Labs exploded, I've had the ability to manipulate electricity streams. Pushing, pulling, redirecting. The only catch is that there has to be electricity already available to use. Simple physics, the law of conservation of energy.

This might seem like a blessing. It's a pretty neat party trick and comes in handy for self-defense. What's not to like?

But my abilities came at a cost. That explosion set off a series of events seemingly determined to ruin my life. My mother's death. Being driven into the arms of my abuser. Leaving him while stumbling headfirst into the embrace of another. Pushing Astrid away, not trusting her to know the secrets I hid for so long.

I tried to protect her, to keep her from the dirty truth of my past. She knew me not as Sparks, but as Anise, due to my love of black licorice and star anise. When she found out about the double-life I led, our relationship crumpled. She walked away without so much as a glance over her shoulder, so I was determined to not look back either.

Derek scraped me off the floor and helped me build this empire. Together, we organized underground casinos, fighting rings, street racing... If you can bet on it, we host it. We also have a few clubs around town, partially to clean money, partially just because.

It wasn't easy. There were times he had to throw a bucket of ice water on me after I found the bottom of too many bottles. A different man every night, not eating due to "lack of appetite," trashing my apartment just to feel a semblance of control. Derek decided that my grief wasn't allowed to kill me. He set me straight, forced me to take care of myself.

I don't know why he did it. Maybe it's because he genuinely liked my friendship. Or I remind him of his late little sister. Or it could be as simple as that I was too valuable of a weapon to die. I prefer to think it's one of the other reasons though. Through the past few months, he's become the closest thing to a brother that I've ever had.

But I'm better now. Jack's dead, and I'm alive. Astrid broke up with me, but that's her problem, not mine. I'm done being responsible for anyone else but me. The bartender passes me a shot and I throw it back, relishing in the warmth of my cheeks. Tonight, I'm getting laid.

I strut onto the dance floor. The horde of bodies jump and sway in a chaotic frenzy. Sweat glistens on limbs clinging to each other. Skimpy straps slide off of glossy shoulders. Button-ups lose a few of their buttons. This is my kind of crowd. A blonde woman catches my eye, her long hair whips around as she spins to the melody floating through the air. She reminds me of Astrid. Carefree, vibrant, radiant. I...

No. Take a breath. Refocus.

A few male candidates swagger toward me, raring to throw their hats into the ring. That's more like it.

I size them up, admiring their muscular forearms and broad shoulders. One man extends his hand to me. Intrigued, I take it, and he twirls me into him. He places his hands on my hips, swaying in time to the music.

"My name's Peter," he says in a sultry voice. "What's yours?"

"You can call me whatever you want to, baby," I purr. "So long as you can show me a good time."

"That can be arranged." Peter winks, pulling me in closer. I can feel the heat of his body through his shirt. His hands slink lower, cupping my ass.

I take a moment to analyze Peter. Dark hair, check. Green eyes, check. Probably a major douche, check. Nothing to remind me of her, check, check, check.

The top two buttons of his shirt are undone, revealing a peek of his chest. I run my fingers along the edge, releasing another button. Peter chuckles and plays with the hem of my dress. If he lifts it any higher, it'll be a shirt.

"Do you want to find a hotel?" I whisper, toying with his collar.

"Lead the way." He steps toward the main entrance, gesturing for me to walk in front.

Luckily, there's a cheap hotel just down the block, a pay by the hour kind of place. I frequent the establishment often enough that they have my card on file. The clerk slides a room key across the counter as we walk in, and I grab it as I call the elevator.

"Do they know you here?" Peter asks skeptically.

"Do you care?" I raise my eyebrow.

I grab his hand as the elevator arrives. Within a few moments, the doors close, and we are locked in a fiery embrace. His hands tangle in my hair as I yank his lapel. As the doors reopen, we stumble out and stagger toward our room.

His hands grip my thighs and lift me around his waist. I wrap my arms around his neck, trailing kisses down his-

Thud.

Ow.

"Sorry!" Peter takes a step back and carefully steps through the doorway, being more mindful to not slam me into the wall.

Deep breath in. Deep breath out. Just keep going.

Peter not-so-gracefully dumps me onto the bed and crawls over. He gently slides the straps of my dress down, exposing my bare breasts. As he fondles them, his lips reconnect with mine. His tongue nudges my mouth open, and he explores wildly. Whatever makes him happy, I guess.

I push him off when he goes up for air. We can salvage this. I stand and my dress falls to the ground. I straddle his lap and pull his shirt off, throwing it on the floor. He leans back as I unbutton his jeans. His dick springs up, eager to be free of his briefs. I slide my finger beneath the waistband, ready to oblige—

I yelp as Peter flips me onto my back. He braces himself on an elbow and his other hand grabs my thigh.

"Hair! Hair!" I push on his arm, which was planted firmly on the strands of my hair. "You're pulling my hair. Please move."

"Fuck," Peter curses. He adjusts and I relax as the pressure on my scalp subsides. His shoulders tense. It's clear he's getting frustrated with his performance.

"Here." I slide off my thong and guide his fingers between my legs. I coach him on the best speed and shapes to make, and slowly, I start to enjoy myself. My eyes close, and I feel my back arch. A small moan escapes. Finally, we're getting somewhere. He starts to experiment with his technique.

"No, no," I murmur as the magic begins to fade. "Go back."

"Trust me," Peter says boastfully. Then he pinches my clit. Hard. Instinctively, my knee jerks up and nails his shoulder as I curl away from him. He rubs his shoulder in pain. "Ow, what was that for?"

"What was that for?" I stand up in disbelief. "For fuck's sake! Stop trying to show off. I don't need flashy, I just need to get off! Jesus."

"I'm trying," Peter whines. So attractive. I groan and turn back to him.

"You're done." I push him flat onto the bed. "Hands to yourself, no touching. I'll take it from here."

He protests feebly but goes quiet when I pull out a condom. I discard his briefs and slide it on. His cock stands at attention, large enough to get the job done satisfactorily. At least one part of him isn't trying to fuck this up. I lower myself onto his dick and grind, slowly and deliberately. I brace myself against his knees to allow for full hip movement. Relaxed, I throw my head back, fully embracing his shaft inside me. Man, this is what I needed.

"Oh god," Peter cries. "Oh god, oh god, oh god!"

He did not.

"Did you just..." I cannot believe this. "It's been like three seconds."

I dismount and can't stop from groaning when my fear is confirmed.

"Sorry," Peter says sheepishly. "I can still help you get there though."

"Forget it," I fume. I grab a robe from the closet and cover myself. "Just go home."

"No really," he insists. "Let's figure this out together."

"I think you are misreading this situation." Goddamn it. I hate when they get clingy. "This isn't some sappy rom-com where we find the clit together. Get out so I can take care of this myself." I don't bother waiting for a response, instead I throw Peter his clothes.

"This isn't fair," Peter protests. "Give me a second chance."

His hand darts out and grabs my arm. My training kicks in with the unexpected contact. I twist around, pinning his arm to his back, and shove him to the floor.

"Get dressed or I'll kick your ass out naked," I seethe. "I don't care either way."

With that, I lock myself into the bathroom and fill the tub. As I slide into the bath, I feel the muscles in my back loosen. The warm water soothes my shoulders. I lean my head back against the headrest, breathing a sigh of relief. Finally, it's time for me to have some pleasure.

I start out slowly, using my fingers to make circles below my clit. Slow, meticulous circles. I can't imagine how Peter couldn't figure it out, Astrid always knew exactly what to do.

Shit, don't think about her. Think about yourself. Enjoy the feeling of the sensation.

I resume the circles a little faster this time, as if my fingers could distract me from her.

I've been waiting to touch you for weeks. We're on her dining room table. She's straddling my lap, coming up for air. Her voice sounds like caramelized honey, so sweet yet so dark. *To feel your body against mine, run my fingers through your hair, to learn how you taste.* My flannel has fallen off my shoulders, but it's not stopping me from exploring every inch of her body. *I am reveling in every fucking moment.*

Wait, no! I'm thinking about her again. Fuck! I don't need her, I can get off by myself. My eyes roll to the back of my head as my fingers make contact with my clit. I allow my moans to pass freely, loud and unrestrained.

I earn every sound that crosses those lips. Her voice plays through my head again. *Don't keep my prizes from me.*

Fuck it.

I lean in, giving myself permission to think of Astrid. Riding my motorcycle, her hands inching up my thighs. Oh god. Smearing pink and blue body paint on each other until it turned purple. Oh god. Her eager smile from between my thighs. Oh god. Kissing in the snow on Christmas. Oh god!

My core clenches as a wave of euphoria washes over me. As I soak in the final moments of my ecstasy, I pretend that I don't notice the memory that pushed me over the edge.

I love you.

CHAPTER 3
ASTRID

My alarm is ringing in the background, but it's fairly redundant at this point. I'm awake. I've been awake, staring at my ceiling for the past... hour? Who knows. I can't sleep. My bed is too big, too cold. I never had trouble sleeping when Anise lived with me. She would wrap me in her arms, petting my hair as I drifted off.

But she's gone, probably moved on months ago. How could she be fine when I'm the one who broke up with her? I would laugh at the irony, but I'd probably cry instead.

That night is all I can think about. Every time I close my eyes, I'm back on that beach. She's on her knees, desperately pleading for me to listen, to give her another chance. But I can't even look at her. Saltwater drips from my hair as I cave to my agony, my bitterness, my grief. I just... walked away.

I know I had to break up with her. I know that she was bad for me, that she was deceitful and a liar. If we didn't break up, she would just hurt me again. I know this, but yet I wish I didn't.

I wish she was here to hold me as I slept. I wish she was here to kiss my forehead. I wish she was here to tell me that I'd be okay. I wish she was here.

But she's not here, and I'm not okay.

I fumble with the alarm clock, trying to quiet its piercing cry. Dragging myself from my rumbled sheets, I stumble into the kitchen, pouring water into a kettle. I adjust the temperature to boiling with a wave of my hand.

As the owner of a coffee shop, I have no shortage of mugs. Tall mugs. Short mugs. Mugs with funny sayings. Mugs in the shape of cute animals. The cabinet above my sink is solely mugs. I probably have enough to use a new mug every day for a month, but I always use the same one.

Strands of crimson and scarlet weave together. Every so often a thread of silver glints in the background. I painted this mug for Anise, inspired by the vibrancy of her hair. She used to drink her hot cocoa from it every morning.

There's a second mug on the counter, one she painted for me at the same time. Splotches of blues and greens are layered over each other behind specks of white foam. Water, she said. She claimed it was based on a conversation we had, but looking back, I don't know how I didn't see it earlier. God, there were so many signs. She was always out at odd hours. She would come home with cuts and bruises. She knew who I was the whole time, but I didn't piece it together until it was too late. How did I not notice? Some detective I am.

I nurse my coffee as I replay my memories, searching for details I missed. With a sigh, I set down my cup. This isn't healthy. I can't keep doing this. There's only one person I can turn to for help – Mimi.

Several hours later, I pull into the driveway of my childhood home. I grew up in a sleepy town called West Haven, Pennsylvania. I haven't been home since Christmas, hoping to avoid questions about my breakup. Of course, I call my family every few days, so they already know, but it's different seeing the look on their faces. My family loved Anise, especially my brother Liam. However, being around noon on a weekday, only Mimi should be home. I fish the secret key from its hiding spot and unlock the door.

"Hellooo!" I call out. "It's Astrid. Anyone home?"

"Astrid, what a wonderful surprise!" My grandmother comes around the corner and squeezes me in a hug. "It is a surprise, yes? Did I miss your call?"

"No, Mimi." I return her embrace. "I didn't call. I just really needed your help."

"I see." Mimi steps away, much more serious. Mimi is the spiritual matriarch of our family, and she knows it must be important if I am singling out her advice. "Please, let's sit down."

We curl up on the couch and it's not long before I break down, recounting the story to Mimi. The lies, the breakup, the heartache, her moving on and leaving me in the past. Mimi doesn't push when I skirt around certain details – namely my vigilantism and Anise's involvement with the mob. She just tuts and rubs my back, passing me a tissue to dry my tears.

"There, there," she coos as my sobs turn into hiccups. "How can I help? Do you need a sleeping draught?"

"No," I sniffle. "I just want to forget she was ever a part of my life."

"Oh dearie." Mimi pulls me into another hug. "Are you sure this is what you need? Sometimes pain is a message to unravel, not to sweep under the rug."

"Please, Mimi," I beg. "I'm tired. I'm done. I can't do this anymore."

"Okay." She holds my gaze and nods. "It sounds like you need a cord cutting ritual."

"Will it fix me?" Please, please, please.

"You don't need fixing, granddaughter." She strokes my hair. "You aren't broken, just hurting. Come into my room and we shall prepare the ritual."

After a final dab with the tissue, we both retreat to the back bedroom. A large altar lines the back wall. It puts my small altar to shame, complete with delicate vials of moonwater, crystal beads, and pouches of herbs. Mimi scans the collection before pulling out two red candles. She carefully carves my name in one, and Anise's in the other, along with some runes. Once satisfied, she stands them on top of some herbs and ties a piece of twine between the wicks.

"Astrid, please listen carefully as I explain the ritual." Mimi clears her throat before continuing. "A cord cutting ritual is very serious and should not be done without significant introspection to be sure you are committed to cutting the spiritual ties between you and the other person. If it is truly time to split ways, this can bring much needed peace to the both of you. When you are ready, light both candles and allow them to burn fully. The wicks should light the cord and allow your connection to be cut. Do you have any questions?"

"No, Mimi." I shake my head.

"Please take a moment to explore your spiritual intentions, and if you deem the time is right, there are matches in the top drawer." With that, she walks out, leaving me alone with the candles.

I take a deep breath. Finally, I can be free. I run my finger against the side of her candle. This is it. This is really it. Our relationship wasn't long, just a few months full of intensity and passion, but it's finally time for it to end. I wipe away a stray tear from my cheek and brush off my clothes. It's time.

The matchbook feels heavy in my hands, despite there only being three matches inside. I pluck the first one from the row and scrape it on the starter. A bright flame ignites, clean and strong. Here it goes.

I lean forward and hold the match over Anise's candle. It goes out before it can touch the wick.

Huh.

Bum match.

I place the spent match in a stone bowl and pick up the next one. The strike pad sets it ablaze. A flickering light, bold and brash. Let's do this.

I go to light the candle. The flame disappears in a wisp of smoke.

What?

No way.

Frustrated, I grab the last match. I hold the matchbook right above the candle. Surely, I can move a lit match one centimeter without it going out, right? This is ridiculous. I take a deep breath, trying to calm myself and focus on my intentions.

I strike the match.

It snaps in two, unlit.

Oh, come on!

I throw the empty matchbook on the ground in a fit of exasperation. An empty shoebox on the floor catches my eye. I sweep the candles and twine into the box and shut the lid. If it won't work here, I'll do it at home. I'll even grab a butane lighter if it makes the wicks catch. I tuck the box under my shoulder and find Mimi in the kitchen, sipping a glass of iced tea. She raises an eyebrow at my shoebox of shame.

"I think I need to do this at home, at my own altar." Only partially a lie.

"Yes, your energy will be more in tune there." Mimi nods approvingly. "Very wise choice."

"I need to start the drive back if I want to be home before dark." Bold lie, but I want to do this ritual as soon as I can. "Thank you for your wisdom, Mimi."

"Please be careful, granddaughter." She pulls me into another embrace. "I worry about you."

"I'll be okay, promise." I hold up my pinky finger and Mimi wraps hers around mine. After another hug, I am shooed out of the house, shoebox in hand.

Seatbelt buckled, mirrors checked, keys in the ignition. I head out of town, but a strange feeling takes hold of me. Up ahead is the back road I used to take as a shortcut to my favorite childhood hangout. I can't tell you why, but I take the road. A short jaunt later, I arrive at the lake.

It's not a big lake. As far as I know, it doesn't even have an official name. I've never seen it mentioned on any hiking or wilderness brochures of the area, but my friends have been coming here for ages. It's the perfect size for a small group to play and feel like they own the world. The water is always cool, staving off the sharp heat of the summer sun. Of course, it's hardly swimming weather – it being April – but the cold has never really bothered me.

I shimmy out of my shorts and lay my t-shirt on the hood of my car. I watch my step, navigating sticks and small stones as I tiptoe through the dirt shore into the chilly water. Each step disturbs the silt, creating clouds where I walk. I push off from the ground, diving into the lake. The water parts easily, glinting in the sun as my hands cut through. I could use my powers for a million things right now – to keep myself dry, to warm the lake, to propel me to where I'm going. But now, I just want to swim.

I've always craved being in water. They called me a little fish when I was a toddler playing in the bath. Then as I learned to swim, I would stay long past my skin pruning and wrinkling, only coming out to reapply sunscreen. Star athlete on both the high school and collegiate swim teams.

Just being in the lake, I feel all of my pent-up emotions floating away. The chill feels good on my skin, soothing and calming. I duck underneath the surface, admiring the fish skittering below. Their scales refract the few available sunbeams and scatter stunning rays of color.

Eventually, I resurface, gasping for fresh air. Past the tree line, I see the ruins of the old research facility. It's decrepit now, but it wasn't always that way. I remember when they first built it. The owners were very secretive, so everyone in town assumed that they were working on something confidential, maybe research for the military. The rumor mill spiraled and soon the legacy of the place became larger than life, haunted and cursed experimentations or nuclear weapons or whatever seemed interesting that day.

But they always say there's a bit of truth in every lie. Whatever they were working on, it was surely cursed. After all, something had to cause the explosion. The explosion that killed me.

The birds were singing in the trees. My friends were splashing in the shallows. Liam was fiddling with the sunscreen. Our dads were all standing by the grill, overanalyzing the frozen hamburger patties while the moms were sipping lemonade in the shade.

I threw my flip flops underneath a tree and jumped in. My friends were finishing up a competitive game of chicken as I was aimlessly drifting further into the lake. Floating on my back, my hair sprawled out around me. Carefree flutter kicks slowly steered me onward.

It was peaceful, serene. Laughter. Birds. A subtle gust of wind. It was the perfect moment in time.

But perfect moments rarely last.

Everything that happened next happened all at once. The loud boom, as if a bomb had detonated. Screams barely cutting through the distance. Birds taking flight in a panicked frenzy. A bright light burst from the facility.

Our parents shouted, crying for us to get out of the water. My friends clamored to the shore. But they were in the shallows, and I was in the deep. The bright light was coming toward us, and I just knew, I couldn't outswim that.

So, I made a gut decision and I prayed, and at the last moment...

I ducked beneath the surface.

The bolt hit the water, and I could feel everything. My nerve endings lit up with agony. The air was ripped from my lungs, replaced with water from the lake. I couldn't move. I couldn't breathe. I sank to the bottom as the life left my body.

It felt like seconds later when I opened my eyes. Everything was the same, but different. The water against my skin was alive. I could feel it as an extension of myself. I pushed off the ground and broke the surface almost immediately, without kicking my legs. I coughed as air refilled my lungs, but no water came out.

I didn't have time to examine these new sensations any closer as screaming drew my attention. Someone grabbed my arm and started towing me to shore. Hands. Hugs. Crying. Apparently, what felt like seconds was actually several minutes. I drowned. I shouldn't be alive.

We drove to the hospital. The emergency room was full of burn and shock victims. A redhead a few years younger than me was crying in the corner as her older brother held her close. We learned later that everybody who worked at the facility died, either on the scene or in the hospital later. My family couldn't believe I was okay, but the doctors didn't find anything wrong. No burns, no brain damage, no water in my lungs. I was discharged.

They held a mass funeral for the dead scientists. I stayed home.

My friends and family never came back to the lake, but I couldn't shake this feeling of connection. I never told anyone about my newfound powers, heck, I barely understand it even today. But something happened in that explosion. Something changed me. Perhaps now it's time to understand why.

꙯   ꙯   ꙯   ꙯

The deteriorating asphalt crunches under my tires as I pull up to the fence surrounding the research facility. Signs are zip-tied to the wires – "No Trespassing," "Condemned," "Warning – Danger." I pull off to the side, wishing I had my Water Weaver disguise to hide my identity. Typically, I try to stop crime, but I figure just this once, a little breaking and entering won't hurt anybody. I easily scale the fence and walk up to the building. The front door is locked, but I am able to easily jimmy a window and slip inside.

The lobby is coated with a thick layer of dust. I make my way over to the reception desk and try to boot up a computer. Nothing. There's no power. Okay, we're going analog then. I open a drawer and pull out a notepad, noting the name on the letterhead. Huh, Synergy Labs. Never knew what this place was called. Wait, Synergy Labs? Where have I heard that before?

Oh god.

Anise.

Or well… Sparks. The only time I got her to talk to me about whatever she was involved in, she mentioned Synergy Labs. She said she got her powers from them and the machine she was recruited to fix was actually a weapon. She destroyed it, and all hell broke loose. She was tortured, Jeremiah – a close friend of mine – was executed, and I killed a man. That was also the day we broke up. It was probably the worst night of my life.

My mind spins as I try to piece together this information. She got her powers from here, but how? I pace around the room, hoping to settle my thoughts. Were they doing human experiments? God, I hope not.

I think back to all of the fragments of Anise's past that I can remember. She always claimed that people were after her, thinking she had some kind of special insight into her mom's work. That's why it was so important that she had to be secretive and anonymous. I never took her seriously, thinking she was being melodramatic, but I humored her. Now, I'm starting to think that was the most honest thing she ever told me.

How did her mom die? Crap, I don't remember. I fiddle with the edge of my sleeve, trying to trigger the rest of the memory. Yes! A workplace accident. I remember because it was so vague and ambiguous. I couldn't figure out what she meant but had enough tact not to pry.

Oh no.

I pause my pacing mid-stride. I know how her mom died. She must have been a scientist here during the explosion.

But wait, what does that mean for her? Did she get her powers from the explosion like I did? But her mom died…

Oh. Oh goodness. Please no. Anise was here. I compare the details, hoping I'm wrong. Grew up in rural Pennsylvania. Lost her mom eight years ago. She had to have been here.

The muscles in my stomach clench as waves of emotion wash over me. In my mind, a teenage redhead runs across the room. Her screams fill the air with pain, grief, and devastation. The moment that your entire life changes.

Oh Anise. I'm so sorry. I look up, trying to blink back the tears threatening to fall. I can't feel bad for her right now. I need to figure out what was so important about this place that people are still killing each other so many years later.

The rest of the reception area bears no fruit, so I move on through the only hallway. A door on the left has a faded plaque, "Human Resources." Sure. I walk into a cobweb and swat at my face as the door shuts behind me. Worker's rights posters line the wall. I pick up a poster from the floor. The corners are ripped, still stapled to the corkboard. "What To Do in Case of Emergency." A file cabinet in the corner is ajar, the records hastily gathered.

On a desk in the corner is a binder. Flipping through the pages, I find an employee roster. Each page lists a few key pieces of information – name, title, address, emergency contact. I can't imagine having to make those calls. Notes are scribbled among the margins. "DOA," "DOA," "Critical Condition," "DOA." I grab the binder and take it with me as I continue searching the area.

Back in the hallway, offices line the corridor. Most of them are locked. I try to shoulder my way into one but end up with a firmly shut door and a bruised arm. But I continue jiggling the handle of each office until I find one that gives. I wipe the dust off the desk nameplate and match the name to one in my binder.

"Holly Jennings," I read aloud. "DOA, sorry to hear that. It seems you were the Director of Research Integration. I'm not sure what that means, but it sounds impressive. You lived nearby in Danver Hills, a nice town. Huh."

I pause as I continue reading. Her emergency contact was scratched out. I open the binder rings and hold the sheet up to the window, hoping the light would reveal something more. Nothing.

"That's odd, Holly," I muse. "Who would have done this?"

Perplexed, I snoop in her office. I find a few notebooks in a desk drawer filled with drawings and diagrams I can't decipher. The word "energy" is circled in red. There's a sketch of some machinery on the next page.

"You know who would be super helpful right now?" I ask aloud. "Anise. Probably the one person I can't talk to about this."

I close the notebooks and continue my search. There's a bookshelf on the wall filled with worn textbooks. A few of them have dogeared pages and highlighted sections, so I add those to my pile of things to take home. Maybe those will help me decipher the notebooks.

On a second look, I notice a much-loved journal tucked on the bookshelf. The edges are worn from being opened and shut so many times. I lift the cover and see "For Lottie" written on the inside in an elegant script. I flip through the pages and see letter after letter written to someone named Lottie. There are so many letters that only a few pages remain blank. It doesn't say who Lottie is. Maybe a friend or a wife? I skim a few more before shutting the book. It's too personal, too intense, digging through the possessions of a dead person who obviously had somebody they loved. But I can't leave the journal. Maybe if I find Lottie, I could deliver it. I find a box in the Human Resources office to hold my clues and leave that in the hallway.

There's a large metal door at the end of the hallway. I try to open it, but it won't budge. I can tell there's some kind of electric lock, but without power, I can't even try 1234 or 0000. I walk outside and scout for a different window to sneak through, but the windows appear to only be on the office side of the building. Dang.

Defeated, I grab my box and head back to my car. I make the trip to Danver Hills to try and find Lottie, but the current resident of Holly's house has no helpful information. He didn't even know who Holly was. I sigh and lean against the headrest in my car, grieving the lives of people I never knew.

CHAPTER 4

SPARKS

Have I mentioned how much I fucking hate coffee? Bitter, harsh, yuck. But Derek believes in this thing called a routine, so every morning is the same. Coffee and team meeting, gym time, and then work. Derek says it's to promote serotonin and shit, but I know it's just so he can keep an eye on me, make sure I'm not slipping back into the hole that he dug me out of. In an annoying way, I appreciate it. I've never liked coffee, always ordering a hot chocolate or a tea instead, but I've sworn off hot chocolate after her. It wouldn't be as good as hers anyway. It would bring up memories that are best kept away, so Derek always pours me a cup of brew. But I still hate coffee.

Oliver is on his third cup, gradually waking up, while Derek only needs one cup to be a functioning human. We've gone over all of the standard agenda points. The final topic is a potential expansion opportunity. A betting establishment up north is failing and is looking for an investor. Oliver confirms we have the cash flow to back it up, but Derek is worried about sharing stakes in the ring.

"If they're keeping ownership, we lose control," Derek argues. "Then it's up to them to ensure all payments are honored and that standards are held. It's not a good look on us if they get lax."

"I think we're ignoring the obvious issue," I add. "Why do they even need cash? More money isn't going to fix poor business practices. I say we offer to buy them out completely or walk away."

"But think about the territorial implications!" Oliver contributes. "We're making waves, but just imagine how much noise we'll make if we take 87th and Cardiff Street. It's practically unheard of for syndicates to set up that far north."

"We don't move to be flashy," Derek warns. "We move when we are stable enough to support it. Stability is strength. That being said, I do think we have enough manpower to extend our borders."

"Oliver, can you set up a meeting with their staff?" I ask. "I want you to take a look at their books directly."

Oliver nods and takes his coffee cup to his office. Derek and I pound knuckles as we walk into the gym. We wrap up our hands and wrists to spar.

"That was a good call, Sparkie." Derek beams with pride as we step into the ring. "You are really growing into your role as a mafiosa."

"Stop buttering me up." I roll my eyes. "Just punch me already."

"No, no, no," Derek teases. "The goal is to not get punched."

I groan and raise my hands. We circle each other for a few seconds, getting reacquainted with the rhythm of the gym. I duck as Derek swings a right hook, but don't see the left jab until I barely have time to block. I throw a kick and catch him below his ribs. He curses and I smirk, challenging him to do something about it. He does. I block what I can, and try to return fire when there's an opening, but I end up receiving the rough end of the sparring. Derek is pulling his punches, but I know I might have a few light bruises regardless.

Behind me, I hear a loud crash. I glance to look, just as a roundhouse catches me in the ribs. The breath is knocked from my lungs as I skid on the floor. I roll onto my hands and knees to recover.

"Shit, Sparks." Derek jogs over. "Are you okay? I've told you, focus on the fight inside the ring."

I don't hear what he says. Instead, I'm back on that goddamn boat. Powerless, fragile, weak. Crawling away as I am pulled back by my ankle. Defenseless as his hands roam my body. Gun pointed at Astrid. I won't let him hurt me again. With or without powers, I won't be a victim again. I won't stop until I'm stronger, faster, better.

I punch the floor, anger flaring. I recognize the lights of the gym are flashing. Other exercise enthusiasts clear out, weary of the massive shitshow that often accompanies my outbursts. I stand, reigning in my powers. Derek and I lock eyes, and I raise my fists.

Derek swings first, and I dodge while shooting a jab that catches his shoulder. We go back and forth again. This time I hold my own. We exchange blows until sweat drips from our arms and our knees are weak with exhaustion. Eventually, we both fall onto our backs, too tired to walk to the showers. Derek and I lie there in a comfortable silence, panting for air.

"He's dead," Derek says suddenly. "He can't hurt you anymore."

"I still have nightmares." I stare at the ceiling, unable to meet his eyes. He doesn't have to say Jack's name aloud. We both know who we're talking about. "I'm just waiting for him to pull the trigger, knowing there's nothing I can do. The target changes, sometimes it's Astrid or you. Other times, it's Jeremiah."

We don't talk about Jeremiah much. He used to work with Derek and Oliver when they were a part of the now-collapsed gang, the Tributaries. He died last December protecting me. Jack tortured us together before he just...

shot him. No warning, no real reason. Just to feel powerful. I know Derek and Oliver think about Jeremiah a lot. Neither one of them disagreed when I suggested we send a cut of our earnings each month to his mother. We've never said anything to her. Simply mail a check with "In Honor of Jeremiah" on the memo line. It's the least we could do.

"You're a better fighter than you were then." Derek's voice cuts through my internal spiral. "You know how to control the situation."

"I know," I whisper.

"You can protect yourself," Derek reassures.

"I can protect myself," I repeat.

I can protect myself. I can protect myself. I can.

⚡ ⚡ ⚡ ⚡

After a shower, we paid a little visit to the failing gambling ring. Derek and Oliver sit at the table, negotiating with the current owner. I stand behind them, posing as one of the bodyguards. A few more of our men stand outside, ready to intervene if necessary. It's poor taste to launch an attack during formal meetings, but we like to be prepared.

I try to pay attention to the discussion, but I don't really care. Revenue, profit sharing, blah, blah, blah. Oliver will summarize everything to me later anyway. That's good enough for me.

We take the show on the road as the owner offers a tour. This is where I come in handy. I slink into the shadows, preferring to observe from a distance. I study the body language of the small crowd – who's winning, who's losing, what the protocols seem to be. There must be some reason why this place is failing, and I'm determined to find it out.

After a few minutes of sleuthing, it's painstaking clear what the problem is. Patrons are betting more than they can spend, and no one is checking for collateral. Losers don't have anything to collect, so to prevent winners from getting ripped-off, the difference comes from the pocket of the house. This certainly won't do. If we want to play in this establishment, serious change is in order.

I regroup with Derek and Oliver as the tour wraps up. I can tell that they are also not enthused with the state of the place. The owner is frazzled, trying to save the investment. He must really be desperate.

The door opens and I casually observe a man walk to the bar. He's backlit so I have trouble making out specific features, but I know who he is. I feel my shoulders tense as I break off from the group. Derek notices my unusual reaction and subtly gestures for the group to split. Half of the guards stroll behind me without drawing attention from the owner. The mystery man is turned away from me, talking to the bartender. I can hear his voice clearly.

"Rum and Coke," he orders. I know that voice. I know it all too well.

"We're all out," the bartender says flatly, rubbing the counter with a towel, glancing at me. All out? There's plenty of rum right behind him.

Suddenly, the man takes off sprinting. Damn it! The bartender tipped him off!

"The bartender doesn't leave!" I shout as I take off after the runner. Blinded as I burst into the late afternoon sun, it takes me a second to locate the man. When I find him, he's already got a block lead on me. Fuck. We weave through crowds of people. I'm gaining on him as he scrambles down a staircase, taking the steps two at a time.

The metro! I make it to the platform just in time to see him board a train. I throw myself toward the doors, but they close before I can board.

The man turns to face me from the relative safety of the train car. The same goddamn cocky smirk. Jack has risen from the dead.

Waves of fury waft off of me as I return to the gambling den. The security detail gives me a healthy berth, but Derek holds his hand out to stop me. I sidestep him and walk straight up to the bartender, socking him in the face.

"Where is he?" I roar, clutching his lapels and pulling him down to me. Derek and Oliver grab me and drag me away, kicking and screaming. "You fucking bastard! Where is he?"

Oliver closes the door of the supply closet as Derek holds me against the wall, still squirming.

"Sparks, pull yourself together," Derek scolds. "Take a fucking breath and talk to us. We look like we have our thumbs in our fucking assholes out there!"

"Jack's alive!" I can't breathe. My vision goes fuzzy. My heart is beating a mile a minute in my chest. Derek releases his hold on me in shock, and I fall to my knees. Is the world vibrating, or am I shaking that hard? "He's alive. The fucking bartender tipped him off. I chased him to the subway, but I didn't make the train. But it's him, I'm sure of it."

Derek kneels next to me and guides my head between my knees.

"Deep breaths," he coaches. "In through your nose, hold, and out through your mouth."

I take a breath, then another. This isn't what I want! I'm pissed. I'm hurt and confused and feeling too many things to be calm. I slam my hand and the ground and stand, fists clenched by my side. Oliver stands before the doorway, blocking my exit.

"I'm going to break something," I threaten. "It could be that bartender's nose or that door. Take your pick."

"If you want to run this, you have to compose yourself." Derek steps back in front of me again. I'm getting real tired of this shit. "You can be angry. Fine, I don't care. But you're being irrational and rash. Use your rage, channel it, control it."

"What's your plan, Sparks?" Oliver asks. "We'll back you up."

"The bartender knows something." I roll back my shoulders. "Knows enough to have coded warnings. Interrogate him, then go from there."

"Oliver, talk to the owner," Derek delegates. "Since his deal is dissolving before his eyes, we might be able to renegotiate for favorable terms. Complete ownership or nothing. I'll go with Sparks and see what information we can extract."

The door opens and I stalk through. The crowd parts like the Red Sea as I walk straight up to the bartender. A trickle of blood has dried beneath his nose. He is being restrained by some of our men. It's time we had a little chat.

The men lead the bartender into a secluded room in the back. It looks like they had the forethought to set up an impromptu interrogation room. Single chair in the center, table with some makeshift tools on the side. I'll have to remember to give them a bonus when we get back to base. The men tie the bartender to the chair, and I dismiss them to guard the door outside. Derek drags in a second chair and reclines in the corner, whistling to himself.

"Do you need your boss to babysit you?" The bartender sneers.

"Nah," I reply, dragging my fingers along the table edge. "He just likes to watch a good show. Unfortunately for him, I'm in a bit of a hurry, so let's wrap this up quickly. What do you like to be called?"

"William." He spits at my feet.

"Hiya Billy, nice to meet you." I lean against the table, fiddling with a screwdriver. "I really only have one question. Where's Jack?"

"Who?" Billy smiles with mock innocence.

"I guess you're at a bit of a disadvantage," I ponder aloud. "I know who you are, but you don't know who I am. Jack never told you about his ex, I suppose?"

"I don't know who Jack is," he sneers. "But even if I did, I wouldn't care about some bitch ex-girlfriend."

"Do you hear that?" Derek chuckles amusedly. "You practically have a fan club."

I take a step forward, allowing my power to surge through the room causing the lights to flicker.

"Whoa, whoa, whoa!" Billy panics, tugging at his restraints.

"Does that jog your memory?" My mouth curves into a malicious smile. "Where's Jack?"

"This can't be real," Billy stammers.

"Are you willing to stake your life on that claim?" I glare at him as I move closer with slow deliberate steps. "Where's Jack?"

"I... I don't know, probably back at the compound."

"What compound?" I pick apart his wording.

"He's planning on making a move, reinstating the Tributaries. But that's all I'm going to say." He raises his chin indignantly, confidence suddenly regained.

"What do you think, Derek?" I banter. "Want to see a show?"

"Kill the lights." He gives a nod.

For a split second, I see the realization cross Billy's face as he realizes just how real I am, but before the gravity of the situation can sink in, I pull the electricity from the room. Billy shrieks as the room goes black.

I cackle as I play around with the energy coursing through my veins. Silver sparks cascade from my fingertips as I stride toward the center of the room, casting a feral glow on my face. I snap as I launch a flash of light over his shoulder. He cowers in the brief ray of the beam before the room is once again encased in darkness.

"I'm sorry!" Billy cries. "I'll talk, I'll tell you everything!"

"How boring," I pout. "I was just beginning to enjoy myself."

"Jack was planning on taking out Derek," he blubbers. "He's bitter that the Tributaries was being replaced by a former member. I was supposed to warn him if I thought he was compromised. When I saw you walking toward him, I figured you knew."

"Where is the compound?" I seethe.

"I don't know." A lie. Not acceptable. I charge my hand with electricity and grip his shoulder. He howls as the energy courses through his body.

"I believe I mentioned earlier that I was in a hurry." I drag a fingernail along his jaw. "Do not make me repeat myself."

"571 Northridge Avenue," Billy says dejectedly. "Jack will probably be in the panic room in the basement. The code is 772757. It spells 'Sparks.'"

"Thank you," I purr. I restore power to the lights. I glance at Derek who is blinking from the unexpected brightness. "Kill him."

I walk out of the room and Derek rises, pistol in hand. Billy's screams are cut short by the ring of a gunshot. I lock eyes with one of the guards.

"Activate the team," I order. "Everyone who is on call. I want them at 571 Northridge Avenue in fifteen minutes. Everyone else, get ready to roll out. Check your weapons, we're going in hot."

In the corner, Oliver and the owner are arguing, probably unable to agree on a deal. Frankly, I don't give a shit about this place anymore, but I do need Oliver focused on our next venture. I barge into their conversation.

"Look," I interject. "This den is shit. Your operations are shit. I'm pretty sure your books are also shit. You won't be in business for much longer, so either accept our deal or don't. Oliver has given you our final offer, which is only on the table for..." I look at my imaginary watch. "Fifteen more seconds. After that, we're leaving."

"Hold on." The man waves his hands. "This is my livelihood."

"Five, four, three." I tap on my watch. "Oh, look at that. My clock was off. You're out of time. Oliver, let's go."

We turn to walk away before the man grabs Oliver's arm.

"Three percent ownership," he pleads. "Something for me to retire on. I'll be a silent partner, you'll never hear from me."

Oliver waits a beat, doing calculations inside his head before shaking the owner's hand. I guess ex-owner.

"Pleasure," I say. "Now, we have people to kill and I'm tired of waiting."

Without checking to see if anyone was following me, I stride out of the den and straddle my bike. I hear the group clamoring behind me, but I rev my engine and veer onto the road. Within minutes, the group catches up and I am leading a cavalry of very dangerous people. Little does the world know, I'm the one to fear.

We pull up to a nondescript house in a seedy part of town. I don't even bother turning off my bike as I stalk up the porch steps. There's too much electricity running through this house, this isn't residential. Good to know we're at the right spot. My powers connect with the building, and with a solid yank, they lose their lights. Thuds and clamors can be heard inside, as the inhabitants struggle in the dark.

A team member rushes forward with a battering ram, and with a swing, the doors crack. Derek kicks through the splinters and I flood the lights back on. The hostiles fumble for their weapons, temporarily blinded, but they unfortunately won't have time to grab them. I reach toward the ceiling and bring my fist down, shooting bolts of electricity into the first group of men. They fall to the ground. Dead? Unconscious? Who gives a flying fuck.

Derek leads the charge, motivated by the knowledge of the failed assassin attempt. Fights break out on either side of the room as reinforcements flood in, but my men engage with them before they can reach me. My mind is set on my target. Jack.

I leave the fighting behind me and hustle down the staircase. Three men with pistols guard a metal door. Looks like that's where I want to go. I slowly slip my right hand behind my back and pull a small metal disk out of my belt, loading a pulse of electricity into it. This idea worked once before, maybe it'll work again.

"Hey guys, do you think we could just talk this out?" I hold my arms out non-threateningly. "No? Fine. Catch."

I flick the disk toward the leftmost man. It smacks his forehead, and the charge causes him to collapse. Bullets riddle the staircase behind me. I feel something pierce my bicep as I jump to the right, but I don't have time to worry about that right now. I pull electricity into my suit as the closest man tries to grab me. He seizes as he comes in contact with the charged aluminum running through the fabric, falling onto me. I hold him up to shield myself from the final gunmen before heaving his body toward his companion. Not super effective, as the gunman just sidesteps him. But that's what I wanted. Focused on his friend, I kick the gun out of his hand and land a jab directly on his nose. He rears back, eyes watering. Tired of this unnecessary distraction, I shock him into unconsciousness.

Finally, the path to the door is clear. This is it. I thought Jack was dead earlier, but no matter, I'll make sure of it this time. I roll my shoulders back and wince, remembering the gunshot I took. Pull yourself together, Sparks. You'll take care of that later.

I approach the door and place my hand on the cool metal. I allow myself to sink into the electricity, probing for any booby traps or nuisances. Everything seems to be in order. I reach up to the keypad – 772757.

The room is dimly lit, but I can see well enough. A few bunk beds line the far wall. In front of me is a coffee table with two lounge chairs. There's a note on the table, alongside a small gift box. I unfold the note. "With Love, —J." Inside the box is a single rope of black licorice. Damn it!

He's not here. I scream as I kick over the table, sending the box flying.

I'm going to kill this motherfucker, no matter how long it takes.

CHAPTER 5

ASTRID

Mimi's not surprised when I show up back at the house. But then again, Mimi is never surprised at anything. She just knows things. She doesn't bat an eye when I faceplant on the sofa, groaning into a pillow.

"Not driving up to Boston, I presume?" Mimi jests, a mischievous glimmer in her eye.

"I simply cannot fail at another thing today." My voice is muffled, so I'm not sure how much Mimi hears, but she tousles my hair anyway. "No more big life decisions, no more big mysteries, no more nothing."

"Mysteries?" She lowers herself onto the floor next to my head. "Bad book?"

"No." I flop onto the floor next to her. "I... What can you tell me about Synergy Labs?"

"Astrid." Mimi sits up, all levity vanished. "You are not to be snooping around Synergy Labs."

"I'm not!" I say defensively. Oops. That was a lie. I've been telling too many of those recently. "I think I know someone who was related to a victim of the explosion."

"I thought you were cutting the cord with Anise?" Mimi questions.

"I am, but it's just bothering me." I pick at my cuticles. "Like she never talks about her mom, so something serious must have happened there. But... wait. How did you know it was Anise?"

"Honey, you were distraught over the girl just a few hours ago." She tuts her tongue. "It's not a huge logical jump to think you're still hung up on her."

"What happened at the labs, Mimi?" I pose the question again. She sighs.

"I don't know more than anybody else, which is to say, I know nothing." Mimi shakes her head. "Those folks were secretive. I did play bingo with one of the scientists over in Danver Hills. He said they were going to save the world. Full of excitement and hope. It's quite the shame he was one of the casualties." She takes a moment to reminisce.

"All that aside, you know I'm skilled at speaking with the spirits," she continues. "In times of great tragedy, I try to help them cross over. I'll sit at the site and commune with the deceased. The spirits at Synergy Labs were unsettled. They felt betrayed and vengeful. A terrible act led to the explosion, and I want you nowhere near this."

"Did you ever speak to a Holly Jennings?" I ask, fully pushing my luck at this point.

"Yes." Mimi gestures for me to help her stand, and I do so. "Now, scurry along back to Boston. You know I love your visits, but your parents will be home soon. If you don't leave now, you won't be back to your cafe until Easter."

"But Holly—"

"Astrid Larson." Mimi gives me a pointed look. "Holly is okay. Leave her and her companions to rest in peace."

"Yes, Mimi."

I know that Mimi said to stay away, but I just can't shake the feeling that something is deeper here. Something that connects me to Holly, something that connects my powers to the horrible accident. I can't just drop it. My divination is nowhere near as good as Mimi's, and I'm not bold enough to engage with upset spirits. With the way my luck is going today, I'll just end up possessed.

But you know what I can do? I can read through these notebooks and physics textbooks, slowly trying to piece together what they were working on. I flip a few pages back in the textbook, loosely matching some symbols to the notebook. "$K + U = $ constant." "$K_1 + U_1 = K_2 + U_2$." Huh. Did I just say I can do this? Yeah, I got nothing. I set my mug down and lean back. After three cups of coffee, I have nothing but papers and textbooks scattered over my rug. Oh, and insomnia. Whether it's the coffee or the swirling letters in front of my eyes, sleep is not a remote possibility.

The same thought loops on my brain. It's unhelpful and irksome, and I'm growing more frustrated each time it shoves its way front and center of my consciousness. *You know who would be able to read this? Anise! She was always so great at science.*

Quite frankly, that's a stupid thought. Anise didn't finish high school. There's no way she would be able to read formulas designed by professional scientists. I've probably made it farther than she would. *What do you mean? You haven't made any progress.*

Grr! I shut the textbook harder than I probably should given its old age. I pace around my living room, biting at my shredded cuticles. Maybe I could attend a physics lecture! Maybe I'd luck out and I can find one covering Ks and Us... whatever those are. Ugh, this is pathetic. There's just one more place I can try.

I glance at the For Lottie journal, set carefully on my entryway table. I gently flip to a random page. The penmanship is delicate, letters filled with love and care for a mystery loved one. Maybe Holly talked about her work. Maybe...

No. I shut the journal. Holly and Lottie deserve privacy, even in death. It wouldn't be right to intrude. Unless, maybe Holly left clues as to who Lottie was. It's not prying if I'm trying to return the journal, right? No. Well...

I open the journal and the pages fall to the last entry.

Dear Lottie,

I just got the news that I will be missing your birthday tomorrow, and I don't know how to tell you. Any other year, nothing would pull me away, but I want you to know that I'll be thinking of you every moment. I promise that this weekend, I will make it up to you. I'll make your favorite dinner, and we'll eat birthday cake and ice cream until our stomachs ache.

We are so close to finishing our project. I know you don't understand it now, but the work I do, I do it for you. You inspire me to want to change the world. When this discovery is revealed, so many things will change, all for the better.

Leadership is getting restless. We're not getting the profits they want. It turns out, scientific research is quite a shoddy investment. I feel like I could have told them that. It is now a race for us to complete our research before they pull the plug on spending. Once we have concrete proof that our theory has merit, we're publishing the research. It's against our contract, proprietary information and all that, but this knowledge is too important, too valuable to be privatized.

But don't you worry. All will be well, I'll make sure of it. Happy Birthday, my dearest Lottie.

Holly ends the letter with a swoopy signature. It's dated the day before the explosion. Lottie never got her birthday celebration.

The question now posed is, what caused the explosion? Did their theory not pan out, or did something happen? And who is this leadership? I pull out the staff binder and flip through the pages, looking for important sounding titles. Nothing really catches my eye.

I gather my materials off the floor and reshelve it all back in the box. I'm back at square zero, stumped by taking college psychology instead of physics. I'll have to try again tomorrow.

Or you could have Anise take a look. The unhelpful voice in my head butts back in.

No. I'm not dragging my ex into nearly a decade old drama. She would barely speak to me about Synergy Labs while we were together. Now that we're separated? Forget it.

Besides, what would she even do if she saw me again? I don't deserve to be welcomed with open arms. I briefly saw her the other day and I couldn't think straight. Being in the same room with her? I doubt I'd be of much use.

You aren't of much use now.

Regardless, this is my own mystery to solve. I won't get her involved.

CHAPTER 6

SPARKS

I didn't get much sleep last night. Screaming interrogation victims tend to do that to you. Good news — the Tributaries are really disbanded now. I doubt their numbers can recover from this loss.

Only a few members are still alive. After about, eh, thirty hours give or take without sleep, I imagine it won't be much longer until they spill the location of Jack's safehouse. Derek sends me upstairs to get some rest and recover, so I begrudgingly leave the interrogations to him. He has more experience with them anyway.

The medic intercepts me in my post-adrenaline stupor, spotting the injury on my arm. I had honestly forgotten about the gunshot wound below my shoulder, but now that I was reminded, it throbs like a bitch. He leads me to a bedroom away from the chaos of the group for a closer examination.

"Ma'am, my name is Luca," he introduces himself in a confident and professional manner. "Would you feel comfortable unzipping your suit so I can have better access to the wound?"

"I'm fine. Let's just make this quick."

I unzip the top of my suit, exposing my black lace bra. One of these days, I will start wearing a tank top underneath my uniform, but today is apparently not that day. Luca averts his eyes, focusing on guiding my arm free from the fabric. The cold air stings. I bite my lip and look away, focused on keeping my shit together.

"Looks like a deep graze, but nothing too dramatic." Luca assesses carefully. His fingers trail along the lightning scar along my forearm. I can see the questions forming in his mind, but he tactfully refocuses. "You'll need stitches, but you'll regain full movement of your arm in a few days."

"Just give me some pain meds and I'll be fine," I grunt as I roll my shoulder, forcing the movement through the pain.

"Ma'am," Luca says sternly. "I have had many macho patients eager to get back in the field. I understand you are in a hurry to go and get shot again, but if you don't take care of yourself, the next bullet will be harder to shake. Now, sit still while I give you some anesthetic."

I huff and lean back in my chair as he preps his equipment. He's right of course, but that doesn't make me feel better. I stare off in the distance, planning my next move. While Derek is a talented interrogator, we might need an alternative method to locate Jack. There's got to be some clues here somewhere. A sudden sting recaptures my attention. I jerk my arm away, but his firm grip holds my bicep in place.

"Sorry," Luca mumbles, focused on administering the anesthetic. "Should have warned you there."

He slowly removes the needle from my arm before swabbing the wound with a disinfectant wipe. The medicine hasn't quite kicked in, so it stings like a bitch.

"Motherfucker," I hiss as I clench the arm of the chair.

"You just got shot and an alcohol pad is what brings you down?" Luca teases. "No, you're right, I'd rather get shot. Now, here comes the stitches. Look or don't, I don't care."

I'm not ashamed to admit, I close my eyes. I rest my head against the wall and focus on my breathing, long and deep. Fortunately, my arm is numb, so I only vaguely feel some painless tugging. I hear the scissors clip, and then soft gauze rolled around my arm.

"That should do it." Luca claps his hands together and stands up. "You live in the compound, right? I can swing by when those are ready to come out. Keep that clean, there's extra dressings in the med bay. Or if I'm bored, I might give you the star treatment and wrap it myself. Don't fuck up my good work by getting it infected."

"Thanks, Luca." I give him a tired nod. "I'll be seeing you soon."

"Not too soon," he scolds, and leaves to check on other team members.

While in the bedroom, I figure a quick power nap wouldn't hurt, but nightmares haunt my dreams. The world is blurry, except for Jack's smirk taunting me. He's saying something to me, but I can't hear the words. I panic. What is he saying? I can't make it out, but I know it's important. The sounds are muddled as if we are underwater. Suddenly, the bubble pops and I can hear him clear as day.

But that also means, I don't need you.

No!

I know what's coming before it happens. The gunshot rings in my ears. Hot liquid splatters across my body, dripping down my cheek. Blood. Jeremiah's blood.

His body hangs on chains suspended from the ceiling. Limp. Broken. Lifeless. The red puddle at his feet grows larger as the blood pools. This is all my fault. I couldn't stop him.

Behind Jeremiah, I see more figures, hidden by shadow. The lights flick on. Derek. Astrid. My mother. No, no please.

But that also means...

I shoot up in bed, chest heaving as sweat drips from my brow. I wipe my face and force myself to calm down. I'm safe. Derek is safe. Jeremiah... Jeremiah made his own decisions.

I get dressed and leave the bedroom. Derek is sitting at the kitchen table, dark circles under his eyes. He shakes his head when he sees me, nothing yet.

"Go take a nap," I order. "You're no good sleep-deprived. I'll see what I can figure out."

Derek moves to protest but thinks better of it. He staggers toward the bedroom I came out of. I walk to the kitchen sink and splash some water on my face, hoping I look more alert than I feel.

There's a shift change happening. Guards clock out as their replacements arrive. I'm glad we can get some fresh troops, but I do feel envious of those going home. I raid the fridge and scrap together a meager sandwich. Fed and somewhat rested, I start snooping.

I pass by a few extra rooms with barracks before I find what I'm looking for – an office. A laptop is resting on the only desk. I power it up and groan when it asks for a passcode. On a whim, I type in the code to the door downstairs. Huh. What would you know? I'm in.

I click through the folders. Downloads. Documents. Pictures. All blank. Motherfucker. I open the email app. It's logged in. Here we go! This could have something. I read email after email. Spam. Spam. Boring operations nonsense. Spam. Ugh, I'm so glad Oliver likes doing the admin work. It would be torture having to do all of our paperwork. Maybe I could have the assholes in interrogation downstairs sort through some. Now that would get them talking.

Wait. Hold on.

It's pretty clear that Jack cleared out everything of any importance just in case we were able to get past all of his security – which we did pretty easily. I'm not going to find any clues laying around in the open. Hell, the men downstairs genuinely might not know where Jack's safehouse is.

But does Jack share my disinterest in paperwork? I can't picture him hunched over a desk filling out tax forms. Is it possible...

I reopen the email I formerly discarded. It seems to be a utility bill of some kind. I click to view the itemized invoice. There's a listing for 571 Northridge Avenue. No surprise there, that's where we are, but there's a second charge on the line below. I got him.

The team assembles quickly, packing up gear and dispatching the remaining captives downstairs. It isn't long before we are back on the road. I lead the caravan on my bike, speeding down city streets. The light turns yellow right as I enter the intersection, and a slew of curses leave my mouth as the red light stops the group behind me. While we pay off the local police force, we try not to push our luck too far. A red-and-white striped barrier descends, blocking the road for the light rail train. You have got to be shitting me.

I glance back at Derek, then at the open road in front of me. I know I should wait, but my nightmare flashes before my eyes. Derek hanging from the ceiling, gunshot wound to the face, blood dripping onto the floor.

I can't let him get hurt. I'm sorry, Derek. He calls out to me, but I rev my bike and shoot down the road.

I cut my engine as I pull up in front of a quaint house. The shutters are painted a crisp white and the garden is blooming. It doesn't look like a safe house, but I don't have the luxury of doubt. In one swift kick, I bust through the door ready for a fight. But that's not what I get.

"It was unlocked," Jack calls out from a side room. "But whatever works, I suppose."

I hesitantly round the corner into a sitting room. Two recliners face each other. Jack is sprawled in the furthest one, holding a glass of whiskey. A second cup is sitting on an end table next to him. The ice cubes haven't even melted. He gestures for me to take it.

"Please sit, have a drink." He takes a sip.

"I'll stand." This is a trap. Something is wrong.

"What took you so long?" He questions. "I've been waiting."

"It's over, Jack." Venom laces my voice. "The Tributaries have collapsed. I don't know how you survived the fall from the ship, but I'll make sure this next fatality sticks."

"Funny, I thought you died too," Jack chuckles, ignoring my threat. "It took me by surprise seeing you yesterday. Although it makes sense, Derek doesn't have it in him to run a mafia on his own. How's your girlfriend?"

I try to hide my emotions, but it doesn't matter. Jack has always been able to read me.

"Trouble in paradise?" He muses. "Who broke up with who? Let me guess, you broke it off with her." He pauses, scanning my body language. "No? She broke up with you?" I flinch involuntarily. "Tsk, tsk. Too bad."

"You don't know what you're talking about." My voice trembles, and I hate myself for it. I hate how Jack can always find exactly what button to push.

"Sparks, baby," Jack croons. I used to love the way he said my name, now it makes me sick. "I'm the only person who truly knows you. You can try and deny it, but I get you, more than your girlie, more than Derek, more than anyone."

"I've changed," I argue. "I'm stronger now."

"No, you're not," Jack chides. "If you were, you would have killed me as soon as you walked in. Face it, you can't kill me because in some twisted way, you still love me."

"No." I'm horrified at the accusation. My composure falters, and I stumble back a step.

"Sparks, it's okay." Jack sits up. "I love you too."

I turn away from him, clutching my stomach. His voice is ringing in my head, I can't think straight. I'm stronger now. I have to be.

If not, what was it all for?

His hand rests gently on my shoulder and spins me to face him. He slowly pushes back my hood. I stand before him, feeling vulnerable and exposed.

"You've cut your hair." He purses his lips and places a lock behind my ear. "I can't braid it now. You'll have to wait until it grows out."

I don't say anything. I can't. All of the air seems to have left my lungs. Dejected, I lower my head and stare at the floor.

"When Derek walks through that door," Jack pauses to lift my chin, making eye contact with me. "Shoot him."

He places a gun in my hand. It's heavy. The matte black metal leeches the warmth from my hand.

I know how to use a gun. Derek taught me a few months ago, and we have occasional practice on the gun range. But

I don't like guns. They're loud and foreboding. I much prefer to fight with my hands or my powers. It's more utilitarian, and I can rely on stealth instead of brute force.

I take the gun and check the chamber. It's loaded. I toggle off the safety.

"You can do this." Jack seems excited, like a morbid cheerleader.

Meanwhile, I can't get over the nauseous pit in my stomach. I hear a horde of engines ripping down the street. Jack retreats back to his chair, grinning ear to ear. He takes another sip of his whiskey.

"Sparks!" Derek calls frantically. I can hear the panic in the voice as he barges through what's left of the door.

I take a breath,

Raise my gun,

And fire.

Blood spatters across the wall. I'm close enough that I get covered, the residual heat from the liquid riles my stomach. A whiskey glass tumbles to the ground, splashing on the wood. I engage the safety and tuck the gun into my belt, before stepping through the fluid coating the ground. I pick up the second glass of whiskey and down the liquid. A bloody lip print is left on the glass. I duck past a stunned Derek, straddle my bike, and drive home.

CHAPTER 7

ASTRID

So anyways, I'm on my way to the Lightning Bolt. Do I know where Anise lives? No. But, I do remember hearing the club mentioned when I was eavesdropping on her the other day. So… yeah, I'm going to poke around. The box of notebooks and textbooks are safely secured in my trunk. Once Anise agrees to help me, I'll come get them. She will agree to help, right?

It's been a bit since I've been to a club, so I am kind of excited to get all dressed up. I'm wearing a white bandeau and a metallic navy skirt with stacked gold necklaces. I didn't go too crazy on my makeup, only a subtle amount of shimmer just in case the Water Weaver needs to appear. There won't be time to remove elaborate eyeshadow and lip gloss.

There's a nervous butterfly in the pit of my stomach. I'm going to see Anise again. Dare I say, this could be… fun? I'm driving way over the speed limit, almost giddy. I'm not usually like this. I'm calm and collected, not rushing headfirst into unknown situations. I should stop, turn around, but my hatchback continues onwards.

The bass matches the beat of my heart as I walk into the club. *Tha-thump. Tha-thump. Tha-thump.* I nervously smooth out the wrinkles of my skirt. The lights strobe in an ever-changing myriad of colors – red, pink, purple, green. I can see why Anise likes this place.

I see a flash of red across the way and dance across the floor. Oh, it's not her. Another redhead! No dice. I must have made the rounds at least three times, and I'm getting discouraged. I wander over to the bar and lean against the counter.

"What can I get for you?" The bartender asks. He has his long brown hair in a loose ponytail, and sleeves rolled up to show off the bottom of a swirly tattoo.

"I'm looking for someone who sometimes hangs out here," I confess. "But I can't seem to find her. Her name is Sparks. She has red hair about to her shoulders. Have you seen her?"

"Huh, not ringing a bell." The bartender cocks his head. "I can ask around. Do you want a drink while you wait?"

"Just water is fine."

"You sure?" He sets down his towel and scans me up and down. "Nothing else?"

"I'm good."

He walks away for a moment. I think he's forgotten about my water, but I'd rather he looks for Sparks anyway. I lean against the bar and play with a napkin as I wait.

"My, you've had too much to drink," an unfamiliar voice says. Before I can react, I feel a sharp prick in the back of my neck. "Let me help you find a cab."

My legs go wobbly as the mystery man pulls my arm over his shoulders. He practically drags me as I fight against the blackness creeping over my vision. My arms go numb, I can't feel my legs. Finally, my head lobs forward as I lose my battle and fall asleep.

❧　　❧　　❧　　❧

I feel like my tongue has been replaced with sandpaper. I fight the urge to open my eyes. No, keep pretending you're unconscious. Learn what you can to help you escape. Go down the senses.

Taste. What can I taste? Nothing, but that one's normally a dud.

Smell. I breathe through my nose slowly, trying to not draw any attention. Bleach and copper. Oh god, I smell blood. Don't panic. Three more senses.

Touch. For once, I'm glad to be in such skimpy clothing, as I can clearly feel the metal chair I'm sitting in. It feels solid, not like a rickety folding chair. I wonder if it's bolted down. Either way, I'm stuck to this chair due to the zip ties around my wrists and ankles. They are uncomfortably tight, but not so much that I'm losing circulation.

Sound. I'm not getting anything. I'm probably not in the club anymore, otherwise, I would be able to hear the bass.

This is not good.

I take the risk to open my eyes, leaving my head drooped against my chest. I can't see much from here. White laminate floors, white painted walls. I see a drain in the floor behind me, possibly for easy clean up. Unfortunately, that might be where the smell of blood is coming from. I think I've learned all I can without "waking up." I take a deep breath and lift my head.

Anise is lounging in the corner, hugging a knee to her chest. She's sitting on a folding chair and reclining against a table covered with a bumpy sheet. I'm so glad Anise is here, she can help me get all of this mess sorted out.

My smile falters when I examine her more closely. She's wearing combat boots, cutoffs, and a black tank top. Her left arm is bandaged and there is blood splatter along her hairline. It looks like she was interrupted in the middle of her shower, since her hair is stringy and roughly towel dried. Most disturbingly though are her eyes. All of their former light is gone. In its place is resentment, bitterness, and maybe a bit of grief. She's staring at me as though she's been sitting there for hours. Perhaps a bit stupidly, I forget about the gravity of my own situation.

"Are you okay?" I ask. It hurts to see her like this. I thought she was happy and carefree, galivanting with her friends. But the Anise in front of me looks worse than the one I met all those months ago.

"You don't get to ask me that."

"I was looking for you." Seems like a good place to start as any.

"You don't get to do that either." This is not going well. A beat passes. Then another. "Why are you here?"

"I need your help—" Anise scoffs before I can even finish my sentence.

"No." Her voice is firm and decisive. "Anything else?"

"What happened to you?" I question, flabbergasted by her hostility. "The Anise I know would never act like this."

"Don't call me that!" She bristles at my tone. "I don't go by Anise anymore, only Sparks now."

"You once told me that name was given to you by someone who betrayed you." I shake my head. "You can't expect me to believe you want to use it again."

"The person who called me Anise betrayed me worse." Her voice is cold, unforgiving.

"That's not fair." My voice is barely above a whisper.

"No, it wasn't." Her scorn is clear.

"You're the one who was lying to me." My voice cracks as I start to lose my composure. "I did what I had to."

"I was protecting you." She stands, her chair falling over from the abrupt movement. "Everything I did, everything that happened, was for you."

"Your protection looks an awful lot like throwing others under the bus," I snap. "Everyone would be better off if you weren't involved."

"Go ahead, say it," she challenges.

"I had to go in blind, no planning." I jerk in my restraints. "I could have done something."

"That's not what you meant." There's a tone of derisiveness in her voice. "Don't be a fucking coward."

"Fine! Jeremiah is dead!" Angry tears start to well up in my eyes. "My friend was murdered, and I was home twiddling my thumbs, all because you were scared."

"You put an awful lot of blame on me while he was making his own decisions!" Anise screams, whatever hold she had on her temper long gone. "He knew he wasn't making it out, but he chose to stay!"

"You didn't even know him!" My throat is raw, but I couldn't be bothered. "He was my friend!"

"I was being tortured too! Do you ever think about that?" Her hands clutch her stomach as she subconsciously curls her shoulders defensively. She scrunches her eyes shut and I can almost see the phantom wounds on her body. "I don't think you do."

She's right. I don't. I can't. That night is too painful, even without picturing what happened on that boat.

"I killed a man." Big, fat tears roll down my cheeks. "I don't know how to live with that."

"No, you didn't." Anise's voice turns cold as her face goes blank. No anger, no resentment, just a vacancy behind her eyes.

"What?" I sniffle, confused. "What do you mean?"

"He survived," she states like a catatonic doll. "Don't worry though, I shot him. He's dead now. I killed him." Her hand brushes the residual blood splatter on her hairline, and she stares at the red coating her fingertips.

"Anise..."

"It's Sparks!" She snaps out of her stupor. "So there you go, you can stop bitching and moaning about your tarnished moral report card. You're in the clear again."

"Ani— Sparks, I don't think you're okay."

"No shit, detective," she retorts. "But you lost the right to worry about me."

"It doesn't matter," I reply softly. "I still do. I haven't stopped."

Sparks take a breath, and I can see her body reset. Her mask slips on and I just know, I've lost Anise. The thought breaks my heart a little more than it already was.

"What do you want?" She asks. "Why are you here?"

"I went to Synergy Labs and I—"

Sparks holds up a hand. I stop mid-sentence.

"Excuse me, I must have misheard you." A maniacal laugh slips out of her lips. "Or else I must be hallucinating, because to me, it sounds like you said you went to Synergy Labs and that can't be the case. It couldn't be. I mean, they are only responsible for every shitty thing that has literally ever happened to me, including the colossal fuck up that was me and you. So I swear to fucking god, if I just heard that you null and voided everything I went through to keep you safe by visiting it like a goddamn field trip, I am going to lose my shit."

Sparks stares at me. I am too scared to say anything. She walks over and crouches in front of me.

"Now is the time where you tell me I misheard you," she coaches.

"I don't think the explosion was an accident," I whisper.

Sparks stands up suddenly and faces the wall. I notice she has a gun tucked into the waistband of her shorts, and I am now deeply regretting my decision to come. Without warning, she grabs the edge of the table and throws it. Several metal instruments clatter to the ground as the sheet billows gently. Screwdrivers, meat tenderizers, pliers, knives. This... this is a torture room. Oh god. I feel the blood drain from my face. Sparks kicks the upturned table in frustration. She runs her hands through her hair.

Sparks turns to me exasperated. She gestures vehemently and I flinch, ducking my head. I hold my breath, bracing against the incoming blow. But it doesn't happen. I cautiously open my eyes. She's standing there crestfallen. I've never seen her in such anguish.

"You thought I was going to hurt you?" She says feebly. I can't tell if it's a question or a statement, but I can't think of a response either way. "I would never. Astrid, I..."

She looks around at the havoc strewn across the floor. Without another word, she turns and walks out of the room.

CHAPTER 8

SPARKS

What was it all for? What was any of it for? The suffering, the heartbreak, the loss. Was it all for nothing?

I killed Jack. Raised my pistol and fired. I felt his blood smear on my cheek. He raped me, abused me, tortured me, but when I killed him, I felt nothing. No, worse than that, I grieved. All of this training, fighting to become stronger. It's all a lie. I'm still weak and broken.

And Astrid. I fall to my knees overwhelmed by the pain crashing into my body from all directions. I lost what felt like the love of my life, and for what? I spent my entire life trying to destroy those responsible for Synergy Labs, needing to prevent another tragedy. I was willing to give that up for her. Truly, I was. To let my mother's memory die and allow myself to dive into a childish crush. I know now that's all that it was. Fleeting infatuation between two incompatible people.

Then I got dragged back into the whole Synergy mess, but it was okay, because I could keep her safe. I've learned since then that I was the only one who survived the Synergy Labs explosion. Jack lied to me for years, telling me ghost stories about an organization that goes bump in the night, wanting to turn me into a weapon. I don't know what is true anymore, and I don't want to find out. I'm done with it. But for her to walk straight into the mess herself? It's a slap in the face to every sacrifice I've made.

I was done. I walked away from it all. Fuck duty and honor and love. It was time for me to put myself first.

Exercise, healthy habits, a career, financial success. I feel so empty. The hole inside of me aches and threatens to drag me down into it. Haven't I given enough?

I burst into the gym. Empty. Good. I lock the doors to keep it that way. I find the nearest punching bag. Fuck the gloves, fuck the hand wraps. I throw the hardest punch I can. I feel the impact from my wrist to my shoulder. The agony is brutal, but it doesn't drown out the anguish from my trauma.

I punch again.

Again.

Left. Right. Left. Right.

It's too much. I can't take it anymore.

I collapse on the ground. All I want to do is scream, to yell and shout and wail, but no sound comes out. I want to throw a tantrum and bang on the floor and kick the walls. Instead, I curl into a ball as silent tears rack my body.

I miss my life before. I miss the coffee shop, ice skating, dancing in the living room. I miss a warm bed at night, a tender hand soothing an injury, a voice calming my fears. I miss her.

What was it all for? I don't have a clue.

Once all of my pieces have been carefully taped back together, I walk back into the interrogation room, a slice of watermelon in hand. I find my chair on the ground and sit across from Astrid, painfully aware of how closely she watches my movements. I truly didn't mean to scare her.

"Are you thirsty?" I ask, extending a proverbial olive branch. She stares suspiciously as I extend the watermelon.

"This isn't water," Astrid states.

"I'm not stupid," I reply. She begrudgingly takes a bite of the watermelon.

"Am I a prisoner here?" She asks delicately.

"No." I shake my head and take a bite of the fruit for myself.

"Then can I leave?" She follows up.

"No." I hold my finger up as I swallow. "Well, you can, but we'd have to drug you and find your car and it's a whole thing."

"I see." It doesn't sound like she does.

"We can't have a known vigilante knowing where our base is," I elaborate. "Bad for business."

"Did you do something worth reporting?" She narrows her eyes at my knuckles, bruised from my earlier meltdown.

"Oh fuck off, Astrid." I roll my eyes. "It is completely legal to beat up a punching bag."

"You're bleeding," she states nonchalantly.

"What?" I glance at my hands. Bruised yes, bloody no. She juts her chin toward my shoulder, and a fresh trickle of blood has dribbled free of the gauze. I must have popped a stitch. Luca is going to kill me. I shrug. "So I am."

"It is alarming how comfortable you are with being injured," Astrid observes. I'm getting really tired of this conversation.

"Synergy Labs." That got her attention. "You have two minutes, say whatever you want to say, then I'm leaving."

No sooner have I finished my sentence than she is rambling at full speed.

"I got my powers the day the explosion happened. I began thinking that they were related so I decided to start digging. Then I put together all of the details you told me about your mom, and I think it's safe to assume she died in the explosion. Then I was like, duh, the explosion probably gave you your powers too!"

I blink at the rapid amount of information she just threw my way. It's startling to have someone recite my past back to me, especially due to how tightly I keep it under wraps. She doesn't seem to notice my visceral reaction, continuing on with her saga.

"So then I was looking into what caused the explosion, and I think it was some kind of foul play! The scientists were planning on publishing data that would ruin the profitability of their research, thus ticking off the big wigs. Plus, Mimi said the spirits were angry and unsettled, which isn't as likely with a standard accidental catastrophe. And you know how..."

She continues on with whatever point she has next. I'm not listening. I stand and wander aimlessly around the room. Is it possible that I've got this all wrong? I thought my mom was developing a weapon, but it's been so long, I don't even know why I thought that. And if she was murdered... that changes everything.

Does it though? I have no incentive to get involved. If anything, it would bring pressure down on my organization, which I've put so much time and effort into building into what it is today. I glance back at Astrid, apparently finished with her spiel, waiting for an answer.

"Please," she begs. I don't know what she's asking, I stopped listening.

"How could I trust you?" I allow my vulnerability to show through the cracks of my shell.

"I've never done anything to intentionally hurt you." Astrid's eyes are round and sincere. "The night I broke up with you, I made so many mistakes. If I had the chance, I would do everything differently. But I have always cared about you, and I still do. So much so that it is supremely bugging me that you're not applying pressure to your cut. You're bleeding, Sparks. You need to take care of that."

"Promise me one thing."

"Anything."

"If all of this goes sideways, you can't turn us into the cops." I hold her gaze. "I can't work with you if I'm constantly worried that you'll learn something you shouldn't."

"Okay." She nods. "Your crew gets immunity. I won't touch them."

I grab a knife from the floor and cut off her restraints. Astrid immediately grabs my arm and places her hand over the bandage.

"Fuck, Astrid," I hiss through my teeth. "Could you warn me before you grab where I was just shot?"

"You were shot?!"

Oh boy. This is going to be exhausting.

After a quick stop in the med bay at her insistence, we go up to Astrid's car to grab the box of "evidence" as she calls it. I think she's being a bit overdramatic. I type my code into the keypad and set the box on my living room floor.

"Is this where you live?" She scans the room.

"Yeah." I shrug. "This is my place, I guess."

"It's... nice." Astrid is trying to be polite, but it doesn't feel sincere. "Very crisp."

"What's wrong with it?" I look at the living room, suddenly defensive. Everything is in its place, the table is dusted.

"Nothing's wrong," she reassures me. I stare at her until she continues. "It's just sterile. Cold. There isn't anything here that makes the space a home."

I pause, letting her words soak in. Nothing I hadn't heard before. I shake my head and refocus.

"Grab whatever you want from the kitchen, water included." I gesture accordingly. "Bathroom through there. I'll be right back."

I walk into my closet and grab a t-shirt and sweatpants. I come back to find Astrid munching on potato chips. I toss the clothes to her.

"Not sure if you wanted to change out of your clubbing outfit," I suggest. "I mean, you look nice, just not super comfortable."

"Thanks." She blushes and steps inside the bathroom to change.

I notice she's set out a notebook. I flip it open to the first page and scan through the chicken-scratch writing. Something about this feels familiar, but I can't quite place it.

"Are you able to understand any of it?" Astrid peers over my shoulder. I'm startled by the familiar scent of her shampoo – peaches and honey. I didn't realize how accustomed I grew to that smell until it wasn't there anymore.

"Um, I guess I recognize some letters." I point to a formula on the page. "'K' is kinetic energy, and 'U' is potential energy. But do I understand the notes as a whole? Not really. Maybe if you give me an hour with the textbooks I'll have more."

"That's more than I understood." Astrid plops onto the couch beside me. "Oh wait, your mom worked at Synergy Labs, right? I guessed that correctly?"

"She did, yeah." I nod and look away, hoping to hide the lump in my throat.

"Did you ever meet any of her coworkers?" She asks. "I know it's a long shot, but I found a series of letters and I'm trying to figure out who to deliver them to."

"I went to the labs once, on the day of the explosion." The memory is foggy, but I try to remember as much as I can. "I was mad at her for something that's so stupid in hindsight, so she took me to work with her to try and perk me up. I don't know why she thought that was a good idea because it was so boring to me. But I did briefly meet some of her coworkers."

"How about Holly Jennings?" Astrid digs into the box and pulls out a leatherbound journal. The pages are frayed and yellow. She passes the book to me. "She wrote a ton of letters to someone named Lottie."

"I knew Holly," I whisper, feeling my throat tighten. I open the journal to the first page, and my suspicions are confirmed.

Dear Lottie,

First day at the new job! So exciting. I can't wait to tell you all about it when I get home. I know you didn't want to move, but I'm sure Danver Hills will grow on you.

"Sparks?" Astrid shakes my shoulder. I ignore her and continue reading.

The work I'm doing here at Synergy Labs is important. It's been my dream to use my physics doctorate to better the world, not simply optimize engineering to increase profits. That was my old job, but this, the research I'm doing now, it actually matters. If progress means we have to move to rural Pennsylvania, I think that's a risk the two of us have to take.

All of my coworkers are excited to meet you. They'll give us time to settle in, but they're trying to persuade me to throw a housewarming party. I think it's a marvelous idea. And who knows, you might enjoy hanging out with their families?

This move is going to be good for us, Lottie. I can feel it. I hope you feel it too. Just know that I love you more than anything in the world.

I thumb through the journal. It's full of letters. There must be close to a hundred, if not more. I force myself to swallow the lump in my throat.

"You're Lottie, aren't you?" Astrid whispers.

"It's what my mother called me." I nod, still in shock. "Short for Charlotte. She always said that Charlotte was my public name, but Lottie, that was just for the two of us."

"I'm so sorry." She places her hand on my back. "I should've figured that out earlier. I can't believe I just dropped these on you like that."

"No, it's fine." I shrug off her hand. "I didn't know she wrote these, but it doesn't matter. These look to be more like diary entries than real letters anyway."

"Sparks, it's okay to feel sad."

"It's late." I stand up, placing the journal on an end table. "There's a spare room you can stay in overnight, and then we can regroup in the morning."

I don't give her a chance to object, quickly ushering her into an empty dorm, pointing out the main kitchen and bathrooms along the way. Once I return to my apartment, I lock the door and rest my head against the wood.

My liquor cabinet is fairly empty. I normally go upstairs when I want to drink, but tonight, I really want to be alone. Luckily, I find a bottle of whiskey and a clean glass. Smooth pour, two fingers, bottle back in the cabinet. I lean against the counter and take a sip.

Pour a glass, put the bottle back. That's a Derek-ism. Something about making each drink a conscious decision instead of mindless consumption. That technique can be really helpful, but not tonight.

I down the rest of my glass and grab the bottle back out of the cabinet. I curl up on the rug, reclining against the couch. I thumb through the frail pages of the journal before returning to the first page. My fingers glide across the script, tracing her scrawling ramblings. Holly Jennings. Charlotte. Lottie. Names I haven't heard in so, so long.

The whiskey burns my throat as I take a deep pull from the bottle. I don't know how long it takes me, but I read the rest of the letters and get through most of the bottle. Memories dance through my head. Picnics in the park, pancakes cooked into silly shapes, my infatuation with this one boy band. I'd forgotten all of these moments of my childhood. I close the journal and stumble into my bedroom. Instinctively, I tuck the book into my sock drawer, hiding it beneath the hosiery. No one else needs to know it's there.

I step into the hot water of the shower, wanting to finish what was interrupted before. Red-tinged liquid pools by the drain, the last remnants of blood finally scrubbed from my hair. Soap bubbles slide down my torso taking the grime of the past day with them. I crumple to the floor, letting the shower stream cascade over me.

Jack's dead. My mom's dead. My shooter didn't have the decency to kill me. I survived, and for what? What was it all for?

N   N   N   N

"Sparks, you are not allowed to skip this morning's coffee meeting!" I hear banging on the door. "Do not make me come in there."

"Fuck off, Derek!" I groan and cover my face with a pillow.

My head is pounding, my arm is throbbing, and my hands are aching. I'm not in the mood. The keypad beeps as Derek enters his code. The lights emit the glare of a million suns. I hear Derek shuffling around in my closet before clean clothes are tossed on top of me.

"Get dressed, Sparkie," he teases. "I'll be in your living room."

I throw my pillow at his receding figure before peeling my body from my sheets. The fabric of my athletic shorts is rough against my skin, but the t-shirt is worn and soft. I stagger into the living room and flop onto the couch.

"I was going to ask how you were handling things." Derek holds up the bottle of whiskey, eyeballing the dwindling amount of remaining liquid. "I think I have my answer."

"I'm fine." I brush him off. "What's so important that you just had to wake me?"

"Sparks, I thought we agreed not to lie to each other." Derek sits across from me. "You're the only thing on the agenda today. I sent Oliver home. It's just the two of us. Talk to me."

I sit up as he slides a hot mug of coffee in front of me. I hate coffee, but the warm mug can be soothing to hold. Derek takes a sip from his own mug, patiently waiting.

"I don't feel any better," I confess. "Wasn't that what we were working toward? Get stronger, so no one can hurt me again. Get my shit together. Well, I killed Jack, Derek. I shot him in the face, felt his blood on my hands. He's dead, and I'm here, but everything still hurts."

"What happened before we got there?" Derek asks. "You left us. I saw the door busted in, but I couldn't find you. I panicked, I thought he... I thought I was too late. But then you had a gun. I know that wasn't one of ours."

"He told me he loved me," I mutter.

"Classic manipulation," Derek scoffs. "He only has one trick."

"It almost worked." I hate to admit it. "Not because I love him. No, I despise him, he just knows how to get under my skin."

"You won though!" Derek exclaims. "Can't you see? This was all you. You got yourself through this."

"I s'pose." My hair falls into my face, and I drag my fingers through trying to push the strands back. "He gave me the gun to shoot you."

"And?" Derek shifts in his chair, unsettled but listening. "Still mulling it over?"

"Oh god, no!" I panic, waving my hands, nearly spilling my coffee in the process. "I just didn't want you to hear it from anyone else!"

"Calm down," Derek chuckles. "I trust you."

"Good." I look at the brown liquid in my drink.

"By the way, we looted his safehouse after you left." Derek fishes around in his pockets. "Standard protocol, you know. Make sure he doesn't have any incriminating evidence left behind or what not. I found this."

He gently pulls out a sparkling chain with a small pendant on the end. I recognize it immediately. My mom's missing necklace, one I used to wear every day. Jack stole it from me last year after I left him. It was a deep blow, but now, I don't know what to feel. Derek extends the necklace to me, but I can't move. I just sit there in some combination of shock and surprise. He awkwardly sets it on the table.

"I heard that while I was... cleaning up, you had a late-night visitor," Derek probes.

"That is correct." I set my coffee on the table and curl up nervously on the couch.

"Was it taken care of?" He asks, bluntly.

"In a sense."

"Sparks." He narrows his eyes. "Do not let her leverage your past relationship over you."

"She's not here about the gang." I play with the ends of my hair. "I actually negotiated for immunity. She won't touch us."

"And what does she get in return?" Derek sits up. "I don't like the feeling of this."

"She just needs my help on a side project," I answer vaguely. "Nothing related to the team. Just something I know more about than her."

"I won't stand in your way." Derek leans back in his chair. "But I want you to remember how badly she hurt you last time. Stay distant and keep your guard up. I care about you too much to let you fall back into that rut."

"I'll be fine." I shrug.

"Yeah?" Derek says, frankly. "What happened to your fists? Or that bottle of whiskey? It's been one night."

I take a deep breath and rub my bruised knuckles. He's not wrong. I haven't taken seeing Astrid again well.

"I'll be careful," I concede. "If I remember right, the next part of our routine is exercise?"

"Yeah." He gives me a small smile, acknowledging my Derek-ism. "Let's hit the gym."

CHAPTER 9

ASTRID

Sparks opens her apartment door, and I freeze with my fist in the air, raised to knock. My breath catches as we stand face-to-face, only a foot away from each other. I haven't been this close to her in months.

A man steps around Sparks, shoving me with his shoulder as he passes in a way I can only assume is intentional. I stumble back a step, stunned at his brazenness and a little embarrassed.

"Was that the guy who fought alongside me on the boat?" I ask Sparks, doing a double-take at his retreating form.

"Yes." Sparks's voice is distant as her eyes glaze over.

"I still can't figure out why he did that." It was one of the strangest things that has happened to me as the Water Weaver. I stormed the boat to rescue Sparks, and then this man turned on his cohorts, slashing and stabbing with ease. We fought well together, covering each other's blind spots. "I was so confused, but I wasn't about to complain."

"Derek did it because I asked him to." Sparks shrugs, as if it was just that simple. "He asked what I needed, and I said to keep you safe."

"Oh." I pick at my fingernails, on edge from being in this unfamiliar place where I am clearly not wanted, talking about the worst night of our lives. "Thank you, I guess."

"Don't mention it." I get the feeling she means that literally. "Anyway, Derek and I are heading to the sparring ring. Care to join?"

"I don't know if I'm brave enough to go head-to-head with him." I shiver, remembering his skilled movements from our fight. "His glare alone could kill."

"You could skirmish with me," she offers casually. "I'm a bit tired of Derek whooping my ass."

"So you think that you can just bowl me over?" I raise my eyebrow, trying to decide if I should be offended.

"Nah." She shakes her head as she leads me toward the gym. "But it'll be fun to get beat up by a different person."

Something about her frankness catches me off guard, and I throw my head back laughing. Sparks glances at me over her shoulder. Her eyes don't have their usual malice, instead she seems almost amused.

In the gym, Sparks shows me how to swathe my fists with the wraps, to help protect our wrists or something. What kind of fighting does she think we're about to do? Derek stands nearby, overseeing our conversation. He seems to serve as some kind of trainer for Sparks, teaching her how to fight. I wonder if that extends past the walls of the gym to how the inner workings of the crime syndicate are structured. I shake my head, sending the thoughts away. Sparks has amnesty, we shook on it. None of this concerns me.

Still though, a pang of jealousy cuts through my chest. She has someone in her corner to guide her, show her the ropes. The Water Weaver never did. My fighting technique relies on a very simple principle – don't get hit. Evade, glide, move like water. If all goes to plan, I use my powers to apprehend criminals, never having to interact with them at all. That being said, several years of trial by fire have taught me enough to hold my own. Wait for the right moment, dodge, find your opening. Then get the heck out of there.

"Alright you two, standard fighting rules apply," Derek recites passively. "No hits to the neck, spine, or groin. No use of your powers. If one contender yields, all contact is to cease immediately. Any questions?"

Sparks stands across from me, shaking out her hands. Her expression is hard and determined, taking this perhaps a bit too seriously. Okay then, I raise my hands. Maybe this could be fun?

Derek blows his whistle and Sparks immediately steps to my left, starting to circle. I've really only seen her fight once. It wasn't the most impressive performance I've seen, but to be fair, she was restrained at the time and freshly beaten. I have no idea what to expect from her. What are her strengths? What are her weaknesses? She throws out a soft jab, testing my defenses. I duck underneath and evade easily. Sparks is not surprised that her blow doesn't land but raises her eyebrow when I don't try to block, instead preferring sleek movements to a firm stance. It seems Derek taught her to fight like a guy, a brick wall of force. Oh, this is going to be so much fun.

Sparks throws a right hook next. I slink underneath, trying to weasel my way behind her, but Sparks is a fast learner, catching on to my plan. She sticks out her foot and I trip, smoothly transitioning into a somersault instead. My ponytail whips around as I stand, chuckling to myself for falling for Sparks's trick. She's better than I gave her credit for.

"Fighting dirty, huh?" I taunt, a mischievous gleam in my eyes.

"I don't know what you mean," she feigns indignation.

I move in and she strikes, testing how good I am at evading her blows. Left hook, right uppercut, left side kick, right hook. I dodge the first three easily, but as I sidestep her kick, I move directly into the incoming right hook. She catches me directly on my cheek.

"Ow!" I stumble back, holding the side of my face. I bend over as I reel from the blow. "Motherfucker!" This is no longer fun.

"Shit, are you okay?" Sparks drops her guard and places a hand on my back... just like I wanted.

I grab her arm and yank it forward as I sweep her legs. Sparks falls on her stomach. I try to use her momentum to pin her arm behind her back, but she squirms out of my hold, twisting to face me. I straddle her, but she bucks her hips to throw me over her head. I slide cleanly into another somersault, rising to a crouched position matching hers.

"That was a dirty trick," she grumbles.

"If you don't like it, then do something about it." I wink, having fun again. God, I missed our banter. No one can dish out sass quite like she can.

After letting her lead the offensive, I decide it's my turn. Lithe and graceful, I pounce. We grapple for a moment. I'm slipperier than she is, but she's strong. Sparks gets control of my wrists and forces me to the floor, straddling my hips. Her hair dangles freely, not in a ponytail like mine. I scrunch my nose as her curls tickle my face. She whips her hair back, a polite gesture, and our eyes meet. I can see the deep flecks of silver and gray in her iris. I can feel the warmth of her breath. I notice the outlines of her muscles, more pronounced than when I'd seen her last. Her strong thighs around my hips, her firm grip on my wrists. Focus, Astrid. Focus.

I suddenly jerk my arms down and Sparks loses her balance. I slide out from under her agilely, while she topples clumsily. She curses at herself under her breath as we stand and reset our defenses, circling each other once more. Sparks feints toward my left side, hoping I'll flinch due to her landing the right hook earlier. Not the case. Instead, I reach across my body with my right hand, firmly grasping her arm, and in one fluid movement, I spin and lash out with my left elbow. Her head is knocked back as I connect with her brow. Oof, that looked like it hurt. She stumbles back as Derek blows his whistle.

"That's enough, girls." Derek eyes me distrustfully. "Take a break."

I relax immediately, completely shifting my body language from the Water Weaver back to Astrid. I hold a hand up to my cheek and mutter profanity under my breath. That really hurts.

"Come on," Sparks offers apologetically. "Let's get you some ice."

"Don't you get tired of being covered in bruises all the time?" I moan, following her dutifully to the kitchen freezer.

"Haven't thought about it." She shrugs. It's unsettling how used she is to being injured. She tosses me a bag of frozen vegetables. "I do get tired of peas though."

"Ugh, I hate peas." I wince as I hold up the peas to my face. Yeah, that's going to bruise. She grabs a bag of frozen corn, pressing that to her brow.

"So, about Synergy... how thoroughly did you search the labs?" Sparks asks hesitantly. She grabs a croissant and picks at the layers.

"Not fantastically." I sit on an island stool, grabbing one of her croissant flakes and popping it in my mouth. "There were a lot of places I couldn't get to. Lots of locked doors for an abandoned building."

"Why didn't you pick the locks?" Sparks goes to the fridge, pulls out some fruits, and sets them in front of me.

She also slides over the rest of her demolished pastry, encouraging me to eat.

"Pick the locks?" I raise an eyebrow. I look over the fruit before selecting a nice peach. "Why would I know how to do that?"

"Do you need me to teach you?" She offers. "Derek's like a total lockpicking pro. He's shown me a ton."

"Umm, no." I shift on my stool. "I try not to make petty crime a habit." Sparks rolls her eyes, annoyed at my comment.

"Answer me honestly." She scoots onto the counter, pulling one leg up in front of her and letting the other dangle. "Is there anything I can do to get you to stay away from Synergy Labs, or is this going to be something that you'll go behind my back to investigate?"

"Sparks, I don't see how I can stop." I fiddle with the peach pit. "I mean, this connects to our powers and to the death of so many people. I need to figure out what happened, maybe even find justice for their families." I avoid looking at her during that last sentence.

"I don't think it's a good idea," she huffs. "Synergy Labs has been and will always be bad news, even disbanded." There's a beat of silence. "But if there's no stopping you, then I don't want you to go there alone."

"Really? Oh, thank you!" I leap up from my barstool and hug her. "This is going to be so much fun!" She quickly squirms out from my embrace, uncomfortable with my affection.

"This doesn't change anything," she blurts coldly. "We're still not friends."

"Sorry." I wipe the crumbs from my shirt. Sparks cringes as I pull away awkwardly. For a moment, I almost think she feels bad for her snipe, but then I force myself to remember. We broke up – no, I broke up with her. She doesn't care about me anymore. "When are you available to make the trip?"

"Do you have your suit?" I nod, and she sighs. "Then we're going today. I need a shower first."

We get ready quickly, each take a shower – separately – and she grabs a prepacked go bag. I subtly peek inside. It has some standard equipment: rope, flashlights, glass cutter, sunscreen. Apparently, this is what they consider to be the bare essentials. We agree to take my car, as it doesn't make sense for us to drive separately. Plus, I think Sparks would sooner walk than give me a ride on her motorcycle. I stand by the elevator, unable to go up on my own due to their security measures. Derek passes Sparks some sack lunches and I overhear a bit of their conversation.

"I hope you know what you're doing," Derek warns, clenching his fists at his side. "You shouldn't be going on this road trip with her."

"I wouldn't if it wasn't important," she promises. "I'll have my phone on me, so call if there's an emergency here." He pulls her into a tight hug, and she doesn't pull away like she did with me.

Derek whispers in her ear and tussles her hair. I used to be Sparks's best friend, the one she could banter with, trust with some of her secrets. It turns out, I was easily replaceable. I try not to let the hurt show on my face.

"I'm not a child," she whines in response to his whispers.

"No, but you're practically my sister." Derek whips her around and locks her in a noogie.

"Stop it." She tries to sound intimidating but can't stop laughing. I used to make her laugh. Used to mean something to her.

Eventually, Sparks escapes the headlock. Derek gives her a smile and waves, before glaring at me. Message received. I'm not welcome here. Sparks doesn't notice as she presses her thumb into the elevator, taking us to the parking garage.

My Water Weaver costume catches the small amount of light illuminating the garage. There's a mindset switch when I don the costume. Astrid is gone, and I become someone more surefooted, confident in my actions. That being said, I also love the outfit. The fabric really does shimmer like water. The gossamer tulle is also quite stunning. I notice Sparks staring. She's never really gotten to look at my disguise up close before. Her eyebrows scrunch together, and I can tell she's wondering why there's fabric flowing from my waist and sleeves. Reasonable question, it doesn't seem practical at first glance.

"It's slippery." I answer her unspoken question. She snaps out of her trance, not realizing she'd been staring. "If someone grabs it, I slide right out. Go ahead, touch it."

She hesitantly runs her fingers along my forearm before grabbing my wrist tightly. I slide right out of her grasp. Her eyebrows raise in surprise at the ease in which I do so. Trust me, many people have tried to restrain me when fights go south. It never works out for them.

"Very neat," Sparks agrees. "Thanks."

"No problem." I grab her bag and place it in the trunk. "Any fun tricks in your suit?"

"Yeah, actually." Her eyes light up as she gestures at her suit. "It's super cool. See the silver lines? That's aluminum threads. It allows me to electrify my suit! I don't get to use it very often because my powers are range-based, but someone did get zapped just the other day!"

"Hmm." I eye her suspiciously. "Nifty."

"Try it!" She holds her arm out and I scurry back a step, not eager to feel her electricity in my veins.

"You've shown me already," I counter, keeping a fair distance between us. We've come to blows before, long before I knew Sparks was Anise. The encounter was rough, even though both of us were pulling our punches. I am not in a hurry to relive the feeling of her powers coursing through me ever again.

"What?" She lowers her arm, confused. "When?"

"Second robbery, the armored trucks," I reply, shuddering as I think about the jab I landed on her abdomen.

"Oh." A moment of awkward silence passes. "Sorry about that. If it makes you feel better, that was a baby shock. Normally, it's a lot more of a deterrent."

"It doesn't." Trust me, the baby shock was quite a deterrent. I step into the driver's seat. "Oh god, the poor people you give a full shock to."

"Don't worry about them." Sparks shrugs. "They're all dead."

I lean my head against the steering wheel. Goodness gracious, Sparks.

It's a long drive to Danver Hills, and it passes about as quickly as you can expect. I hum along to the radio, tapping my fingers on the wheel occasionally. Sparks just curls up against the door and stares at the Pennsylvanian countryside passing by. She gets tenser the closer we get, especially when she appears to start recognizing landmarks. I do my best to soothe her without being too overt about it. I switch the radio to slower music and hum a little louder, but she just tightens her seatbelt and scrunches her eyes closed.

Slowly, the tires roll to a stop. We're here. I observe her cautiously as she takes a deep breath and opens her eyes. I can see the thoughts cross her face clearly, as if she was saying them aloud. *Oh god, we're here. I can't breathe. It's not safe. We have to go. We have to leave.* I pull my door handle to open the door. *It's not safe. I'm not safe.* She closes her eyes and her hand darts out to squeeze mine.

I freeze at her touch, unsure of how to respond. We're not friends. She made that clear. She doesn't want my affection. But I know I have to do something as she curls up into a ball, rocking slightly. Slowly, I close my door and start humming again. I gradually shift to sit on the center console and pull her into my chest, stroking her hair. We sit like that for a few minutes, humming along to a lullaby my mother used to sing to me. Eventually, her heartbeat returns to a normal rhythm and her eyes flutter open. I hold Sparks for a few moments longer, reluctantly letting her go. She rubs her palms on her thighs, embarrassed by her episode. I don't say anything, just sit in the silence patiently.

"You've been in before?" She whispers. "It's safe?"

"It's safe," I promise.

CHAPTER 10
SPARKS

Normally, I would force myself to roll my shoulders back, walk into every situation with my head held high, no matter how much it terrifies me. But that's not what I do.

My shaking hands fumble with the door handle as I exit the hatchback. Astrid grabs my go-bag and then holds my hand the entire walk up the driveway. I'm trembling so bad that my vision is blurry, but I keep putting one foot in front of the other.

Astrid slips through a window to enter the front lobby before unlocking the main doors for me. I walk in. Everything looks the same, dusty as hell, but the same nonetheless. Shadows of memories flash through my mind. The smiling receptionist. The ringing phone. Astrid's footprints from her earlier visits are still clear. I can see where she paced along the back wall, probably trying to piece together some part of my past.

I shake my head and walk through the lobby, past all the offices. I know where we need to go. I find the metal door at the end of the hallway, the entrance to the lab. There's an electric lock on the door. Well, that's what they want you to think, but I know the secret. I lift the lock off to reveal a normal keyhole.

"What's that?" Astrid asks, confused.

"The electric lock was just a cover," I explain, remembering stories from my mom. "Budget cuts, couldn't afford proper security features."

I pull my lockpicking set out from a small case concealed in my belt. Never know when you'll need a good pick. Within a few seconds, I turn the door handle and we are in.

We walk along the catwalk overlooking the main lab. This is where it happened. This is where I was. I take a few steps forward to the exact tile and kneel to the ground.

"Mom, can I just go home?" I complain. I've been here for hours. If I hear one more thing about the Law of Conservation of whatever, my head might explode.

"C'mon, Charlotte." My mom tries to get me excited. "Let's go look at the machine again! I think we're getting ready to turn it on. If you ask nicely, maybe Zach will let you push the button."

"I don't want to push the button," I complain, looking over the railing. "I just want to go home."

"Lottie, I know this isn't the birthday you wanted, but we can try to make this fun!" For a second, I almost believe her. "I think Glenda from HR brought some ice cream." Now, I believe her.

"Excuse me." Someone bumps into my mom. That voice sounds familiar.

Mom just steps aside and leans against the railing. I notice my shoe is untied. I crouch down and pull on the laces, making sure the shoe is tight on my foot. I don't even get to finish making my bunny ears when I hear it.

BOOM!

My mother's face goes pale. She opens her mouth to scream but the airwave's impact takes the sound away.

No! Mom!

I leap up to grab her as she flies over the railing. My fingers tighten around her necklace. The pain is unbearable. Is this what dying feels like? I clutch to the necklace as my mother hangs limply. I know she's dead. I can just tell. But I can't let go even as the electricity pulses through my body. I can't let go. I won't let go. The chain snaps and I watch in horror as she falls to the floor below, her skeleton posed in an unnatural position. Mom...

An arm wraps around my shoulders as Astrid kneels next to me.

"I didn't know Holly," she begins solemnly with her head bowed. "But I know she was a brave, intelligent mother who only wanted the best for her daughter. She was a caring woman, with a passion and a zeal for using her knowledge to improve the world around her. I hope that wherever she is, she finds peace."

"Thank you," I whisper.

We sit there for a few moments, paying our respects. Then we proceed down the walkway towards the special experiment division. I don't know what experiments happened in the lab below, that wasn't where my mom worked. She was a specialist brought here to work on one thing and one thing only – the machine. Whatever it did.

Every room we have gone through thus far has felt like a time capsule, sealed in the moments just after disaster. It was as if they removed the bodies and then abandoned the lab deeming it cursed or more likely, too much work to restaff. Dust lays over every surface as a thick blanket.

This next room, however, is not that way. Footprints disrupt the fine powder, leaving evidence of a large horde trampling through. Traces of handprints linger on walls and counters. A pristine rectangle of clean flooring is along the far side of the wall, with dolly wheels leading away. I know immediately what left that imprint. The machine.

I can instantly see why so many mechanics before me had failed to repair the machine. Half of it was still here, screwed into the wall. We were all doomed from the start. Cords dangle limply toward the ground. I open the cover panels and study the mechanics I can see, while trying to remember the details of the inner workings of the machine. But it's no use, I have no idea what's going on. I really am more of an electrician than a mechanic. I take photos of what I can see to reference later.

While I was examining the remnants, Astrid was doing her own investigations. She returns with a paper map ripped from the wall. She lays it on the counter, and I look over her shoulder.

"We're here." Astrid points at a spot on the diagram. "It looks like there's a security office not far, over here. I think it's worth checking out."

"Lead the way." I follow her down another hallway.

More memories flash through my mind. My mother introducing me to coworkers, the intern trying to entertain me with magic tricks, and an older man condescendingly explaining electrons to me. I wince and try to clear my head, but the ghosts of the past keep knocking on my door. Astrid grabs my hand, noticing my distant stare. I feel warmer somehow. She gives me a gentle squeeze and holds it all the way to the security room. I pick the lock and we are in.

Computer monitors line the walls, their black screens reflecting our image back to us. I avert my eyes, not wanting to look at myself. A computer tower is nestled under a desk. Other than that, this room is barren.

"Dang," Astrid mumbles. "If only there was electricity going to this building. I would love to see if there was any security footage left."

"What do you mean?" I look at her quizzically.

"The recordings could show us what happened..." Her voice trails off, unsure of where I got confused.

"I know what security footage does." I roll my eyes dramatically. "I meant, what do you mean if only there was electricity?"

"This is an abandoned building, no way anyone paid the power bill the past decade." Astrid makes a strange face.

"I don't know what to tell you." There's been electricity since we stepped into the lab, I've felt it with my powers. I reach down and press the power button. The computer tower whirs to life, slowly booting up.

"... that makes no sense." Astrid stares in disbelief.

I shrug and pull out a chair for her, while sitting in a second. She pulls up the last recording. I gulp as I notice the timestamp. The day of the explosion.

"I... I can't watch." I stumble out of the chair. "Let me know what happens."

I stand just outside the room, leaning against the wall. I hear Astrid gasp. I scrunch my eyes, trying to block out my own visualizations of what she's seeing. She is silent after that. I only hear mouse clicks as she navigates through different footage angles.

"Sparks," she calls. "I need you to look at something for me."

"Something good and happy and filled with rainbows, right?" I stay at my spot on the wall. "Right?" I repeat weakly.

"Umm..." I hear through the wall. "No rainbows, no."

Dammit.

"Pull yourself together," I whisper angrily at myself. "You are not allowed to break down. Get your shit in order."

I brace my forehead against the wall, taking in one last deep breath before pushing off. I stride into the security office and sit down. The monitors are frozen on a still shot. Past me is kneeling, tying my shoe. My mother just got bumped into. From this angle, I can see who bumped into her.

"This is a joke, right?" My face pales, and I turn toward Astrid. She looks just as uneasy as I do. "That's not..."

"I was hoping it wasn't." She wrings her hands. "I'm asking you."

I stare at the screen, eyes locked on the man who bumped into my mother, the voice that sounded vaguely familiar in my flashback. I should have recognized it sooner, should have put it together. It seems my subconscious was determined to forget. On the screen in grainy black and white, yet clear as day, is Jack. He's several years younger, maybe eighteen or nineteen, but he still has his signature smirk. It's him for sure.

"The directory you found, was he listed?"

"No." Astrid shakes her head. "But he could have had an alias."

"What happens next?" I demand. "Where does he go?"

"I don't have great angles," she admits. "But he goes into the room with the machine just a few moments before the explosion. If you look through the window, you can see him fiddling with it."

"I swear," I curse under my breath. "That motherfucker keeps showing up."

"We need to figure out why he was here," Astrid declares. "That might help us find our answers."

"Rewind the tape." I lean close to the screens. "Did he do anything before he got here?"

Astrid clicks some keys, and the film plays in reverse, like a nightmarish cartoon. We follow him backwards from screen to screen. I struggle to find him a few times, but Astrid quickly points him out each time. It seems when I was in the hallway, she got well acquainted with the angles and layout of the cameras. He walks casually through the building, blending in with his white coat. Internally, I'm screaming. *Notice him! Imposter!* But no one finds any reason to be wary.

Jack slides a phone under a door. It looks like a supply closet? Why would he do that? We continue rewinding even further. He doesn't speak to anyone, just walks through various labs. What is he doing?

I squint at the screen, trying to pick up on subtle details. He holds up a clipboard as he walks by a whiteboard. The phone peeks over the board.

"That doesn't look right." Astrid points at that frame. "Why would you hold a phone like that? You can't see the screen at that angle."

I cock my head, examining his body position further. I scan the room and find a sheet of paper. It's not a clipboard, but it'll do. I hold the paper out, mimicking Jack. Astrid helps me line up my phone with the edge of the paper, matching the angles from the feed.

"See?" She gestures. "That's unnatural."

"No," I disagree. "It's perfect."

"For what, scratching your camera lens on the clipboard?" She mutters.

"Close." I open an app on my phone to test my theory. After a click, I know I'm right. "For taking photos."

"Sparks," Astrid's voice is quiet, full of disbelief and shock. "Was he trying to steal your mom's research?"

"Fuck." I pinch the bridge of my nose. "Maybe?"

He told me he had a brother who died in the explosion, that's why he was at the hospital later. We bonded over our shared grief. I can't believe he lied about that too.

I think back on Jack's paranoia. No names, no paper trail, no setting down roots. We moved frequently, always to urban areas, always in a hurry. He was always well-connected, prone to criminal behavior. Yet, after eight years, I really knew nothing about him.

We spend a few minutes in that room, sitting with the gravity of our theory. Well, that's what I do. Meanwhile, Astrid pours over the blueprints, muttering to herself as she references security cameras. This is crazy. Who would want to steal research from a random facility in rural Pennsylvania? My mother wouldn't shut up about her experiments, they could have just asked. Then again, in all of her journals, she never said what she was working on. Fuck, I wish I listened to her better.

"We need to find that closet," Astrid declares suddenly. "It's not on the map. That means it's important, or secret, or some combination thereof."

"You're not being for real, are you?" I ask incredulously. "Do you not realize how serious this could be? If Jack really was a spy or something, that means all of his paranoia and delusions of secret evils were valid. That means..." My face pales as I consider the possibilities. "We need to leave."

"Don't you want answers?" Astrid checks her map once again. "You have no idea what Jack was looking for. Did he intentionally cause the explosion? Was it an accident? There's still so much we don't know."

"I know that your curiosity could get us killed." I stand authoritatively. "Come on."

Astrid begrudgingly stands and walks down the passage with me. She slyly glances at her map.

"Astrid..." I warn.

My admonition falls on deaf ears as she slips down a different hallway, forcing me to either abandon or follow her. I pause, considering it, but as much as I hate her, I couldn't. I huff and trudge after her. She finds the closet in question, jiggling the stuck handle.

"See!" She exclaims, much too excited. "Why would a storage closet be locked?"

I roll my eyes, knowing her next question. Before she asks, I kneel and pick the lock. She steps forward as I back away. The door handle twists, and the door swings open.

Bwaaah! Bwaaah! Bwaaah!

Instinct takes over. I fall to the ground and pull my mask up in one fluid motion. My hood falls over my head, and I see Astrid inside the storage closet, hurriedly looking around.

"The fuck are you doing?" I shout. "Time to go!"

"This could be our only chance!" She desperately peeks under desks and in drawers.

I scan the closet. It's clear it's not actually a closet. High tech computers and other electronics cover the wall, but no papers, no cell phone, nothing easy to grab. A computer tower is set next to me, hard drive removed. I know instantly we aren't going to find anything.

"Now!" I command.

I'm done waiting. I grab her arm, and thankfully, she comes with me. We burst through the front doors and sprint to the car. I beat her there and slide across the hood, popping into the driver's seat. Astrid fumbles for her keys, but I've already jump-started the car – great time to have powers. I peel out of the driveway before she's even finished buckling her seatbelt. Minutes pass before I ease off on the accelerator, content that we are safe among the side roads I've taken. I pull my mask off and take a deep breath, heart still beating loudly in my ears.

"So, that could've gone better." Astrid breaks the silence.

"Fantastic deduction," I snipe, still angry about her ignoring my warnings.

"Look, I know we didn't get all the answers that we wanted, but we learned so much!" Astrid grins, enthusiastically. "We'll figure the rest out!"

"No, we won't." I grip the steering wheel tightly, knuckles turning white. "This stops now. I won't risk everything I've worked so hard to build, just so you can play superhero dress-up. I've put Synergy Labs behind me. I suggest you go back to stopping petty crimes and leave me out of it."

"You're really going to let your mother's legacy end like that?" Astrid argues. "She's your mother!"

"Exactly! She's *my* mother." My temper flares. "So stay the fuck away from her!"

"It's like you don't even care." Her words sting.

Fuck it. I pull the car off the side of the road and slam my door.

"Where do you think you're going?" Astrid yells out the window.

"Boston!" I continue stomping along the road.

"You can't walk to Boston from here," she calls out, annoyed.

"Try me!"

Astrid shrieks in frustration and walks to the driver's side of the car. She lowers the window further and rolls the car next to me. "Get in the car, Sparks."

"No." I turn away, hoping she can't see the tears threatening to fall.

"Anise, please get in the car." Her voice is strained, still annoyed but with a forced placidity. "Let me drop you off at the club. Then we can go our separate ways and never talk to each other again. Please."

The wind ruffles my hair as a few raindrops fall on the road. I look to the sky as water drips from the stormy clouds above. Astrid leans over and pops the car door open. Begrudgingly, I slide into the passenger seat. I pull my hood back on and curl up facing the door, pretending to be asleep. In reality, I stare at the rain trickling down the car window, matching the trails silently forming on my cheeks.

FRAGMENT 1

"This is your target." A dossier is slid across the table to me. "Her name is Charlotte Jennings. Common alias, Sparks. The picture on the left was taken eight years ago during the Synergy Labs incident. We captured the image on the right from security footage half an hour ago."

A person's appearance drastically changes over eight years, but the resemblance is still clear. Her cheekbones are still round, but more defined. The gray in her eyes is more saturated, yet there is a depth to them. I can tell the past eight years have not been kind to her. Perhaps most striking though, is her vibrant red hair. She's cut it shorter as she's grown. It's now shoulder length, but her curls are still just as bold as the first photo.

"During the failed mission, the explosion appears to have given her powers to manipulate electricity. The full capacity of her abilities is unknown. We don't have her full history since a rogue agent, Jackson Davis, concealed their movements. He has since been dispatched by Miss Jennings. She is considered armed and dangerous at all times. Please consult the dossier for further details."

"Yes, ma'am." I flip through the pages. It's a pretty slim file, but I've worked with less. The director turns to another agent.

"This is your target, Astrid Larson. Common alias, Water Weaver. Former romantic interest of Miss Jennings. There are rumors that she also has powers, except hers are focused around manipulating water."

"I look forward to gaining more intel." Agent Chadwick responds. What a suck-up.

"Deliver these messages. Then observe and wait for further instructions."

"We won't disappoint you, Director." Chadwick responds. I nod in agreement.

This will be fun.

CHAPTER 11
ASTRID

What a selfish, narcissistic, heartless bitch! I'd almost forgotten why I broke up with her. Thank god for that breath of fresh air. She refused to speak to me the entire car ride yesterday, just stared out the window wearing that stupid hood. What a child. It doesn't matter. I'll never see her again. Good riddance.

I trudge up the stairs after grabbing my mail. Bill, spam, spam, letter, spam. I examine the letter closer. *You are hereby invited to the Saving the Children Gala. We look forward to your attendance.* Weird. I wonder how I got on that mailing list. The mail joins the stack of papers to deal with on my entryway table. Normally, I'm more on top of everything, but I haven't been sleeping well. It's hard to care about bills when I'm perpetually exhausted.

Under my arm, I'm carrying the box with the ritual from Mimi. It's time. I'm going to cut the cord. My altar is not nearly as elaborate as hers, but it works enough for me. I clear enough space for the two candles and sprinkle the herbs around.

"Pure intentions." I chant aloud. "Pure intentions. Ridding my life of negative energy. Self-reflection."

I visualize my apartment, devoid of her boxes, another woman in my bed. Isn't that nice? Isn't that lovely? Deep breath. I grab my matchbox and strike the stick along the starter. Bum match. Am I going crazy? Are these some newfangled matches that don't work like every other match in the known universe?

"Calmness," I say, taking a deep breath despite my frustration. "Serenity, peace, independence."

Once calm, I walk toward my kitchen to find a lighter. If this doesn't get the job done, I'm asking Mimi for new candles. Lighter in hand, I kneel back in front of my small altar. I fumble with the trigger of the lighter. It's a cheap lighter, sure, but has it always been this finicky?

Knock! Knock! Knock! Knock! Knock!

Loud banging disturbs my meditation. It's getting hard to have pure intentions in this apartment.

"Coming!" I call, trying the lighter one more time.

Knock! Knock! Knock! Knock! Knock!

The banging continues, faster and more urgent. Jesus, this better be important. I roll my eyes and open the door.

Sparks barges in, nearly bowling me over. She slams the door and engages the lock. She jumps onto my couch pulling my blinds shut. Her chest is heaving and sweat glistens on her forehead. She peeks underneath the blinds, eyes scanning frantically.

"I don't think I was followed," she sputters. "I didn't park nearby. No one saw me. They couldn't have followed. They couldn't have."

Understandably, I'm starting to get concerned.

"Now would be a great time for some context," I demand.

"They found me." She's breathing so fast, I'm worried she's going to pass out. Sparks puts a hand on her chest, and I bet she's thinking the same thing. "They found me. I don't know what to do. Jack never told me what to do!"

"What do you mean 'they found you?'" And why do I care, I add in my head.

Sparks pulls a folded envelope out of her shorts pocket. The envelope was messily ripped. I look inside and find an invitation to the Saving the Children gala. Same as the one in my mailbox.

"Oh, I got the same one," I say, unconcerned. "You just got on some weird mailing list. It happens."

"Not to me," she replies, hard stare in her eyes. "Not the day after we stumble onto a secret spy room inside some defunct research facility, not placed on the handlebars of my motorcycle, and most importantly, not addressed to Charlotte Jennings."

What? I flip the envelope over. "Charlotte Jennings" is written in elaborate cursive along the front. Oh. Well. That's not great.

"That's creepy." Not a very helpful response, but my mind has gone blank.

"Ya think?" Sparks says exasperated.

"Do you..." I think quickly, trying to offer a viable solution. "Do you want something to drink? Hot chocolate?" Crap, that wasn't a good one.

"No, I don't want a fucking hot chocolate!" Sparks yells.

"What do you want me to do?" I shrug with my arms out wide.

Sparks takes a deep breath, trying – and failing – to calm down. She snatches the letter from me and shoves it back in her pocket.

"I don't know, I just... Nevermind. Forget it. I'm leaving. If I hurry, maybe I can catch the next train to... fuck, I don't know, wherever."

"Wait, wait, sit down." Now I'm the one who's frazzled. "Give me a second to process this."

Ignoring the perfectly good couch, she plops down on the floor. She holds her knees to her chest and starts softly crying into her arms. For a moment, I am overwhelmed with sympathy. Her entire adult life, she was warned to stay anonymous, to be an enigma floating without a trace. Then to get a letter addressed to a person you once were... that's a lot.

"Shh, you'll be okay." I kneel next to her and stroke her hair, hoping my voice is more soothing than I feel. "You want a drink, I'll put on the hot water. You want to stay here tonight, I'll grab a pillow. Need an escort home, someone to worry about you, or a phone to call Derek? Whatever you need, I've got it. What would make you feel safe?"

"I don't know," she sniffles. I pass her a tissue and she blows her nose. "Do I take off? God, I'm so tired of running. I knew I shouldn't have settled down. It makes leaving so much harder."

"Then don't." I rub her back. "Face them. You have Derek and your team. You can fight this."

"We don't even know what this is." She buries her head again.

"I know how to find out."

❧ ❧ ❧ ❧

The night of the gala arrives, and I'm still not certain Sparks is going to show. She's been a nervous wreck all week, throwing herself into running on the treadmill and sparring in the ring. Of course, I haven't been back to the compound, but I was able to convince her to give me her cell number. We don't text much, but I can read between the lines.

I don't know what she told Derek, if anything. That man really does hate me. I'm content to keep our interactions nonexistent, but I'm still bitter. I used to be the one to make sure she made it home at night, to worry when she was out late and came home with new cuts and bruises. Guess that's someone else's problem now. That's fine, doesn't bother me.

I'm standing in front of the hotel listed on the invite. Other well-dressed attendees walk by, and I breathe a sigh of relief seeing I got the dress code right. I'm wearing a navy dress with an off-the-shoulder neckline landing right below my collarbone. Instead of my standard ponytail, I've twisted my hair into a low bun. My skirt swishes in a satisfying way as I walk, though it does little to assuage my pacing. If she doesn't show soon, we're going to be late.

Where are you?! I shoot off a text, grumbling to myself.

Here.

I look up as a taxi pulls into the circular driveway. A long, toned leg steps out, followed by a woman in a stunning emerald green halter dress. The dress hugs her curves with a slit high enough to raise a few eyebrows, especially with the black garter sitting on her thigh. She turns to thank the driver, and her smooth skin is complimented by her backless dress swooping down to her waist. Sparks shuts the door and catches my eye as I try to catch my breath. Goddamn.

"Sorry, I'm late," she apologizes. "I couldn't find the knife I wanted."

"Excuse me?" I blink.

"Don't worry." She pats my shoulder. "I found it."

"Why do you have a knife?" I whisper under my breath. She looks at me, bewildered.

"Do you mean to tell me you don't?" She hisses.

"Why would I?" I will never understand this woman.

"You are unbelievable." She rolls her eyes as we enter the hotel. I try not to scoff out loud. I'm not sure if I succeed.

Hotel staff direct us toward the ballroom. Grand streamers decorate the vaulted ceilings as posters of happy children are scattered on easels along the floor. We walk along a silent auction with numerous items up for bid. A weekend at a cabin in the Catskills, a private five-course meal cooked by a celebrity chef, tickets to an upcoming movie premiere. All bids are already in the several thousands.

"This action is a bit steep for me," I joke.

Sparks doesn't laugh. Instead, she subtly scans the room, studying the movements of the crowd. Anytime someone gets close to her or me, she stares at them, prepared to act. I sigh at her dramatics.

A waiter walks by with tray-passed hors d'oeuvres, and I flag him down. Oooh! Shrimp tartlets. I offer one to Sparks and she politely refuses. I take one for myself and the waiter continues on. The two of us silently meander through the crowd. I enjoy my tartlet and later a small piece of bruschetta. Sparks abstains from that as well. It isn't until I accept a flute of champagne that she says something.

"Are you really going to drink right now?" She smiles as she speaks out of the side of her mouth. Any passersby would have no idea she's being such a hypocrite.

"You're one to talk." I copy her smile and give her a mock toast before sipping my drink. "Besides, one isn't going to hurt."

"Haha, you're so funny." She shoots a cross glare at me, though her smile remains plastered on. "You can't guarantee they didn't spike the food."

"If they did, I'd die happy." I ponder for a moment. "And then you'd be right, so you'd also be happy. Win-win."

Her smile falls, revealing a stone-cold demeanor.

"You should be taking this more seriously." Her voice is apathetic, but I can sense the hurt behind her criticism.

She disappears into the crowd alone. I turn away and mingle with some of the other attendees, enjoying my champagne and their company. A balding man stands behind a podium and clinks his glass, drawing the attention of the crowd. We listen patiently as he gives a canned speech about children and happiness and how the money we contribute aids the cause. He never actually shares what we're saving the children from. Polite applause follows his spiel. A few other chairmen of the foundation speak, a toast is given, and then a band strikes up a fun jazz tune.

"Miss Larson?" A member of the waitstaff taps on my shoulder. I turn around confused. "I have been requested to invite you upstairs for a private meeting. Our benefactors wish to speak to you about a unique business opportunity."

I acquiesce and follow him, dreading the inevitable timeshare pitch that must be coming. This is how they get you. They feed you shrimp and goat cheese, loosen you up with jazz and champagne, and boom! You just signed a contract for a property in Jamaica. My uncle fell for that once. Now, us Larsons know better.

My theory becomes less plausible as we step off the elevator on the second floor. Sparks is waiting in the hallway, twisting a strand of hair around her finger. Her eyes meet mine and I can almost feel her telling me, *See! I told you so!* The waiter steps back onto the elevator and the doors close behind him. Sparks walks up to my side, nonchalantly.

"If things go like I think they're about to," she whispers quietly. "There is a knife tucked in the back of my garter. Don't move outside of arm's reach of me."

"It is not going to come to that." I try to sound confident.

"How sure of that are you?" She spots my bluff. "That's what I thought."

A door opens and a kind, middle-aged woman stands in front of a long table.

"Good evening," she greets with a cheery disposition. "Come in! Come in! We're so glad you could make it."

We step into the conference room as the lady walks around behind the table. Two men sit on each side of her wearing suits and ties. Sparks positions herself ever so slightly in front of me. She's always been overprotective, and I try not to roll my eyes at her possessiveness. I step around her and take a seat. Sparks slowly pulls out her chair and sits down, alert and suspicious. The lady across the desk watches our interaction carefully.

"Have you enjoyed the gala thus far?" She claps her hands together excitedly. I'll admit, this is a very strange timeshare pitch.

"It's very nice, Miss…" I answer, hoping she'll fill in her name.

"Excuse my manners." Her manicured nails dramatically flourish. "You can call me Marissa. These are my associates."

"Nice to meet you, Marissa." I nod politely. Sparks says nothing.

"Could I offer you anything to drink?" Marissa folds her hands in front of her. "Water, sparkling water, juice, soda, more champagne?"

"I'll take some water." I accept her offer graciously.

"Sorry, all out of water." Her plastic smile doesn't waver. "Anything else?

"No, thank you," I decline, confused. Didn't she just offer water? Marissa turns to Sparks.

"I'm fine," she says tersely. I sigh as Marissa cocks her head, almost like she's glitching. Could Sparks be any more off-putting?

"Alright then, on to business." She smiles again. "My organization offers a very exclusive service to high-level clientele. To be brief, we make their problems go away. I believe you two would be valuable assets to the team."

Her smile is starting to get unsettling. I shift in my seat and subtly move my hand towards Spark's thigh. She senses my discomfort and pretends to fix her hair. She uses that motion to adjust her legs, giving me easier access to the slit in her skirt.

"I don't know what you mean," I chuckle awkwardly. "I make a killer latte, but my mochas could use some work."

"Oh, I think you know what I mean." Her sickly-sweet facade drops. "And I have no doubt that the Water Weaver's mocha is of excellent quality."

"Who?" I tilt my head. Marissa ignores my denial and turns to Sparks.

"And Miss Jennings, we would like to offer our condolences on the loss of your mother." Her sympathy doesn't reach her eyes. "How tragic."

"Yes, tragic." Sparks keeps her expression neutral. I have no idea what she is thinking.

"Thank you for dispatching Mr. Davis for us." Now her smile is real. "His insubordination was... vexing for us."

"I assume you mean Jack?" Sparks leans back in her chair as if she were in total control of the situation. I hope she is. "We were on more of a first-name basis."

Marissa doesn't react. I can see her calculating her next move.

"I'll consider your offer of employment," Sparks continues. "But I have some questions first."

"I can't guarantee you answers." Marissa's plastic smile has returned.

"Did you cause the explosion at Synergy Labs?" Sparks locks eyes with Marissa, who ponders the question.

"That was not the goal." She chooses her words carefully. "The intention was to create a duplicate hard drive, however, a rogue asset did cause a mistake which resulted in an unfortunate chain of events."

"So that's a yes?" Sparks clarifies, giving nothing away with her expression. I look between the two, following the conversation like a spectator at a tennis match.

"That is not the way I would classify the incident," Marissa responds, hands folded together. "Perhaps we should discuss the job opportunity."

"Whatever you think is best."

Sparks picks an imaginary piece of lint off the front of her dress and smooths the fabric of her skirt. As she does so, she moves the panels of her skirt. While Marissa is distracted with Spark's disinterest, I slide my hand under her leg. I find the hilt of the knife easily and slip it between the folds of my skirt.

"Our position offers the opportunity to travel to exotic locations all over the world with a comfortable per diem," Marissa pitches. "Imagine, a trip to the island of Costa Rica—"

"We're not interested," Sparks interrupts icily. "Thank you for your consideration."

"You didn't get to hear about the benefits package," Marissa growls, suddenly aggravated. "But more importantly, you missed a key qualification for the position. We weren't asking."

Time stands still. Marissa and her associates rise to their feet. Sparks whips to me, her eyes focused and resolute. She only says one word before the lights go black.

"Run."

CHAPTER 12

SPARKS

I flip the table as I shut the power off to the room, hoping to buy us a few seconds to get away. Astrid yelps as she opens the door to the hallway, finding three burly men blocking the exit. She dives between them as their meaty clubs for hands grab at her. Enraged, I flick bolts down from the ceiling, striking each of the men. They crumple to the ground, and I jump over them, seizing Astrid's arm and dragging her into the hallway. We turn toward the elevator as the doors open. I groan as more men file out.

"Stairs?" Astrid suggests, a bit frantically.

"Stairs," I agree.

We turn on our heels as Marissa's henchmen stumble out of the conference room. I'm a bit annoyed to be doing all of the work. Astrid got us into this mess, she could at least help save our hides. It is at this time I recognize a critical issue.

"There's no water," I pant as we run.

"Nope," Astrid squeaks.

No doubt she thought of this much earlier, essentially powerless. I pull a fire alarm as we pass, hoping to engage the sprinklers. Nothing happens. No alarm, no sprinklers, nada. Fuck.

We come to a three-way intersection. Astrid looks around wildly, not seeing a sign for a staircase. More hostiles approach from the right. An emergency exit sign is lit up on the left. I make a split decision.

"Go left!" I order. "I'll buy you some time."

She turns to challenge me, but I already have sparks dripping from my fingertips. She wisely decides to take off down the hallway, hiking up her dress to run faster. I only hope she uses my knife if she gets stuck. But I can't worry about her right now, I have my own problems. I face the men brave or stupid enough to face me.

"Who's first?" I taunt.

I don't wait for an answer. The lights flicker in the hallway as I sprint toward the mass. I move as a banshee, flinging electricity as I spin around the first hostile. I don't check to see who I hit as a scream cries. The truth of the matter is all of these men will die tonight. The order doesn't matter.

My body is electrified. Every punch, kick, and jab take another man down. I slide between the legs of another, popping up behind him and twisting his neck in one fluid motion. Someone draws a firearm. I duck and the bullet flies into the unlucky bastard behind me. After the other day, I am not as forgiving of getting shot at. I throw a bolt and discharge him quickly. Soon, only one man is left. He stares at me with fear in his eyes before turning to run. I slowly pick up the fallen rifle and fire. He crumples to the ground. I drop the weapon, satisfied.

I can't find Astrid as I trot down the left hallway. Hopefully, she was able to find her way out. I twist and turn through the standard hotel labyrinth before finding a staircase. I take the steps two or three at a time, in a hurry to leave this godforsaken place.

On the ground floor, I speedwalk toward the exit, smoothing my dress as I go. I notice a man guarding the main doors. Slyly, I change course, meandering with a small group of socialites back into the ballroom. The guard takes a step away from his post, trying to determine if I was his target.

"Dance with me." I grab the arm of a man standing nearby and pull him toward the dance floor.

"Oh! Um, sure." He follows me, a bit surprised but not opposed.

"I just love this song," I lie, hoping to cover for my abrupt actions.

"Yeah, those cats are cooking." The man gives me some cheesy finger guns before extending his hand.

I give a flirtatious curtsy as I accept. A residual trace of electricity shocks him, and he jerks away. He laughs it off as he shakes his hand.

"I guess I was *shocked* such a stunning woman asked me to dance." He retakes my hand and gives me a slow spin. I glance at the guard over his shoulder, relieved when he retakes his place by the door, unconcerned. "But I'm glad you did."

"You're laying it on a bit thick," I tease, but smile at his compliment.

The truth is, he wasn't too bad to look at himself. He's a bit older than me, maybe late twenties. His black hair is trimmed close to his head, but he has a little bit of length on top, swept out of his face. His hazel eyes were warm, with a charming glint. He moves gracefully and powerfully, with a firm control of his body.

"What's your name?" He asks, placing his warm hand against the small of my back.

"I could tell you." I coyly look at him through my eyelashes. "Or we could live in the moment. Just a man in a suit and a woman in a dress, crossing paths for just one night. It's everything all at once, and then it's nothing."

Bullseye. He swoons, gazing starstruck into my eyes. Men fucking love when you look at them through your eyelashes. He pulls me in a hair tighter, though not too much to no longer be gentlemanly. We sway together for the rest of the song. A spin here, a small dip there, he leads with evident practice. I have just enough coordination to not embarrass myself, especially as I keep making small glances over his shoulder looking for a navy dress or a battalion of muscle. I don't see either. The band ends with a flourish, and I give my mystery date a polite curtsy.

"I'm afraid that's my cue," I apologize. "I have to be going."

"Are you sure I can't interest you in another dance?" He accepts the shake of my head graciously, albeit a bit disappointed. "Then please, allow me to escort you out."

Miraculously, the guard posted by the door takes this moment to move. Although I don't know what that means for Astrid, I acquiesce, and my suitor extends his arm. Together we stroll outside to the front of the hotel. The stars shine in the sky, and he stops for a brief moment to examine them.

"Stunning," he says after he turns back to me. I'm not sure which he is referring to. He takes my hand and kisses my knuckles. "Until we meet again."

He hesitates, not wanting to step away. His eyes look into mine and I can feel his indecision. Any other day, I might take him to a hotel for a bit of fun, but I'm on the clock. He's a pawn, helping me blend in while I make my escape. Unfortunately, he never stood a chance from my manipulations. I feel guilty, using him this way.

I make his decision for him, gently placing a hand on his neck and pulling him down. My lips brush his cheek, leaving a soft smudge of red lipstick in their wake.

With that I turn and walk away, fishing out my phone. Do I call her? What if she's hiding, and the ring of her phone gives her away? I type out a text, thinking a single beep isn't too bad, but then I get nervous and delete it.

But what if she needs help? God, I hate this bitch. I feel like I'm babysitting the most useless child. I debate this back and forth, ending up sending a text with only a single question mark in the message.

There's a clatter down the alley toward my left. I roll my eyes, already dreading what I'm going to find. I peek around the wall as I see Astrid burst through the door. Her hair is flying wildly, her previous coiffed bun long since ruined. She falls to the ground as the door gives. Apparently, she had to force it open. She quickly stands, slamming the door shut on someone's head. He crumples to the ground, but he wasn't alone. Astrid doesn't see me, instead takes off toward the other side of the alley. A second hulking man is hot on her tail, just a foot behind.

Fuck. My knife is on the ground. Astrid must have dropped it when she fell. I scoop it up as I trot after them. The blade is clean. Jesus, Astrid, do you not know how to use a knife?

A scream draws my attention from down the alley. The man has caught up to Astrid, enveloping her in his arms. To be fair, Astrid is putting up a formidable fight, squirming and thrashing in his grip.

Deep breath in.

Take aim.

Don't miss.

I fling the knife down the alley, lodging it directly between the man's shoulder blades. Astrid screams again when she notices the magically appearing knife.

"Shut up," I hiss, pulling her up. "Are you trying to attract more? Let's get out of here!"

"You could have hit me!" She says as I drag her along, partly in shock and partly pissed. Whatever.

"Don't be insulting," I retort. "I don't miss." I do actually, but that wouldn't make her feel better right now. Little white lies never hurt anybody. Knives do.

Astrid stumbles as we run, having lost her shoes somewhere between the first and second floor. Despite the filthy Bostonian sidewalks, I kick mine off too, discarding my heels to prioritize speed as we flee beneath dim streetlights.

We make it to the train station, and I go to my locker, punching in a code. The door swings open and I grab my duffel, slinging it over my shoulder.

"Let's go." I wave for her to follow. "What train is leaving the station next?"

"What?" She blinks wildly, shaking her head. "Go where? What? No!"

"Astrid, I have enough cash for us to have a solid start." I pat the bag. "But we need to go before they catch up to us."

"I'm not going anywhere with you!" I hope that tone of voice is shock and not disgust. Bitch.

"Actually, you're right. They're looking for the two of us." I unzip the bag and rummage around. "We should split up. Do you want to go north or south?"

"No!" Astrid pulls my duffel away. A shirt falls out of the bag and onto the floor. "We can't just up and leave. I have a life here! Brew for Two, my apartment, my family. Oh god, my family!"

She starts to hyperventilate, and for a moment, I pity her. It's always hard to leave. This is my what? Fourth? Fifth? And I still mourn the people I leave behind, like Derek.

"They're safer if you leave," I reassure her. "Think of the opportunities! You can go anywhere you want. Have you ever been to Chicago? I've heard the pizza is great. Or you could go to Miami, or Atlanta..." I snap my fingers. "San Francisco! You look like a San Francisco fan."

Despite my best efforts, she just starts to bawl. I'm starting to get flustered. I feel vulnerable standing in the middle of the train station.

"Pick where you want to go," I plead, desperately. "I'll come with you. We don't have to split up. You'll land on your feet, I'll make sure of it."

"No," she whimpers as her tears dry. "I'm staying."

"We don't have time for this," I groan. "I need to go."

"Then leave." Astrid turns away from me. "You're good at it."

"Are you trying to tell me something?" I stand, taken aback at her dig. "Also, now is very much not the time."

"When things get hard, you walk away," she spits. "You just turn and hide. That's not how I work."

"Are we talking about the same people?" I gesture between the two of us. "I seem to recall *you* leaving me."

"I never saw you again!" She glares. "You didn't come by the shop, you didn't come back to the apartment, nothing!"

"What does a breakup mean to you?" I am honestly flabbergasted. Bewildered. Dumbstruck. "Did you want me to come back?"

"Of course I did!" She sobs. "I wanted you to knock on my door in the middle of the night, begging for us to try again, saying we could make it work if we tried. I wanted you to throw snowballs at my window until I came onto the fire escape. I wanted you to show that you cared that we broke up, not just disappear like a whisper of smoke. I waited for you for weeks, but you never came."

"This isn't fair." Tears sting my eyes, and I sniffle embarrassingly. "You made it pretty clear that you wanted me gone."

"Can you blame me?" Astrid sits on a bench, scratching at the skirt of her dress. "That was the worst night of my life."

"Look," I sigh. "Let's talk about this on the train. You can yell and scream and whatever you need, I can take it. Let's go to San Francisco."

"I'm not going." She plants her feet. "Go by yourself."

"They'll kill you," I say. "I can't keep you safe."

"You're not responsible for me." She leans back, arms crossed.

"I can't just leave you like this." I wave my hands at her disheveled form.

"Go." She glares.

"Fine," I sigh, defeated. "I'll text you my number when I get a new phone. If you decide to hide, you can join me in San Francisco."

Astrid won't look at me, just sits on the bench. I rezip my duffel and sling it over my shoulder, crossing the tracks until I get to my platform. I find my own bench and hunker down, watching her across the station. My train arrives, and Astrid looks up as I board. We lock eyes. I stand there in the aisle. I should find my seat. I should try to get some sleep so I can hit the ground running tomorrow. I should do a lot of things.

I should not step back onto the platform. I should not watch the train leave, chugging along without me. I should not restuff my go-bag into my locker. But I do.

Astrid stands as I approach her, wiping her tears off her cheeks.

"We're still not friends," I grumble.

"Wouldn't want to be," she gripes.

Fuck.

The chemistry was undeniable. Sparks literally flew when our hands touched. It pains me to wipe her kiss off my cheek. Out of everyone in that ballroom, she chose me to dance with. I still can't believe it.

There was something enchanting about her. Her gray eyes, her red lips, her playful banter. We were meant to be together. I'm sure of it.

One day, she'll be sure of it too.

CHAPTER 13

ASTRID

Sparks and I meet up once a day. Always a different place, always a different time. We don't always speak. Letting a simple nod confirm we are both alive and okay. Sometimes, we sit in a ripped vinyl booth and eat together. I tell her stories of the customers at the cafe and try to ignore the sadness in her eyes when I mention Dolores. She tells me vague stories about her organization, using euphemisms to avoid obviously telling me the crimes they commit. I suppose that's for the best. We aren't exactly warm to each other, most chats ending with one or both of us storming out, but we are civil. Sometimes.

We both silently agreed to never bring up what happened at the train station. My meltdown. Her stepping off the train. I don't know what went through her head when our eyes locked. Heck, I don't even know what was going through mine. But she let the doors to the train car close without her, and I'm not brave enough to ask why.

Today, we are meeting in the park. We met here before, many months ago. It was the first time Sparks and the Water Weaver were really able to talk to each other. I didn't realize who she was under the hood, but she knew it was me. I can only imagine how stupid I sounded from her perspective.

Sparks is already by her old tree when I get there, sitting cross-legged against the trunk. She has a stick in her hand, drawing loose squiggles in the dirt. I place a bag with a maple pinwheel in it next to her before sitting at my tree across from her. I open my own bag and pick at a cinnamon roll.

"You can take it back," she says, indifferently. "I'm not hungry."

"You don't need to be hungry for dessert," I tease. "It goes in the second stomach."

She doesn't touch her pinwheel. They used to be her favorite, unless she was lying about that too. I can't keep up with my own mental gymnastics today. Exhausted, I tilt my head back to rest on the bark.

"Rough night?" She asks. Does she care, or is she just nosy?

"I haven't been sleeping well recently," I explain.

"How long?" Sparks sits up, apparently more concerned now. "Since the gala?"

"Longer."

"Oh." She relaxes again. "That's a bummer, I guess. You always slept so soundly when..."

Her voice trails off. It's okay, I can fill in the blank myself. When we shared a bed, when we slept together, when she would hold me tight until I woke the next morning.

The silence is deafening. The longer we sit in it, the more tense it gets. A stick snaps in the distance and Sparks in on her feet in an instant, gun in her hands. A squirrel scampers out from under a bush, racing up a tree in the distance.

"Relax, Annie Oakley," I chide. "The squirrel isn't going to hurt you."

Sparks stands there for a moment, and I realize her calm demeanor is a facade. She scans the horizon and treetops once more before retucking her gun in her waistband. Her eyes continue darting to the sides and her shoulders don't fully relax, despite her casual stance.

"Glad you're alive." Sparks looks, at best, indifferent. "See you tomorrow."

"Hold on, you forgot your pinwheel." I grab the bag, but when I look up, she's gone. Guess she's the one storming off today.

The sun isn't due to rise for another hour, yet I toss and turn in my pajamas. I've tried everything. More blankets, new pillows, adjusting the thermostat. Cutting out caffeine nearly killed me, so I resumed my coffee habit.

I give up on drifting off again this morning, stumbling to the kitchen. I heat up water in my mug on the counter. In my carelessness, it sloshes over the rim and splashes against my arm. I slam my hand on the tile, biting back spews of profanity. My vision blurs as tears well up in my eyes. I stagger to the sink, turning on the tap. The cool water stings as it runs over my burn, but I grit my teeth and suck it up. Thankfully, the wound doesn't blister, though there is an angry red splotch on my arm. I wrap my wrist in gauze, annoyed at my clumsiness.

Things just... haven't been going right for me lately. Mimi always says to get good karma, you have to give good karma. It has been a hot minute since the Water Weaver was out and about. I figure nothing could be worse than sitting with my own thoughts right now, so I slip on the blue suit.

There's a lot of skill and research that goes into being a vigilante. I have a carefully crafted network of informants to provide intel on crime predictions. However, sometimes there's also a fair bit of luck and random hunches. This morning is one of those times.

I'm perched on a roof by the harbor, observing the passersby below. There's not much going on, but crime rarely occurs in interesting places. Normally, I can make peace with the boredom, almost meditatively. But today, I can't sit still. Maybe today just isn't the right day. I vault to another roof, meandering back home.

Out of the corner of my eye, I see a trail of sirens chasing a speeding car. That's something. I slide down a ladder, landing at street level. The car is swerving, the driver likely panicking. He veers down a corner without looking. His car flies through a guardrail and into the brisk harbor water. Without thinking, I dive from the rocky shores into the bay, pulling myself through the murky water.

I am able to locate the vehicle quickly. Thankfully, the driver is the only occupant, so I don't need to take several trips. My powers help me drag his unconscious body to the surface, though I have to lug him over the rocks on my own.

Vigilantism is a contentious topic with police forces. Most of them tend to shrug me off. After all, they get the credit for the arrest. I prefer anonymity. Ninety times out of a hundred, I am gone before they arrive, leaving the culprit restrained in some way. Nine times out of a hundred, they get a pleasant wave from me as I bounce, clearing out from the area. Ninety-nine times out of a hundred, we find some way of ignoring each other. This was not one of those times.

I start compressions on the driver as the police clamber over the railing. They yell and point as they run, probably directing the EMTs.

"There!" "She's right there!" "Hurry!"

They're getting the EMTs, right? Right?

"Freeze!" "Stand with your hands up!"

Right?

The first firearm is drawn, and I decide that it's time for me to exit. Shots cut through the water as I dive back into the ocean. Holy shit. This is... um... new. I propel myself through the water before coming up for a breath.

Shouts carry across the water, and I hear splashes as people jump in after me. Are they being for real right now? I yelp and duck underneath as another wave of gunshots ring out. I swim along the coastline, trying to come up with a plan. Unfortunately, no great ideas are coming to mind. Even more unfortunate, plenty of bad ones are. Most unfortunate, I go with one.

Underneath my feet, my powers solidify the water until I am standing on a sheet of ice. In a fluid motion, I force the ice sheet up and springboard off of it. I fly through the air, landing roughly on the roof of coastal property. I jump from roof to roof, running toward... not sure yet. I'll get there.

My plan goes awry quickly as I run out of close enough buildings to jump between. Improvising, I clamor down the fire escape and take off down an alley. I can hear the policemen close by. I can't outrun them. New plan, quite possibly, worse plan.

I strip off my disguise, grateful to be wearing a sports bra and athletic shorts underneath. Desperately, I throw my suit and mask inside a trash can. If I live through this, I can come back for it. I jog for a few blocks, hoping I look less flustered than I feel.

A pair of arms wrap around my torso as I am roughly tackled to the ground without warning. I cry out as my arm is twisted forcibly behind my back, and more hands grab my ankles.

"I'm not resisting!" I plead, as I am aggressively dragged to my feet. "I'm not resisting!"

My pleas are ignored as cuffs encircle my wrists, much too tightly. I scream as the metal digs into my burn. I am thrown in the back of a squad car, trembling as the police car starts driving.

My thoughts spin wildly. Am I really being arrested? I've never even gotten a speeding ticket or a warning. I didn't drink a single drop of alcohol until I turned twenty-one. Pirating movies? Never me. Look up law-abiding citizen in the dictionary. It's just a picture of me, smiling with my swimming scholarship.

Are they going to call my mom? Liam is never going to let me live this down. Wait, am I going to go to jail? Or prison? I don't even know the difference. There's no way you get coffee in prison. What if my last cup of coffee ever was this morning? I didn't even drink it! Oh god, what if I go to jail forever?

The car rolls to a stop and rough hands drag me into the station. Camera flashes disorient me as I am processed. Mug shots, fingerprints, questions. *What's your name?* Astrid Larson. *How old are you?* Twenty-six last month. *What were you doing at the Boston Harbor this morning?* Jogging. *Are you the vigilante known as the Water Weaver?* Who? No, that's ridiculous. *Where's your cell phone?* I left it at home. *Didn't bring it with you?* I want my phone call. *Where's your disguise?* Phone call. *How many arrests are you responsible for?* Phone call. *Are you trying to embarrass the Boston police department?* Phone call. Phone call. Phone call.

It felt like hours before I was brought to a phone. It could have been minutes though, I have no way of knowing. Who are you supposed to call when you've been arrested? No one ever told me. Not that it mattered. I don't have any numbers memorized. Not my mom's. Not my dad's. Not Liam's.

Actually, that's a lie. I do have one phone number memorized, but I can't call that one. An officer stands behind my shoulder, staring at my back. They didn't give me anything to cover up with, and my sports bra is not as conservative as I now wish it was. I take a breath and dial the number.

Sergeant Benson? Her voice is crisp on the line. *Your payment isn't due for two more weeks.*

"No, it's me." I sniffle and wipe my nose. "Astrid."

Why are you calling me from a police station? Sparks asks. I can almost hear her roll her eyes, annoyed at my voice.

"I'm in trouble." My voice squeaks, and I hate how scared I sound. "I've been arrested. I don't have anyone else to call."

Am I really your emergency contact? She munches on something crunchy. Is she eating right now? Seriously? *Girl, that needs to be updated.*

"Can you please bail me out?" I beg. "I'll pay you back."

I can just bust you out, she offers. *That's free.*

"Absolutely not!" I hiss, covering the phone with my hand. Hopefully the guard behind me didn't catch that, although I don't think he's supposed to be listening. "Please, can you help me?"

Ugghh, Sparks groans. *Fine. Were you arrested doing what I think you were doing?*

"I don't know what you could possibly mean," I say, more for the officer than for Sparks. "I was just out for a jog."

That's a yes. I hear a deep breath. *Do yourself a favor. Don't talk to the cops. I'll take care of this.*

"Okay." My voice cracks, and I can feel my chin tremble. The officer taps his foot impatiently, gesturing for me to wrap up my call.

Keep your head up, Astrid. I've got you.

The officer reaches around and disconnects my call. I am led to a cold holding cell with a few people inside. Are they criminals? What did they do? I sit on a bench along the wall, keeping to myself. A man glances my way, raising an eyebrow at my scant clothing. I scooch further down the bench, and he thankfully leaves me alone.

More time passes. Minutes. Hours. Time has lost all meaning.

"Larson!" One of the guards calls.

I scamper to the door. This is it! I can go!

Amendment – I could not.

I was ushered back into the interrogation room, one way mirror and all. My restraints are shackled to the center of the table. The metal chair is cold against my skin. Goosebumps line my arms and I shiver. Did they turn the air conditioning lower before I came in? Two guards storm in and slam a file on the table.

"Lovely afternoon," one says to the other. "Nothing like a nice, warm April day to lift my spirits."

"I had a lobster roll on the pier during my lunch break," the second officer responds. "Delicious."

"What did you have for lunch?" The first guard asks, looking at me.

Sparks's voice repeats in my ear. *Don't talk to the cops.* I left my apartment this morning close to 5 a.m. *Don't talk to the cops.* How is it past lunchtime already? I'm hungry, thirsty, and scared. *Don't talk to the cops.*

"Hello?" The first officer waves his hand in front of my face. "Are you listening?"

I just start sobbing, shaking hard enough to rattle my chair. The cops look at each other awkwardly.

"We haven't even started the bad cop bit yet," the second one whispers to the first. The first doesn't have a response. He slides a box of tissues to me, and I blow my nose.

"Good afternoon, officers." A man in a flashy suit bursts through the door. "Chris Rimes of C. Rimes Law. We seem to have a slight problem."

"... excuse me?" The first officer stares dumbstruck at the intrusion. I am just as startled.

"Yes, you are excused," the lawyer responds. "If you feel so inclined, you may also kiss the rings." He extends a hand with ostentatious rings on each finger. The policemen roll their eyes as the lawyer withdraws his hand. "Only kidding, only kidding. Now let's get back to business, shall we?"

"Why are you interrupting our interrogation?" The second officer stands angrily.

"Advocating for my client's constitutional rights," Chris speaks quickly, whipping his words at the officers. "You have heard of those, correct? And laws? I find those all to be very helpful for police officers to know."

"We know laws." The first officer stands as well, trying to be intimidating. It's not effective.

"Your parents must be proud."

Chris slides off his jacket and drapes it around my shoulders as he sits in the chair next to me. I gladly accept the jacket, thankful for the small amount of modesty. He gives me a cheeky wink, as if to say "enjoy the show." Ever so slightly, the pit of dread in my stomach subsides. Maybe everything will be okay.

"My client has had several infringements on her rights in the several hours she has been in your custody." Chris leans back, slamming his briefcase on the table and unclipping the latches. "For starters, she has been given neither food nor water, has not been informed of her rights, and has not been kept in a holding facility separate from members of the opposite gender. Those are just the ones I have the paperwork ready for."

Chris reaches into his briefcase and pulls out paper after paper after paper. He pats his shirt before remembering I was wearing his jacket.

"Dearie, would you mind pulling out the pen in the coat pocket?" He points to several lines denoted by sticky flags. "I need you to sign these."

"Hold on now," the first officer stammers. "Let's talk, shall we? We can offer a plea deal."

"Good for you, we decline," Chris says, condescendingly. "Because while Astrid Larson was in your custody, the Water Weaver – the very same person you allege my client to be – has been seen gallivanting around West Boston. I have witness statements and photographic evidence. Could you possibly explain to me how Miss Larson was both here and there?"

Chris pulls a stack of photos from his briefcase and flings them across the table. I catch a glimpse of someone in blue. Wait, what? The officers seem just as confused as I am. The three of us examine the photos. These are pictures of the Water Weaver, or at least someone in the costume. But I left that in the alley? I look closer and see Sparks having an absolute ball, wearing a blonde wig and running through the streets. She has a squirt gun in each hand, and she sprays water at random bystanders while darting between cars. In a different picture, she spins, laughing at how the fabric flows with her movements. This is so embarrassing.

"Stop looking so interested," Chris chides under his breath. I drop the photo reluctantly, and he chuckles. "I'll get you copies later."

"This isn't possible," one of the policemen mutters. "We caught her."

"That's not the way the media will see this." Chris stands slowly, planting his hands on the table. "The story they will run is that of the upstanding, moral citizen you dragged here. The fine, respectable woman, practically a child, who was crying alone in an interrogation room wearing nothing more than her undergarments, as two male police officers coerce her into false confessions for fear of her own safety."

"But—" an officer tries to cut in, but Chris isn't done.

"Now, I advise you to get on the phone and apologize to your bosses," Chris threatens. "Because after my client and I leave here, I am going to draft much, much more paperwork. I am going to rain hellfire down on this precinct until you can't take a shit without getting a papercut. I'm talking harassment, unlawful arrest, violation of constitutional rights, and whatever else my interns can think of."

"You don't have the grounds!" The officer doesn't look too confident in his rebuttal.

"I don't care." Chris shrugs. "You have to respond to them regardless. I get paid to waste your time. Unless... no, that's crazy."

"What?" The first officer probes. "Unless what?"

"No, I won't even consider it." Chris dramatically looks away.

"Spit it out." The second guard is losing his patience, but Chris doesn't let it disrupt his performance.

"Maybe if you would drop the charges and release my client..." He wraps his arm around my shoulders. "I could be persuaded to waste my time in other precincts. Maybe."

Within minutes, Chris and I are walking out of the police station. His jacket has been returned to him since the Boston PD so nicely provided me with a shirt, requested of course by Chris. The sun is high in the sky, and I squint at the unexpected light.

"Nice to meet you, kid." Chris thumps my shoulder. "Stay out of trouble."

"Yes, sir," I promise. "Thank you!"

He gives a pageant queen wave as he walks away, surely to hassle some other police officers in Boston. I continue down the steps and spot Sparks parked on the street. She's laying on her bike, resting her head against the handlebars. Her cropped tank shows off her toned stomach. She sits up when she sees me, adjusting the brim of her baseball cap over her sunglasses.

"How was life on the inside?" Sparks mocks, smiling lightheartedly. "Did you join a gang? Please tell me you got a tattoo."

I don't say anything, just sit next to her on the bike. She pulls me into a hug, and I nestle my face in her shoulder, exhausted, strung out, and emotional.

"There, there," she soothes. "I've got you."

"Thanks for your help, and for Chris." I mumble into her neck, savoring the residual smell of the sandalwood and bergamot body wash Sparks always uses.

"Ah, Chris Rimes of C. Rimes Law," Sparks chuckles. "For when you need a frosty motherfucker. He's a total schmuck, but he knows his way around the courtroom. Love that guy."

"Today really sucked."

"Sorry we couldn't get you out faster. Our legal defense took a bit to set up," she whispers softly. "They were playing hardball, so we had to get creative. Your suit is back at your apartment."

"I think it's time to retire." I kick at a rock with my foot. "They freaking shot at me."

"Up to you." She shrugs. "You hungry? Let's go get you something to eat."

"It's fine." I stand and wave her off. "I'm just going to go home."

"Why do you think I'm here?" Sparks asks dryly. "You need a ride wherever you're going."

"You shouldn't have," I protest. "You've already done so much."

Sparks stretches as she straddles her bike. The sun rays highlight the small of her back, her smooth skin, the gun in her waistband. Wait, gun?

"Get on the fucking bike, Astrid," Sparks commands, stuffing her baseball cap into a saddlebag.

"You have a gun," I state. "Why did you bring a gun to a police station?"

"Don't worry about it," she laughs. "Chris Rimes is my lawyer."

My hands wrap around her waist as she peels away from the curb. It feels so familiar, yet so strange, like the hauntings of a memory. Neither of us are wearing a helmet, she used to insist I did. I tried to force her to as well but had less success.

Sparks rounds a curb quickly, and I instinctively squeeze her waist, flinching away from the hard concrete below. She slows the bike, adjusting to my discomfort. Despite my apprehension, Sparks pulls up to my apartment without incident. She cuts the engine as I get off.

"Thank you for everything," I say awkwardly. "I know it was a lot to ask. I'll pay you back."

"It's not a problem." She looks sincere, but I don't know. We aren't friends. "Honestly, Chris is on retainer, and I probably had a bit too much fun taking those photos."

She gets off the bike and walks toward the stairs.

"No!" I blurt out. "It's okay. You can go home."

"Astrid, I don't think you should be alone right now." She looks hurt.

"I'm fine," I reply stubbornly. "Thank you."

"Okay." Sparks sits back on her bike, watching as I climb the stairs by myself.

"Astrid," she calls as I unlock the door. I turn to face her as a small amount of water splashes on my arm.

"Pew pew!" She waves the squirt gun in her hand and drives away.

I step back into my apartment and lock my door. It feels duller than it used to, like it's missing something. I know what it is, but I won't admit it to myself. The dishes have been done. The rugs are vacuumed. A fresh tea bag sits on the counter next to a mug filled with water. She's so thoughtful, but I'm not in the mood for tea right now.

A small bag sits at the foot of my bed. I unzip it and my disguise is folded inside. I used to wear this proudly, like a badge of honor, but it seems like I'm not wanted anymore. I lift the fabric intending to set it back in its hiding place, but the subtle scents of sandalwood and bergamot tingle my nose. It smells like her.

I flop onto the bed, holding the suit to my chest. Burying my face in the clothes, I savor the lingering scent. I can't do this anymore, can't keep lying to myself, refusing to face what I've known to be true for months now. Distractions haven't worked, every road leads back to here, to this moment. The missing part of my life, the reason I toss and turn all night. Anise. Sparks. Charlotte. The name doesn't matter.

I still love her.

I cradle the bodysuit, pretending she's in the bed next to me. For the first time in four months, I effortlessly drift asleep.

CHAPTER 14

SPARKS

You know what they say, if they can't get it done right, then do it yourself. I'm tired of being disappointed with unsatisfactory results, so I'm taking matters into my own hands. The vibrator buzzes as the switch is flicked on. The lights are dim, and low music drifts from my radio. Let's do this.

My sheets are soft, cushioning my bare skin. My fingertips glide across my ribs, following the curve of my body to my breasts. My nipples perk at the sensation. I force myself to release the breath I was holding and relax. I'm not in a hurry, I can just enjoy the feeling of my touch for a minute. My head pushes back into my pillow as I pinch my nipples, casually rolling the buds between my fingers. Yeah, this is what I want. I smile, giddy and excited.

I part my legs, shivering at the cold air on my bare skin. One hand stays massaging my chest while the other ventures south. My fingers slide between my folds, already dripping with anticipation. My eyes roll to the back of my head as I find the spot I'm looking for. My hands move with a practiced precision, touching exactly where they can elicit the maximum pleasure.

The tension in my gut is growing. It's time. I gasp as the vibrator connects with my sensitive nerves. My toes curl and I arch my back from the mattress. Fuck. The pulses send jolts up my spine, and I'm trembling from need. Suddenly, my hands aren't mine. Soft skin. Blue eyes. Blonde hair.

Someone pounds at my door.

"Not now!" I roar.

"Sparks, we need you upstairs," Derek calls through the door.

"Take care of it yourself." My voice is strangled. So close, I'm so close.

"We need you." Derek pounds on the door again.

"Five minutes," I plead. Go away. Go away. Go away.

"Now!"

I scream in frustration as the orgasm that was so close fades away. Fucking hell. I throw my vibrator across the room, the batteries roll across the floor.

Because I'm needed upstairs, it's implied I need to get dressed up in club attire. I am so not in the mood for sequins and rhinestones. I pull out a leather miniskirt and a black corset. I need to throw out this skirt. It's short, even by my standards, but it's good enough for now. There's probably not time for makeup since Derek is pounding at my door again, but I can't go upstairs barefaced. I grab a stick of lip gloss and eyeliner, shoving them in my bra as I fumble with my heels. Derek ushers me to the elevator, and I use the door's muddled reflection to draw winged liner on my eyelids.

"LaRusso's here." Derek brings me up to speed. LaRusso is our main competitor. We've been joshing with each other for territory lately. Things have been heating up. "Showed up out of the blue with a whole team. I don't like the look of this."

"We'll hear him out." I swipe red gloss over my lips. "And we'll handle it." I hand my makeup to Derek who looks at the tubes blankly.

"What do you want me to do with these?"

"I don't have any pockets." I gesture to my outfit. "You do."

Derek grumbles and stuffs them in his pants pocket as the doors open. He walks out first, commanding the scene. I sway my hips as I follow him to our booth. LaRusso is already sitting, flanked by three men. His eyes greedily follow my legs until I sit down. This is going to suck. I lean back, all too aware of how much this top pushes up my boobs. It seems LaRusso has also caught on.

"We typically require appointments," Derek calmly states to LaRusso. "Bold of you to ask to be the exception."

"Funny." The older man doesn't laugh, eyes narrowed. "I don't remember asking."

"Can I offer you a drink?" Derek suggests icily.

"I'll pass," LaRusso scoffs.

"Fine." Derek shrugs, before turning to me. He runs his index finger along my jaw. "Can I get you anything?"

"Please, baby," I purr.

I don't know what Derek's angle is with this faux flirting, but I trust him enough to go along with it. Derek flags down a member of the waitstaff and orders two drinks. I lean into his shoulder, and he places an arm around me protectively. LaRusso says nothing, only glares at Derek.

After a moment, the waiter returns with two whiskey sours. Derek tips my chin up and dangles the cherry into my mouth. I bite the fruit off the stem, sensually licking my lips after.

"LaRusso, didn't your wife recently leave you?" Derek asks with a pretend innocence. Found his angle. Derek's trying to make him jealous! Oh, I can help with that. I nestle into his side, playing with the top button of his shirt.

"That's not the way I would tell that story." LaRusso grips the table, indignant from Derek's boldness.

"Either way," Derek runs his fingers down my arm, "I find it's easy to keep a woman if you keep her satisfied." Derek doesn't realize how ironic that statement is, my vibrator abandoned downstairs.

"I did not come here to be insulted," LaRusso declares with a quiet anger. He stands, knocking his seat to the floor.

"No?" Derek looks up nonchalantly. I watch LaRusso suspiciously, unnerved by his escalating temper. "You haven't told me why you're here. I just guessed."

"I'm here to reclaim the territory you stole from me by whatever means necessary." His tone lowers, and the implication is clear. "You will give it back, or we will be having a different discussion."

"I've been a gracious host," Derek says, warning in his voice. "You would do well to avoid further transgressions."

"Then you would do well to die quickly." LaRusso whips out a pistol. Men on both sides draw their firearms, and I feel Derek stiffen underneath me. Fuck. LaRusso is definitely going off script.

"Finally," I groan, thinking fast on my feet. I slide out of the booth. LaRusso's eyes dart to me, getting stuck on my chest. "I've been waiting for a chance to leave this loser."

"What?" Derek says, hurt.

"LaRusso." I flutter my eyelashes, slowly striding toward him. "Do you think I could keep you company tonight?"

"Apparently you can't keep them satisfied," LaRusso cackles with glee. He keeps his pistol squared on a resentful Derek while extending his other hand to me.

I saunter into LaRusso's arms, cradling his face with my hands. We lock eyes, and I gasp quietly. My lips meet his, deeply and passionately. I wait a few beats, and I feel his other hand drop to embrace me, the barrel of his pistol no longer aimed at Derek.

"See you in hell," I whisper maliciously.

His eyes widen in surprise as electricity courses through his veins. The lights in the club strobe dramatically. Before his guards can react, I send bolts toward the three of them as well. They collapse to the ground without firing a shot, and the crowd below dances oblivious to the skirmish above.

"Yuck." I grab a napkin and wipe the feeling of LaRusso off my lips. "That was disgusting."

Derek doesn't move from his seat. He stares off in the distance as the flashing lights return to their normal cadence. I grab his hand and pull him into the elevator, shielding him from the watchful gaze of our staff.

"I never thought that someone would actually..." His voice trails off. "He pulled a gun on me in my own club."

"It's okay, you're okay." I force him to look at me. "We're a team. I've got your back."

"I didn't realize you were acting." His expression shows his hurt and guilt. "I thought you were going to whore yourself out to him. I made you kiss him, I put you in that position."

"Hey, snap out of it." I wave my hand in front of his face. "It was a kiss. I'm an adult. I kiss random strangers all the time. I would kiss a hundred more to keep you safe. But not a hundred and one, I have to set a limit somewhere."

A faint smile breaks through his stupor. He lets himself laugh at my joke.

"Thank you." Derek pulls me close.

"Anytime." I hug him back. "But if you ever feed me a cherry again, I am going to spit in your eye."

"That was such a bad plan." He shakes his head, embarrassed.

"And like, ew." I punch his shoulder. "Never gonna happen."

"Yeah..." He scrunches his nose. The elevator doors open and Derek steps out, waiting for me.

"I'm actually going to pop up to the roof."

I smile and wave him off. He nods, and I hope he goes somewhere where he can process things. His entire family was assassinated due to mafia politics. I'm sure those memories are resurfacing right about now.

The elevator takes me up to the roof. I come here occasionally when I need space to be alone. It was quite nice in the winter, feeling the bitter cold of the snow on my skin.

I like to read up here, where no one can judge me if I need to sound out words. I dropped out of high school when my mom died, but Astrid showed me that I can keep learning on my own. Since then, I've been obsessed with textbooks. I've read quite a few, with topics ranging from the Italian Renaissance to psychology and business strategy. At one point I was working on a book about statistics, but I got lost in the math. I keep the books in a waterproof tub next to a plastic lawn chair,

I unfold the chair and fish out my astronomy book. The stars are shining brightly tonight. There's something soothing about them. No matter what happens down here on Earth, they are up there twinkling. People thousands of years ago used to look up at the constellations, telling stories about legends and heroes. Sometimes I wish I could float into the sky and live amongst the stars. It would be a simpler life.

Dark clouds filter in from the southwest, and I tuck my book away as the rain starts to pour down. Typical for a Boston spring. The water comes down in fat drops, and it only takes a minute for me to get completely soaked. I sit back, watching the storm move in until the entire sky is obscured and the stars are hidden from view. Thunder rumbles as lightning flashes through the dark. My scar itches as I watch the bolts, remembering the time I was struck.

There's still a lot we don't know about lightning, but we know enough to understand the gist. Negative charge in the clouds, positive on the ground. A violent reaction happens when the two charges connect, and the static energy erupts into electricity. I accidentally turned myself into a lightning rod many months ago, resulting in this burn. I haven't been too keen to experiment since. Instead, I just watch. I've learned to sense in the air when the moment arrives, the exact second that the lightning will crack, sending thunderous shockwaves through the air.

I know lightning should scare me. Fuck, it nearly killed me. But I can't find the fear inside me. Just respect, admiration, jealousy. Lightning can let loose, react vividly and dramatically. It doesn't have to stay contained inside the shell of a cloud.

I close my eyes as the rain coats my skin. My eyeliner is streaking down my cheeks, but I could not be bothered. What would it be like to explode? To erupt and bring the world down with you? To force others to feel your pain and sadness and anger? I sigh. Must be nice. Lightning flashes in front of me as if to gloat. *Look at me! Free, volatile, uncontrollable!*

I move from my chair and sit on the edge of the roof, dangling my feet over the street below. Cars drive by, headlights shining as the windshield wipers flap wildly. My hair is stringy from the rain, hanging in front of my face in heavy tendrils. I sweep it back, but it just swings back again. The consequence of cutting my hair I suppose. A clicking sound draws my attention, but I can't tell where it comes from. I must be going crazy. I shake my head, clearing the thoughts from my mind. Cold from the rain, I decide to tuck in for the night.

⚡ ⚡ ⚡ ⚡

The floor sways beneath my feet as the ship rocks with the waves. Lightning fills the sky with vivid, bright flashes. I stand on the deck as the ocean roars, splashing against the guardrails. LaRusso stands in front of me, gun leveled at Derek. I try to run, to stand in front of him, but the boat lurches violently and I lose my footing. I crawl, scratching at the wood until my fingernails bleed. I won't make it in time! He pulls the trigger and Derek falls to the deck. I scream as LaRusso turns to me, laughing maniacally. The lightning flashes again, striking the ship. The impact sends me flying through the air and I fall into the murky water below.

I splash through the water and end up not in the ocean, but at the gala conference room. Astrid's on her knees, being held down by two burly men. Her eyes are wide with panic, and she screams through a gag. I reach toward the ceiling, pulling electricity from the lights around, but nothing happens. No bolts, no lightning, not even a few measly sparks. Marissa cackles as she walks in front of me.

"I told you we weren't asking." Her plastic smile is gone, replaced by a sinister sneer. "Welcome to the team."

"Sparks!" The door to my bedroom flings open, and Derek crashes in, gun drawn.

I hear someone screaming. Bloodcurdling, shrill, terrifying. Who's screaming? Make them stop! Somebody make them stop!

"Sparks!" Derek jumps onto the bed and grabs my arm. "What's wrong? What happened?"

What happened? I don't know! I don't know! Ash coats my sweaty body. My sheets are gone. Did somebody steal my sheets?

Smack! Derek slaps me across the cheek. The screaming cuts out abruptly. Wait, was that me? My chest is heaving. I can feel my heart beating so fast that I think it might burst.

"Are you okay?" Derek asks, sitting next to me. He's set his pistol on my bedside table.

I take a moment and scan my bedroom. Upon closer inspection, my bedsheets are scorched, leaving behind a sooty residue. It leaves a dark smear on Derek's pajamas. I am coated in it. Fragmented lightning shapes decorate the ceiling, burned into the paint. My nightmare comes back to me, and I realize I caused this destruction. Derek sits there, waiting for an answer.

"Spider," I stammer. "There was a spider."

"Must have been a big spider." Derek lets me save face, but he knows the truth. His eyes are lined with pity and compassion.

"Huge." I nod. "Massive."

"How about you rinse off in the shower while I hunt around for the spider?" Derek suggests. "Just to make sure it's gone."

I'm too exhausted to protest. The water runs black as it carries the soot off my body. I sit on the floor for a moment or two, just holding myself tight. Derek's alright. Astrid's alright. I'm alright.

I'm not alright.

By the time I've toweled off, Derek has replaced the sheets on my bed. He can't do anything about the burns on my ceiling, but we'll have maintenance take care of it tomorrow.

"Do you want to talk about the spider?" Derek offers, fluffing my pillows.

"No." He's got enough on his plate, I can't add my nightmare to his list of responsibilities. He already feels the weight of the world on his shoulders.

"Well, I'm all set up on your couch, just in case the spider comes back." Derek steps back, hands on his hips.

"Dude, you live across the hall." I roll my eyes. "Go back to your bed."

"I'm fine on the couch for a night." His eyes meet mine, and I feel the fraternal warmth of our makeshift sibling bond. He's not going anywhere. I give him a tight hug.

"Thank you," I whisper in his ear.

"Anytime."

⚡　　⚡　　⚡　　⚡

"I swear I left my hat here." I dig through the saddlebag on my motorcycle. Ponytail, sunglasses, lose twenty-dollar bill. No baseball cap. Did I give it to Astrid yesterday? Whatever. Frustrated, I grab my sunglasses instead. I had some spare time and figured a walk would lift my mood. Seems less likely at this point.

Regardless, I set out towards nowhere and anywhere. Puddles splash my boots, but the leather keeps my feet dry. My flannel keeps the sun off my arms while also letting the gentle breeze keep me cool. Something draws my attention down an alley. I leave the main road and crouch down near a garbage bin. A small black fuzzball shivers in a puddle. After a quick search, I can't find the cat's mother or any siblings, just the little kitten. I extend a hand, allowing her to sniff me. She opens her eyes and licks my finger. Aww, shucks.

Carefully, I scoop up the kitten and hold her to my chest. She's cold to the touch. Quickly, I run to the nearest vet hospital.

"Help me, please." I go up to the receptionist, sweaty from running this whole way. "I found this cat and she doesn't look very good. I'll pay whatever, just make sure she's okay."

The receptionist calls for the vet and we are ushered into an exam room. I don't know what kind of tests the vet runs, but the little kitten doesn't complain the whole time. I pet her nose when she gets her vaccines, trying to give her some form of moral support.

"Great news," the vet says. "She's a perfectly healthy little cat. Bummer she was abandoned. We can't find a microchip so she's probably a stray. I'll call the local shelter and they'll come pick her up soon."

"Wait, what? No!" I crouch next to the kitten and cradle her to my chest. "I can't just abandon her too."

I know what it's like to be on your own. Neglected, isolated, alone. This cat is only a few weeks old, she doesn't deserve to be abandoned.

"Do you want to adopt her?" The vet asks, raising her eyebrows. "A cat is a big responsibility."

"She's mine." Her breath is soft against my skin. "I'll take care of her."

"Okay then. Have a great rest of your day."

It's that easy? Shouldn't there be a background check or some kind of readiness test? I stare down at the little creature in my arms and meander back home. This is going to be tough to explain to Derek.

It was not, in fact, tough to explain to Derek. As soon as he saw the kitten, his puppy-dog eyes grew three sizes. He coddled her and played with her paws. A shipment arrived less than an hour later with all the cat supplies we could ask for – litter boxes, food, treats, beds, toys. I thought the kitten would get overwhelmed, but she contentedly chases a string in between stopping for scritches.

"You've got to name her," Derek prods.

"It feels rude to just give her a name." I gesture to her. "Like, that's just deciding who she is without her opinion."

"It's a cat." Derek rolls his eyes. "She needs a name."

"Fine." My mind spins, searching for a suitable name. "How about Licorice?"

"What do you think, Licorice?" Derek coos. Licorice responds with a squeak. I hope that means she approves.

Derek lays on the floor with her for over an hour, giving her constant attention. Maybe he needed this as much as I did. My phone buzzes, Astrid. She's wondering if we are planning to meet today. Shit, I have something I need to do first. I sneak out, content that Licorice will be fine with her new pal.

I have to check on one of our franchises. We can meet after. I shoot off the quick text to Astrid.

Do you want to meet there? Save you a drive. Her response.

Fine, but don't come inside. The clientele there is a little... temperamental.

Cool, text the address.

This is going to bite me in the ass, isn't it?

CHAPTER 15

ASTRID

Of course I go inside. Did she honestly think I wouldn't? But I do take her warning seriously. Instead of dressing how I normally would, in a skirt or lacy top, I wear my best Sparks-lookalike outfit. And by that, I mean I steal her clothes from the boxes in my closet. My final look consists of ripped jeans, a faded t-shirt, and a flannel. I leave my hair down around my shoulders, embracing my naturally wavy hair.

Sparks didn't lie, this place is super grungy. There's a fighting ring in the center, which I try to avoid. I grab a cheap beer from the barkeep and keep to myself, wearily eyeing those placing bets on the results of the fights. Some women who must be supermodels line the outside of the ring, cheering for the fights and flirting with the victors. I don't think anyone who steps in that ring would be my type. The latest duo were both heavily tatted, and one didn't have all of his teeth. The fight ends with a lot of commotion. Some celebrate their winnings, while others gripe about their losses. Don't bet what you can't afford to lose, my dad always says.

I sip my lager as the announcer calls forth the next fighting duo. I nearly choke as I see a familiar redhead step into the ring. What the heck? I stand and move closer to the ring, jostling with the crowd.

The bell sounds and Sparks sizes up the lunk in front of her, lightly bouncing on her feet. He lunges toward her, and she ducks under his arm, kneeing him in the ribs. The man whirls toward her, angry. She just smirks and pops him in the nose. He curses as blood drips down his face. They circle each other, searching for weaknesses. He steps in front of Sparks, and slowly guides her into the corner. Move! I want to shout. Don't get trapped. But I doubt she would hear me over the crowd.

Sparks stalls, waiting for the right moment. Suddenly, she smiles and strikes. She feints left, and as he exposes his side, she jabs his torso. She darts around his legs, running back to the center of the ring. Sparks flips her hair out of her face, and somehow, locks eyes with me. Her cocky expression falters. I point, but the warning comes too late as her opponent knocks her to the ground.

She skids across the floor. He's on her before she can regain her footing. He kicks at her stomach, and Sparks arches her back, barely missing the blow. The fighter loses his balance and Sparks takes advantage of the mistake. She jumps on his back and puts the man in a headlock. He throws himself to the ground, landing on her, but Sparks keeps her grip. Finally, the ref calls the fight and Sparks is crowned the victor. She showboats to the crowd, winking at the ladies swooning on the ring ropes. I try not to gag.

I elbow my way to the ring, forcing my way through the bidders and other fighters. Sparks slinks under the ropes and walks down an isolated pathway. I jog to catch up.

"Hey," I call out. She ignores me. "I wish I knew you were doing this sooner. I could have been whipping my shirt around with all of those floozies."

"Eh." She rolls her eyes. "They sleep with you and run off with your winnings. I don't pay them much attention."

"Nasty fall you took up there." I study her gait. "How are you feeling?"

"I'm fine," she snaps. Now I've annoyed her. "I thought I told you to stay outside."

I follow into a locker room and Sparks grabs a duffel, ignoring the men changing and showering. They don't ignore her though, they stare at her body as she walks to the exit. A few of them eyefuck me, so I hustle after Sparks before they can act on their fantasies.

"You knew I wasn't going to wait when you sent me the address," I defend. "This isn't my fault."

"It never is," she huffs. "Look, are we good? I've got things to do. Oliver needs me to grab the books, I need to file a maintenance request, my cat needs—"

"You got a cat?" I interject excitedly. "Oh my goodness, when can I meet him? I already love him."

"Firstly," Sparks whips around to face me. "Her. She's a girl. And you don't get to love her. You don't have Licorice rights."

I gasp, hands on my face.

"You named her Licorice!" I gush. "That is adorable. Let's go."

"Did you not just hear me?" Sparks groans. "It's like I'm talking to a wall."

We exit the gym and Sparks straddles her bike. I stand in front of the tire, blocking her path.

"Please," I beg. She sighs.

"Only if I get my flannel back before you leave." She flicks her eyes to the shirt I'm wearing. "Don't think I didn't notice your change in wardrobe."

"Deal." We shake on it, and Sparks speeds off, leaving me to remember where I parked my car.

Sparks meets me in the parking garage and escorts me down to her bedroom. Derek is there, lying next to a snuggly ball of black fur. Licorice squeaks when she sees me, excited to have a new friend to play with. I am thrilled to oblige. She somersaults over her clumsy paws as she chases a laser pointer, stumbling every few steps. Derek and I alternate fawning over the kitten. It's strange to see such a large, muscular man dote on such a small creature, but Licorice seems to love him.

Licorice falls asleep in Derek's arms, and I lean back on Spark's couch. Wait, where's Sparks? I think back and realize she must have ducked out a while ago.

"Took you that long to notice, huh?" Derek scoffs, disapprovingly.

"Excuse me?" I bristle at his disdain.

"You heard me." Derek pets the cat while shooting daggers in my direction.

"What's your problem?" I shake my head. "I barely even know you."

"Well, I've heard plenty about you. Nothing that explains why she tolerates you being here."

"She never mentions you," I snipe. "Who's to say that you have the moral high ground here?"

"Because I take care of her!" He whisper-shouts, trying to not disturb the kitten. "Every time you take a piece out of her, I'm the one trying to patch the cracks. And you know what? She's running out of fragments for you to steal."

"You don't know what you're talking about." I cross my arms.

"The fuck I don't." The kitten stretches her paws. Derek freezes until she curls back into a little ball. "Every nightmare, every binge drinking episode, every reckless attempt to get herself killed, I'm there. She made so much progress, but you had to step back in. Now she's getting worse, and I can only do so much."

"Why do you care, huh?" I stand, rage overflowing my body. How can he accuse me of being bad for her? "Just wanting her for your meal ticket? You're using her for her powers."

"How dare you!" Derek yells for real this time, setting Licorice on the ground. "She's like a sister to me. I would die for her!"

I scoff, shaking my head. I don't believe this.

"Did you know that night, Sparks begged me to keep you safe?" Derek speaks slowly, ensuring that every word punches my gut. "After being tortured for hours, she didn't want me to help her escape. She accepted her death, but she pleaded for me to help *you*. I should have let you die instead."

I turn and walk away from him, devastated by his words but trying to hide the pain. I don't have to listen to him belittle me.

"You know what?" Derek moves to stand in front of me. He is much taller than I am, but I refuse to let him intimidate me. "You don't get to do this. You don't get to come in and wriggle back into her life. Stay away from her."

"I'm not leaving." I poke his chest. "I'm in love with her."

"Too late." He spits at my feet. "You threw away your chance."

His words cut deep, partially because I know he's right. I had her in my arms, but I pushed her away.

"I know." I fight back the tears pricking my eyes. "But I'm here anyway. I'll make it up to her. Whatever it takes."

"Do you ever think she might be better off without you?" He backs away, having made his point. "Do the right thing and leave. Or ignore me and follow her up to the roof. I'll be here to pick up the pieces either way."

The door slams behind me as I run into the hallway. I repeatedly push the elevator button, flustered and agitated by Derek's backhanded remarks. I take a breath as I enter the elevator. Luckily, someone is getting off, so I don't need to beg Derek for his fingerprint. Not that he would help.

Derek's words stick to my back. Am I bad for her? I can't be. I love her. How could I be hurting her? I lean my head against the cool metal of the elevator. After a beat, I press the button to the roof.

Sparks is sitting on the edge of the roof, reading from a book. I nervously perch next to her, apprehensive of the far drop to the street below. The silence stretches for a bit, until she sets aside her book and lays on her back, staring at the twinkling stars. I lean back with her, our shoulders barely touching.

"Why were you fighting in the ring today?" I break the silence. She takes a breath, and for a moment, I don't think she'll respond.

"Has it occurred to you that I enjoy it?"

"No, it hasn't." I turn on my side, analyzing the minute movements of her face. We didn't date for long, but I got pretty good at reading her expressions. "I don't think that's the reason though."

"It's not." Her eyebrows scrunch together, and she combs her hair back. I stumbled onto something personal.

"It's okay, you don't have to explain." I return to my back and lace my fingers over my stomach.

"Do you remember that night on the boat?" Her voice shakes.

"I'll never forget it." Unfortunately, I mean it.

"Do you remember the cuffs Jack used to restrain me?"

"You mean the barbaric ones with the spikes?" Anger laces my voice. The sight of blood dripping down her forearms is etched into my memory.

"Yeah." She takes a moment to compose herself before continuing. "When metal pierces my skin, it disrupts my ability to channel electricity. The energy goes through me before it gets directed elsewhere. It means I can't use my powers without hurting myself first."

"So that night when you shocked Jack..." The moment comes to the front of my memory, staring down the barrel of his gun. Both of their screams haunt me.

"I was electrocuting myself too."

"Oh." My brain spins, processing this new information.

"I felt so useless the whole night." A tear falls down her cheek. "I couldn't help, couldn't stop him, couldn't protect you or Derek or Jeremiah... I won't feel like that again. That's why I learned how to fight."

I find her hand in the dark and she squeezes mine tightly. With my powers, I can sense her tears rolling toward the ground. It hurts to try and picture what she could be thinking about right now.

"I've never thought of you as useless," I whisper, unsure if she's listening to me. "Brave, headstrong, determined, self-sacrificial to a fault, but never useless."

She chuckles at my joke and wipes the water off her face.

"I've been reading about astronomy lately." She changes the topic.

"Is Mercury in retrograde or something?" I tease, hoping to draw out another laugh from her.

"Very funny," she says dryly. "That's astrology, not astronomy." Dang, it didn't work.

"My textbook said that it takes hundreds to thousands to millions of years for the light from our planet to reach those stars," Sparks continues, "depending on how far away they are, of course. If you were able to stand on one of them and look through a telescope pointed at Earth, you would be looking at the past, almost like a time machine."

"That's pretty crazy." The stars glow in the sky, almost as if they too were proud of that fact.

"Somewhere, on some star out there, the dinosaurs are still alive." Sparks smiles sadly. "On another, so is my mother."

"Maybe on another..." The words fall from my lips, hesitant and uncertain. "We're still together."

Time seems to stop, and I almost wish I could take it back. Almost.

A beat passes.

Then another.

Her shaky breathing is the only sound from the rooftop, nearly drowned out by passing cars and far away construction workers. Finally, she breaks the silence.

"The dinosaurs went extinct for a reason." Sparks drops my hand. "Maybe we did too."

She stands and walks toward the elevator. I slide through the doors before it can close. She won't meet my eyes.

"I made a mistake, and I'm sorry," I admit. "I was harsh, and angry, and I ended our relationship without a second thought. You were everything to me, and now, you won't even look at me and I can't take it anymore! If I could undo it, go back and try to work things out with you, I would. I would go back in a heartbeat. But I can't. All I can do is beg for you to let me try and make it up to you, try and be friends again." I fall to my knees, hands clasped in front of me. "Sparks, please. Let me back in."

The doors open and she steps out. I scramble to my feet, following her to her bedroom. She doesn't acknowledge me, but she doesn't kick me out either.

"Anise, please," I beg, following her to her bedroom. She flinches at the name. "I'll spend the rest of my life making it up to you. Please, just look at me."

"I can't forgive you." Her voice is strained.

"Why not?" I don't understand. "You got off the train. You didn't run to San Francisco, or Chicago, or wherever. You stayed and that means something!"

"It doesn't mean anything!" She faces the wall, unable to face me. "I didn't want you to get yourself killed."

"Stop lying!" I place my hand on her shoulder. "You feel something, I know you do!"

"Fine, you want to know what I feel?" She whips around and shrugs off my hand, glaring into my eyes. "I hate you! I hate you, Astrid!"

"Why?" I probe deeper. "Why do you hate me?"

"Because you left me," she growls. "After all I did for you, you turned and walked away."

"Close, but that's not it." I can read her face, I can read her tells. I'm not leaving until I get the truth.

"The fuck you mean that's not it?!"

"If you can't be honest with me, at least be honest with yourself," I scoff. "Why do you hate me?"

"Because after everything, all the bullshit you put me through," her voice cracks with anger, "I'm still obsessed with you. I can't stop thinking about you. The smell of your shampoo, your hair draped across my pillow, the way it felt to hold you in my arms, all of it! I hate you because for a moment, I thought I found my soulmate, and I'll never feel that way again."

Sparks whirls away from me, holding her head in her hands. Then she explodes, screaming at the wall. She chucks the pillow from her bed. It flumps softly on the ground, which seems to aggravate her further.

Her rage is overtaking her. She needs an outlet. Something to blame, something to use. I can be that for her. I grab her arm and her eyes snap to mine. The intensity of her fiery glare startles me, but I won't lose my nerve.

"Slap me," I request, placing her hand on my cheek.

"What?" She pulls her hand away. "Don't be stupid."

"Do it!" I yell, goading her on. "Just this once, get it out of your system. I give you permission. You need to, otherwise you'll just resent me forever. Slap me!"

"I'm not going to hurt you." She bristles. I can feel the tension in her voice, see the turmoil in her eyes. She needs this, to let out the turbulence that's been locked inside her.

"I left you," I provoke, intentionally throwing salt in her wounds. "You were on your knees, begging and pleading, but I wasn't listening. I just threw you away like everyone else in your life has, like—"

My face whips to the side as her palm strikes my cheek. I ignore the sting as I stare into her pained eyes.

"Hit me again," I urge.

CHAPTER 16

SPARKS

"Hit me again," she urges. A red blotch is already forming on her cheek.

She left me. Everyone leaves me. My breathing is labored and rapid, but I don't feel like I'm getting any air. I clench my fists and look toward my ceiling, trying to calm myself down.

"Do it!" Astrid gets in my face. "Get it all out now because I'm not doing this anymore. After today, we're going to be friends again and you're going to like it. So whatever it takes to get out all of your pent-up resentment, now is the time."

She stands still, jutting out her chin, a challenge in her eyes. This is stupid I know, but the first slap felt so cathartic. No, I'm not going to hit her again. She catches my eyes again, a slight nod. I swing without thinking.

She stumbles to the side, scrunching her eyes. I feel as though a weight has lifted off my shoulders. Astrid stands and strides to me. I brace for her to hit me back – it's only fair – but she grabs my head in her hands and kisses me with a violent ferocity. Stunned, I tense in her arms and push her off. She takes a step back, dejected.

"I'll see you tomorrow," Astrid says, crestfallen.

Something comes over me at that moment. She yelps as I roughly grab her t-shirt, pulling her lips to meet mine. I force my tongue through the gap between her lips, feeling the edge of her teeth. She clings to me as I hitch her thighs around my back, carrying her to my bed. I throw her down on the mattress, caging her in by leaning on my forearms. Heat radiates from her body as my knee presses between her legs. She squirms beneath me, flustered by my sudden shift of behavior.

"Do you want me to fuck you?" My voice comes out somewhere between lust and contempt. "I'm not going to be gentle and loving. I'm going to pull your hair and—"

In one fluid movement, Astrid wraps her legs around my waist and flips our position. I slam onto the mattress as Astrid flings her shirt to the ground. My shirt quickly finds a spot on the floor next to hers. Her nails scratch against my bare skin as she holds my wrists above my head. She kisses me carnally, driven by desire and need. I hiss as she bites my lip before moving to leave a hickey on my collar bone.

I buck my hip to regain the top position, ripping off her jeans. Two fingers plunge into her without warning. She cries out at the sudden intrusion, arching her back. I aggressively thrust my fingers in and out as I massage her chest. Once her breasts are free of her bra, I take a nipple in my mouth, pinching the sensitive flesh between my teeth. She fists my sheets as her eyes roll back in delirious ecstasy.

"I hate you," I seethe. "I can't stand how stubborn you are. Your optimism borders on obliviousness. I feel like I'm always saving your ass from things that are your fault."

"Yeah?" She retorts. "I hate you too. You're selfish. You think you have a monopoly on suffering and depression? You're only miserable because you're scared to be happy. You—"

I force my lips onto hers, shutting her up momentarily as her words hit too close to home. Astrid sees through my plan and slides out from under me. She shoves my shoulders onto the mattress, her eyes flash with lust.

"There are better ways to keep me quiet," she admonishes.

Astrid slides to the floor and nudges my legs apart. She drags her nails down my thighs, discarding my shorts and underwear at the same time. Her nail catches on my thigh and a single drop of blood dibbles down my skin. Jesus, that was so hot.

Nestled between my thighs, she demonstrates how to better silence herself. Moans escape my mouth as hers is focused on me. My hips rock, infatuated with the sensations coming from below. Astrid chuckles and pins me to the bed. Her breath tickles as she gasps for air before going back down.

While this is a fantastic use for her mouth, I think there's slight room for improvement. My foot guides her shoulder to the floor, and she lays on the conveniently-placed pillow I threw earlier. Her neck cranes as I sink to my knees, hovering just out of reach. I tsk as I weave my fingers in her hair and pin her to the ground. She grins impishly as I straddle her face, slowly lowering myself onto my awaiting seat. Her tongue eagerly lashes out, flicking at the most sensitive parts of my body. I cry out as she nips at my clit, yanking her hair in retaliation. She wins the battle as she sucks on that spot, swirling her tongue with malicious precision. I brace myself as I grind on her, feeling closer and closer to climax.

"I hate you so much, you fucking bitch," I groan, throwing my head back. "I seriously can't stand you."

Astrid speeds up her torment as my thighs clench. The muscles in my stomach tighten as I cry out her name. She pushes me over the edge, and I collapse onto the ground, panting. But my work isn't over yet. Too many incompetent men have left me unsatisfied, and I refuse to let any of my partners experience the same disappointment.

Astrid moves to get up, but I violently push her back onto her pillow. She's going to climax, and she's going to like it. I position myself between her legs, hooking one over my shoulder for easier access. Astrid tugs at my hair, craving release. I can make that happen.

I go to work, fingering, licking, nipping where it garners the biggest reaction. It doesn't matter how long it's been since Astrid was in my arms, I could never forget how to draw out her little gasps and moans. Within minutes, her gasps have turned to screams. Her legs twitch as she nears her peak. Her breath catches in her throat as I send her over the edge.

Panting, I lay down next to her. Sweat glistens on her bare chest, and for a moment, I allow myself to appreciate how beautiful she is. Her lightly tan skin, her toned stomach, her tousled hair. I force myself to look away before she notices my gaze.

"I still hate you," I mumble.

"Didn't feel like it two minutes ago," Astrid teases.

"I'm serious." I turn my head away from her. "This doesn't change anything."

"You're not allowed to hate me." She rolls onto her stomach, propping herself on her elbows. "Remember? You were supposed to get everything out of your system. We're friends now, like it or not."

I huff and cross my arms. Astrid slides a finger along my bicep.

"Do you need to go another round?" There's a hint of sincerity behind her condensation.

"...yes."

And so, we undergo another tour of each other's bodies. By the end of the night, we both have new bruises and scratches decorating our limbs and torsos. Astrid goes to leave but is surprised when I pull her under my covers, holding her against my chest while tracing little circles on her back. I don't know why I do. Maybe it's because I miss having another warm body in my bed. Maybe it's because I miss the smell of her shampoo. Either way, she doesn't complain as she nuzzles into my shoulder and drifts asleep.

⚡ ⚡ ⚡ ⚡

Astrid leaves early the next morning after saying goodbye to Licorice. I'm sure she has to go man the cafe or whatever. I go through my normal routine and try not to notice Derek's disappointed glances at the hickeys on my neck. He pushes me hard today, sprints on the treadmill, maxing out my weightlifting, and after all that, full out in the sparring ring.

"You won't always be fighting boys," Derek taunts, as one of his right hooks catches me a bit too hard. "You'll have to fight men."

I spit blood on the floor, staggering back to my feet. I barely have my blocks up when Derek barrages me with another string of blows.

"They'll fight dirty," he continues. "They'll be bigger than you, stronger than you. You need to be smarter than them."

Right now, it doesn't feel smart to let Derek take out his aggression on me. I duck under his arms and dart to the other end of the ring, chest heaving from the exertion. My arms feel like lead, weighing me down. I fall to my knees.

"Stop," I pant. "Time out, I'm done."

"No, you're not," he scoffs under his breath as he ducks under the ropes.

"No more, Derek." I stand, woozy. "I need to sit down."

"That's not what I meant." He unwraps his hands aggressively. He's never talked to me this way before.

"Are you punishing me for something?" I slide out of the ring and grab a bottle of water. "Is that why you're pushing me so hard?"

"I'm pushing you hard because you need to focus." He throws his hand wrap into his cubby. "I won't always be there to protect you."

"Is this about LaRusso?" I place my hand on his shoulder. "You're safe, we took care of him."

"This isn't about LaRusso," he snaps. "This is about how when faced with a decision, you always take the one that hurts you. It's like you don't have a bone of self-preservation in your body."

"Are you mad about Astrid?" I laugh, bewildered. "We're not together. I just used her for an orgasm. You'd be surprised how hard those are to find nowadays."

"I told her to walk away." Derek kicks over a stack of towels. "I told her to leave you the fuck alone, but she just had to dig her talons into you deeper. I'm going to kill her."

"Whoa, whoa, whoa." I get in front of Derek and wave my hands. "Firstly, huge overreaction here. She and I are not together. We are not friends. Second, you have no say in who I fuck. Ground rule. Boundary. You stick your dick in whatever you want. I don't care. But you can't police who I sleep with."

"Sure," Derek scoffs. "It's not my problem until you nearly set your bedroom on fire."

"That's not fair." I recoil as his words hit deep.

"You're right," he sighs. "I'm sorry. I just… You were so hurt when she left. I don't want you to go through that again."

"Why don't you trust me?" I take a step back as he tries to approach. "I might be younger than you, but I'm not a child. We're partners."

"I trust you, but you're my family." Derek holds his hands out. "I'm supposed to protect you."

"Maybe you should focus on bettering the syndicate and leave my sex life to me." I sidestep his arm as he tries to stop me from leaving.

"Sparkie, stop," he calls after me. "Wait, let's talk this out."

I'm done talking. I jog into my apartment and barricade the door, just in case he feels like using his code to come in. The cold shower rinses away all of my sweat, but my muscles still throb after the intense workout.

After I'm dressed for the day, I decide I still don't want to see Derek, so I go to the one place he would never look for me – Oliver's office. Heck, even Oliver wasn't sure what to do when I walked in, but I was so angry, I was willing to spend my entire afternoon doing *shudder* paperwork. My eyes glaze over after staring at numbers for way too long, so Oliver shoos me away. I've hit rock bottom.

Derek has a lot of rules. Sorry, *guidelines.* Only pour one glass of alcohol at a time. Don't date people you work with. Always wear a helmet when you ride a motorcycle. Well, fuck it. I can tell myself how to act, and I'm going to start right now.

The elevator doors open, and I stomp into the parking garage. I think it's time to go for a ride, sans helmet. Yeah, that'll spite him. I go to throw something in my saddlebags, but the clasp was already loosened. That's odd. I always cinch them after I open the bags. I pull back the flap and peek in.

A new bag of cat treats sits on top with a ribbon tied on it. I stumble back, dropping my keys on the concrete. Did I see that right? Slowly, I pull the bag out of the saddlebag. Yep, brand new bag of unopened cat treats. Derek wouldn't do this. He knows we already have enough treats. Heck, he bought most of them.

Hesitantly, I dial Astrid's number. She answers after a few rings. I can hear the comfortable chatter of the cafe in the background. I miss that place.

Didn't think I'd hear from you today after I left. She sounds surprised. *Everything okay?*

"Yeah, yeah. No worries at all." Is this how nonchalant people talk? Think subtle. Think casual. "No biggies over here."

Sparks? You sound weird. Shit. *Is this about last night?*

"No, I just had a random question for you." I'm crazy. This is just my imagination. "Did you put something in my saddlebags? You know, on my bike?"

No, why would I?

If the treats aren't from her, who could they be from? I didn't tell anyone about Licorice.

Earth to Sparks. Hello? Is everything okay?

"Sorry, yeah. Lost in thought." My mind spins and another question pops into my head. "Also, next time we see each other, could you bring back my baseball cap? It was my favorite."

What cap? I hear her shuffling in the background. *Did you leave it here last year? I could check the boxes of your stuff. You know, you can really come get those anytime. I'm not holding them hostage or—*

"No, Astrid," I interject, a mounting feeling of hysteria rises in my chest. "When I picked you up from the police station, I was wearing a hat."

Oh, yes! I liked that hat. You put that in one of the bags on your bike.

"Oh, silly me." So I was right. I'm not crazy. That thought fills me with dread. "I've got to go."

Sparks, Astrid warns. *Are you hiding something from me? I thought we were past that.*

"No, I'm just... no. Bye!"

I hang up despite her protests, and I know she didn't buy my act. But I have other things to worry about. I completely dump out my saddlebags. Zip ties, jumper cables, loose cash, ponytails, a random rock. Hat – no. Cat treats – yes. Someone has been touching my stuff.

Paranoia reclaims its familiar hold. My head whips around until I get dizzy. Is someone watching me? How do they know about Licorice? What do they want with my hat?

My earlier plans of reckless driving go on hold as I dash back into my bedroom. Derek tries to flag me down, but I ignore him. He calls after me. I have to go. I need to hide. I scamper into my closet and shut the door. My pistol is loaded and at the ready. I sit there in the dark, holding my breath.

My phone screen lights up, casting a glow on my face. A text from Astrid.

I'm coming over.

No, stay home. I text back. My lungs stop taking in new air.

You're not going to keep things from me anymore. I'll be there in twenty.

I'm not going to let you down. She's not in the system. She can't go down the elevator by herself.

Then I'll punch the bartender. I'll see you in the interrogation room.

Can't this wait until tomorrow?

No response. Shit. I debate staying here, tucked away in my closet, but I don't think she's bluffing. Dreading this next conversation, I fumble with the zipper of a bodycon dress. Smudged eyeshadow is fast eyeshadow. Who really cares what I look like anyway? I leave the gun on my nightstand. They're loud, messy, and I have other ways I can defend myself.

Up inside the Lightning Bolt, I order a double shot of whiskey. Astrid appears on the stool next to me. The bartender raises an eyebrow after recognizing her, but I wave him off.

"What's wrong with your motorcycle?" Astrid doesn't beat around the bush.

"Nothing." I swirl my glass.

"Look me in the eyes and try that again."

She stares at me, cold and unmoving. I open my mouth, but no words come out. My shoulders droop and I finish my drink, signaling for a second.

"It could be nothing." I try to sound unbothered, but Astrid's unblinking eyes can read my apprehension. "Do you want a drink or something? I'll add you to my tab."

"Don't change the subject." Wisps fall out of her ponytail. It seems she also got dressed in a hurry. She looks gorgeous in a skimpy iridescent dress.

"I think someone stole my hat." The bartender delivers my second drink.

"And that warrants four shots of whiskey?" Astrid is unimpressed, or doesn't believe me, or I don't care. "Was it a magic hat?"

"Fuck you," I bite back. "I didn't ask for you to come."

"Well, you always hide things from me!" Astrid gestures wildly. "I always feel like I'm on my back foot with you."

"Hide things from you?" I chuckle cynically. "You know more than Derek does. I don't know what else you want from me."

"Wait," Astrid pauses, putting the pieces together. "He doesn't know about the gala?"

"No, because it doesn't concern him." I play with the ice in my drink. It clinks satisfyingly against the edge of the glass.

"This proves my point," she groans. "You need to tell him."

I spin in my chair, leaning against the bar. The liquor slowly starts to dull my senses. Perfect. A sexy blond catches my eye, and he smiles. I give him a small wave and he saunters my direction. He'll do for tonight.

"Between you and Derek, I'm done being lectured today." I throw back the last of my drink. "So do me a favor and leave me alone."

Astrid shoots daggers at me as the blond extends his hand and I gracefully slide off the barstool. We dance together and his hands venture south and cup my ass. He gives me a playful squeeze and I whisper sultry nothings in his ear. Time to seal the deal, I flutter my eyelashes.

"Do you want to find somewhere more private?" His creamy voice makes me tingle in all the right places. Boom, the eyelashes always work.

I lead him outside, intending on going to my standard hotel. We don't make it that far. He grabs my hand, and we duck inside an alley, giggling like highschoolers. My suitor hitches my legs around his waist and holds me against the brick wall. My hair catches on the rough material, but his sweet kisses distract me from the sting. His hands push up the hem of my skirt, playing with the lace of my underwear. A rapid succession of clicks draws his attention, I almost don't hear it.

"Is someone taking photos?" He squints down the alley, looking for the cause of the noise.

"What?" I ask confused.

"I have a girlfriend, I can't be here!" He drops me suddenly and takes off.

I catch myself before I can fall on my butt, in awe of his brazen cheating. What an ass. The clicks continue, and I recognize the sound somewhere in my subconscious. I've heard it before. I creep down the dark alley, but the sound stops. I should just head back to the club, try to find a new date.

I turn around at the perfect time. A needle jabs my muscle at a weird angle, and my movement rips the syringe from a man's hands before he can fully push the plunger. My attacker runs away into the night. I should chase him. The needle falls to the floor.

I should... what?

The world slows around me, shapes blur and color leeches away. Help, I need help. My hand grips the crumbling brick and pieces come off in my hand. Someone should take a look at that.

Wait, help.

Help first, bricks second. I need to get back to the club. Where am I? Where is the club?

I turn onto a street, praying my subconscious can remember the way home. My heartbeat slows and every step is like I'm dragging cinder blocks. There's a voice. I can't tell what they're saying. Help me, please help me. A pair of arms catches me as I collapse, and I can only hope that this is not the person who drugged me.

Something about her hair in the streetlights looks so perfect. Maybe it's the way the yellow glow turns her hair copper. Or maybe it's because she's drunk, causing her hair to swing as she walks.

The bastard pushes her against the wall, not even caring enough to take her somewhere private. Anyone could see her panties as he forces her dress over her thighs.

Click. Click. Click.

I would treat her better. Lay her gently on a soft mattress, caressing her skin as I coax the oh-so-tight fabric over her hips. She would moan my name, no one else's.

Observe and wait for further instruction. It's killing me. I've never felt this way toward a target, toward anyone. I'll only ever feel this way about her.

Click.

"So do me a favor and leave me alone." Sparks saunters away with some random blond.

Typical. Avoid your problems. Drown them out with liquor, and apparently, random sex toys. Was that all last night was to her? Am I just another person who would sleep with her? I know we're not together, but I was hoping... Well, I wasn't hoping that she would sleep with someone else when I'm right here.

I still think she's hiding something. Back to her same tricks. Doesn't she know that we only want to help her? All of her secrets and lies only lead to trouble.

And that blond guy? Yuck. She could do better. He's obviously looking for a quick lay. She deserves someone who will woo her, make her come first, who cherishes how soft her skin is. He won't even notice.

"Stare any harder and he'll explode." Derek stands next to me. I didn't notice him walk up.

"Don't tempt me," I gripe bitterly.

He leans against the bar, and we stare at Mr. No Good for a few minutes, until he breaks the silence.

"It has been pointed out to me that I can be a tad overprotective of Sparks." Derek doesn't look at me, instead examines his fingernails. "I think it's possible that our last conversation got out of hand."

"Is that your version of an apology?" I look at him sassily. "It's a pretty bad one."

"It's the one you're getting. Take it or leave it, I don't care." He crosses his arms. "I still don't like you."

"Glad to know where we stand." I still don't like him either.

"I really do see her as my sister," Derek sighs. "I had a biological sister once. She was everything to me. She died too young. I just want better for Sparks."

"I do too," I promise. "We're on the same team."

"Is she in trouble?" Derek asks bluntly. "I know you two are up to something, I'm not stupid. I just thought she'd tell me eventually."

"I'm not sure I'm the one to share the story." I roll my shoulders back, relishing in the leverage I have over Derek.

"Are you seriously going to make me beg?" Derek's voice wavers slightly, twinged with worry. I almost start to pity him, but then I remember that he's a jerk.

"You could beg." I shrug. "Or add my fingerprint to the elevator and I'll tell you."

"Deal." He drags me from the bar. "Let's go."

Derek escorts me up the stairs to a lofted area. It's crazy how I didn't notice it sooner. It blends in with the ceiling unless you know what you're looking for. He points to a booth, and I sit down, waiting as he gives orders to the armed men standing guard. Dang, this place is serious.

"What do you want to drink?" Derek asks.

"I'm fine." I brush him off.

"Honey, this is organized crime." He rolls his eyes. "It's tradition to do business over drinks. It means that you trust each other or something. Whatever, just let me get you a cocktail."

"Fine." How am I already this annoyed? "A paloma good enough for you?"

Derek points at me, then at a guard. The man walks away quickly and comes back with two drinks. Derek picks up his whiskey and we clink glasses. My fingerprint is added to the security system, and I tell Derek everything. Breaking into Synergy Labs, the ambush at the gala, the cryptic questions about her bike. I do leave out the details of her almost leaving at the train station. It felt too mean to share. Derek listens intently, growing more concerned at each twist of the story. He finishes his drink with a pensive grimace.

"Damn." He scowls. "How did I miss all that?"

"Unfortunately, Sparks's biggest talent is keeping secrets." I grip my glass tightly, remembering all of the lies she's told me.

"Is that why you broke up?" I can almost hear the gears clicking into place inside his brain.

"More or less," I sigh. "I stand by the decision. We didn't trust each other, and a relationship can't survive that. I just thought that this time, she would be more open with me. Not that there really is a 'this time.' She's making that clear with Blondie over there."

We glance over the railing as Sparks leaves the club, her lover for the night in tow. I look away as tears prick my eyes, Derek doesn't need to see me like this. I take a cue from Sparks and shoot back the rest of my drink.

"Against my better judgment, I'm going to give you some advice." Derek leans back in the booth. "I know Sparks better than anyone, and I assume you knew Janice really well."

"Sorry, Janice?" I'm lost. "Did I miss something? Who's Janice?"

"Sparks." Derek gestures, as if that was obvious. "She used to go by Janice, didn't she?"

"Do you mean 'Anise?'" I ask. "I used to call her Anise."

"What kind of name is Anise?" Now Derek is confused. "Never mind, it doesn't matter. The point is, I know Sparks and you know Anise or Janice or whoever, but does anyone actually know who she is behind all that?"

"You mean Charlotte?"

"Who the fuck is Charlotte?" Derek sighs exasperatedly.

"Her birth name is Charlotte." Duh.

"There's too many fucking names." Derek lays his head on the table. He breathes a moment before looking back at me. "Get to know Charlotte, not Sparks, not Janice, but Charlotte. Then maybe you'll have a chance. Now get out of my booth."

I head down to the dance floor. It crosses my mind that maybe I should get my own date, but my heart's not in it. I've never been one for casual sex. It's best I get home and try to sleep. Last night in Sparks's arms was the best sleep I've gotten all year. I'm not as optimistic about tonight.

The cold air bristles my skin. Though it's April, it can get quite chilly as the sun goes down. A splash of red catches my eye a few blocks down. Sparks is clinging to the wall, the liquor is hitting her hard it seems. Now I have to help her back to the club. Great.

I start to walk toward her. Quickly though, I realize something is wrong. Her eyes are unfocused, her knees are trembling. Jogging, I'm jogging toward her.

"Sparks? Can you hear me?" She doesn't respond. Running, I'm running toward her. "Sparks!"

A thin red line of blood dribbles from her shoulder. I start to make out her mumbling.

"Help me, please help me."

Her eyes roll back in her head, and she falls into my arms.

"No, no, no." I shake her shoulders. "Sparks, stay with me. Help! Help us!"

There's no one around. I need to get her to the club. Derek would know what to do. I grab Sparks's wrists and pull them over my shoulders, orienting her in a piggy-back style. I've never been a strong person, focusing on cardio instead of weightlifting, but I manage to drag her back to the club doors.

"Derek!" I scream as we step inside. The music is loud, the lights are dim. Somehow the club patrons are oblivious, maybe it's due to the strobing lights and pulsating bass. There's no way I can find him. The bouncer steps in front of me.

"What's going on here?" He asks aggressively.

"Help us, please." Sparks slides off my back, and the guard steps back alarmed. "We need Derek, he's the owner. Please."

"Code lightning!" He radios. "Code lightning, front door!"

I kneel by Sparks. Her breathing is shallow, but consistent. Please be okay.

"Step away, ma'am." The bouncer pulls a weapon, aiming it at me.

"You need to help her!" I plead, cradling her head in my lap. "Why aren't you doing anything?"

Armed men converge around the entrance, guns drawn and at the ready. I cover Sparks with my body protectively.

"Don't hurt her!" Tears stream down my face. "Stay with me, Anise. Please."

"Stand down!" Derek pushes through the guards and lifts Sparks into his arms. Her head flops back, almost lifelessly. Oh god, no. "Clear a path! Elevator!"

The guards get to work doing something actually productive now, and the three of us are on the elevator in seconds.

"What happened!" Derek roars, cradling Sparks against his shoulder.

"I don't know!" I am near hysterics, petting Sparks's hair. "Come on, baby."

I try to hum a lullaby, but I'm crying too hard to make any consistent sounds. A medic is waiting when the elevator doors open, and Derek places Sparks on the gurney. The medic jumps on to begin his examination while a team runs the gurney into another room. The door closes behind Derek, and I am left in the hallway, trying to hum through strangled sobs.

Minutes pass, then an hour. I don't leave my post, right outside that door. My shoes are abandoned, long since kicked off. There are sofas down the hallway, but I don't dare walk away. I hold my vigil on the floor, praying to every god I can think of. I draw runes in the air, ones for protection and health. Please be okay. Please, Sparks, be okay.

Eventually, Derek comes through the door. His eyes are puffy and rimmed with red. He sits on the floor next to me.

"She's okay," he whispers, as if he doesn't believe the words himself.

"She's okay?" I can't breathe.

He nods, and something cracks inside me. I break down sobbing in the middle of the common area, clutching my chest. Derek cries too, more dignified than me. He leans his head against the wall, silent tears dampening his face. He extends an arm and folds me into a hug. I cry until his shirt is soaked and he hums, mimicking the lullaby I croaked out earlier. Eventually, we both run out of tears.

"What happened?" I dry my cheeks. "Can I see her?"

"She was drugged." An edge laces his voice. "When I find who did it, you won't want to be there."

"Don't worry," I sigh. "I've hung up my cape."

Derek examines me before standing. He extends a hand, and I take it. He enters a keycode and the door unlocks. There's shelving in the med bay with staple medical supplies – bandages, ibuprofen, the like. A second set of doors separates the exam room. Derek holds the door open, and I walk in. Well, I like to say that I walked, but as soon as I saw Sparks sleeping on the cot, I dashed to her side. An IV bag drips into her pale skin. I kiss her forehead gently and stroke her hair. Her eyes flutter open and meet mine, dazed and confused.

"Astrid?" Her voice is hoarse. "What happened?"

"You're okay," I soothe, trying not to cry for the millionth time.

"Camera," she stammers. "Clicking noise in the alley."

"Shh," I hush. "Just rest. You're safe now."

"Hey there, Sparkie." Derek sits on the other side of the bed and squeezes her hand. "Don't think this gets you out of sparring practice tomorrow."

Sparks smiles at his joke. Derek offers her some water, but she strains to sit up. I guide her back down to the bed and use my powers to bring the water to her. She takes a drink from her personal water fountain before falling back asleep.

The medic, who I learned is named Luca, keeps Sparks under observation for a few days. Derek and I rotate keeping watch at Sparks's bedside. She insists that she's fine and that we have better things to do, but you can't pry us away. I practically move into one of the spare rooms after Derek sends one of his men to pick up some of my clothes. Licorice also gets to come into the med bay for playdates and cuddles. Luca grumbles about the sterile field, but a stern look from Derek shuts him up.

Eventually, Sparks is back to her normal self, bouncing at the walls to leave the med bay. Luca insists she needs more time to recover, but she just rips out the IV and walks out. Derek drags her back by her ear to have her hand bandaged, but then relents and lets her escape to the rest of the compound.

On one condition.

CHAPTER 18

SPARKS

I'd do anything to leave the med bay, but does it have to be this? The three of us are gathered in my living room. Licorice is purring contentedly on my lap, swishing her tail intermittently. Astrid made coffee for all of us after hearing about our "legendary" coffee meetings. Well, she made coffee for Derek and herself, a hot chocolate for me. It sits on the coffee table untouched.

"You told him!" I roll my eyes at Astrid. "What the fuck, man?"

"Excuse me," Derek interjects. "You should have told me this when it happened. There's no good reason why I found out from Astrid."

"You were so stressed about the syndicate." I twist a strand of my hair. "I didn't want you to worry."

"Bull." Astrid narrows her eyes. "I've learned your tells, Sparks. Give it up."

"How did you let the two of them become friends?" I ask Licorice. She twitches an ear in response. "Traitor."

The duo stares at me, arms crossed the same way. Their partnership might become my undoing.

"No more secrets, Sparkie." Disappointment lines Derek's voice. I hang my head ashamed.

"I don't want anyone else getting hurt," I sniffle. "I just want to take care of it myself."

"But we also don't want you getting hurt." Astrid gestures at me, tears pricking her eyes. "Do you know how scared we were? I thought you were going to die in my arms."

"We also need to teach Astrid all of the code phrases," Derek mentions. "She almost got herself shot because she wouldn't leave your side on the code lightning."

Code lightning. Oof. Boss down, reserved for Derek or me. The team tends to take that one pretty seriously.

"I'm sorry." I mean it. "I'll tell you everything, nothing held back."

"I think we're both caught up," Derek says. "But just, no more."

"Actually…" I run my fingers through my hair. "I have one more."

"Motherfucker," Astrid curses under her breath.

"Hey!" I defend. "I figured this one out the day I was attacked. Not a lot of time to tell people."

"Is this about the motorcycle thing?" Astrid stands, frustrated. "You definitely had time to tell me."

"I'm telling you now!" I carefully move Licorice to her cat tree. She mews angrily but falls asleep quickly. I bite my lip nervously. "I think I have a stalker."

"Did not expect that one." Derek breaks the silence after a moment.

I tell them about the missing hat and the cat treats, as well as the clicking noises that have been following me. How the blonde guy I was with panicked, thinking it was a camera shutter. I don't have a better explanation.

"Do you think your stalker drugged you?" Astrid looks as though she could freak out any second. I don't feel too dissimilar. I shrug.

"Show us the cat treats," Derek says. "Maybe there's a rational explanation."

We go on a field trip to the parking garage. I think it's a waste of time, because cat treats are just cat treats, but they insist. When I arrive at my bike, I am stunned. A "Get Well Soon" balloon is tied to my handlebars, and an envelope sits on the seat.

"I'm going to assume this wasn't you guys..." I ask the group. Both shake their heads.

I apprehensively open the envelope. There's maybe ten or so photos inside, me in the alley with the blond man. The photographer took the photos from a low angle, ensuring my panties are in the frame. I'm centered in all the shots. Some are cropped closely on my face, others on my hips. Most disturbing though, the blond man is X'ed out in every photo he was in. The thick black marker completely covering his face, leaving a disembodied pair of hands roaming my body. A note falls out with messy, scrawled handwriting. *He doesn't deserve to touch you.*

My hands shake as I stuff the photos back into the envelope. Derek unties the balloon as Astrid searches the saddlebag for any more gifts. Thankfully, it's just the cat treats. Derek is on the phone as soon as we reenter the compound.

"What do you mean we don't have a camera there?" He screams into the microphone. "She is your boss! I don't care what you have to do, get a security camera up there immediately. Now!"

"You don't go anywhere alone anymore." He whirls to face me.

"That's not fair," I protest. "I'll go crazy on house arrest."

"Then take Astrid or me with you." He shrugs indifferently. "Fuck, take a whole squadron of men with you. I don't care. You don't go anywhere alone."

"But—"

"No," Derek cuts me off. "Do not make me put a GPS collar on you. You know I will."

Everyone knows Derek has an overprotective streak, but this is a bit much, even for him. I glare at him and slam my apartment door, before reopening it.

"Astrid can come in, but I'm protesting against Derek for the immediate future."

Derek throws his hands in the air as Astrid scurries in, sticking her tongue out at him. She flops onto my bed, letting Licorice bat at her fingers. Her shirt rides up slightly, exposing a small sliver of her back. Since high-waisted shorts and skirts are her go-to, it's a rare sight. I brush her hair to one side, revealing her neck. God, I love when she wears her hair down.

"Do you maybe want to mess around?" I twist a strand of her hair around my finger. "Have some fun?"

"Sparks, you just got out of the med bay." She rolls her eyes.

"We both know I'm perfectly healthy," I whisper in her ear. "Let me show you a good time."

"Maybe later." She shrugs away from me.

Astrid sees me examining her and sticks her tongue out at me, trying to be silly, but her heart isn't in it. I sit on the ground, perching my arms on the mattress. I look up at her from the floor as she keeps playing with the cat.

"Did I do something to upset you?" I ask, confused. "I'm sorry if I made you feel uncomfortable, we don't have to have sex."

"No, you're fine." Licorice bats at her fingers. She avoids looking at me.

"I don't think you are." I pull the cat away, setting her on the floor. She chases a bug, unperturbed. "Talk to me. No more secrets, right?"

"I guess I just thought..." Astrid trails off, searching for the right words. "I hoped that things would be different."

"I know," I sigh. "No more secrets. I've fucked up again and again, but truly, I've told you everything now."

"It's not that." She absentmindedly picks at her cuticles. "Well, actually I guess that too, but it's not that."

"Hey." I scooch on the bed to sit next to her. "What's wrong?"

I brush her hair from her face, but her eyes gloss over. She turns away. How did I make this worse?

"You looked so happy the other night in the club, dancing with that blond guy." She folds her hands together, squeezing her fingers tightly. "I know it's not fair to you, and I'm not proud of it, but I was jealous."

"We can fix that," I chuckle, nudging her shoulder. "Let's go to the club tonight. I can be your wingwoman. We'll find you a stunning girl to take home and it'll be great!"

"I don't want some random girl." Astrid's voice is soft but accepting, resigned to whatever is causing her melancholia.

"What do you want then?" I gently lift her chin with my finger, bringing her gaze back to me.

Our eyes meet, and I realize my mistake. A lone tear falls, her hopelessness dripping onto her arm. The one thing she wants is something I can't give her.

"You." She shakes her head. "I want you."

"Astrid," my voice cracks. "I—"

"I know," she cuts me off as she wipes the tear from her cheek. Her shoulders shudder as she continues. "You don't need to say it. I know."

"I can't lose you again." My voice catches in my throat. "It took so long to put myself back together. I couldn't... I can't..."

"I know." Astrid presses her forehead to mine. "I... I know."

Now it's my turn to cry, a few silent tears leaving damp lines down my cheek. We lock eyes, and she glides her thumb across my cheek, erasing my tears.

"I love you. I never stopped," she whispers, a pained smile on her face. "Don't say it back, whether or not you feel the same. It would hurt too much to hear you say it again. I just couldn't live with myself if I didn't tell you."

Our lips are inches away. My breath catches in my chest. I close my eyes, expecting her to kiss me. Softly. Gently. But she doesn't.

The mattress shifts as she stands, arms hugging her stomach. Licorice scampers to her feet. She doesn't mind the tears falling on her fur as Astrid scratches her tummy. She takes Licorice into the living room, but I'm stuck to the bed. The mattress has a hold over me. Maybe it's because the world outside my bedroom is falling apart, leaving me trying to catch the pieces. Maybe it's because from down here, I can pretend that the dinosaurs aren't extinct.

Eventually, it's time to face the outside world. Licorice chases a laser controlled by Astrid. She's back to her usual bubbly self, as if nothing happened. I suppose that's for the best.

"Do you want to grab lunch?" I ask, extending a proverbial olive branch. "There's a new sandwich place a few blocks away. I'll buy."

"Sure." She jumps up. Her hair bounces around her shoulders. "Do you want to take your bike?"

"Great idea." I grin, eager to feel the wind. I grab two leather jackets from my closet, throwing one to her. The helmets are already in the garage. I open my apartment door, and Luca is there, about to knock.

"Oh, hi Luca," I say, surprised to see him. "Everything okay?"

"I need to see you in the med bay again."

"Nooo," I groan. "I'm fine."

"Derek wants me to double check one of your vitals." He shrugs as if he's about as excited as I am. "It was a little high earlier. Five minutes, I promise."

"Sorry, Astrid." I roll my eyes. "I'll come grab you when I'm cleared by the doc."

"She can sit in the waiting room," Luca offers. "Truly, just five minutes and then you two can bounce."

"It's fine with me." Astrid gives Licorice one last pet as we head out.

Astrid takes a seat in the waiting room, and I turn to her.

"Do you want to come back with us?" I ask. "I feel bad leaving you alone."

"No," Luca interjects quickly. "She needs to stay here."

My eyes dart to Luca as my eyebrow raises.

"It's fine, Sparks," Astrid assures me. "Go make sure you're healthy and everything."

Luca leads me back to the exam room. I sit on the bed as he takes my temperature, scribbling numbers down on a clipboard. He gestures for me to remove my jacket as he unwraps a blood pressure cuff. I shrug it off one of my shoulders and he takes his measurements.

"One last thing before you go, flu shot." Luca draws a syringe of liquid before flicking the needle.

"Does this really have to happen right now?" I groan. "I have other things to do."

"You can explain to Derek why you're sick this flu season if you want." Luca gives me a knowing look.

"Fine."

Luca lightly grabs my shoulder, his hand trembling. I notice a bead of sweat dribbling down his forehead. This isn't like Luca. Where was the steady, confident medic who stitched my shoulder after I got shot?

"Actually, I think I'm going to come back later." I pull my shoulder away, but Luca tightens his grip.

"I already have the medication drawn, just relax your arm," Luca mutters.

He looks in my eyes, and I know. Worse, he knows that I know. He jabs the needle into my shoulder as I pull away. The syringe falls to the floor before the full dosage can be administered. I stomp on the plastic casing, spilling the liquid on the floor.

"Damn it," he curses. "Now you'll need a second dose. Can't have either of you waking up early."

Either? Astrid. I need to warn her. I crawl on the floor, my legs already going numb. Luca walks around me, heading toward the door. I reach out with my powers, feebly launching a bolt toward him. It's not very strong, but it hits.

"Ow!" Luca cries out. "Motherfucker!"

There's rustling on the other side of the door. Luca panics, drawing a gun and running back to me. No, Astrid! Go away!

"Run!" I yell, hoping she hears my warning. "It's a trap!"

The door flings open, and Astrid stands confidently in the entryway. She pulls water from the sink along the wall, creating a sphere floating in the air. The syringe, the traitor, the gun flush with my temple. She takes a moment for it all to sink in.

"Drop the gun," she commands.

"I think not." Luca flicks off the safety. "Release the water. Now."

Astrid glances at me. I shake my head. Don't. Please. Save yourself. Luca pulls my hair, and I whimper from the pain. Her eyes soften and the spheres turn to puddles on the floor.

"Kneel to the ground," Luca orders. He releases my hair to slide a syringe to Astrid, keeping the gun trained on me. "Inject yourself."

One leg at a time, Astrid lowers herself to her knees, eyes never leaving Luca. She plucks the syringe from the floor.

"No!" The lights flicker as my strength is slowly sapped away, but I can't do anything to stop her. She flinches as she jabs the needle into her thigh, pressing the plunger all the way down.

"I love you," Astrid mouths to me as the drug rapidly takes effect. She collapses on the cold linoleum, her blonde hair splayed around her.

"See." Luca gestures at Astrid's unmoving form. "Isn't it so much nicer to get the full dose? Partial doses just drag out the inevitable, especially since this is the second time we've had to go down this road. But hey, now I get a bonus for securing both girls."

"How could you?"

It's a struggle to keep my eyes open. A team of men step off the service elevator. One hoists Astrid limply over his shoulder. I reach for her desperately, knowing there is nothing I can do.

"Shh," Luca soothes. "You're going right behind her."

A second needle pricks my skin, and her blonde hair is the last thing I see before the world goes black.

⚡   ⚡   ⚡   ⚡

My body is jostled as we drive into a particularly large pothole. Soft hands hold me tightly, stroking my hair and humming a lullaby. I groan as I struggle to open my eyes, remnants of the drug still in my system. Astrid pulls me tighter as I stir, glancing nervously through the clear divider blocking us from the rest of the car.

Thunder rumbles outside of the SUV, the dark clouds making it hard to get my bearings. What time is it? Where are we going? I don't know the answer to either. The SUV looks fairly standard, the only difference being the thick piece of glass separating us from the front of the car. Astrid and I seem to be in the trunk. A second black SUV follows behind us. The car finds another pothole, and she protectively squeezes me to her chest, absorbing the blow for us. I hear a metal tinkling caused by the handcuffs around her wrists. I have a matching pair. Fortunately, these are the standard variety, so they shouldn't be too hard to pick with my tools. I reach for my belt before remembering I'm not wearing my bodysuit. Fuck.

"What did you do?" I tuck a flyaway strand of hair behind her ear. "You were supposed to run."

"I'm not leaving you," she says, stubbornly. She adjusts her legs, pulling me further onto her lap. "We're a team."

"How long have we been driving?" I nervously look outside. The standard hilly plains have been replaced with mountains. I don't think we're in Massachusetts anymore.

"I woke up about half an hour ago." She glances out the window as well. "But I don't know how long I was out. Assuming this is the same drug as you had the last time, that would be a smidge over an hour."

"I didn't get the full dose last time," I correct, remembering how the syringe fell from my arm. "It could have been hours."

"I don't want to know where they're taking us," Astrid mutters. "We need to escape."

"Is that SUV following us with them?" I ask.

"I think so." She nods. "They've been with us for the past half hour, so it's a fair assumption."

"If we can pull over, I could take at least two guys at once," I grimace, not seeing any obvious sources of electricity, like streetlamps. "More if I can get these cuffs off."

"I can take care of the cuffs once we get outside." She strains her wrists. "I just need some water."

"Good news." The thunder crashes as we drive deeper into the storm. The rain pelts the windows outside. "We have plenty of that."

The rain obscures the horizon, blurring the text on street signs. I wish I could just clear it away so I could see where we were. The SUV behind us has their windshield wipers swishing rapidly.

"Astrid, remember that time last year you caused a blizzard?" An idea forms in my head. A very bad idea. A very stupid, no-good idea.

"I don't like where this is going..." she responds hesitantly, "but yes."

"Can you do that with rain?" The fragmented pieces of the plan click together in my brain. "Force the car to crash?"

"The car that we are currently in?" Astrid thinks I'm crazy. She might be right. "We're not even wearing seatbelts!"

"How else could we get them to pull over? Unless of course, you're okay with jumping out of a moving vehicle, likely into the SUV following behind us."

"I don't like this." Astrid's eyebrows scrunch together. "We could get hurt."

"Think of it this way." I stare out as the terrain passes beneath us. "We could get roughed up now, or we will be killed later. I'd rather take my chances here."

Astrid sighs but doesn't disagree.

"Listen." I hold her hands in mine. "You force the car to crash. Cover the windshield, make it hydroplane, whatever. We'll bust out this window and then run as fast as we can."

"I won't leave you," Astrid argues.

"I'll be right behind you," I promise. "But don't stop running. No matter what."

"Why do I feel like you're saying goodbye?" I don't have a response. Astrid pulls me in, and her lips graze my cheek. "No matter what happens next, I'm so grateful to have met you. I wouldn't trade a single second."

"We're going to be fine," I say, trying to convince myself as much as her. "Both of us."

With that, Astrid rises to a kneeling position to get a better vantage point. It's subtle at first, but the rain falls faster and faster. Quickly, the windshield is completely saturated. The men inside the car freak out, pulling on seatbelts and grabbing the door handles. Astrid's face scrunches as she concentrates, and the car swerves. The driver yanks on the wheel, but he loses control of the car. A flash of lightning streaks across the sky, lighting up the outline of a large tree.

"Brace yourself!" Astrid shrieks. I cover my head as we ram directly into it.

Immediately, I kick out the trunk's window. A trickle of blood drips from Astrid's eyebrow, but I can't care about that right now. Instead, I shove her through the opening. She helps me out, and we take off. The second car follows us, not concerned with their injured comrades. I drag Astrid off the road into the tree line. We duck behind a ditch, and I extend my hands.

"Take off the cuffs, Astrid," I order frantically. "Quickly!"

Water seeps into the locking mechanism. Just when I think she's overstated her handcuff-removing abilities, the water freezes and shatters the lock. The cuffs fall off in a fluid motion.

"Thanks." I rub my wrists. "Do yours. I'll buy us some time."

"Wait!" She calls, but I'm already creeping back toward the road.

The second car has slowed, scouring the darkness for us. They roll down their window, and I hear voices shout. They've spotted us. I reach out with my powers, feeling the polarization of the air. Any second now. I just need to be patient. The SUV pulls over.

"C'mon, anytime now," I mutter.

Astrid crouches beside me, pulling on my arm.

"We need to go!" She whispers.

"Hold on." I yank my arm free. "They'd just follow us. I'm going to stop them. Stand back a few feet, I have a plan."

She obliges, trusting me. Focus, any second now. The men scramble out of the SUV. Wait for it. Static shifts in the air. Now!

"Astrid, get down!" I shout as I reach for the sky.

The static energy crackles as it converts into electricity. I grit my teeth as I grab the strongest current I have ever redirected, hurling it at the SUV. Lightning bursts from the sky, igniting the gas tank into a fireball. The shockwave knocks the breath from my lungs, and I am thrown through the air.

CHAPTER 19

ASTRID

"Sparks!"

She slams into a tree and crumples to the ground. I rise from the muddy grass and dash to her side. Sparks staggers to her knees, disoriented from the impact.

"Did it work?" She asks. "Did they survive?"

I glance toward the blazing car. There are a few agonized screams, but they are fading quickly. Everyone else is either dead or will be soon, but I don't want to stick around in case I am wrong.

"Let's go," I urge. "Can you walk?"

"Don't think I have a choice." She grimaces as she stands, and the blood drains from her face.

"Come on." I lay her arm across my back, supporting some of her weight.

Together, we stumble deeper into the forest. We travel at a slow pace, more of a trudge than a walk, tripping on tree roots and rocks in the dim light. The rain drenches our clothing, despite our leather jackets. Normally, I would use my powers to keep us dry, but Sparks insists I save my energy. I'm glad to at least have the jacket, but I would kill for pants and hiking boots right now. I don't know how I haven't twisted my ankle in these sandals. While we're at it, I would also kill for a flashlight or granola bar. Luckily, we have plenty of water. Sparks's head slumps and she jerks herself awake.

"We need to stop for the night." I decide, scanning the horizon for anything remotely similar to a shelter.

"No, we need to keep going," Spark's words slur together. She shivers as the wind gusts stronger. "It's not safe."

"You're practically sleepwalking," I point out. "Plus, I'm the one dragging you, so I'm making an executive decision."

She protests weakly but relents when I find a small cavity in a cliffside. It's small, but it has a roof and walls, so it's close enough. Sparks slides off my shoulder and I stretch in relief. Despite being protected from the wind, Sparks continues shivering.

"I'm going to look for some firewood," I say.

"No, they'll be able to see it." She shakes her head. "It's too risky."

"Sparks, we're no longer just running from our kidnappers," I chide. "We're also trying to survive in the middle of some random forest. We don't have the luxury to go without fire. You're practically turning blue."

"Okay," she relents. "Just a small one though."

"Fine," I compromise and head out to gather some kindling.

I return a short while later with some grasses, twigs, and wood. Sparks is leaning against the cave wall, holding two rocks.

"What are those for?" I eye her stones.

"To start the fire, duh," she teases. "What was your plan?"

"I hadn't gotten there yet." I shrug. "One thing at a time."

Together, we arrange the firewood the best we can figure. Sparks tells stories of camping with her ex and some of the techniques they would use. She admits that it had been a while and they weren't very good at it, but it worked well enough then. I use my powers to dry the kindling, and while I was at it, dried our clothes before Sparks could protest.

"Astrid, you need to conserve your energy," she lectures.

"Sparks, I cannot explain to you how little effort that took." I roll my eyes. "Just start the fire."

She kneels over the grasses and strikes the two rocks together. Some sparks fly from the friction, but nothing catches. She tries it a few more times, getting frustrated.

"Hey, my turn." I grab the rocks from her.

On the first strike, sparks latch onto the grass. I quickly lean down and gently fan the embers until we have a small flame in our campsite.

"I loosened it for you," Sparks huffs.

"Yes, you did." I tousle her hair jokingly. "Either way, it was your idea, so props there."

"We're going to need to prioritize finding food tomorrow." Her eyes flit back and forth, compiling an invisible list of concerns. "We also need to find a way out or get help."

"I've been debating if we should find the road again." I twiddle my fingers in my lap. "On one hand, we could flag down someone driving by. On the other, we could flag down the wrong person."

"I don't think we can risk it."

Sparks runs her fingers through her tangled hair. Mud is streaked on her forehead, and her color is still paler than

I would like. That being said, I probably don't look much better.

"So, you can make lightning." I try to lighten the conversation. "Didn't know you could do that."

"I can only redirect lightning, can't create it myself." She grimaces as she flexes her left hand, the one with the strange scar. Mimi claimed that Sparks was struck by lightning, but I never knew the full story. "That was only the second time I've done it. The first was an accident, and I struck myself. That hurt like a motherfucker."

"I can't tell if that was brave or reckless to give that a go today." I pinch the bridge of my nose.

"Oh, completely reckless," she asserts. "It took a lot out of me. I feel like shit. But hey, I didn't give myself another scar this time, so that's great."

"Yay for little victories." I circle my fist. "Woo!"

Sparks smiles before a dark look flashes across her features. She sighs before looking back up at me.

"Astrid, I need to ask you something serious," she starts, nervously.

"What's wrong?" I'm concerned.

"These people aren't going to pull their punches." Sparks rubs her forehead. "Can I trust you to kill them if it comes to it?"

"What?" I heard her, but she caught me off guard.

"Astrid." She grabs my head in her hands. "If they come after you, there is no other option. You need to fight tooth and nail to survive, and that includes taking their lives."

"But—"

"No, Astrid, no buts. They will come for us. They will have guns. Even if they hold a pistol to my head, I want you to give them hell. Use your powers, steal their weapons, whatever it takes."

"I can't let them hurt you," I sniffle as tears threaten to fall.

"Then they will use me to get to you." Sparks softly rubs her thumb on my cheek. "And I couldn't live with myself if that happened."

"I don't know if I can." My voice wavers.

"Promise me you'll try." Pain overtakes her eyes. "Please."

"Okay." I nod and Sparks pulls me into a hug.

"It's getting late," Sparks says after a minute. "One of us should get some sleep."

"I'll take the first watch," I volunteer.

For once, Sparks doesn't argue. Probably because she's already about to pass out. I gesture for her to lay her head in my lap. I stroke her hair and hum the lullaby that my mother always sang to me. Her breathing slows within seconds.

The night passes quickly, sans for a few squirrels scaring me half to death. I keep thinking they are our kidnappers, rounding the corner to catch us, but they just keep chittering, scrambling from tree to tree.

I slink outside, gently lowering Sparks's head from my lap. The rain has ceased, leaving muddy puddles in its wake. I grab a few sticks to add to the fire, ensuring it doesn't burn out. Sparks is awake by the time I return. She shrugs off her jacket and bundles it into a pillow for me. When I remind her I have my own coat, she just shrugs and says the fire will keep her warm. I smile as the scents of smoke and bergamot lull me to sleep.

The smell of roasted meat rouses me and my grumbling stomach from sleep. Sparks has a few kebabs propped against the embers. I don't ask her where the meat came from, but the squirrels have gone quiet. She washes the blood from underneath her nails in a puddle. Her face is grim. I feel a bit of shame. She's always been strong and tough, I hate seeing her have to harden herself again. I wish I could take this burden from her.

She hands me a stick and we gnaw at our squirrel kebabs. We sit in a comfortable silence, enjoying the sunrise and soft birdsong.

"You can have the last stick," I offer to Sparks.

"There's no way you're not hungry." She holds it out to me.

"Same goes for you." I don't take the stick.

"Fair." Sparks takes a bite and then passes it to me. "We'll share."

We alternate bites back and forth. Granted, there's not much to eat, but it's the thought that counts.

"Ready to head out?" Sparks asks. Her skin is no longer pale, having recovered from her overexertion last night. She stretches her arms.

"Let's kick it," I say, trying to sound optimistic and excited. I think it worked.

We make faster time now that Sparks can walk on her own. As we hike, I notice some herbs and flowers that Mimi taught me about. Her intended lessons focused on witchcraft and spells, but edible is edible. I show Sparks the wild violet flowers, dandelions, and chickweed. The dandelions are bitter while the other two are milder. It's not the most filling thing in the world, but beggars can't be choosers. I breathe a sigh of relief as we stumble upon a river but Sparks quickly pulls me away.

"What are you doing?" I yank my hand from her grasp. "There's water over there. I'm functionally powerless without it."

"And that's why they'll be looking for us there," Sparks whispers. "We have to stay away from water sources, especially while there are plenty of puddles we can drink from."

"Don't you feel vulnerable being so far away from electricity?" I probe. "I can protect us by the water."

"Of course I feel vulnerable!" Sparks says. "It's like I only have one hand, but trust me, this is safer in the long run."

A twig snaps in the distance and her eyes widen in panic. We don't stop to check whether a rabbit is messing with us. No, we just grab each other and run. I trip on a tree root, landing sprawled in the damp soil. Sparks hauls me up by my arms, forcing me back to my feet. We run until we can't anymore, until our chests are heaving and sweat coats our bodies. I put my hands on my knees as Sparks leans against a tree.

"We need to keep going." Her paranoia is working overtime. "It's not safe here."

"It's not safe anywhere, Sparks." Oh god, my ribs hurt so bad. "I need a break."

"Come on, Astrid." She pulls me back to my feet, and we resume our trek to nowhere.

"I'm surprised you stopped for me when I fell." I smirk. "Figured you would be too much in a hurry to wait for me."

"Don't say that." She whips to face me, stunned by my comment. "I would never leave you behind."

"It was a joke," I pant, trying to keep up with her. "Just kidding."

"Oh."

We fall back into a steady cadence of walking. Sparks eases up slightly, but I know she's still antsy. But luckily for me and unfortunately for her, the sun once again dips toward the horizon. We can't find a suitable cave, but since the sky is clear of clouds, we figure it would be fine to camp in the open.

We split up to search for firewood and small game to eat. I kneel down to harvest some wild garlic. It's not much, but it might make the squirrel or whatever we eat a bit more enjoyable. I stuff a bundle into my jacket pocket.

"Found ya." A gruff voice comes from behind. Someone grabs a fistful of my hair and drags me backwards.

"Let go of me!" I struggle in his grasp, clawing at his hand.

He lets go as he curses. Blood stains the tips of my fingernails. I scramble to my feet, putting distance between me and my attacker. He's strong and burly. Good for him. I'm small and nimble. Let's dance.

He lunges toward me, and I jump to the side. My hands grab a hefty branch and swing it at his face. It connects with a solid thunk, and he falls to the ground. He grabs my ankle as I try to run away, but I kick at him with my other foot. The man manages to grab both of my legs, pulling me down until he's lying on top of me. The smell of his body odor is assaultive, and I resist the urge to gag.

"If I let you up, will you run or be a good girl?" He asks.

"I'll be good," I lie. He doesn't believe me.

My attacker pins my arms to the ground, and I buck my hips, trying to throw him off. It is not effective. He chuckles, enjoying seeing me struggle beneath him. Think Astrid, think! I close my eyes, reaching out with my powers. Any water will do, even dew on a leaf. There's nothing.

He zip ties my hands together and drags me to my feet. It appears that he thinks being restrained makes me defenseless. Dumbass. I drive my heel into his foot. As he instinctively bends over to grab his foot, my elbow is already in motion, breaking his nose. His head whips back, and I ram my knee into his groin. I'm already ten feet away by the time he's recovered from my attack.

Run, run, run! Don't lead him to Sparks. I can't remember where our meeting point was. I decide to just keep going straight, hurdling over boulders in the way.

My sandals decide now is a great time to cause a problem. They snag on an exposed tree root, and I crash to the dirt. I try to catch myself, but my restraints limit my motion. I land on my wrist and immediately feel a sharp pain. I shriek as I hold my wrist to my chest. It hurts! Oh god, it hurts!

Keep moving. I have to keep moving. I force myself to get up, blinking back the tears. He's getting closer, I can hear him. Keep moving. Don't stop.

Arms surround me as I'm tackled. My wrist screams as I land on it again. Or maybe I do. His momentum carries us forward, and we tumble down the hill. Branches scratch at my skin, and I'm bleeding from several shallow cuts by the time we reach the bottom of the slope. I'm back up to run, but the man has learned by now. He latches onto my wrist, and I fall to my knees. The pain is debilitating. I can't think, can't focus. Only pain.

"Aw, did the little girlie hurt her wrist?" The man squeezes tighter, and I scream. He pulls out a knife, the edge glints in the moonlight. "The Director wants you alive, she didn't say unharmed. You're not going to run away from me again."

My attacker shoves me to the ground, aiming his knife at my leg.

A scream cuts through the silence of the forest. This time it's not mine.

CHAPTER 20

SPARKS

I don't know how much longer we can keep hiking. It would be one thing if we were well-fed, taking frequent breaks, and had proper gear. Two people can't survive on just squirrels and random flowers. Astrid doesn't even have proper shoes. I think I walked through some poison ivy earlier today as an itchy red rash has developed above the edge of my boots. Maybe Astrid knows of a poultice that can help.

I shake the thought from my head. We can't waste time on silly rashes. Every mile we trek makes it that much harder for them to find us. Astrid probably thinks I'm being overbearing, pushing us too hard. What she doesn't realize is that Jack has been preparing me for this moment my entire life. I know how to run, how to hide.

My firewood stack feels sufficient, especially since I'm still against making a fire. Between the smoke and the glow, we'll be easily tracked. But Astrid insists, and I have to compromise somewhere. I navigate back to our agreed upon meeting point, beating Astrid back. I begin to stack my kindling, she'll be back any second now.

The firepit is ready. I pace around anxiously. Any second now, her blonde hair will pop over the ridge. I look up, as if my manifestation could summon her. No dice. It's fine. She's just picking some flowers or something to surprise me. Yeah, she's fine.

She's not fine. She was supposed to be back by now. I don't have a watch. Has it been seconds or minutes? Hours?

Don't go looking for her, I tell myself. What if you leave and she comes back? We don't need two lost hikers. I'll just grab some more firewood. One branch, a twig, a second branch.

A shriek pierces through the air. My sticks tumble from my arms. I'm already moving before they hit the ground. She's hurt. She needs help. Astrid. Hold on, I'm coming.

I can't think straight. *I can't lose her again.* Memories flash through my head. Hot chocolate in the morning. *I can't lose her again.* Sparing with her in the ring. *I can't lose her again.* Shooting her with a squirt gun after she got arrested. *I can't lose her again.* Feeling her bare skin beneath my fingertips. *I can't lose her again.*

I race through the tree line as a second scream sounds further to the left. I adjust course. She's on the move… or being pursued. The possibility spurs me to run faster.

Tree branches crack and I finally catch sight of Astrid. She grapples with a man as they roll down a chasm. Several small twigs are embedded in her hair. I slide down the pitch, popping up as soon as it flattens out.

She shrieks again. A knife. I have to reach her. Her attacker hesitates, hearing the grass crumple beneath my feet. That's all the time I need. *I won't lose her again.* I leap forward, wrapping my arms around his neck. My inertia forces us to the ground. He screams as he flails with the knife, but I pin his hand to the dirt with my heel. In his frenzy, he lets go of Astrid. She stands and kicks his ribs repeatedly, I hear several crack. Good girl.

Eventually, he passes out and I release my hold, panting from the effort. Astrid struggles with the knife to cut through her restraints. I take the blade from her and carefully saw through the zip tie.

"Thank you." Astrid winces as the plastic snaps. "He snuck up on me. I didn't—"

She doesn't get to finish her sentence. Instead, I take her head in my hands and crash my lips into hers. My fingers weave through her hair drawing her in deeper. She tenses in shock, but quickly melts into my embrace, pressing her body into mine. I pull away and rest my forehead against hers. I'm not surprised that tears have already fallen down my cheeks.

"You don't get to do that again." I choke out, as sobs rack my body. "You don't get to scare me like that ever again, you hear me? I love you. I can't…"

Astrid brushes her lips against mine, softly this time. One of her hands cups my cheek. Her touch has a tenderness I haven't felt in months.

"I'm okay," she whispers. "We're okay."

"I heard you scream." My voice is strained, and I struggle to put my feelings into words. "I didn't know where you were, if you were okay. I came as fast as I could."

"I'll recover." Her thumb wipes the tears from my cheek.

"Recover?" I ask, forcing myself back. "What happened?"

The panic rises in my chest again. Her wrist, she's hurt. The pink skin is swollen, and she whimpers as I examine the injury.

"I fell and landed on it wrong," she grunts as she tries to move it. "I can't really use it."

"I'll come back to it in a second," I assure her. "First I have to deal with him before he wakes."

"Check his backpack." Astrid points to the bag. "He has zip ties. We can restrain him."

"We can't leave him alive." My voice is low. I don't get any pleasure from this, but we have to kill him.

"Can't we just leave him tied up or something?" Astrid pleads. It breaks my heart to have to expose her to this.

"If we leave him alive, he'll call for reinforcements," I explain. "If we leave him tied up, he'll just die from starvation or the elements, especially since you broke several of his ribs. It's crueler than if we give him a quick death."

"Oh." Her voice is quiet.

"Turn away, Astrid." I pick up the knife from the ground, stalking toward his unconscious body like a predator. "You don't have to watch."

"Let me do it." She grabs my arm, pulling me back.

"What?" I turn back to face her. "No."

"Please," she begs.

I don't understand. I could see vengeance or anger driving her to volunteer, but she has none of that. A deep sadness is in her eyes, for a moment, I think it might be shame.

"Why?"

"I need to." Astrid tightens her grip on my arm. "I need to learn, to grow stronger. I can't put this weight on your shoulders. You don't deserve that burden. Let me take it from you."

Part of me thinks that she's right. There could come a time in her life where she will need to be comfortable with taking a life. But the other part of me breaks. I made her into this. Stole her light. Coached her on the necessities of survival. I won't be able to protect her forever, but I can shield her for one more day.

"Close your eyes," I whisper, placing a soft kiss on her hairline.

She buries her head in her hands, sobbing. I only hope she was loud enough to drown out the sound of my knife slicing through his neck.

His backpack is heavy. I dig through it quickly. Flashlights, sleeping bag, first aid kit, rations, satellite phone. A few other knick knacks. Finally, some good luck. I grab the phone and pop out the battery, ensuring nobody can track us. We'll see what we can do with it in the morning. Bag slung over my shoulder and knife stuck in my waistband, I grab Astrid's good hand.

"We have to keep moving." I forgot about the way his blood splattered on me. A red handprint now circles her arm. She tries not to look. "If I heard your screams, it's possible others did too. Let's go."

It feels like an hour has passed, but I've always been bad at judging time. The bag falls from my sweaty shoulders as I kneel in front of a puddle. The water is dirty, with particles floating on the surface.

"Hold on." Astrid crouches beside me. "Dirty water isn't safe to drink."

She uses her powers to lift an orb of water to my lips. I gratefully swallow the cold liquid. We both drink our fill. Once finished, I wash the blood off my hands, grimacing as the water gains a red tint. Then, I clean the blood off Astrid. Her arms are covered with small nicks, I presume from when she fell down the hill, plus the handprint I left.

There's not a chance I'm risking a fire tonight. Instead, I fluff out the sleeping bag, telling Astrid to slip inside. She protests, wanting to take first watch, but there's no way I'm sleeping tonight. I stroke her hair until she falls asleep, and then for a short while afterward. I need to keep her safe. No one is going to touch her again.

Eventually, I pull myself away and rummage through the bag again. The first aid kit has plenty of gauze and wound dressing, as well as a compression bandage. I'll splint Astrid's wrist when she wakes. The flashlights could come in handy but could also give away our position. I'm not sure if they're safe to use. Either way, I stuff the batteries in my pocket, feeling a little more secure. It's not much electricity, but I can still fuck up someone's day if needed. There are a few packs of rations in the bag, but with two of us eating, we'll go through them quickly. We'll need to hunt tomorrow when it's safer to light a fire.

The sun gently bobs above the horizon and Astrid stirs. I kneel next to her, waking her with a gentle caress of my lips. She moans contentedly as her eyes flutter open, lighting up as they meet mine. I'm sure after three days without a shower, I'm pretty grimy, but she doesn't seem to mind. That being said, I think she looks beautiful as the morning sun glistens in her hair. She pulls me down for a second kiss, before realizing it's morning.

"You didn't wake me up!" Astrid fumbles with the zipper of the sleeping bag. "You need to sleep."

"No, I need to set your wrist." The first aid kit is already open beside me. "We can't let you reinjure it."

"I'll wrap my wrist." She stubbornly tucks her wrist behind her back. "You nap."

I chuckle and lean forward, lips centimeters away from hers. She closes her eyes, her breath hitched in her chest. Sucker. I seize her arm, turn, and wedge it under my shoulder.

"Hey!" Her other fist pounds on my back. "That's cheating. You can't— ow, fuck!"

"Sorry babe, almost done," I laugh as she curses, not normally one to drop an f-bomb. I secure the compression bandage and line two sticks up with her wrist, using zip ties to create something resembling a splint. "There you go."

She rips her arm away fuming.

"Stop it, right now," she snaps. "This whole self-sacrificial thing, it's done, it's over. We both need to sleep, we both need to eat. If you keep treating me with these kid gloves, we will never make it out of this forest."

"Astrid, it's fine." I shrug it off. "I wasn't tired. It's—"

"Nope," she interjects.

"What—"

"Nuh-uh."

"Oh, come on—"

"I don't want to hear it."

She turns away. I take a deep breath. She's right. I could maybe win this fight if I had a full night's sleep, but fatigue slows my thoughts.

"I'm sorry." I sit on the ground. "You're right."

"Maybe I do want to hear it." She faces me, surprised that I'm not pushing back harder.

"I would kick your ass if you did the same to me." I drag my fingers through my hair. They catch on the tangles and matts that have set in during our camping trip. "I've been so focused on you that I'm starting to slip. I'm going to make a mistake, you're going to get hurt. It's all my fault. It's all my fault."

"Shh," Astrid hushes me. "You're not thinking straight. Take a nap, you'll feel better with some sleep."

She zips me into the sleeping bag, and my eyelids close of their own volition. I feel her lips on my forehead, and it might just be my imagination, but I swear I smell the last remnants of her shampoo. As I fade asleep, I dream of soft hair, peaches, and honey.

⚡ ⚡ ⚡ ⚡

Astrid wakes me after a few hours. I groggily roll up the sleeping bag as she hands me a granola bar. We should save these, we don't know when we'll get more food. I'll put mine back. But Astrid gives me a look and I quietly eat breakfast.

"He had a satellite phone." I set it in front of her. "I don't know what to do with it."

"Duh, let's call someone." Astrid fiddles with the phone, disappointed when it won't turn on. I hold up the battery but slide it back in my pocket before she can grab it.

"It could be tracked," I warn. "They could ping our location, read our texts, see what number we call... I'm worried they'll intercept us before help can arrive."

"Do we have a choice?" Astrid sighs, looking up at the rain clouds forming in the skies. "We can't stay out here indefinitely."

"I know." I stab the dirt with a stick. "It's all just fucking impossible."

"We have to try something, Sparks." The Water Weaver persona comes out, confident and assured. I wonder how much of her conviction is an act. "Give me the battery, let's open a map."

We huddle around the phone as Astrid slots the battery in, quickly navigating to the GPS. I scratch the coordinates in the dirt as Astrid zooms in on the map, looking for nearby towns. According to the phone, we are in Eastern Pennsylvania. How did we get this far from Massachusetts? It looks like we've been heading roughly east the past few days.

"Look, if we continue east, we'll run into this town – Riverdeep Pass."

"That's where they expect us to go," I counter. "There's another town to the southeast, just a little bit further – Birch Rapids. I think that's the better option."

"If you're sure…" Astrid hands the phone to me as I dial Derek's private number. Please pick up. Please pick up.

"Hello," a familiar gruff voice sounds.

"Birch Rapids, Pennsylvania." I talk quickly, trying to hold back my panic. The phone has been on too long, they're going to catch up to us. "We are en route and need an evac. ETA tonight or tomorrow morning."

"Birch Rapids," Derek confirms. He knows I can't talk long, we've trained for this. I can hear both relief and concern in his voice. "I'm coming, be careful."

"Ignore the incoming text." A partial idea crosses my mind. "Birch Rapids."

Before he can respond, I end the call. I shoot off a quick text – *Riverdeep Pass, Pennsylvania. Send help.* Then I rip out the battery.

"Wait, the text was wrong," Astrid interjects.

"I know." I smirk. "That's not for Derek. He knows, Birch Rapids."

"You sneaky bitch," Astrid laughs. "Let's hope that buys us some time."

We quickly gather our supplies, wanting to get far away from where the phone pinged from. Astrid takes the backpack before I can sling it over my shoulders. Still cradling her arm, she leads the way southeast.

Half an hour later, a helicopter hovers above the tree line. We duck beneath some denser foliage and sit horrified as four men slide down a rope onto where we camped. The phone was definitely tracked.

"Come on," I grab Astrid's hand and we dart between trees, trying to stay obscured from the circling helicopter above. Thankfully, it looks like my diversion worked, and the team focused on searching toward the east. Either way, we don't want to be any closer than we need to be.

The sun is high in the sky when we come across a valley, with a swift-moving river cutting through. Rocks line the shore and also jut out from within the rapids. The water breaks around these blockages, releasing a spray of white foam. Small saplings pop up here and there, thriving in the riverbed. Astrid visibly relaxes and kneels at the shoreline, splashing water on her face. She moans euphorically.

"The water is so cold." She dunks her head below the surface, before whipping her hair back, sending cold rivulets flying. "Babe, you have to feel this."

"I'm okay." I stand back, wearily eyeing the coursing water.

"Sparks, I love you, but you smell," Astrid teases. "I know this because I also smell. Come rinse off."

"I don't do water." It's taunting me, begging me to slip and fall in.

"You do me." She smirks, waving me toward the bank. "Now get over here."

I crouch and creep toward the malicious torrent. I lean over and scoop some water with my palm, holding my breath as the water wets my face. My hand trembles as I reach for a second. Astrid doesn't notice my apprehension, basking in the cooling sensation the river provides. She dives in, happily splashing in the current.

"Let me help you in." She wades back to me, eyes sparkling from the water's reflections. "I'll slow the rapids slightly so you can have fun too."

"I'm content staying on dry land."

"We have to cross the river regardless, Birch Rapids is past the rapids." Astrid gestures downwards.

She's right. Sparks, pull yourself together. Get in the fucking river.

I take her hand and carefully step off the bank. The river comes up past my waist. Though Astrid has slowed the current as promised, the river still pulls at my ankles, threatening to drag me under at a moment's notice. Which it does. The rocks slip beneath my feet, and my arms flail as the current pulls me under.

All at once, I am transported back to that December night. Sinking into the ocean deep. Hair billowing toward the surface. The moonlight glinting off the handcuffs piercing my skin, until the depths of the water block all light and the world fades to black. I'm going to drown. I'm dying. Strong arms drag me upwards, but it's too late, it's too late!

As soon as my lungs take in a breath of air, I'm already shrieking. Astrid's look of elation turns to shock, and then alarm. Does she know? She's going to drown. The river will take us both. I can't swim, I can't swim!

"Shhh," Astrid desperately tries to quiet me. "Sweetie, you're okay. You have to be quiet. Sparks, please stop."

The water tugs at me, eagerly tugging and yanking. It's going to pull me back down. I writhe in Astrid's hold. We need to get out! With her injured wrist, she's not strong enough to restrain me. My arm slips free, and my elbow accidentally bangs her nose. Her head whips back, and she momentarily loses her hold on the river. The current overtakes me, and I am back under the fray.

It's stronger now, relishing in its preemptive victory. I thrash, but it's futile. Swimming in this torrent would be difficult even for those that know how. My body slams into a rock, and another. I choke on the water, still screeching. It's not safe! Astrid, get out!

Her arm wraps around me, and the river slows. It's a trap, biding its time until we let down our guards.

"Sparks, you need to stop." She covers my mouth with her hand. "They hear you, they're coming. Anise, stop!"

I'm dying. I'm drowning. Her powers can't save me. I can't save myself. Her eyes flick to the bank, terrified. She glances between me and the bank, me and the bank.

"Anise, I'm so sorry."

Astrid pushes me back under the water. This time, she dives down with me. I don't know how far we've floated down the river, but this section is much deeper. Astrid holds me against the river floor, lying with her chest against mine. A globe of air surrounds our heads, but it doesn't matter, we're going to drown.

"I'm sorry, Anise," Astrid whispers as tears fall down her face. She presses her hand against my mouth tightly. "Please stop screaming."

I can't breathe. I can't breathe. There's no water but it doesn't matter. I'm drowning. Astrid, I'm drowning... Astrid...

CHAPTER 21

ASTRID

Her shoulders rise as she takes a breath. Thank god. I've never seen someone faint like that. I press my hand to my own mouth now, trying to muffle my sobs. She was screaming so loud. She wouldn't stop. I heard the men calling out, they heard her. Branches snapped, they were close. We had to hide, she just kept screaming. She wouldn't stop.

I've never used my powers like this before. I didn't know I could trap air underwater like this, and I don't know how long it will last. The river roars above us. Hopefully, the rapids will obscure us from view. Please, please, please. Underneath me, Anise shifts, slowly awakening. I quickly cover her eyes.

"Please be quiet, baby." My voice cracks as I whisper in her ear. "Shh, please, you're okay."

"Astrid, what's going on?" She goes to sit up, but I hold her down with my arm. She tilts her head, trying to see past my hand. She sounds so scared.

"Please Anise, please," I shush. She flinches at the name. "I really need you to be quiet right now."

"Why won't you let me see?" She whispers. Her frightened body trembles. "Why can't I move?"

"I know you're scared," I murmur, petting her hair with my injured hand. "But I need you to trust me, okay? Please?"

"I found their tracks." A deep voice. I can only hear it faintly, as the water distorts the sound. I hold my breath, clinging to Sparks. "No, I don't see them. I think one of them fell in. There's no way anyone could swim through this. Too fast, too rocky... Maybe the river was too strong for her powers? I don't know what to tell you. They're not here. I'll follow the river and see if I can find their bodies."

I lay atop of Sparks for a few more minutes, until my quickened breathing calms. She's been quaking this whole time. I don't think she's figured out where we are, but she is aware enough to understand the danger. Her eyes are scrunched tightly shut, but I don't dare remove my hand.

"Sparks, I need to check whether it's safe to leave," I say softly, brushing her hair. "To do that, I need to step away from you for a brief moment. Can you stay right here with your eyes closed?" She nods. "Promise me you won't open your eyes."

"I promise," she says meekly.

"Okay, I'll be right back. Stay put."

I focus on maintaining the air bubble as I swim to the surface. Glancing across the shorelines, we are alone. Thank god. Back down to the air bubble. As promised, Sparks is laying still with her eyes closed. I straddle her again, thinking about how I plan on calmly getting her out of here. Unfortunately, my thinking time is cut short. A fish jumps out of the water, smacking Sparks. Startled, she opens her eyes. I clamp my hand over her mouth as her eyes dart around wildly.

"Shh, shh, shh, you're okay," I reassure. "I'm right here, you're safe."

She squirms underneath me. I lean over her, my stringy hair dripping water.

"Look at me, hey!" I whisper harshly. "Look. At. Me." Her teary eyes meet mine, full of grit. "You cannot freak out right now. I got you, you are safe. Just look at me, not the water."

Her struggles cease, trusting me despite her panic.

"Here's what is going to happen," I continue. "You are going to close your eyes and take a deep breath. Then, you are going to feel some water. It will be cold, keep holding your breath. If you get scared, cling to me, okay?"

Sparks nods, and I slowly remove my hand. She whimpers, but she doesn't scream. Big improvement. I very slowly slide off of her. As soon as her hands are free, she clutches me close to her.

"Big breath." I breathe in with her and push off from the ground.

My powers propel us up toward the shore. I drag us onto the rocks, and Sparks is instantly scrambling for the grass. She fumbles onto her back and scoots away. Her clothes are drenched and clinging to her limbs. I dive back into the water to retrieve our bags from the other side. As I drag myself out of the water for the final time, I feel shaking hands pull me further from the river.

"I take it you're afraid of drowning?" I groan, sitting up. Sparks doesn't answer, hugging her arms to her chest. "That would have been helpful to know earlier."

"I don't know how to swim," she mutters. "And in case you've forgotten, I have drowned before."

Well now I feel like a dick. I dry the both of us with my powers. Sparks just grabs the backpack and walks away, still pale and trembling.

"Wait for me." I jog to catch up to her. She's sniffling quietly, holding back tears. "Sparks, I'm sorry."

"You don't have anything to apologize for," she says briskly. "I'm the one that caused the problem."

"I did kind of push you under." I cringe inwardly. "That wasn't my finest moment."

"Ah," she exhales. "I was hoping I imagined that. Still, my fault."

"Do you want to talk about it?" I grab her shoulder, forcing her to stop her sullen march.

"There's nothing to say." Sparks hangs her head. "I wasn't strong enough. I almost got us killed. I need to be better."

"That is a completely one-sided take," I defend. "It's a bit more complicated than that."

"Is it?" She looks up at me. "I don't think so."

With that, she turns away, trudging up the hill. I sigh, but don't push the issue further. I hate when she beats herself up like this. I can't wait until we can leave this stupid forest and put all of this behind us. After what feels like forever of uncomfortable silence, I speak up.

"I want to get to know you better."

"What do you mean?" Sparks raises an eyebrow. "You know me better than anyone, except maybe Derek. You might actually know me more. You two can fight over it."

"I know Anise really well," I ramble. "Derek knows Sparks, but neither of us know Charlotte." She stumbles, caught off guard by the name drop.

"They're really all the same person." She clears her throat. "It doesn't matter."

"You matter to me," I encourage. "I mean, isn't it exhausting to always be wearing a mask? To always have this wall up, keeping yourself closed off?"

"Yes." A twig snaps underneath her feet.

"Let me in," I plead. "Introduce me to Charlotte."

"What do you want to know?" She asks quietly. Shucks, I didn't think I would get this far.

"When we get out of here, what is the first thing you are going to eat?" Not my best question, but it's what I got.

"Are you an option?" She winks. Oh god, I want that to be an option.

"All love and respect, I don't think I could keep up with you until I get an actual meal," I joke. "I'm thinking... chicken and waffles."

"Good pick." She licks her lips. "I think I want a really greasy cheeseburger and tater tots."

"Tater tots?" That's interesting.

"I would literally kill someone for some tots right now." Her stomach growls. I pity the fool that stands between her and food.

"What makes you happy?" We walk several feet as she mulls it over.

"Not much recently," she confesses. "I used to love playing the viola, but I haven't touched one since... well, you know when. Nowadays, I just work, have sex, and sleep. Simple life, except it's not simple at all."

"I still have your viola." I look down at the ground. "It's in the closet with the rest of your things."

"I figured you would have thrown all of that out months ago." A sad laugh. "It doesn't matter though. I don't have anything to play for."

"Sparks," I pause, trying to stay composed. "Why didn't you come back for me?" She looks up, staring into my eyes.

"I didn't have the strength to lose you twice." Her walls are down. I'm looking straight into her center, her most honest version of herself.

"I'm sorry." A lone tear falls free. "I fucked us up. I had everything I ever wanted and then—" Sparks cups my head in her hands, gently leaning in until our lips meet.

"Just promise you'll stay with me," she whispers, tucking my hair behind my ear. "From now until forever."

"I promise," I say breathlessly. "From now until forever."

She kisses me again, the kind where neither one of you is in a hurry, where your lips meet and the world stops, and you find yourself leaning forward as they pull away, trying to extend the kiss even a second more. Sparks laces her fingers in mine, and we continue walking southeast. The birds sing, the breeze tousles her hair, and perhaps, for a moment, everything is right in the world.

But then again, that's when things do typically go to shit.

There's a crack in the distance, and we freeze when we see a man cut across the clearing ahead – one of the kidnappers. Somehow, he doesn't know we're here. Sparks and I slowly creep behind some shrubs for more cover.

"Sparks, throw your knife at him," I whisper.

"Why would you think I know how to throw knives?" She looks at me like I've grown a second head.

"You threw a knife the night of the gala," I remind her. "You know, when that one guy grabbed me? You hit him square in the back."

"Ah, yes, well, about that," she stammers. "That was actually a lucky shot."

I slowly turn to face her, glaring at her through my eyelashes.

"You mean to tell me, you threw a knife at me and just *hoped* you didn't kill me?"

"To be fair, there was an entire person between me and you," she hisses. "And I might have acted a bit impulsively."

"Later, I'm going to kill you."

"Later." She nods.

"New plan," I suggest. "I'll sneak around to the left, you sneak to the right. I draw his attention and you stab him."

"That's a shit plan."

"I'd love to hear a better one."

"I have one," a third voice whispers. "Raise your hands behind your head."

Sparks and I lock eyes. Oh crap. I blink and Sparks is already on the move. She flings out her leg and the man falls to the ground. Unfortunately, that is enough to draw the attention of the other guy. Sparks throws out her hands and electricity shoots from her pockets towards the man on the ground. He convulses until he is still. Out of juice, Sparks unzips her pockets and starts chucking batteries at the other approaching guy. It doesn't do much besides irritate him. I lean behind her and grab the knife. Seems like we're back to my plan.

I crawl through the bushes. The thorns pull my hair and scratch at my arms. I glance up and see a third pair of hiking boots a few feet in front of me. I look up further and we lock eyes. Or... maybe not my plan.

The man is rather amused, smirking at my poor version of an army crawl. I rise to a crouched position still gripping my knife.

"That looks sharp. You should put that down before you get hurt," he chuckles, still bemused. He then sees my wrist in its makeshift splint. "Aww, you already are."

"I'm fine." I grit my teeth. "I can still make your day considerably worse, unless of course, you are smart enough to walk away."

"There's no ocean for you to jump in," he taunts, stepping closer. "What are you going to do without your powers?"

"Oh sweetie." It's my turn to be condescending. "Those are just an added bonus. I'll still kill you without them."

He lunges at me, and I dodge toward the left, swiping with my blade. I graze his forearm, and he curses at me as blood stains his sleeve. He whirls around, but I am already following up with a second swing. This one misses, but he takes a step back, reconsidering his strategy. I don't give him the chance. I jump forward, jabbing at his torso. He grabs my wrist and twists. The knife clatters to the ground. Ow, ow, ow! My wrist!

I wrench my arm away as he reaches for my hair. I narrowly avoid his grasp and somersault past him. He grunts, frustrated with my stubborn insistence on being difficult to capture. Suddenly, a choking noise gurgles from his throat. He reaches behind himself and pulls out a knife, covered in his own blood. As he falls to the ground, he flings the knife with alarming speed. Sparks tries to dive out of the way but is too late. The knife plants itself up to its hilt in her thigh.

"Sparks!" I rush to her side, applying pressure to her leg.

"We've got to move," she grunts, breathing quickly through the pain. Her skin is pale and sweaty. "There's more coming. Grab the rope from his bag and apply a tourniquet."

I do as she says, tightening the cord as she bites down on a stick. When the tourniquet is secured, I help her to her feet. Her leg gives out as she puts her weight on it, but I catch her before she falls.

"Come on, babe," I encourage. "Birch Rapids is so close."

She bites her lip as she leans on me, and we hobble over the last hill. Birch Rapids is clear on the horizon. Derek is waiting. Please, Derek, be waiting. We hear the sounds of another team coming in behind us. Sparks's eyes meet mine and we both know she's not making it to Birch Rapids. We're out of time.

"We can fight them off," I claim. "We'll be fine."

"No, we can't." Her thumb brushes my cheek. "You need to get help."

"I won't leave you." I place my forehead against hers. "From now until forever, remember."

"Go, get Derek and come back for me." She pushes me away. "Run!"

I spare one last glance at the woman I love, before turning to run. I sprint down the clearing, pushing myself faster and faster. I burst into town and see a convoy of black vans waiting.

No... not like this. It can't end like this.

But instead of more hostiles, Derek and a whole squadron of men pour out. Derek sees me, sweaty and out-of-breath. He only says one word.

"Where?" We both know what he means.

I turn and run, leading the charge of angry gangsters. Despite being tired and hungry, I sprint faster than any of the reinforcements. I have to get back to her.

A scream cuts through the air. A blur of red is surrounded by men in black. She writhes in their arms, trying to escape their clutches.

"Sparks!" Derek calls.

The two forces collide. Bullets fly, knives flash, fists connect. Me? I dart through it all. With the kidnappers distracted, I grab Sparks's arm and start dragging her to safety. A hand grabs the back of my neck, yanking my hair.

"Don't touch her!" Sparks cries, throwing rocks at my assailant.

A gunshot rings out and the man falls to the ground. Derek nods from across the fray and continues to battle.

"Time to go." I grab her arms again and keep dragging her. A light trail of red follows our path. Her hands are clammy and cold in mine. She breathes softly, her head sagging forward. "Stay awake, Sparks. Talk to me."

"Ask me a question," she teases. Her voice is weak and hard to hear.

"What is Charlotte's favorite subject?" How far is this stupid town? "I know you dropped out of school, but before then."

"Science," she mumbles. "I was always good at science. My mom liked physics, she taught me..."

"What did she teach you?" She doesn't respond. I kneel down next to her. "Stay with me, baby."

By that point, Derek swoops in and lifts her into his arms. I sprint with him, not bothering to look back at the remnants of the bloodshed behind us. We load into a van with a medic – not Luca thankfully. He already has a blood transfusion prepped and gets to work. I sit next to Sparks, holding her hand. Derek tries to examine my wrist, but I shoo him off. Sparks is important now, not me.

After some time, the medic has finished sewing up Sparks's leg. As he weans her off the anesthetic, her eyes flutter open. She smiles faintly when she sees me.

"Why so sad, babe?" She whispers.

"Because I was worried about you, silly." I lightly kiss her knuckles.

"I told you I would be fine," she smirks. "From now until forever, remember?"

"How could I forget?" I roll my eyes.

"Now is someone going to explain why my girlfriend still has a shitty-ass splint on her wrist?"

CHAPTER 22

SPARKS

A few weeks have passed since our foray into the wilderness of Pennsylvania. Astrid's wrist was only sprained, not broken, so that healed really quickly. My stab wound took a decent while longer to heal, but I made damn sure that didn't hold me back from getting the meal I was craving. I also got the cheeseburger and tater tots.

Derek has increased security around the compound, furious at the Luca betrayal. Honestly, he had nothing to worry about. While other criminal organizations treat their muscle like shit, Derek and I have always prided ourselves on giving our men respect and above-market-rate compensation, including dental. My abduction struck a nerve within my loyal crew, and they found a few other wolves in sheep's clothing on their own.

Some of the men organized a round-the-clock security detail to follow me whenever I leave the compound. They even wait outside when I go to Astrid's. While I'm sure some of the volunteers are just excited for the overtime pay approved by Oliver, most value it as being a part of an honor guard. It's a bit much at times, but I appreciate their fidelity.

However, despite our increased efforts, my stalker still finds ways to interact with me. A "Get Well Soon" card was left in the club addressed to Charlotte. Nobody saw who dropped it off. An unknown number calls me in the middle of the night. They never say anything, there's only the sound of him breathing. When I got too freaked out to answer anymore, the number would send texts instead. Always just a few words. *Sleep well. Good morning. Lovely weather today.* I tried changing my number but got a text less than an hour later. *Keep in touch.*

Gifts still appear in my saddlebags. I had to clean them out since all of my things kept going missing. Ponytails, sunglasses, pens. Nothing was sacred.

I stopped leaving the compound, even stopped going to the Lightning Bolt. My world consisted of my apartment, the common area, and the gym. But Derek and Astrid say that I need vitamin D, so Astrid's dragging me out on a date. She says we're going to the fair. I say we have corn dogs at home. She says I'm going anyway.

And that's why I'm outside, driving my bike toward the carnival. Everything is fine as I coast through the parking garage, but as soon as I get on the road, I feel a strange wobble. I carefully pull my motorcycle off to the side of the road. Damn it, flat tire. Because of the crazy thief, I took my tire repair kit out, so my bike is shit out of luck. I send a quick text to my protection detail asking them to bring a spare tire. I stupidly left before they were ready, thinking they would catch up without an issue.

"Everything okay?" A standard four-door sedan pulls up next to me.

"I'm fine." I wave off the good Samaritan. "I've already texted a friend. They'll be here in just a minute."

"Are you sure? I could give you a lift."

"I'm sure, thanks." I look up. The man inside the car looks familiar. Late twenties, black hair, hazel eyes, strong build. I tilt my head. "Do I know you?"

"I don't think so." He pauses. "Wait, jazz girl?"

"Oh my goodness," I chuckle. "Are you my dance partner from the gala?"

"The very same." He gives a mock bow from within his car. "I didn't recognize you in street clothes."

"Sorry, evening gowns and motorcycles don't mix."

He eyes my outfit. It's my standard garb – leather jacket, cropped black tank, shorts.

"I think you look amazing." It feels sincere.

"Thanks." I blush.

With that, my security detail pulls up and the two of them get to work replacing my tire.

"Thanks for stopping." I wave. "Hope to bump into you again sometime."

He nods lightheartedly and drives off. Before too long, my tire is fixed and I am back on the road, detail in tow this time. Together, the three of us navigate through the busy Boston traffic until we make our way to the front entrance. Astrid runs over and nearly tackles me with her hug.

"You made it!" Her blonde ponytail bobs as she jumps excitedly. "This is going to be so much fun. Hi Noah, hi Trevor."

She waves at my security detail, and they give her a subtle nod before blending into the crowd. Her teal skirt swishes as she twirls, skipping toward the ticket booth. A matching ribbon is tied around her ponytail. I nervously glance at the mass of people before following her in. This is going to be fun, right?

I don't remember the last time I went to a carnival. Crowds cheering, lights flashing, attractions catching your eye every few feet. I hold onto Astrid's hand as she drags me deeper. We do everything. She screams as she clings to me on the roller coaster while I whoop and holler. Powdered sugar tickles her nose as we sample a funnel cake. We save half for Noah and Trevor. Even though they're working, they can still enjoy the festival too. The line to the Ferris wheel is short, so we ride it twice. Once to fully take in the grandeur of the city, a second for me to take in the beauty of the woman sitting next to me. And by that I mean we make out the whole time.

After she wins me a plushie at one of the boardwalk games, we stumble onto the mirror maze. The ramshackle hut doesn't look like much, but you can briefly see panes of glass lining the walls from floor to ceiling, creating intricate reflections and illusions.

"I bet you one corndog that I could beat you in the mirror maze," Astrid boasts.

"Oh really?" I nudge her arm. "I am fantastic at mazes."

"Watch me." She sticks out her tongue.

The attendant gives each of us a pair of cotton gloves so we don't smudge the glass when we touch it. Astrid goes first, slinking through the curtain into the entrance behind. A timer on the wall claims she makes it to the exit in three minutes and twenty-one seconds. I scoff and puff out my chest. This will be easy.

"Three, two, one, go!" The attendant cheers as I duck behind the curtain.

Immediately, I am faced with my reflection multiplied endlessly in the glass. Everywhere I look, a version of me is staring back. My heart skips a beat as I am forced to engage with my reflection after avoiding it for so long. Look away, focus on the maze.

I stumble through a hallway before smacking my head on a pane of glass. I stagger back a step, faltering as I try to discern the way through. My hands wave in front of me, tapping the walls. I veer left as I feel an opening in that direction.

A glass wall disrupts my path as mirrored panes block either side of me. Damn, dead end. I've been ignoring the images in the mirror so intently that I'm spooked when something in the reflections catches my eye. Another figure navigates the mirrors alongside me. Odd, I thought only one person was allowed in at a time. His leather gloves trail along the glass, but he walks with a calm assurance as though he knows the path by heart.

Wait, leather gloves. The attendant gave me these ridiculous white, cotton gloves. I didn't know we could bring our own. I turn around, trying to find the exit of this stupid passage, but my breath catches when I see the rest of his reflection. A bandana is tied around the lower half of his face, while the rest is obscured by a ballcap.

My ballcap.

Shit.

I dart down the hallway, feeling for an exit. Where is it? Where is it? My hands find a gap to the right, then to the left. I follow the walls blindly before slamming into a mirror. Motherfucker!

Frazzled, I whirl back around. Do I go left? Right? I don't remember which way I came from. Images of the man surround me. No matter where I turn, his slow pursuance follows me. He doesn't rush, instead he walks in a steady cadence, confident in his relentless shadow.

His assurance unsettles me, causing me to panic further. I try to move faster, banging into more mirrors. I don't know where I'm going. I don't know where I've been. His reflection is getting larger and larger and—

We collide. I ram into his muscular chest, reeling from the sudden impact. I would have fallen, but he wraps an arm around my back, pulling me close to him. A gentle hand glides across my temple, softly tucking my hair behind my ear. I scream.

Startled, he loosens his hold and I fall to the floor, scooting away from him until my back hits the glass.

"What do you want with me?" I cry. The lights flicker from my fear. "Leave me alone!"

He doesn't say anything, just stares with his brown eyes. I hear a commotion from the front.

"You can't go in there!" The attendant shouts. A thud, and then he is quiet.

I stare at the man in front of me. He slowly reaches into pocket and pulls out a photo, handing it to me. My hands tremble as I take it from him. The subject of the photo is me, as to be expected. It's framed tightly, focused on my bright smile. I'm laughing, deboarding the roller coaster earlier today. It's cropped so tightly you can't even see Astrid. "I missed you" is scrawled in permanent marker on the back. I look up from the photo, and he is gone, vanished from the mirrored reflections. The only evidence I have that he even existed at all is the photo in my shaking hands.

A flash of teal darts through the mirrors, and Astrid is kneeling at my side. The lights still as I release the breath caught in my lungs, feeling safe with her there.

"What's wrong?" She examines me quickly, paling at the photo in my hands. "He left that for you?"

"Worse." I shake my head. "He handed it to me."

"We need to go."

Astrid grabs my arm, deftly weaving me toward the exit. Trevor and Noah assume their formation, one clearing a path and the other covering the rear. The crowd parts easily and I am escorted off the fairgrounds. Trevor hops on my bike while I ride in Astrid's car. He zooms ahead as Noah trails behind her hatchback. Astrid grips the steering wheel fiercely, daring someone to cut her off.

I just curl up in my seat, staring at the photo in my hands. I look happy. The moment captured is one of joy and elation. My jacket slouches off one of my shoulders, carefree in the moment. How naive I was. Astrid snatches the photo from my hands and shuts it inside the glovebox.

"Don't go down that path, Sparks," she warns gently, placing a hand on my thigh.

"What path?" I say glumly.

"Whichever is closing you off right now." Her thumb makes tiny circles on my thigh, unknowingly decorating my fading scar. Is this what life is now? Stabbings and stalkings?

"Hey!" Astrid interrupts my spiral. "What did I just say?"

I don't respond, just sigh and lean my head on the window. Astrid squeezes my thigh, concerned by my silence. I give her a half smile. She doesn't buy it. I guess I don't either.

We pull up to Astrid's apartment. I thought we were going to the compound, but it doesn't really matter either way. I go where I'm told, every moment supervised like I'm a small child. It's for my safety, they say. The mirror maze was the first time I've been alone outside the compound in weeks, and the vultures swooped instantly. *I missed you.* I miss myself too.

I climb the steps to Astrid's apartment as Trevor passes her my keys and Noah finds a good place to park. They'll be here until their shift replacement takes over, and so on and so forth. I'll be here until I'm needed somewhere else. I meander through the living room after discarding my jacket, settling onto Astrid's sofa. I lean over the frame, gazing through the window at the streets of downtown Boston. People walk by, not noticing the onlooker from above.

Astrid sits next to me, placing a warm mug in my hands. Drinks are how she soothes others, tea and hot chocolate flow endlessly around here. I set the beverage to the side, content to ruminate in my self-pity. Unfortunately, Astrid is not. She grabs my drink and wraps my hands around it. I stare at the swirling brown liquid. I haven't had cocoa in months, not since we broke up.

I close my eyes as I bring the mug to my lips. The rich liquid warms my insides as the flavor of anise dances on my tongue. Her recipes are just as good as I remember, if not better. It feels like home.

The mug is empty quickly. I cradle the ceramic to my chest, allowing the last of the residual warmth to reach my body. Astrid stays next to me, people-watching in silence.

"I love you," I whisper, not knowing what else to say.

"I love you too." She glances at the mixed expressions flicking across my face. "What's Charlotte thinking?"

Astrid started asking about Charlotte a lot since our forced camping trip. It's an understood code between us now. When she asks about Charlotte, she's asking about the thoughts I hold tight, buried beneath my layers of defenses. I don't always answer, and she respects that, but I try to give a good faith effort to be more open.

"She's thinking…" my voice trails off, "that she lives in a fishbowl where others can sit and watch as long as they like."

"Do you want me to close the blinds?" She offers.

"No, leave them open." I hold her hand back. "It's no use pretending otherwise. That feels worse."

Emboldened, I go around the entire apartment, flinging open curtains and blinds. Bright light floods the rooms. I lay on the bed, soaking in the sun rays. Astrid flops down next to me, propping her head on a pillow.

"What's Astrid thinking?" I tease.

"What I'm thinking is not super helpful right now." She smiles and rolls onto her side.

"Well now I'm even more intrigued." I grin up at her.

"Fine." She pauses before she continues. "I'm thinking that when your tank top rides up, it drives me crazy. Every time, I just stare at the sliver of skin and wish I could unwrap the rest."

"Why don't you?" Her pupils dilate at my question.

"I didn't think you would want me to." Her gaze flicks down to my hips, eyeing the gap between the fabrics before tearing her eyes away. "I wouldn't ever want to pressure you or—"

I shush her as I guide her hands to the hem of my shirt.

"Show me," I request.

Astrid shifts to straddle my thighs, gently lifting the cloth covering my torso. I arch my back, allowing her to discard my tank. Her fingertips graze the muscles of my stomach. God, I'm glad I did a core workout this morning. Astrid moves slowly, intimately caressing my sides before unbuttoning my shorts. She folds the denim down, exposing my hip bones to her affectionate revelation. The lace of my panties peeks through, and Astrid tenderly removes my shorts the rest of the way.

I'll admit, I had a feeling our day would end like this, and I chose my underclothes accordingly. A skimpy thong accentuates the angles of my body, while my low-cut bra doesn't leave much to the imagination. The straps fall off my shoulders, taunting us both. Astrid cups the lacy material, stroking the hem along the curve of my breast.

"You look beautiful right now," she whispers. "The red of your hair is so vibrant in the sunlight, and your skin is so soft, and you are just stunning."

"I love you." I mean it.

Her lips brush mine, lightly at first, but craving more. She leans in closer, kissing me deeper as if she could never get enough. Her tongue slides against my teeth. She pulls away slowly, savoring every second we touch. Astrid unclips the hooks of my bra, and the material falls to the floor.

Her tongue finds something else to explore, circling my erect nipple. Her hand massages the other tenderly, kneading and caressing. My eyelids flutter as I tilt my head back, high on the sensations tingling my nerves. Her hand ventures lower, skimming the last bit of lace I still have on. She slides a finger past the mesh, moving as if she had all of the time in the world. I moan, anticipation taking hold of my heart. It beats faster and faster. I wonder if her tongue could feel my pulse through my chest. I rock my hips forward, leaning toward her touch. She tsks and withdraws her hand.

"Please," I beg breathlessly. "I need you."

"Since you asked so nicely..." Her mischievous eyes meet mine and she crawls lower.

Astrid bites the fabric of my panties between her teeth, gradually dragging it over my thighs. Kisses line the path all the way to where my legs meet. Her breath tickles, and my toes curl into her sheets. I shudder as she flicks her tongue out, sampling how I taste. Pleased, she dives in, sucking and licking to her heart's content. She enjoys her meal leisurely, savoring me indulgently. She moves at her speed, no matter how much I beg for more. It turns out, Astrid knows best. Slowly but surely, the tension mounts in my core. I grip the rungs of the headboard. Astrid reads me like a book, holding my hips down as I squirm.

Time slows. Nothing exists outside of this bedroom. The whole world consists of just the two of us. Her name graces my lips as I crash from the peak, falling into the throws of her embrace. She's there to catch me, she's always been there. Her hands are in my hair, my lips find hers.

We spend the rest of the day exploring each other's bodies. Tracing, massaging, kissing. Not in any particular hurry, not for any particular goal, only to seek pleasure in the touch of the one we love. Both thoroughly satisfied, we drift asleep in each other's arms.

Click. Click. Click. Click. I stir in my sleep, somewhere between awake and dreaming. My eyelids blink lethargically, sleep pulling me back under. A loving hand strokes my hair, the leather soft against my skin. I moan drowsily, turning over to wrap my arms around Astrid.

Wait? Astrid's over here?

I groggily sit up, rubbing my eyes to see through the dark. No one's there. I shiver at the breeze coming through the open window, lightly blowing the curtains. Shaking my head, I pull the covers over Astrid and myself.

The morning sun cuts through the room, sharply glinting across my eyes. Normally the curtains diffuse the light, but I was an idiot and threw them open yesterday. Astrid stretches, rolling onto my chest.

"Good morning," she murmurs. Her smile glints in her eyes.

"Good morning, gorgeous." I brush her hair over her shoulder, pulling her in for a kiss. Her soft lips brush mine, lingering before she pulls away. I can't imagine how I went so long without waking up next to her every day.

Eventually, we crawl out from under the covers. I can't find the underwear I discarded yesterday, it's probably tangled in the sheets somewhere. Luckily, I have several boxes of clothes in Astrid's closet. I dig through and pull out a comfy, oversized t-shirt and some extra underwear.

Astrid pulls on a robe and heads toward the kitchen, rubbing the sleep from her eyes. I hear her fiddling with some mugs, before she shrieks and I hear the ceramic shatter.

"Astrid!" I hurdle over the bed, running toward the door.

"No, stay in the bedroom!"

But it's too late, I've already opened the door.

I freeze, taking in the sight before me. Photos are strewn all over the living room. There must be hundreds, no thousands, of them. On the couch, on the rugs, on the end tables, on the bookshelves. Astrid steps in front of me, trying to usher me back into the bedroom. What doesn't she want me to see?

I step around her. The scalding water puddling on the floor burns as I pad barefoot into the living room. I pick up a photo, lifting it from the ground. My naked body is framed in the shot, focused on my arched back. The picture flutters to the ground as it falls from my fingers.

My scarred hand fisting the sheets.

My hair sprawled on a pillow.

My head rocked back, exposing my neck.

There's so many. All of them are pieces and parts of me, somehow cropping Astrid out of every shot.

Biting my lip.

Clenching the headboard.

Grinding my hips.

The pictures are crystal clear, as if he was standing in the room with us. Every inch of my skin in perfect clarity. He's watching me. He's always watching.

My lips.

My thighs.

My breasts.

I stumble away from the horrific display. Astrid's words blur as they leave her mouth. I can't be here. He's watching me.

I dart to the door, flinging it open and taking the stairs two-at-a-time. The rocks cut my feet as I sprint down the alley. He's watching me. I have to get away.

I bolt around the corner, faltering as I enter a park. Heads turn to look at me. He's watching me. They're watching me.

There's nowhere to hide. Concerned faces, someone asks me a question, a hand brushes mine. I jerk away. He's watching me. They're watching me. They're all watching me.

I back away as the crowd inches closer. Don't look at me. Leave me alone. *Click. Click. Click. Click.*

I can hear the camera shutters. I turn over my shoulder. Where is he? I whirl around. He must be here somewhere. Watching. Staring.

Click. Click. Click. Click.

Eyes staring at me. Everyone's looking.

Click. Click. Click. Click.

He's watching.

Astrid's here, along with a man from the security detail. She grabs my shoulder, and I fall to the ground. My guard lifts me in his arms, carrying me to the van parked along the road. He drapes a jacket over me before shutting the door. Astrid pulls her robe tighter, worriedly watching the van drive away.

I slouch in my seat, pulling the jacket over my head. I can't hide from him. He's everywhere. I cry quietly until we park in the garage.

They said to observe and wait for further instruction. I know I shouldn't have approached her at the carnival, but she wanted me to, I know she did. It was so worth it. To hold her in my arms. To have the subtle scent of bergamot tickle my nose. It was everything I've been wanting to do for weeks now.

I didn't mean to scare her. She just wasn't ready to love me yet. It's okay, I can be patient. Plus, I made it up to her with her gift. All of those gorgeous photos celebrating her body. Her curves. Her toned muscles. Her desperate expressions.

Of all the photos I took, there was only one I didn't give her. I couldn't, it was too perfect. The moment of release. All of the pent-up tension leaving her body in a glorious flash of euphoria. The way she arches her back as she cries out. I trace the outline of her figure. One day, it'll be my name on her lips. One day. Soon.

CHAPTER 23
ASTRID

She won't come out of her room.

Won't eat. Won't say anything. Won't even take the whiskey we left by her door.

Derek gave her one day before punching in his code and storming into her living room. Her bedroom door was also locked, but that barely slowed Derek. He flicked on the lights, but she turned them off. That was the only indication that she was there. Otherwise, we couldn't find her. I mean, there wasn't a lot of furniture in the room, pretty much only the bed. Derek looked under the bed frame, but she wasn't hiding under there.

I slide open the closet door and there she is, curled up in the dark. Her eyes are hollow. She's still wearing the t-shirt from yesterday, hasn't even put on shorts.

"Sparks, it's time to eat something." I reach a hand down. "Come on."

"He can't see me here," she mutters. Her phone buzzes from the end table and she flinches, a tear falls down her cheek. "He can't see me."

Derek picks up the phone, anger crossing his face.

"What the fuck?!" He scrolls through the texts. I peek over his shoulder. Photos of Sparks line the text history, some explicit, some not, none of them posed. *I miss you.* Sparks riding her motorcycle. *Come outside.* Sparks out for a jog. *I just want to see you again.* Sparks kissing a stranger. *This could have been us.*

Another notification, a new text. I snatch the phone from Derek and power it off. He doesn't need to see that picture. Derek walks into the closet and kneels by her side.

"Kiddo, you need to get up." Derek tousles her hair. "Time to rejoin society."

Sparks doesn't respond, just buries her head in her arms. I go to the kitchen and grab a glass of ice water. I nudge Derek out of the way and sit next to her.

"Drink up, babe." I extend the glass. No dice. "This is your last warning." Still nothing.

I use my powers to remove the ice from the glass, leaving the brisk water. I fling the cup at her, splashing her with the chilled liquid. She jerks up, startled to reality by the cold. I grab her hand, forcing her to hold an ice cube.

"Listen, Sparks." I gesture toward her hand. "This ice, that's real. It's frozen in your hand. Feel it. Notice how the cold stings, how it melts and starts to drip off your palm. That's real. Right here, right now."

Sparks actually listens to me, studying the ice cube in her fist.

"That guy out there, he doesn't matter," I whisper. "You're here. You're safe. We'll protect you. But if you shut down, he wins. If you stop eating, stop taking care of yourself, you are playing into his hands. You're better than that, baby. Tell me, what does the ice feel like?"

"It hurts," she says quietly. "It's really cold."

"What about these?" I toss her a pair of shorts.

"They're rough, but the kind of soft that you can only get from well-worn denim." She squeezes the fabric. "They're my favorite pair."

"Put them on." I brush her hair back, using my powers to dry her off as I do so. "Then let's go get something to eat."

Derek follows me, and together we cook a full breakfast for the three of us. Pancakes, eggs, bacon, fruit. I smack his hand as he reaches for the coffee machine. As we set plates out on the bar, Sparks emerges from her bedroom, freshly showered and wearing a complete outfit. She's right, those shorts fit her perfectly. I pass her a plate and she picks at it with her fork. She pushes the same blueberry across her plate three times.

"Derek, I think we're out of eggs. Can you go grab some from the kitchen in the common area?" I smile at him sweetly.

"Sure thing." He ducks out.

"Listen to me, Sparks." My voice lowers, and her eyes snap up to mine. "You will eat that entire plate or so help me god, I won't fuck you for a week."

"That's not fair," she protests. Her pleas fall on deaf ears.

"I don't care." I shrug. "I'll sit on your couch wearing nothing but those panties you like, you know the ones, and I'll touch myself until I scream my own name."

"I have ways of convincing you to let me play." She looks at me sultrily, batting her eyelashes as she twirls her hair.

"You know what's really sexy?" I tease. "What really gets me going?" I drop the fun banter, switching back to seriousness. "You not starving. Eat."

Perfect timing, Derek walks in with a carton of eggs.

"Wait, there are eggs right here?" He gestures at the counter, confused.

"Oops," I say bluntly.

He huffs and sets the eggs down. Begrudgingly, Sparks stabs the blueberry and slides the tines of her fork against her teeth. Slow-moving progress. Licorice jumps on the counter, and Sparks holds her in her lap, still eating with her free hand. Derek and I help ourselves to breakfast, and soon, all three plates are empty. Sparks makes a point to show me hers. I roll my eyes.

Derek clears the dishes and Sparks sulks to the couch, laying upside down with her head dangling off the cushions. Suddenly, she bolts up and throws a pillow.

"I can't do this anymore!" She screams, chucking cushions across the room. "I can't stay in this lifeless apartment on self-inflicted house arrest. I can't be followed everywhere I go like a toddler. I'm going crazy."

"Where do you want to go?" I ask. "Let's make it happen."

"It doesn't matter what I want," Sparks sniffles. "He's out there. I can't do anything without him watching. I used to just hop on my bike and drive wherever I wanted, whenever I wanted. Now I practically have to ask permission to visit my fucking girlfriend."

"You and me." I grab her hand. "Let's go."

"Wait," Derek protests. "You don't honestly expect me to be cool with this. It's dangerous."

"He's right." Sparks slumps her shoulders.

I swear I could see the life drain from her eyes. Maybe this is stupid, maybe it isn't. Either way, it needs to be done. I walk to the sink and pour myself a very tall glass of water.

"Derek, I want you to know that I've really come around to you." I take a sip of my water, as he looks at me suspiciously. "That's why I want you to know that I'm sorry."

He moves abruptly, but he doesn't stand a chance. I shape my water into a tendril, whipping it around his wrists. It freezes, forming a temporary restraint. I grab Sparks's hand, yanking her to her feet despite her weakening protests. Sparks throws her head back laughing as we sprint through the compound. With each step, a bit more color returns to her skin. Her security detail follows us to the parking garage, but Sparks sucks the energy from the van battery. They struggle with the ignition, confused when it won't start.

"Go, go, go!" I grab my helmet and jump onto the bike behind her, tightening the strap as she peels out of the garage.

The engine purrs as she merges onto the interstate. Her shoulders finally start to relax. She didn't grab her helmet, so her hair flies freely in the wind. It's been forever since I've truly ridden with her. I'd forgotten the way the open road feels when it's just us on a bike. I loosen my grip on her torso, enjoying this nearly as much as Sparks is. Sparks leans down, pressing her chest against her handlebars. Without her body to block the wind, it gusts into me unrestricted. The air pulls at my shirt. I cautiously let go of Sparks, squeezing the motorcycle with my legs. Feeling more confident, I fling my arms in the air, cheering the adventure. Sparks sneaks a look back, and I see her chuckle. She sits back up and I rewrap my arms around her, cherishing our time together.

We drive until we run out of gas and pull over at some greasy truck stop to grab some burgers and milkshakes. The light returns to Sparks's eyes. I drip my french fries into my shake as she relentlessly mocks me. She throws her head back laughing. I take the tip money and fold it into a little origami crane. She pats its head and slings her jacket over her shoulder.

I straddle her lap as we sit on the motorcycle after we fueled up. After all, she cleaned her plate. While I wasn't about to get her off in some random parking lot, I was less opposed to making out. Sparks nips at my ear, and I let my head roll back. She grabs the nape of my neck, pulling me back to her lips. My fingers weave in her hair, and I give her a quick yank. She gasps, and I use that as my opportunity to slide my tongue in her mouth, dragging it along the edge of her teeth. Sparks moans, and it takes everything in me to not eat her out on this bike right now.

While I was debating the pros and cons of a public indecency charge, two black SUVs pulled up to the truck stop. They come to a stop in the middle of the parking lot, ignoring the painted lines on the concrete.

"Sparks..." I whisper in warning.

"I see them." She slides her arm past me, and I use it as leverage to scoot to my side of the seat.

"Get us out of here." I cling to her waist. She revs the engine and chuckles as their headlights flash.

"This is going to be fun." I don't like the sound of that.

Sparks burns out of the parking lot, leaving a rubber tread mark on the asphalt. As we drive past the first car, she flings out her arm, and flashes of electricity dart to her outstretched hand. The lights of the first SUV go dim, and Sparks swerves onto the road. She weaves between traffic, dashing between cars and vans to put distance between us and the second SUV. The pursuing vehicle has a different approach, bypassing traffic by driving in the ditch along the road.

We pull onto the interstate and Sparks directs the bike into the shoulder. She leans flat against the bike. I follow suit and Sparks lays on the throttle, accelerating in her "open" lane. The guardrail is inches away from our arms. I hold my breath and tuck in my elbows. Hazard lights flash ahead as signs alert that the road is closed for construction.

"Bridge out." The recommended detour is packed, a traffic jam at a complete standstill.

"Hold on!" Sparks yells over the wind.

"What do you think I'm doing back here?" I don't know if she heard me, but I tighten my grip regardless.

Sparks blows past the detour, not even faltering.

"Sparks, the bridge is out!" How could she miss the signs?

"I'm going to jump the gap!"

Bad idea. Bad idea. We lean into the curve and the bridge looms ahead of us. Or well, what used to be a bridge. A twenty-foot gap is where the bridge should be. I see Sparks doing the math in her head. There's no way we can make it. The SUV slows behind us, ready to intercept us when we brake. Stopping isn't an option.

"Gun it!" I order.

"We can't make it!" Sparks shakes her head and decelerates.

"Do it!" I lean up and force her hand forward, opening the throttle.

"Are you crazy?!"

She tries to pull her hand back, but she can't keep the motorcycle steady. She gives in and pushes the throttle on her own. Where there's a bridge, there's water. Hopefully. I wrap one arm tightly around her midsection and close my eyes. Yes, a river! I force the water up, freezing it into a ramp spanning most of the bridge. It'll have to do. Sparks swears and leans flush with the bike. I hug her with both arms so tightly I'm not sure she can breathe. The motorcycle darts up the ramp, wheels spinning in the air. The bike lurches as we land, but Sparks is able to keep us stable. I turn and shatter my impromptu ramp, flipping off the SUV as I do so.

"Don't you dare tell Derek," Sparks cackles.

I throw my head back laughing as she revs the engine, and we soar through the wind, feeling completely free.

❧   ❧   ❧   ❧

Derek is seething when we pull back into the parking garage hours later. Hands on his hips, he paces back and forth griping about our recklessness and blatant disregard for our safety. But his tirade dwindles as he sees how happy Sparks is as she skips into the compound, twirling me in her arms. He grumbles about her workout the next day before a soft smile replaces his scowl. I give him a knowing nod as the elevator door closes. Don't worry, I've got her.

Sparks sprawls on her couch, cradling a book in her arms. She reads slowly, still struggling with some of the larger words. It doesn't discourage her though, if anything, it drives her to consume harder material. Her lips move soundlessly as she mouths words to herself, eyebrows scrunched in persistence. I make a note to ask her what she's reading about later.

In her kitchen, I fill a soup pot with water and set it on the stove, turning on the burner. Normally, I try not to use tap water for my spells, preferring moon or rainwater, but I don't have any here so tap will have to do. I dump in some ingredients, measuring with my gut. Cinnamon sticks, cloves, apple slices. The water starts to simmer, and the aroma fills the air. A pair of hands rub my shoulders. I didn't notice Sparks set down her book.

"Whatcha cooking?" She whispers in my ear.

"It's a simmer pot." I stir the water, channeling positive vibes into the vessel. "Not meant for eating, just to... I don't know."

My voice trails off, embarrassed. I don't talk about my family's witchcraft often. It's weird and taboo, but I was raised on simmer pots and tarot cards. The arcana is in my blood, and though I don't practice as often as I should, I do believe in it.

"Hey." Sparks frowns, tucking my hair behind my ear. "You don't have to hide any part of yourself from me. Tell me about the simmer pot."

"It's a spell," I stammer. It feels so dumb when I say it out loud. "As the water evaporates, it adds energy to the air. Depending on what herbs and such you add, you can create a specific intention."

"Magic, huh?" Sparks eats a sliver of apple that was abandoned on the cutting board. "What does this spell do? Are you creating Snow White's apple?" She teases me, but there's no malice in her words, just lighthearted curiosity.

"Nothing that crazy," I chuckle, relaxing as I continue to stir with the wooden spoon. "This is a fairly basic protection spell. I was just hoping to make you feel safer in your home."

"Thank you." She twiddles with the apple core in her hands. "That's very thoughtful."

"Don't mention it." I shrug. "I know you probably don't believe in it, but I figured it wouldn't hurt."

"Actually," Sparks pauses, a confused look flashes across her face, "some things happened last year that I can't explain."

Concerned, I set the spoon down and lean on the counter, giving her my sole attention.

"Two main things I guess," she continues. "Your grandma gave me a jade necklace at Christmas. She said it would save my life or something. I was attacked on my motorcycle and crashed. When I woke up, the bead was shattered. Somehow, I survived. I don't think I was supposed to."

I didn't know Mimi gave her a talisman. Mimi must have known more about Sparks than she let on. I squeeze her thigh reassuringly.

"A different time, I saw your tarot deck in the corner." She shivers recalling the memory. "I thought it would be fun to take a card, like a game. But the card I got... that was not fun."

"Which card did you pull?" Different cards flash through my mind, which one could have scared her? Maybe the devil, or death, or judgment? No card is "bad" per se, but those names are off-putting.

"The Hanged Man." The light drains from her eyes. "It was telling me I was going to be killed."

"That's not what that card means." I blink rapidly, taken aback.

"He was being hanged." Her hand brushes her neck. "What else could it mean?"

"Oh sweetie." I pull her off the counter and into my arms. Her hair is soft as I stroke it reassuringly. I grab my phone and pull up a picture of the card to show her. "He's hanging by his foot, Sparks. This isn't an omen of death."

"Huh?" She zooms in on the picture, seeing I'm right.

"The Hanged Man can mean many things," I explain. "Most commonly, he warns you to slow down and think through your decisions. Other times he represents sacrifice or the need to let go and let the universe guide you. It helps to draw a few cards and read them as a whole."

"I still don't like it." She hands my phone back. "This water magic feels better."

"I also lean toward spells." I switch off the burner, content with how much water evaporated. "Divination is hard to understand, and the future tends to not like being controlled. Manifestation is more wholesome."

"What other spells are there?" She leans against the counter.

"Really, there's a spell for anything you want." I place the cutting board in the dishwasher after scraping off the apple remnants. "Fortune, happiness, cleansing, whatever."

"What about love spells?"

My eyes latch onto hers, reading her emotions. Lust. Passion. Desire. She shakes her hair out, arching her back.

"I suppose," I ponder aloud. "A simmer pot wouldn't be the best vessel. I would imagine an oil or ash approach would work better."

"Do it," she challenges.

Her eyes darken with need as I lean past her, rummaging through her spices. She doesn't have what I would typically use, but I find plenty of replacements. I pull a small ramekin out of the cabinet then select an orange from the fruit bowl. My hands move quickly sprinkling the dried herbs and spices into the dish. Red chili flakes, ginger, dried rosemary, basil. I smell the mixture, wafting the scent toward me. More chili and basil. I peel the skin off the orange, tossing the fruit to Sparks.

"Eat that," I command.

"Is this part of the spell?" She separates a segment of the fruit.

"Sure." I shrug. She rolls her eyes but eats the fruit just in case.

I find a matchbook and strike the stick along the starter. First try, the fire is lit. Carefully, I drop the match in the ramekin. Sparks leaves the counter to watch as the spices burn. We wait until the fire consumes it all and goes out on its own. I shake the ramekin slightly, allowing the ashes to mix and cool. I take a pinch and rub it between my fingers. Yeah, that should work.

Sparks steps out of her clothes and lays on her bed. I strip as I follow her, setting the precious ashes on her bedside table. Her breathing quickens as I straddle her, dipping my finger in the ashes.

"Are you ready?" I whisper.

"Cast a spell on me," she purrs, leaning her head back.

My finger leaves a dark streak on her abdomen as I draw the romance rune. It's shaped similar to a three-leaf flower, one petal pointing to each hip and to her sternum. The ashes are still pleasantly warm, and Sparks exhales comfortably below me.

"It's official," I croon in her ear. "You are now irresistibly in love with me."

"My turn." She wraps her legs around me and flips me to the bed. Sparks looks down at the rune decorating her ribs and tries to replicate it on my torso. She purses her lips, unsatisfied. "It's missing something."

A laugh escapes my lips as she draws hearts on the remaining canvas around my collarbones. Her thumb rubs my cheekbone as she cups my face, leaving a smudge of ash. I didn't think I could love her any more, but as the heat from the ash radiates through my skin, I know I was wrong.

"There," she whispers, eyes locked onto mine. "Perfect."

Looking back at her, I would have to agree.

CHAPTER 24

SPARKS

I was half-tempted to get that drawing tattooed across my torso, but by the time our limbs separated, it was smudged past recognition. It's okay, I have the feeling that Astrid's magic will follow me regardless.

The rest of the day passes normally, and I manage to avoid a lecture from Derek about the escapade Astrid and I had earlier. He has a private moment with Astrid. Probably something like "do that again and I'll kill you," but they seem to be on good terms after. It's weird to see them getting along.

The clocks tick on, and soon the day winds down. This is normally where Astrid would go home, sleep in her own bed, but tonight she begs to spend the night with me. She doesn't have to beg, she can stay over whenever. I hold her beneath the sheets. Astrid is so excited, she can barely fall asleep. What on earth has got her acting like this? I ignore her and turn over, drifting off.

"Happy Birthday!" She cheers, bright and early. My alarm hasn't even gone off.

"It's not my birthday," I groan, smothering myself with a pillow to block out her high-pitched squeal.

"Yes, it is!" Astrid shakes my arm. "May 23rd, right?"

"What?" I sit up quickly, checking the date on my phone.

May 23rd. It snuck up on me this year. My chest tightens.

"Happy twenty-fourth birthday!" She practically tackles me to give me a hug.

It's my birthday.

"How did you know it was my birthday?" I don't tell anyone. I don't celebrate. I haven't in eight, no, nine years.

"It was in your mother's journal," she admits. "I read a few pages before I knew who she was."

"Oh."

"I know just how to celebrate," Astrid whispers in my ear, sneaking her hand under the hem of my shirt. I jerk away.

"Maybe later," I say, hoping to ease my rejection. But I know I can't, not today.

"Okay..." Astrid tilts her head, confused by my reaction. "Later then."

"Derek's going to be waiting," I stammer, fumbling with a sports bra. "I need to get to the gym."

"You can take today off." She slides out of bed. "How do you want to celebrate?"

"Treadmill sounds nice." I can't look at her. If I stand still, she'll know. "Or maybe I'll do sprints today."

"You actually want to run?" She is bewildered. "We could go bowling, or rollerblading, or watch a movie."

"I choose running." I finish lacing my shoes. "Feel free to go back to sleep, I'll wake you after I shower."

Astrid calls after me, but I'm already jogging out the door. It's my birthday. I hate my birthday. Every year, I try to avoid it, pretend it doesn't exist. It rarely works, something always reminds me.

All of the treadmills are occupied, but the basketball court is clear. Good enough for me. I stretch my legs and loosen up. I crouch down at one end of the court.

The thoughts cut through my mind, recollections I can't drown out. Well, I can certainly try. I take off toward the other wall, touch the boundary line, and bolt back. *Again.* A memory pops up. *Again.* I can't shake them. *Again.* I relive the moment with each sprint. Down, back. The memory replays.

My shoe slips on the accumulating sweat, and I wipe out, skidding onto my side. I roll onto my knees, unhurt but unable to get up. I look toward the fluorescent lights lining the ceiling, my chest heaving from the exertion. It's my birthday. Derek takes that moment to enter the gym.

"Sparks, wash up," he calls. "I need you in the common area in fifteen."

I nod, lacing my fingers behind my head. Gradually, I stand and make my way back to my apartment. Astrid isn't there. Great, I upset her. I sigh as I dunk my head under the shower stream. She doesn't understand. It's my birthday.

Every way I can make this a normal day, I do. Same shorts, same tank, same flannel. There's nothing special about today. It's just a random day in May. Deep breath in, deep breath out. Okay, what does Derek want?

"Happy Birthday!"

Everyone jumps out as I step into the common area. Streamers and balloons are everywhere. I don't know how they decorated this quickly. A few sheet cakes line the counters. Astrid and Derek high-five as Oliver leads the group in song. It seems we have practically every member of the syndicate here. I force a smile to my face. They put so much effort into this. They don't know that my birthday is a reminder of the worst day of my life.

I blow out the candles as the group cheers. Oliver cuts the cake, passing slices around. The cake's nothing special, store bought with loopy frosting letters reading "Happy Birthday, Sparkie!" I don't know how Derek and Oliver found out, probably Astrid. Everyone's having a great time, racing each other in video games, dancing to the boombox someone brought, drinking fruit punch out of plastic cups. Everyone's having a great time but me.

While they're distracted, I sneak into the elevator, taking it up to the roof. I rummage through my book tub to find my emergency bottle of whiskey, hidden while Derek was trying to get me sober. The pouring rain soaks my hair as I sit down on the edge of the roof, unscrewing the cap and taking a long pull of the drink. I won't get drunk right now, that'll raise too many questions later, but I do need to take the edge off. I rescrew the lid, hoping the rain won't water it down too much.

Cars drive by quickly down below, windshield wipers flicking water onto the damp concrete. In the distance, there's a faint honk. I wonder if anyone else is celebrating something today, or wishing they weren't. I reach back for the bottle, my fingers seizing only empty air. Huh?

The bottle is gone. In its place is a small clear container with a single cupcake inside, set atop a photograph wrapped in a plastic film. Hesitantly, I move the cupcake aside, picking up the picture with shaky hands. It's faded, not recent by any means. Unlike the usual photos from him, this one is posed. A young woman holds a smiling child in her arms, maybe eight years old. They both wave at the camera. It's my mom and me, many years ago.

I stand quickly, scanning the area for any sign of the person who left this, but he's gone, vanished into thin air. Should I be more concerned about how he got onto the roof? Probably, but I don't really care right now. I just sit back down, staring at the happy family in the picture. A few tears slip down my cheeks, and I am thankful for the heavy rain washing them away.

"There you are!" Astrid plops down next to me. Her powers create an umbrella over us, directing the rain elsewhere. With a flick of her fingers, I am dry, tears and all. "Why'd you sneak out?"

"I just needed some air." I shrug, looking down at the street below. "Sorry, I'm not too great at this birthday thing."

"No need to apologize." She holds my hand. She looks at me, gently tilting my head towards her. I resist for a moment but let her turn my head. "Why are you crying?"

"What do you mean?" I sniffle. "It's just rain."

"What's Charlotte think—" She cuts herself off. "Oh. Oh, no."

"Yeah." I hand the photo of my mother to her. "I don't celebrate my birthdays anymore."

It was nine years ago today. Nine years ago, the explosion killed my mother. Happy birthday, me.

"I'm sorry." She passes the photo back. "I didn't realize. God, I'm so stupid."

"Don't beat yourself up over it." I shrug. "Most people tend to avoid having traumatic events on their birthdays. Besides, it's been nearly a decade now."

A decade? I realize the weight of my words as they tumble from my mouth. I try to brush off the pain, but silent sobs rack my shoulders. I lean into Astrid's chest, and she pets my hair.

"I can't remember her," I mourn. "My memories are fading. All I have left are scraps. A shadowed silhouette reading 'Physics for Babies' to me in bed. A bandage on a scraped knee. A fresh cookie from the oven. I can't even picture her face without looking at her photo."

"She knows you love her," Astrid murmurs. "That's what matters."

"My mom loved the rain." I look up at the clouds. "She would always drag me outside and dance with me in the puddles. We would dance and dance until we were soaked through, and then we would dance a bit longer."

Astrid stands and extends a hand down to me. She stops redirecting the rain, and the drops pelt my hair.

"For Holly?" She offers.

"For Mom." I accept.

I lean my head on Astrid's shoulder as the rain soaks my clothes. We slowly spin in wide circles, nothing like the frenzied movements my mom used to do, but it's all I have in me right now.

"I want my mom back." My voice cracks.

Astrid just holds me close. A few tears glide down her cheeks as well. She holds me until I can't tell where my tears end and the rain begins. And then, we danced a bit longer.

⚡   ⚡   ⚡   ⚡

The next few days pass without note. Leftover cake quickly disappears from the communal fridge. If my birthday brought any good, it's a boost in team morale. My men are noticeably happier, and I make a note to add more celebrations to the calendar. But that's something I can do later, I'm a bit busy now.

Astrid moans beneath me as my fingertips blaze a trail beneath her shirt. Her hands are woven into the strands of my hair, gently pulling my lips to hers. I suck on her bottom lip, releasing it after a quick nip. She chuckles before peppering my neck with sweet kisses. God, this woman is intoxicating. She slips a finger into my waistband-

BWAAAH! BWAAAH! BWAAAH!

I jerk away, fixing my tousled clothes.

"What's that noise?" Astrid's eyes lock onto mine.

"The panic alarm," I answer, unnerved. "We need to go."

"What's going on?" She takes my hand as I lead her out of the bedroom.

"That's what I'm trying to find out."

Derek is already at the door, composed as always.

"Unknown hostiles, maybe a hundred of them," Derek rattles off the information. "They've broken into the club. Well-armed, organized, disciplined."

"How many men are in the compound?" We stride toward the armory. Men are passing out automatic rifles as we scrutinize the security footage.

"Maybe fifteen including you two," Derek sighs. "Oliver took a bunch to go do shakedowns and audits. Worst fucking timing."

"How far away are they?" I crunch the numbers in my head. Fifteen versus a hundred is not great, even with Astrid and me here.

"Maybe forty minutes away," Derek estimates. "Other on-call staff can maybe be here in thirty."

The security feed is disheartening. Masked individuals all carry automatic weapons. They nearly fill the club upstairs. Some of them are working on the elevator shaft. If they have any skill, they can be down in minutes.

"Astrid, go grab Licorice," I order. "She has a crate in my closet. Derek, prep the evacuation route. We need to retreat. Set up a rendezvous point with Oliver and whoever you can rally with promises of overtime."

Derek nods, his lips set in a thin line. He drew the same conclusion as me, just didn't want to be the one to say it. On the feed, we see the aggressors pry open the doors to the elevator shaft. We're already out of time. One man pulls out a bullhorn. He seems to be the leader.

"We are only here for the two girls." His voice echoes down the shaft. "Turn them over and we will leave peacefully. You have five minutes."

The man holds a stopwatch up to a security camera and dramatically clicks the button. Astrid glares at the screens while Licorice meows in a crate next to her.

"They will never stop." There's no fear in Astrid's voice, just a quiet acceptance. "It doesn't matter where we run or hide, we will always be looking over our shoulders."

"I know." I've been running for nine years. It doesn't end. "But there's nothing else we can do. I won't lead my men into a massacre."

"Just us then." Her faint whispers are loud enough only for me to hear amidst the bustle of the evacuation preparation behind us. Her hand slides into mind. "I don't want to run anymore."

"We can't beat them." I squeeze her hand tightly, tears pricking my eyes.

"From now until forever?" Her eyes look into mine, a silent proposal lingers in the air.

"From now until forever."

I draw her in close, crashing my lips into hers. My hands shake as I pull away, wiping the single tear off her cheek. Deep breath in, deep breath out.

"We're ready to evacuate." Derek jogs up to us. "Let's get moving."

"Derek, can you hold onto Licorice?" I ask. "She likes you more."

"Whatever, just come on."

All of the men funnel into the escape route single-file. Their rifles are held at the ready, just in case the hostiles know of this tunnel. Derek is the last one to walk through the door before I slam it closed. Astrid slides down the metal bar lock, securing the passage from the outside. It won't keep the intruders from following them, but they're only interested in us. The bar is for Derek.

He whirls around, hearing the metal door latch into place. Rage and hurt dominate his expression. Derek pounds on the door, shouting obscenities through the glass pane. The rest of the men turn, realizing their cherished leader is on the wrong side of the barrier. They try to break through the hatch, using their fists and the butts of their guns. It doesn't matter, they can't break through. Derek made sure of that when he designed the passage. I place my hand on the glass.

"Take care of my men, Derek," I order, keeping my tone firm. "They need you now."

Astrid and I turn away, Derek's pleas falling on deaf ears. At least, I wish they were deaf. I hear every word like a knife through the heart. He keeps screaming, even as my – no, his – men drag him away.

Astrid pulls the fire alarm, flooding the common area. I turn over the tables, setting up some meager cover.

"I love you," I say, hoping it isn't the last time I'll say those words to her.

"I love you, too," she replies.

And as the bullhorn sounds, our five minutes are up.

"We are coming down," the man shouts. "Surrender and no harm will come to you."

Yeah, right.

Ropes fall down the elevator shaft, and men decked in full riot gear descend. Immediately, they raise their guns, firing off several shots for cover. I duck behind a table, but a lucky bullet nails my shoulder.

"Motherfucker!" I curse. The bullet was rubber, but a nasty bruise is already starting to form.

"Don't touch her!" Astrid is feral, flinging razor-sharp discs of water at their heads.

Some of the improvised frisbees lodge in their helmets, others go through. The decapitated men collapse in a pile of limbs.

"Fuck yeah, baby!" I cheer, flinging webs of electricity toward the survivors. More fall down the shaft, their screams stopping suddenly as they hit the bottom.

But the men keep coming. For every one that falls, three take their place. Rubber bullets keep flying, a few bouncing just right and catching Astrid or me. One hits my temple, and my head is rocked back. My eyesight blurs and I stumble to the ground. I blink rapidly, trying to clear my vision. Keep going, you have to keep fighting. But my arms are growing heavy, and they just keep coming. Astrid dives behind the kitchen counter, her position compromised by the ever-growing horde. Her eyes meet mine for just a moment, and we both know we can't hold on forever.

Desperate, Astrid surges a tidal wave, hoping to push the mass back. I electrify her current, and those in the splash zone clutch their chests as they are electrocuted. We can take them, I tell myself. Maybe together, we can be enough.

The megaphone sounds again. All at once, the men pull down their hoods revealing hidden gas masks. Before we can worry about what that means for us, the room goes black. They cut the electricity to the building. I grasp at the retreating power frantically, flinging the last of my reserves into the lights above, hoping Astrid can see just enough to do something. But the flickering lights only add to our horror as canisters fly through the air, spreading a hazy fog in their path. The air burns my lungs. I can't breathe. I can't breathe!

Astrid's voice cries my name. No, don't get taken alive! Keep fighting! But I know it's no use as four hands grab onto my arms and drag me toward the elevator.

CHAPTER 25

ASTRID

... I'm alive?

Oh god, I'm alive!

Oh god... I'm alive.

Five senses, Astrid. You can do this. Pretend you're unconscious and figure out where you are.

Taste. My tongue feels swollen and dry in my mouth. I couldn't taste anything if I wanted to, but I am so thirsty. Goodness, I would do anything for a glass of water right now. My stomach growls angrily. How long have I been out?

Focus. Taste was useless as always. Smell. Uck, sweat. I reek and am in desperate need of a shower. Two senses down, but I have the best three left.

Touch. Smooth, cold metal. My neck is hunched in an unnatural angle, my limbs sprawled at my sides. One of my legs is curled underneath me while the other is bent to fit. There is not enough room to lay down fully. I can touch all four walls from the position I was dumped, sprawled carelessly without a second thought. Good news though, I'm not restrained. Despite that, my joints ache from the cramped and awkward confinement. Other parts throb and I remember the rubber bullets ricocheting into my body. I'm sure I have a few nasty bruises.

Sound. The wind is roaring outside. I think there might also be some birds, but they are faint in the distance. No engines, no cars, no voices. Wait, that's wrong. I hear someone groaning nearby. Sparks!

"Sparks!" I jerk awake, disregarding the five senses strategy. Is she okay? Where is she? "Sparks!"

It looks like I'm in something similar to a shipping crate, about one step wide and one stride long. My shoulders nearly brush the narrow walls, but I could probably sit comfortably enough if I wanted. The box is tall enough that I can't reach the ceiling. All four walls are smooth, except for a covered slot on the door. I push on the door and find it bolted shut from the outside. Holes are drilled near the top of the crate. I'm glad they made air holes, they must not plan on killing us right away. Oh god, what are they going to do to us?

"I'm here." Her voice is strained, coming from outside of my room. "Are you okay?"

"I could use a shower," I say. "You?"

"I have a crick in my neck something awful," she jokes dryly. "But I suppose I'll live." Her voice cracks at the last word as she comes to the same concern as me.

I hug my arms to my chest, hissing as I brush the already-developed bruises on my shoulders. The white lace of my tank top is a stark contrast to the deep purple hues. My stomach growls angrily, a sharp pain amidst the aches I feel everywhere else.

"Good morning, ladies!" A male voice calls. I hear him clap his hands together excitedly as a cacophony of footsteps sound in the room outside my crate. "Who's ready to have some fun? What about the redhead?"

A hand knocks against metal. I see a bright light flash through the air holes and hear a spew of profanity. Finally, I smell something helpful. Burned flesh.

"You fucking bitch!" The man is in pain. Good job, Sparks. "You'll regret that."

The footsteps recede quickly. I chuckle at our little victory.

"Who was the genius that put Sparks in a metal box?" I ask aloud, hoping to get a laugh out of her. She doesn't.

"That trick will only work once." Her voice is calm, but I can sense the layer of fear below. "They'll figure it out when they realize their phone batteries are dead..."

"Well..." I pause. "It was worth it."

"We'll see."

We sit in an uncomfortable silence for several minutes until the footsteps come back. I can almost hear Sparks hold her breath. Or maybe that was me.

"Now it's time to play."

His boots stomp across wooden floors.

Thud. Thud. Thud.

"Who wants to play with me?"

Thud. Thud. Thud.

"I think she needs a time out, so it would have to be..."

Thud. Thud. Thud.

"You."

Metal clangs as the braces against my crate disengage and the door swings open. I am on my feet, cowering against the back corner.

"Don't touch her!" I hear Sparks roar, fists banging on her container. "I'll fucking kill you!"

He grins at me, malice flickering in his eyes. He lifts two fingers, beckoning me out. I shake my head, clinging to the wall.

"Grab her," he orders coldly.

A second man strides into the box. He lunges for my arm, but I push myself off the wall to jump over him. I dart out of the crate, but two other men were waiting for me, catching me in their arms.

"No, no, no!" I struggle in their grasp. "Let me go!"

A fist comes out of nowhere, connecting with my cheek. I fall to the side, slamming into the metal door. Blood drips from a cut on my eyebrow. A knee pushes into my spine as my hands are wrenched behind my back, handcuffs cinched too tightly.

"Astrid!" Sparks desperately calls out. "Take me instead! Please!"

"You'll get your chance," the man croons cruelly. "Perhaps now is a good time to hear the rules?"

Strong arms hoist me to my knees as my blood splatters on the wooden planks below. The man in front of me looks down at me, glancing at my cleavage revealed by my shirt. Disgusted, I spit at his feet. In a flash, his bandaged hand grips my jaw, inches away from his face.

"You would do well to remember who is in control here." He spits back at me, his saliva coating my cheek. He points at Sparks's crate. "The only reason your girlfriend is alive is because I allow her to be."

He takes a step back, still looking at me but speaking to the both of us.

"The rules are simple." His voice sends a shiver down my spine. "Fight back, and I kill the other. Use your powers without explicit permission, and I kill the other. Try to escape, and I kill the other. In essence, do as we say and maybe you two will live long enough to serve our purpose. To prove I mean business..."

He gestures and the other men drag me across the floor into another room. I writhe in their grasp, but their grip is too strong.

"Wait, Astrid!" Sparks's voice is panicked, any of her usual calm demeanor is long dissipated. "What are you doing with her?"

His only answer is a long, drawn-out cackle. The color drains from my face as he slams the door behind him, muffling Sparks's distraught cries. This room is the same as the one we left, thick wooden slabs comprise the floor and walls. A large door stands behind him, taunting me. He follows my gaze and chuckles.

"Already thinking about breaking a rule?" He places a finger under my chin, directing my eyes to him. "I would hate to kill your girlfriend so quickly. I haven't even gotten to play with her yet."

"No," I whisper, shaking my head. My breath comes in shallow pants as he glares down at me.

"Shame." He purses his lips. "I guess for now, I'll just play with you."

His boot thrusts out. I keel over as it connects with my stomach. The men drop me, but he keeps kicking. I pull at my restraints, unable to defend myself as his blows land on my ribs and torso. He spits down on me as he walks away, sobs racking my shoulders. Every breath expands my chest, sending a spasm through my body as my muscles protest the abuse.

"Cry louder," the man taunts. "Scream a little. She can't hear you in there."

No. I won't let him use me to hurt Sparks.

I take a deep breath and force my tears to fall silently. This enrages him. He gestures to the two men, and they lift me to my feet, holding me steady as my legs give out. The man swings his fist, sending an uppercut into my jaw. My head whips back. I roll it around my shoulders, letting it slump on my chest. He hits me again. I groan but hold back the rest of my sounds. My thoughts swim slowly, intermixing with each other and becoming muddled. I exhale, relaxing completely until I am limp in their arms.

"No!" The man complains grouchily. "You need to make this fun."

"Way to go, Chadwick," a new voice mocks. "You couldn't even get a single scream out of her."

I didn't see the fifth man earlier. He's reclined on a folding chair, as if my beatings were a basketball rerun. His blue baseball cap is pulled low over his face. I get the feeling that I've seen him before, but that could just be my oncoming concussion.

"You could help." Chadwick grinds his teeth. "I don't see you doing anything."

"I'm supervising." The man shrugs his shoulders, unbothered. "Don't say you need me to do your job for you? I didn't know you needed help to beat up a defenseless girl."

"Fuck off." Resentment flashes in Chadwick's eyes. His nostrils flare as he grips my jaw, lifting my head. I scrunch my eyes closed, bracing for another blow.

"Chadwick, that's not going to work," the mystery man sighs. "You've already tried that, remember?"

"What the fuck would you recommend?" Chadwick steps away and his men drop me unceremoniously onto the floor.

"Easy, you need a sharper pain." The man says this as though it was obvious. "One she can't dissociate."

"Like?"

"How ironic would it be..." his lips curl up into a sneer, "if we torture her using the symbol of her girlfriend? It should be the one thing that she should be safe from, but her girlfriend is too far away to protect her. Her girlfriend will hear the screams, knowing that in this moment, she was powerless to prevent them."

"What?"

Chadwick isn't following, but I am. I scoot back against the wall, fear taking over my body. The mystery man stands, tossing an object to Chadwick. I yelp as he grabs me by the hair, dragging me toward the metal chair. I struggle, clawing desperately at his hand.

"No!" My pleas fall on deaf ears. "Please, no! Stop!"

A second pair of cuffs constrain me to the chair despite my flailing body. Chadwick powers on the stun gun, smiling as it crackles. The two prongs light up as sparks dance between them. I lean away, but I can't do anything as it comes into contact with my skin.

Chadwick gets what he wants as screams are ripped from my throat. Spasms ripple through my body. The pain cuts through every single nerve ending, dissecting me to my core with piercing agony. The current rips through me until darkness tinges the edge of my vision. Then, and only then, does Chadwick pull away.

My pulse races as Chadwick laughs maniacally. He's enjoying this, relishing in my torment. I squirm despairingly as he fixes his gaze on me once again. His hand wraps around my throat, forcing me to stare into his dilated pupils.

"Cry out for her," he jeers. "Beg her to make it stop."

I know I shouldn't. I know it will only hurt her. I know she can't do anything, can't save me now. But I can't help it.

"Sparks, help me!" My shrieks carry into the next room. I'm vaguely aware of her wails in response, but I'm more focused on the weapon diving back toward me. "Please Sparks, I can't—"

My cries are interrupted as the stun gun returns. My thoughts unravel, unable to form words, I just scream. Shrill. Bloodcurdling. Agonizing. Screams.

With a puff of smoke, the stun gun surges, burning my arm as a bright flash lights up the room. As quickly as the surge came, it was gone, and when it went, so did the pain. My head sags as Chadwick hits the stun gun with his palm.

"Why won't you work?" He curses. His men take a step away from the far room, connecting the dots. The mystery man only chuckles. Frustrated, Chadwick throws the stun gun to the floor.

"Take her back," he seethes. "We're done for today."

The men unlock my cuffs, dragging me back to my crate. I don't struggle. I can't. I don't bother to catch myself as they toss me into the box, allowing the cool metal to soothe my aching wounds. Sparks calls to me from across the way, but I can't find the air to respond.

The slat in my door opens, and a bread roll, a hunk of jerky, and a spoiled slice of watermelon fall to the floor. I weakly crawl over, sucking the water from the fruit. It does little to soothe my parched lips. The stale bread scratches my throat as I force myself to swallow.

"Astrid, please," Sparks cries. "Just say something so I know you're alive. Please."

"I'm here." I worry that my hoarse whisper wasn't heard, but then I hear her relieved sobs.

"I'm so sorry." Her voice cracks. "I shouldn't have shocked them. This is all my fault."

"They were looking for a reason." I try to be rational. I try to be strong. "He would have hurt one of us either way."

"Astrid, you can't give up," she pleads. "No matter what, okay? You have to keep fighting. Promise me you won't let them break you."

I curl myself into a tight ball. Would she be ashamed to find that cracks already line my psyche? I'm not strong like she is. I'm not cold, or tough, or brazen. I'm small, and weak, and quiet. I can't do this.

As if she could hear my inner thoughts, Sparks whispers sweet nothings through the air. Her encouragement only deepens the rift in my soul. She's all I have, but I'm not enough to help her.

I knock three times on the wall. *I love you.* Three knocks echo back. *I love you too.*

CHAPTER 26

SPARKS

Astrid won't speak to me the rest of the day. At least, I think it was a day. Food was tossed through the slot in my door a few times – stale bread, meat, and spoiled fruit. She tries to muffle her cries, but I still hear them. Every sob feels like a knife to my heart. It's as if I could feel her breaking.

I should have killed her. I thought about it. I had the power of the stun gun in my grasp, but I let it dissipate. It was cruel of me. She deserves a quick death, instead of whatever torture lies ahead.

I should have killed her.

But I didn't.

I hear her cries, whether it's from the pain of her body or mind, I can't tell. There's nothing I can do to help. I want to hold her in my arms, wipe her cheeks, leave sweet kisses on her forehead.

Instead, I tell her stories, trying to distract her from our terrible situation. I ramble about my childhood, growing up along the East Coast, what she missed during our break-up. I make up tall tales of dragons and princesses and dwarves. They always end happily, with two women getting married and living together for the rest of their lives. They dance through meadows and bottle the sunshine to release on rainy days.

Does Astrid listen? I can't say. But when my rasping voice trails off, tired from talking for hours on end, I hear three knocks. She doesn't have to say anything for me to know what it means. I return the sound – *knock, knock, knock.*

But the footsteps come back. I hear Astrid whimper, scurrying to the back of her crate. I stand, fists clenched at my side.

"What a lovely day to play with my two favorite girls," Chadwick gloats. I can almost hear his smirk. I'm going to knock it off his face.

"Chadwick, it's my turn to play," I goad. If I had the choice, he'd take me instead of her every day. I can take it. I will take it. But it's not my choice, so I hold my breath, praying he knocks on my door. "Come on, I want to have some fun."

The lock on my door releases, and I exhale, thankful for this small blessing. Astrid is safe, at least for now. Chadwick stands in the entrance to my cell, eyeing me eagerly. Something in his gaze is unsettling, but I will not break. I toss my hair over my shoulder and stride out. Two men stand next to the exit. They grab at me, but I duck under their arms, darting toward Chadwick. My fist connects with his face, and his nose makes a satisfying crunch. I throw my head back laughing as his henchmen force me to my knees, handcuffing my wrists behind my back.

"Man, I love this game," I taunt, shooting daggers toward Chadwick. Beautiful red liquid drips down his chin.

"Be careful," he seethes. "Or you'll get your girlfriend killed."

"You see, I had a lot of time to think about that." The men haul me to my feet, but I resist as they drag me toward the second room. "You're full of shit."

"Yeah?" Chadwick's gaze darkens. "How so?"

"You can't kill her, because if you do, you'll have no leverage over me." My words whip out threateningly. "And there will be nothing stopping me from killing you."

"Interesting theory." He muses, pacing as the door shuts behind him. "My question to you is, are you willing to be wrong?"

"I'm not wrong." I try to steady my voice, but he's called my bluff. My mask slips. Only for a millisecond, but enough for him to see what he needs. Chadwick stalks toward me, gripping my chin in his hands.

"How about this?" He chuckles, deviously. "If you can go the whole game without screaming, I won't kill her."

I clench my jaw, eyes staring a hole in his forehead where I wished a bullet would appear.

"I'm going to enjoy killing her in front of you," he whispers, leaning in close. "Slowly and painfully. Maybe today, maybe tomorrow, but rest assured, I'll be the one holding the knife."

Red clouds my vision. I rear back and heave my head into his. Chadwick falls to the ground as his nose breaks again. I blink rapidly as my head aches. Worth it.

"Chadwick, stand down." I know that voice. I whirl around to face him. My ballcap covers his face. My stalker. I suppose I always knew he was connected to this organization, but it's unsettling to have it confirmed.

"This bitch needs to learn her place," he bites. "And I'm all too happy to teach her. Take off her shirt."

The third goon rips off my tank top, leaving me kneeling in my bra. I squirm in their clutches as Chadwick plucks a whip off the wall and walks behind me. I hear the crack as it flies through the air before it tears at the skin of my back. I bite my lip, holding back my scream. I breathe deeply and close my eyes. You can take this. You've been through worse. *Crack!* I stifle a groan. Blood drips down my back from the lacerations.

"Chadwick, stop!" My stalker stands, the chair he was sitting on skids on the ground. "Chadwick!"

Crack! I can take this. I can take this.

Crack! I've been through worse. I've been through—

Bang!

Blood splatters on the ground. Astrid screams in the other room. Chadwick crumples to the ground, a hole directly in the center of his forehead. The other three men turn to the stalker horrified, his gun outstretched.

Bang! Bang! Bang!

Their bodies fall to the floor behind me, their blood soaking into the wooden planks. My stalker watches me as I shakily rise to my feet.

"Time to head out." He reholsters his gun. "Reinforcements will be here shortly. No way they didn't hear the gunshots."

"We need to get Astrid." I fumble with the doorknob behind my back. "Fuck, I can't get it. Help me!"

"Come here, Charlotte." He extends a hand patiently. "I have someplace where you'll be safe."

"Not without Astrid!" I slam my shoulder into the door. I can't get in. Astrid is wailing in the other room. She doesn't know, she doesn't know I'm okay. "Astrid! Astrid, I'm—"

"It's okay, Charlotte," he shushes me, as a cloth muffles my cries. "I'll take care of you."

No! Astrid! I struggle in his arms, but he's stronger than me and my hands are of no use behind my back. The cloth smells funny, like almonds. My eyelids feel heavy. My stalker carries me through the exit, stopping in front of an old pickup. He gently lays me into the passenger seat and buckles me in. My head hangs limply, and he leans it back against the headrest, leaving a kiss on my forehead. He brushes my hair from my face and our eyes meet.

His eyes.

I know those eyes. I've seen them before, twice. Once at the gala, as we danced to upbeat jazz music. Again, when my bike got a flat out of nowhere. The one man I picked out of the crowd was my stalker.

FRAGMENT 5

I've done it. Finally. She's mine.

She breathes softly in the seat next to me. My hand rests solidly on her thigh, afraid that if I let go for a second then she will disappear, as if she's only a figment of my imagination. I squeeze her firmly, she's really there.

A small amount of crimson is smeared between her back and the car seat. Killing Chadwick was the second best moment of my life, behind the moment I first laid eyes on her. Well, I guess now third. Behind every moment spent with her, touching her body, breathing the same air.

It will take her time to get over her girlfriend. I understand. She'll be sad at first, but soon, she'll see that I can cherish her, protect her, love her. Deep down inside, she already loves me, she just doesn't know it yet.

Charlotte stirs and I pull her against my chest, holding the chloroform rag against her mouth. She settles back down, and I kiss her hair. She'll wake up when we get to the safehouse. When we can start a new life together.

I've done it. She's mine.

CHAPTER 27

SPARKS

Click. Click. Click.

Lethargy weighs on my limbs. Am I back in my crate? No, I'm not in some contorted position, stuffed inside a box with no regard. Actually, I'm comfortable. A soft mattress supports my stiff back, and I seem to have been laid down with care, ensuring the pillow fits my neck.

Click. Click. Click.

There's that sound again. The all-too-familiar camera shutter. Wait, the stalker. Astrid! I force my way through the heavy fatigue to open up my eyes. Logs line the walls and ceiling. The cabin is sparsely furnished, but still feels homey, with a stack of quilts in the corner. There are plenty of windows to let in natural light, but thick bars cross the panes.

As I examine the room further, I determine that the sheer number of windows are necessary due to the lack of electricity in the cabin. No outlets, no lightbulbs, nothing. My stalker stands in the corner, camera in hand. It's amazing how even in this well-lit room, he can blend into the shadows. My breath catches in my chest as the shutter clicks, capturing more photos.

"Welcome home." He lowers the camera and smiles genuinely. My brain spins, trying to think of something to say amidst the fog clinging to my mind.

"Thank you." I sit up slowly, suspicious of his intentions.

A long evening gown is tangled around my legs. Dark green, halter neck, backless. This is the dress I wore to the gala. Strappy high heels, painted nails, and I can feel a light coat of makeup on my face.

"It's you," I state dumbly. How the fuck did I miss this?

"It's me," he chuckles, holding out his hands. "My name is Hudson. I'm sorry it took so long to whisk you away, but we're together now. Just you and me."

"Hudson," I repeat. The name feels eerie on my tongue, but he lights up as I say it.

"How long was I out?" I stammer.

"Not too long." He sits on the bed next to me and tucks a loose curl behind my ear. "Just long enough for me to get you home, make sure you were safe."

"And Astrid?" I ask quietly, equally scared of his reaction and his answer. "Is she safe?"

"Yes." He brushes a thumb over my cheek. "She's with Derek and Licorice."

I don't trust him, but I don't see another option. Fuck, he knows the name of my cat! Maybe Astrid is safe. Maybe I can trust him. But I stare into his eyes, and I can tell. He's lying. Astrid's still in danger.

"Can I kiss you, Charlotte?"

He doesn't wait for an answer, softly brushing his lips against mine. He pulls me in deeper, moaning quietly. I panic. Do I resist and push him away? Or do I play along?

I close my eyes and cup his cheek in my hand, trying to push down the feeling of betraying Astrid. I'm doing this for her. I'll be back for her. I promise. I lean in closer, but he breaks the kiss, panting happily.

"Not yet, darling." He stands and holds up the camera. "We don't want to smudge your lipstick yet. Now, smile for me."

I flinch as the camera goes off, holding up my hands to shield my face from the lens. Hudson lowers the camera and tilts his head confused. I blink rapidly and shake my hands out.

"Sorry," I stutter. "I wasn't ready."

Breathe, Sparks. Astrid needs you. I roll back my shoulders and smile, staring into the lens. I force myself to remain still as Hudson circles me, searching for the best angle. His camera clicks the whole time, taking photo after photo. Suddenly, he pulls away.

"Dammit, I almost forgot!"

He speedwalks into the other room. I hesitantly slide off the bed, following him through the doorway into the main room of the cabin. A sofa and a few recliners are curved around a crackling fireplace. There's a dining table set with fresh flowers near the basic kitchen. There's a door in the corner. I think about running, but there's no way I could get past him and escape in these heels. Patience, Sparks.

Hudson fumbles through a desk. Inside the drawer, hundreds of photos are stacked neatly. Next to those, I recognize several items I was hoping I just misplaced – ponytails, sunglasses, lip gloss, a pair of underwear. Oh god. I turn away, trying to hide the wave of nausea that overtakes me. Hudson spins me back to him, excitement plastered on his face. He places a small box in my hands and gestures for me to open it. I hesitantly remove the lid to reveal a pair of silver earrings.

"You never wear jewelry," he states. "I wanted to get you something pretty. Let me help you put them on."

My hands shake as his fingers graze my ear. There's a reason I never wear earrings. Having metal inside of my body disrupts my electrical flow, crippling my powers. Jack used this against me before, once with the barbed cuffs, but first with a pair of earrings. Since then, I haven't worn a single piece of jewelry, traumatized by the feeling of helplessness. There isn't any electricity here to redirect, but the earrings rub salt into the wound. Does Hudson know about this weakness, or are these genuinely a gift? I shiver at the thought, though Hudson interprets that as a sign of gratitude.

"I knew you'd love them." He leads me to the sofa in front of the fireplace. "Now recline on the couch. This will make such a dramatic shot."

I rub my wrists as I lay on the couch. Hudson adjusts my body, tilting my head and repositioning my arms. It's hard to breathe under his scrutiny, his piercing eyes taking stock of every detail. Fixing my smudged lipstick, moving a stray curl, shifting the skirt of my dress so the slit falls on either side of my thigh. I force myself to lay still, though every part of me wants to cover up, hide from his all-seeing eyes. When he's satisfied, he steps back. Coaching me as he looks through the viewfinder. Look slightly higher. Don't forget to breathe. Part my lips slightly.

"Your expression right now is indescribable," Hudson murmurs passionately. "Glossy eyes with a far-away stare. These are going to look so dramatic when they're printed."

I hold my pose, staring into space. Every photo cuts at my shield. Shallow paper cuts atop each other, scoring deeper and deeper. There must be hundreds by now. I am helpless, on display for him. I draw a shaky breath as a single tear falls. He oohs and ahhs, kneeling to catch the perfect shot, oblivious that this pain isn't posed.

"Let's take a quick break," Hudson suggests after a while. "We'll take more photos in a bit, but there's something I want to do before we change outfits."

More photos? I shudder at the thought, nonetheless I'm thankful for my small reprieve. A small boombox in the corner croons a slow jazz ballad. I know what he wants. I can be who he wants me to be.

"Dance with me." I steel my reserve and look at him through my eyelashes, putting on my sultry mask.

"Absolutely." Hudson sets down the camera and pulls me to my feet, spinning me in his arms. He pulls me close, our bodies flush together. His thumb wipes the stray tear from my cheek.

"I love this song," I lie. My fingers curl into his hair as we start to sway. He takes the lead, guiding me across the floor.

"I love you," he says, staring deeply into my eyes.

"You can't one-up me like that," I banter. Don't make me say it back. Please don't make me. "That's not fair."

"Well, it's true." Hudson's voice is a mere whisper. "I love you, Charlotte."

Time slows as my eyes scan his face. He's waiting. I know my line, but my breath catches in my chest. I can't say it. A beat passes, then another. His eyebrows scrunch together, I've waited too long. I need to do something.

My lips crash into his. The momentum of our spinning causes me to stumble, but his arms securely hold me against his chest. I hitch my leg against his hips, the slit allowing the skirt to fall free. His hand slides against my bare skin, creeping higher on my thigh.

My chest is heaving when he pulls away. He eyes me greedily and I can feel his bulge in his pants. I can do this.

I've done it before. He steps away and shrugs off his suit jacket, tossing it on the sofa.

"I think it's time for the second photo session." His fingers graze my back, and my dress falls to the ground. I shiver when I realize that I wasn't wearing a bra under the dress. "Lay down in front of the fireplace, keep the heels on."

The wood is warm beneath my bare skin. The fire's heat soon causes a thin sheen of sweat to glisten on my body. Hudson returns a second later, camera in hand.

"Take off your panties," he orders, lust obscuring his features. "I want you to be completely bare to me."

My hands shake as I remove the last scrap of fabric. Hudson extends a hand, and I give him my panties. He shoves them into his pocket quickly, eager to start shooting.

"How do you want me posed?" I force my shoulders back, not allowing myself to cover my body with my hands, no matter how much his gaze makes my skin crawl.

"I don't want you posed." The timbre of his voice has lowered dramatically. "I want to capture you in pure, authentic bliss. No coaching, no direction, just you pleasuring yourself."

"What?" I can't breathe. Surely he's not serious. Masturbating on film?

"Lay back, Charlotte," he prods. "You know what you like. Show me."

The soft jazz continues to fill the room. The fireplace crackles next to me. I can do this. My hands glide over my ribs, cupping my breasts. I bite my lip as I close my eyes, feeling my thumbs roll over my exposed nipples. Exposed. *Click.* He's watching. *Click.* He's always watching. *Click.* My muscles tense and my pulse races, not from arousal but from fear. I'm vulnerable, every inch of skin on display for his pleasure. My touch is sickening, my body shrinks away from my fingers.

"Come on, Charlotte." He's upset by my performance. Disappointed. Frustrated. His arousal is fading. "You can do better than that."

This isn't working. Something needs to change.

"I have an idea," I say, sitting up. "Can you please pass me your suit jacket?"

Hudson raises an eyebrow, his curiosity piqued. He silently drapes the jacket over my shoulders, and I lay back down. Does the jacket actually cover anything? Not really, no. But the illusion is enough. He can't see me. It's just me and my hands. The camera clicks fade to the background as my fingertips dance along my skin.

My eyes roll into the back of my head, and in my mind, it's not my hands touching my body, it's hers. Astrid's fingernails gently scraping my sides, her fingertips skimming my thighs, crawling between my legs. I can picture her blue eyes looking up at me, her sensual whispers teasing me as she does. I arch my back, moaning as she touches me exactly where I want her to.

"Say my name," Hudson interjects, his voice strained and desperate. "I need to hear you say it."

"Hudson," I groan breathily. I disassociate, the name dissolves into a series of meaningless syllables. Astrid's hands move faster, confident and experienced. I say it again and again, tilting my head back, eyelids fluttering.

His body nestles between my legs as I hear the camera click for the final time. He sets it aside as he pushes my hands away.

"I've got it from here, love," he purrs.

My legs are hoisted around his bare back. His calloused hands caress my breasts, rolling my nipples between his fingers. I scrunch my eyes closed as he lines up with my entrance, gradually sliding inside. He moves slowly, giving my muscles time to stretch and adjust to the intrusion.

Suddenly, Astrid is laying on top of me, and I am back in that river.

Close your eyes, she whispers, brushing the hair out of my face. I relax in her embrace, knowing I am safe in her arms. *Promise me, you'll keep your eyes closed.*

The image in my mind flickers as his hand brushes against my clit, replicating the circles I made earlier. No, not his hand. That's Astrid's hand. His length fills me as he gradually thrusts faster, focused on his pleasure.

Astrid. I cling to the picture of her in my mind. It's not him, it's Astrid. Just for a little while longer, I need to pretend it's her. But the illusion crumbles the closer he gets to climax.

Keep your eyes closed, she soothes. *It's okay. You're okay.*

"Look at me when you come," he croons sultrily. His touch is tender, as though he thinks I want this. "Charlotte, look at me."

My eyes open, locking onto his hazel ones. They're full of passion, desire, lust. His gaze traps me. I know what he wants. I can give it to him.

"Hudson!" I cry, pretending to tumble over the edge.

"Oh fuck, Charlotte!" He slams a fist on the floor as he unravels, his tired pants tingling my ear. I scrunch my eyes closed, already trying to forget what just happened to me. Hudson lays next to me, staring at the ceiling as he comes down.

Astrid is gone. I don't know where she is, I don't know where I am. I'm low on options, subject to the whims of Hudson's obsession.

But Hudson, he's unpredictable. His infatuation drove him rogue, to kill his companions to secure me in his grasp. His fixation could be the death of me. But for now, I know what he wants.

Hudson stands and carries me to the bedroom, setting me gently on the mattress. He rifles through a chest of drawers to pull out a pair of boxers for him, and a nightdress with matching panties for me. I slide the slinky fabric over my curves, not feeling as concealed as I would like. Hudson slides under the covers, pulling my body snuggly against his. His hand draws imaginary lines down my arm, leaving goosebumps in his wake. We cuddle until his breathing slows and Hudson falls asleep.

But I'm wide awake, mind moving a mile a minute. I need to escape. I need to find Astrid.

I slip out of his arms, padding across the floor. The crackling of the fireplace has died down, embers barely glowing from the ashes. I stumble blindly toward the door, the starlight not enough to see the path clearly. I find the door, slowly turning the knob. The door doesn't budge. My fingers run along the frame, searching for a lock I missed. Come on, come on! Why won't it open?! A pair of arms wrap around me, pinning my arms to my torso.

"Hudson," I stammer, my breathing rapid and startled. "I'm sorry. It's not what it looks like. I—"

"Shh," Hudson cuts me off. He turns me to face his silhouette in the dark and strokes my face. "It's okay. I knew the transition would be tough on you."

"I'm sorry." I lean into his embrace, and he cradles me in his arms.

"You're safe here, Charlotte."

I cry as his lies echo through the room, my tears dampening his shoulder.

"I knew you would try to run away," he whispers, his voice cracking. "I knew that you wouldn't understand right away. I just didn't expect it to hurt this much."

Hudson picks me up, carrying me back through the dark to the bed. He lights a candle, providing just enough light for him to rummage through the dresser again. He pulls out a chain and secures it around the thick wooden frame of the bed. The other end clamps around my ankle. He retakes his earlier position in the bed, snaking an arm tightly around my waist.

I sob in defeat, knowing that there's no escape, that Astrid is out there somewhere, and I can't help her. The candle is just bright enough for me to see Hudson's face, and in the flickering light, I'm shocked to see that he's crying too.

CHAPTER 28
ASTRID

Sparks never returned after the gunshots. Four of them in quick succession. She cried out my name, desperately pleading for me to do something, anything.

I tried.

I threw my shoulder into the door, clawed at the rivets until my fingernails bled, banged against the walls constricting me. I was trapped, but I tried, oh, I tried.

I failed. I couldn't save her. Food fell through the slat of my door what felt like several hours later, but I couldn't touch it. Was Sparks... was she... dead? I sat in the back of my crate, hugging my arms to my chest. Her screams echoed through my mind on repeat, endlessly swallowing any hope I had of her survival. I lost her.

Food falls through the slot, joining my discards from yesterday. Another stale roll, some dried meat, and spoiled fruit – this one seems to be a cantaloupe. But no water, never any water. My throat is parched, whether it's from the lack of water or from my unceasing howls, I don't know. I don't care.

I huddle in the corner, my grief all-consuming. I barely notice the ache of my ribs, bruised from the beating. It doesn't matter. Nothing matters without her.

She wanted to run, flee to San Francisco. She begged me, pleaded on her knees, went so far as to step onto the train. But she got off. God, why did I let her get off? This is my fault. I forced her to go to Synergy Labs with me. I insisted on attending the gala. I didn't take her warnings seriously, but she's the one who paid the price.

Footsteps thud on the wooden planks. They killed her. They killed Sparks. I had just gotten her back, and they took her from me.

The door opens and I leap out, tackling the man who had the misfortune of standing in the front. I claw at this face, but the other men drag me off before I can wrap my hands around his throat.

"You killed her!" I scream, thrashing like a feral animal. "How could you? You fucking monsters, I'll kill you for this. I'll kill you all!"

They ignore my threats, cuffing my hands behind my back and hauling me into the second room. The room where they killed her. The door opens, and I am spurred out of my murderous rage by the blood.

God, there's so much blood. On the floor, the walls, the ceiling. The dried crimson stained the floor where it pooled after flowing out of her body. How is there so much blood?

"No, no, no!" I fall to my knees, tears streaming down my face.

What did they do to her? She didn't scream, not until after the gunshots. How did they do this to her without me hearing her cries? I know, deep in my heart, that she forced herself to be quiet, trying to spare me from the torment of listening to her die. It must have infuriated Chadwick. He's not here. Probably off torturing other victims.

Heels click on the floor. I whirl around to see the lady from the gala walking into the room, unbothered by the gore coating the room. Marissa.

"You killed her!" I struggle in my restraints, wanting desperately to lash out at the bitch responsible. "You killed Sparks!"

"No. We didn't." Marissa straightens out her pantsuit, not even bothering with her plastic facade. She knows she won.

"Yes, you did!" I screech. "I heard her! I heard the gunshots!"

"What else did you hear?" She looks up at me, staring intently into my eyes. I don't want her fake interest. Instead I hang my head, wailing heartbrokenly.

"There's so much blood." I don't know if she can understand me as the sobs rack my body. It doesn't matter. Sparks is dead.

"Relax, sweetie," Marissa says pretentiously. "It's not all hers. Besides, she's still alive." My head whips up, my eyes glaring into hers. "We just moved her to a more secure facility. She's quite a handful you know."

I don't say anything for a moment, I just stare at her. I can't read her neutral expression. She could be lying, she could be telling the truth. I have no way of knowing.

"Prove it," I snarl, disdain dripping from my voice.

"Oh, Astrid." She crouches next to me, condescendingly. She runs a finger along my jaw. "I don't have to. You're in no position to make any demands."

I hope she gets blood on her precious pantsuit. I hope the blood is hers.

"Now, let's start today's lesson."

At her words, every man in the room pulls out a gun and points it directly at my head. I flinch as Marissa takes a plastic cup of water and flings it at my face. The liquid drips from my eyelashes onto the wooden planks below.

"Make me a sphere the size of a marble," Marissa orders. "Use your powers."

What? That's easy. I gather the water into an orb. It hovers a few inches off the floor. Marissa tuts and shakes her head. Out of nowhere, a foot connects with my ribs. My prior injuries flare, and I cry out as the water splashes back to the floorboards. A hand yanks on my hair, forcing me to look at Marissa.

"That was a golf ball," she taunts. "I said marble. Again."

I hesitantly reach out again, forming a smaller sphere. It doesn't pass. A fist connects with my lower jaw, and I spit the blood from my mouth onto the floor.

"If I wanted a blueberry, I'd ask for it!" She seethes. "Marble! Now!"

I struggle to hold the next orb still, shaking as I avert my eyes, bracing for the inevitable fail I would receive. Too big. Too small. Too round. Not round enough. Eventually, Marissa becomes bored with her game and deems one of my spheres to be close enough. My shoulders droop and I hang limply from the two men holding me on my knees. They shrug and let go, and I fall to the ground, the blood from my split skin mixing with what might be Sparks's.

"Take her back to her cell." Marissa saunters away, her heels clicking on the wood as she goes.

I curl into a ball, sobbing as more food is shoved through the slot. I know I need to eat. My options are limited when I'm malnourished and weak. But... I'm already weak. Sparks made me promise to not let them break me, to keep fighting.

Sparks is gone.

Maybe alive. Maybe dead. Maybe escaped. I hope she's halfway to San Francisco by now. I hope she rides the trolley and looks out at the ocean, thinking of me from time to time. I hope she gets the chance to heal, let her guard down, allow joy and happiness a place in her life. But that's a pipe dream because there's no way she made it out alive. She's dead, and I'm alone. I wish I was there to hold her, stroke her hair as she closed her eyes for the last time.

I hate myself for this, but selfishly, I wish she were still alive, back here with me. I wish she was here to tell me to be strong, even if I ignore her. I wish she was telling me stories about princesses who bottle up sunshine. I wish she were here. I reach my hand toward the cool metal wall.

Knock. Knock. Knock.

There's no response.

There's no response again, ever again. The hours blur into days, the days blur into nothingness. The beatings continue. The impossible tests relentlessly mock my abilities. The bloodstains remain.

I stop fighting, barely ducking away from the blows that continually rain down. I pick at my food, only eating when the hunger is so intense that its pain is worse than all of the others consuming my body. I'm sorry, Sparks. I'm not as strong as you. You died with all of your fire still burning. I'm still alive, yet only a charred husk of me remains.

Knock. Knock. Knock.

CHAPTER 29
SPARKS

It's been nine days. Nine small scratches into the wood of the bed frame. Nine days that Astrid has been alone, waiting for me. Nine endless days.

Hudson opens his eyes, rolls over, and threads his arm around my waist. He leaves a trail of kisses along my shoulder.

I hate him.

I hate his puppy dog eyes as he dotes on me like a spoiled housewife. I hate the chain tethering me to this bed any time we're not doing a photoshoot. I hate his camera, constantly capturing my vulnerability, forcing me to smile like a glitzed-up pageant queen. I hate how gentle he is every time his hands caress my body, every time I fake an orgasm despite my utter contempt for him.

I hate him.

His fingertips graze my stomach before pulling my lips to his. I know what comes next. He loves the way my body feels first thing in the morning. Every day is the same. He'll roll over and whisper sweet nothings, worshiping me on the altar he forced me to sit on.

Nothing like Jack. Jack took pride in leaving bruises and welts, choking me until I passed out. It was clear where we stood. Behave, or else. It's not like that with Hudson. His touch is so gentle and tender, it's nauseating. It doesn't feel like what I know abuse and rape to be. Just once, I want him to snap. Yank my hair, bite my neck, growl savagely as he goes down on me. That would feel more real than his adoring smiles and imitated affection. It would feel less like Astrid.

At first, I thought thinking of Astrid was a coping mechanism, a way to detach myself, keep myself strong. Now, I'm not so sure. The way he moves, the way he touches me, the way he talks. It's eerily similar to her. I remember all of the moments he intruded on – Astrid and I talking on the roof, our date to the carnival, making love to her in her apartment. Is it possible he… studied her? It's almost as if he is trying to replicate her affection, copying known strategies of wooing me. To think of Astrid as he touches me just feels like a betrayal to her. No, hitting me would be better, would feel better.

Today will be different. Today I'll lead, forcing him to try a new tactic. It'll be faux passion, but at least it will be something I can control, something I have a say in. God knows there's nothing else that I can do anything about.

Before Hudson can slide onto me, I push his shoulders into the mattress. He raises an eyebrow, but submissively lets me take the reins. I drag my nails over his chest, smiling when I get a faint hiss to escape his lips. He springs free of his boxers as I pull down the waistband. I move to straddle him, but my leg is pulled out from under me and I fall onto his chest. I turn and glare at the thick, weighty chain tautly holding back my ankle. My mask shatters.

"No!"

One thing. I wanted to do one thing. He dresses me, feeds me, touches me. Just this once, I wanted to at least dictate the terms of my rape. I'm sick of this bed, sick of this room. I'm sick of waiting, biding my time, playing the role that he crafted for me.

"Get it off!" I scream, tugging at the chain with both hands. Angry tears stream down my cheeks as the chain clanks, otherwise unperturbed by my outburst. Hudson places a hand on my shoulder, but I shrug him off, hysterically struggling with my restraint. "Get it off! I swear to god I'll break my leg or this bed, whichever snaps first!" That got his attention.

"Charlotte!" Hudson pins my shoulders to the mattress, straddling my hips. I jerk underneath him, still fighting to free my ankle. "Charlotte, stop!"

"Hudson, please." I look through my tears into his eyes, his concern blatantly splashed across his face. I try to think of what I should be saying, instead of the spew of profanity I want to spit so badly. "Please, take it off. It's been a week. I've been perfect. I haven't done anything wrong."

Hudson hesitates, skeptically searching my face for lies and deceit. It just makes me cry harder, certain that he was going to walk away and leave me here.

"Hudson," I beg, my voice cracking. "Just five minutes, please."

"You're right," he whispers, stroking my hair. "I haven't given you a chance to earn back my trust. That's not fair."

I watch him as he digs the key out of the dresser and unlocks the cuff around my ankle. Instantly, I jerk my leg away, hugging it to my chest. Hudson detaches the anchor and places the chain back in the dresser. He comes back to the bed and wraps me in his arms.

Breathe, Sparks. Play the role. Put the mask back together. I lean into his shoulder, burying my face into his neck.

"Thank you," I mumble, although my stomach lurches at the thought of thanking this man for anything.

"You're welcome, Charlotte."

I decide right here and now, I will not be here for a tenth day. Fuck Hudson. Fuck this cabin.

Hudson makes us breakfast – oatmeal with fruit. Hudson does my makeup – red lipstick and eyeliner. Hudson picks out my outfit – yet another evening gown. This one is deep maroon with a sweetheart neckline and long sleeves. Yippee, I can wear a bra with this dress. Fuck Hudson.

"Do you want to take pictures outside?" I offer as Hudson glides the zipper up my back.

"No, we'll stay inside." At first I think he still doesn't trust me – he shouldn't – but he continues, "It's supposed to rain soon."

"Ah, wouldn't want to ruin my makeup." I smooth out the front of the dress.

"The only thing that can smudge your makeup is my lips," he whispers in my ear. He runs his fingers through my hair, detangling my curls.

"Maybe I do want to ruin my makeup then," I purr, leaning my head back. I resist the urge to gag. I know what he wants. I can give it to him.

"Go stand along the wall," he chuckles. "That will be a nice backdrop."

"Actually Hudson," I say demurely, fluttering my eyelashes. "Would you be okay if I stood near the fireplace? I'm a bit cold."

"Of course, Charlotte." The eyelashes always fucking work. He rubs my arms, trying to impart some warmth.

I smile gratefully as I walk toward the fireplace. The truth is, I'm not cold. Honestly, I'm actually a little warm. But Hudson doesn't have to know that.

I kneel in front of the mantle, draping the skirt to show off my curves. The camera still makes my skin crawl. The lens is always there, watching, capturing my image for him to fixate on later. It doesn't change anything. I have to play the role. Smile. Bat your eyelashes. You'll kill him soon. I know the poses he likes, easily cycling through them as the camera shutter goes wild. *Click. Click. Click.*

"You look beautiful." Hudson lowers the camera, taking a second to stand there and admire me. Prick.

I lower my head, hiding behind my hair. My eyes flick up to his, and he is transfixed. Hook, line... I stand up slowly, each move deliberate and precise. My hands sneak behind my back and lower the zipper. The dress falls from my frame, crumpling on the floor. Hudson gasps as the firelight backlights my silhouette. Sinker.

"I'm going to the bedroom." I step out of the dress and kick it behind me. "I hope you'll keep me company."

I stride off toward the bedroom, not waiting for his response. My hips sway sensually as I walk. I risk a glance behind, relieved to find he is following me. Keep your eyes on me, asshole.

In the bedroom, I grab his lapel and shove him against the wall. Hudson tenses before my lips crash into his. He relaxes then, hitching one of my legs against his hip.

"You always touch me so gently," I whisper into his ear. "I've been craving something a bit more... assertive. I think it's time I show you how to fuck, instead of making love."

"I know how to fuck." A deep growl comes from his throat.

"I'm not convinced." Stall, Sparks. We need time.

Hudson takes that as a challenge, lifting me and throwing me onto the bed. He straddles me before the mattress can fully absorb the shock, placing a hand over my throat. A wave of panic washes over me, but I force it down. Be careful what you wish for.

He grips both of my wrists in his other hand, pinning them above my head. I squirm beneath him, hoping it reads as playful and not scared. He's too busy kissing me to notice. His tongue forces his way into my mouth, exploring my teeth. He pulls away suddenly, letting go of me as he does.

"Do you smell something?" He asks, alarmed.

"Just you." I grab his lapel and pull him back down. "And you smell good."

I move to kiss him again, but he's not satisfied by my explanation. Shit, I need more time. He jogs back into the living room, and I slide on the nightgown that I discarded earlier. I freeze as I see the wall of fire enveloping the far wall, already billowing thick black smoke.

Huh. Maybe I don't need to stall any more.

Hudson jumps into action, filling a bucket of water at the sink. It's far too late for that. I sprint to the door, tugging at the handle. Even in broad daylight, I can't figure out why the door won't open. There are no visible locks. The window is barred. How the fuck does the door open?

"Hudson!" I cry out. "I can't open the door!"

"We need to put out the fire!" He flings the bucket of water at the flame. It doesn't slow the growing inferno.

"Hudson!" I'm starting to actually get concerned now. "Hudson, help me!"

He takes a step back, calculating something in his head. His math comes out close to mine and he abandons his firefighting efforts. Hudson races to his desk, grabbing a phone hidden in one of the drawers.

"Hudson!" I shout again. "Open the fucking door!"

"I'm coming!"

Hudson steps in front of me and reaches through the window. The pane of glass hinges and lifts up. I hear him fumbling with a deadbolt on the outside of the door. Motherfucker. I hate this cabin.

He swings open the door and we run into the dry scrublands surrounding the cabin. Small patches of dying prairie dot the steppes as the wind rips through the canyon. My hair violently whips around my face as the billowing smoke rises in the sky.

"I don't understand," Hudson mumbles, staring at the blazing cabin. "I've always been so careful. What happened?"

He turns to me, expecting a submissive, scared captive, but I've let my mask drop.

"You." He stares at me, putting together the pieces in his mind. "How did you know to put on your nightgown?"

"How do you think?" I spit, my rage amplified by my swirling hair. I feel powerful now that we are on level terms.

"How did you know?!" He steps toward me aggressively. I hold my ground, refusing to cower.

"Oh Hudson," I mock, portraying an overly sweet voice. "Let me just stand over here by the fireplace while I undress. Then you can take me into the bedroom and rape me to your heart's content!" My gaze darkens as I drop the persona. "It wasn't hard."

"Rape?" A pained look spreads across his face. "Charlotte, I love you, and you love me."

"This isn't love." I clench my hands into fists at my side as he advances closer. "Where is Astrid?"

"I told you," he growls, anger returning to his features. "She's with Derek."

"Stop lying to me!" I leap across the sand, tackling him to the ground. Right hook. Left uppercut. Right hook. "Where is she?!"

Hudson shoves me off and I jump to my feet. We circle each other, deciding our next moves. Hudson speaks first.

"Charlotte, stop this right now." His voice is edged with warning. He wipes the blood from his lip. "Nothing has happened that can't be forgiven. Kneel with your hands behind your head and this doesn't have to go any further."

"You're never touching me again," I seethe.

"We'll see."

And with that, he pounces. His arm wraps around my waist, but he can't hold onto the slippery fabric of my nightgown. I jerk my knee up, catching his chin. He grapples with me and we roll through the dust, each vying for dominance over the other.

You won't always be fighting boys. Derek's lessons flash through my mind. *You'll have to fight men.*

The hours spent in the ring, getting my ass beat. The bruised jaws, bleeding noses, split lips. It was all for this moment. To prove that I could defend myself. I won't be weak. I won't be vulnerable. I won't.

They'll fight dirty. Hudson wins the grapple, pinning my wrists together.

They'll be bigger than you. I buck my hips, trying to shake him off. He doesn't falter.

Stronger than you. I struggle in his grip. This isn't how this ends. He doesn't get to win this.

"Charlotte, stop fighting!" Hudson growls, inches away from my face. He's been pulling his punches this whole time, trying not to hurt me. This riles me further. How dare he? How fucking dare he?!

You need to be smarter than them. I know what he wants. I can give it to him.

I crash my lips into his, craning my neck to reach. He falters, caught off guard. His grip loosens, not much, but just enough for me to rip a hand free. I lash out, striking him in his throat. He chokes, gasping for air. I feel blindly to the side, searching for anything I can use.

My hand finds something smooth, something heavy. I grab it, slamming it into his head. I hear a crack as the rock connects with his skull, and Hudson buckles, crumpling to the ground. I don't let up. I kneel over him, raining down blow after blow after blow.

His eyes stare lifelessly into the distance. He's dead. I killed him.

I clutch the rock to my chest as I scream, releasing my anger and fear and desolation. I killed him. He won't be showing up four months from now, taunting me with his trademark smirk. He won't lurk in the shadows, intruding on my private moments with the god-awful click of the camera shutters.

I killed Jack.

I killed Hudson.

And if anyone ever dares to touch me again, I'll kill them too.

Wait, shit!

Astrid!

I shake his shoulders, hoping there's a glimmer of life left within him, but it's too late. He's gone. Dead. Lifeless. The knowledge of Astrid's location died with him.

His desk. I need to search his desk. I stumble to my feet, but the fire has spread. The cabin is now entirely engulfed in flames. There's no way in. Anything valuable would be long gone by now. Fuck! Shit! Goddamn it! I throw the rock, finding no pleasure as a plane of glass shatters.

Think, Sparks. Think!

His truck is parked off to the side. It's unlocked, keys in the cupholder. Nothing in the glovebox. Nothing in the backseat. I unlatch the tailgate and roll up the tarp to find two duffels in the bed. Here we go. I unzip one to find standard survival gear. This would have come in handy a few weeks ago. Knives with sheaths, rations, compass, other shit. I grab two knives and set them to the side, zipping the rest back up. The other duffel has two sets of clothes in it. One set is clearly too big for me, I disregard those items. In my size, I find a pair of leggings, a black sports bra, a leather jacket, and combat boots. It will have to do. I slide off the blood-soaked nightgown and toss it to the ground. Once dressed, I clip both of the knives to my legs, one on each thigh.

Then I remember. The last thing Hudson did before evacuating the cabin was grab a phone. I steal it from his corpse, kicking him in the ribs for good measure. Asshole. The screen lights up and I navigate to the maps app. The GPS puts me somewhere in western North Dakota. How the fuck did I get to North Dakota? I remember how hungry I was when I woke up in that shipping crate. How long was I out? It doesn't matter now.

Focus. There are no saved locations on the map. No history tracking. I don't know where he's been. No call history, no text messages, no memos in the notes app. My chest tightens as I face each dead end. I need to find Astrid. I have to.

The last app on the phone is the contacts. Only two names are listed, "The Target" and "The Director." I click on the Target and find my phone number listed in black and white. I delete the contact with a shudder. I select the Director. Same as mine, just a phone number. No other details or context. It's my only lead. Deep breath. Dial. The phone rings once, twice, three times. Then someone answers.

"You have some nerve calling me, Hudson." A female voice comes through the line. Crisp, controlled, venomous. She sounds familiar. Is this that bitch from the gala? "Where is the asset?"

"I'm sorry, Hudson can't come to the phone right now," I speak slowly, forming a plan as I go. "Can I take a message?"

"Charlotte?" The lady laughs. "What a lovely surprise!"

"Fuck off," I snap. "Where's Astrid?"

"Who? Astrid?" She pauses, playing with me. "Oh, Astrid! I saw her just yesterday. Her voice is so precious when she screams. 'Charlotte, where are you?' 'Help me, Charlotte!' Highlight of my day."

"You touch her and I'll kill you." I grip the phone tightly, allowing my malice to seep through the microphone. "Tell me where she is."

"Interested in a reunion?" The phone pings as I receive a text. It's an address. "We're happy to pick you up."

"Don't bother. I'm on my way."

I disconnect the call and type the address into the maps. It's about forty-five minutes away. Raindrops splat onto the truck windshield as I shift into gear.

I'm coming, baby. Hold on.

CHAPTER 30

ASTRID

I hear the beeping outside. My crate teeters as a forklift lifts me up, taking me somewhere else. I don't even lift my head. It's fine. I don't care. There's no difference between a beating in this hell or the next.

My thoughts are interrupted as my box tumbles from the forklift. I yelp as I am tossed around. Up becomes down, becomes up again. Curses spew from outside as men try to load the crate. I lean against the cold metal wall, indifferent. It doesn't matter where they take me. I'm never going home.

Memories of my family flash through my mind. My father tossing me in the lake. My brother, Liam, holding my phone just out of reach. My mother taking me shopping for back-to-school clothes. Mimi teaching me about spirits, showing me how to draw runes. I'll never see them again.

I wonder if Mimi has tried to reach out to my ghost yet.

I wonder if she was relieved when I didn't answer, or if she knew that death would be preferable to where I am now. Sparks told me that once, long ago. Said that I should kill myself before I let them take me. I should have believed her.

Sparks. I'll never see her again either. I keep hearing her final screams, calling my name. I want to remember her happy – riding her motorcycle down the freeway, dancing with me in the club, throwing snowballs through the air. But I can't. Every memory disintegrates, replaced by only her screams. They keep me company throughout the drive to who knows where.

Eventually, we come to a stop and the door to my cell opens. I sit there as a man ties a blindfold over my face, my vision restricted by the black cloth. I am hauled to my feet, arms gripped callously by two men. The truck drives away once we are clear. The men lead me stumbling through the rain.

I fight the urge to keep myself dry. No powers. That's the rule. Breaking the rules only leads to pain and punishment. I lose my footing on a patch of mud, my wet skin slipping through my guards' hands. I freeze, waiting for a blow or a kick to punish my accidental transgression. We must be in a hurry since it never comes.

Instead, they yank me to my feet, and we continue inside. They guide me to an industrial staircase, groaning as I stumble up the stairs. Frustrated, one tosses me over his shoulder for the remainder of the climb. I hang limply, my hair tickling my arms. At the top of the stairs, I am slumped off his shoulder. I move to stand, but a backhand strikes my face. They drag me to a railing, cuffing each hand to a rung. My hands are wrapped around thick metal bars. A metal grate cuts into my knees as I kneel submissively.

This is it. They've finally decided to execute me. Why else would they bother to move me? Mixed emotions run through my mind. I don't know whether to laugh or cry. Soon, the pain will be over. My aching limbs, throbbing ribs, grieving heart. I can be at peace in the afterlife, reunited with Sparks as my last breath fades.

How about one last game of five senses, just to pass the time until the executioner's axe swings?

Taste. Blood.

Smell. Blood mixed with rainwater.

Sight. Nothing, mercifully blindfolded.

Touch. Metal, cold.

Sound. Thunder crashes loudly, and I can sense the man next to me jump. I can't stop the chuckle that escapes my lips. He should be scared.

I hear it again, the storm moving ever closer. Thunder. You know what comes with thunder? Lightning. The thought soothes me, that a part of Sparks will be with me in my death.

I'm coming, Sparks. We can be together again soon. I hold the thought close as heels click along the metal walkway.

I'm coming, Sparks.

CHAPTER 31

SPARKS

Forty-five minutes is a long time. Plenty of time for me to grip the steering wheel, planning forty-five different ways to kill anyone who dared to lay a finger on Astrid. Forty-five different ways to exact my revenge. Red tints my vision as the thunder crashes. Lightning sprawls along the sky, crackling as it feathers out. I flex my hand, my scar a perfect match. Despite being mid-day, the storm darkens the sky.

They know I'm coming. They probably have a plan in place, a way to stop me. I don't feel like making it easy for them. I fumble with the silver stuck through my skin, throwing the earrings to the floorboard. My curls fall around my face in an unruly mess, matching my internal mania.

I'm coming, Astrid. Hold on.

The truck slows as I get closer to my destination. It's a large metal warehouse. The loading doors are wide open, revealing a brightly-lit room inside. A crooked grin spreads across my face. Perfect.

I pull the truck over to the side and climb onto the roof. The rain soaks my hair, dripping from the sleeves of my leather jacket. Men in riot gear pour through the open doors, forming a human barrier to the warehouse. Great, I have their attention.

"Where is she?!" I roar. No answer. Instead, they creep forward as a group.

"How many of you touched her?" I take note of the ones that flinch at my words.

I better handle this quickly. Astrid's waiting. I breathe in deeply as I close my eyes. The storm rages inside me, tumultuous, waiting to be directed. I am all too happy to oblige.

My eyes snap open as the sky flashes brightly. My hand grasps the current and I slam it down, commanding it to fragment and scatter through the group. Screams sound out as lightning strikes the ground, offshoots fling through the air until each man crumples to the dirt. Only one man survives, writhing on the ground in agony. I kneel on his chest, hand wrapped around his throat.

"Where is she?" I spit, leaning close to his ear.

"Inside," he wheezes, barely able to speak.

"Thank you."

I reach for the truck, directing its current into the sorry excuse for a man until the light leaves his eyes. His death was too quick, but I need to find Astrid. I grab his gun and check the ammunition. Rubber bullets. I toss the gun to the side. I can do better with the knives strapped to my thighs. Lightning flashes across the sky once again.

I'm coming, Astrid.

Blue sparks drip from my hands as I walk through the open doors of the warehouse. Machinery and tools cover the floor. It looks like this is some kind of workshop, hastily picked as their last stand. I pick up an iron crescent wrench, content with its weight in my hand. A group of people stand on a metal gangway above, watching me slowly approach. I see the bitch in the center, her pantsuit pressed neatly, hair coiffed without a single flyaway. Marissa, was it? I gather a ball of energy in my hand, preparing to electrify the walkway, killing them all instantly.

"Careful, sweetie," Marissa calls out, her condescension dripping like the rainwater from my hair. "I would think twice about your next choice."

"Where is she?!" Anger fuels me as the wind rips at my clothes and hair. I am a vortex of energy with only one goal. "Tell me where she is or I will kill you right here, right now."

"If you kill me, you kill her." Marissa leans forward, wrapping her hands along the thick metal railing. She glances to the left and I follow her gaze to the trembling figure kneeling at the end of the walkway. A blindfold is ripped off, and blue eyes meet mine.

Astrid.

The breath is ripped from my lungs as I see her again. Her eyes, normally full of light and life, are dull. Her long blonde hair is tangled and matted, its luster lost. She's shaking as her hands grip the railing, her torso covered in dark blotches. My fists clench as I realize that those marks are bruises, layered from several beatings. Dried blood has left trails from a cut on one of her eyebrows and a split lip.

"You're alive?" Astrid says in disbelief. "But... I heard the gunshots. They killed you."

"They gave it a go, but I'm okay." My heart breaks seeing the emotions flickering across her face. I can't imagine what she went through this past week, but I'm here now. "I'm going to get you out, Astrid."

"You shouldn't have come back," she speaks softly, as if every word hurts. Tears well in her eyes. Her head droops, lowering her gaze to her knees. "You're supposed to be in San Francisco."

"I couldn't go without you, baby." I step forward. I just want to run my hands through her hair, tell her everything will be alright. "From now until forever, remember?" A tear rolls down Astrid's cheek.

"How touching!" Marissa clasps her hands to her chest. "I love a romantic reunion, but unfortunately, I have other things to do today. Be a good dear, Charlotte, and get down on your knees, hands behind your head."

"Go to hell, Marissa." I twirl the wrench in my hand. The electricity in the building flickers as I hold it in my grasp. "Let me know when you're ready, Astrid."

"Astrid, do you need me to remind you of the rules?" Marissa hisses, slowly making her way down the walkway. Astrid shakes her head, her white knuckles gripping the railing. Marissa stands next to her before looking back at me. "You see, Charlotte, Astrid has been a very attentive student. She knows the rules, even if you do not. Astrid knows better than to use her powers. It's not permitted."

"Astrid, don't listen to them!" I run forward and hurl the wrench through the window closest to her. The glass shatters, rain falls onto the windowsill. "There's your water! Use it!"

Instantly, everyone on the gangway aims their guns at Astrid. She cowers, ducking away from the barrels. Marissa yanks a fistful of hair, forcing Astrid to meet her barbaric gaze.

"I didn't do anything!" Astrid shrieks, pleading desperately. "I wasn't— I didn't—" She sobs wretchedly as Marissa releases her grip, smiling arrogantly at me.

"Seems our training worked," she taunts as the men lower their guns. She turns to me. "I'm excited to break you too."

Astrid. How did this happen? You promised to stay strong, to keep fighting. Please, don't give up. Don't say I'm too late.

I roll my shoulders back. Her story won't end like this. I quickly count the men standing on the gangway. Ten men, give or take. I can do this on my own.

I spare one last look at Astrid. Tears glisten as they roll down her cheeks. She glances up at me, grief etched over her face. Then, so quickly I think I imagine it, she winks.

CHAPTER 32

ASTRID

Funny thing about tears – nobody pays attention to where they fall. Good example, my tears fell from my cheeks onto my arms, where they crept slowly into the locking mechanism of my cuffs.

Sparks. She's alive. I almost don't believe it, but she's right there. Her fiery temper flaring brighter than her scarlet curls. It's all I can do to kneel here and resist the urge to run into her arms. She came back for me.

She falters when she sees me cowering below Marissa. Sparks has always been strong and brave, even though I know she's been beaten down and broken before. Seeing her raw anger crackling off as streaks of light, it ignites something inside me. I crawl out of my hole, reaching for her hand at the end of the tunnel. And now, it's time to dance.

I wink at Sparks as the water in my cuffs freezes. They fall from my wrists, and I jump to my feet. My left hand knocks aside the gun pointed at me, while my right strikes Marissa in her perfect, plastic face. God, that felt so good. Marissa stumbles back as the man lunges at me. I'm slower than I'm used to, malnourished and dehydrated. I try to sidestep his grasp, but his hand wraps around my throat. Sparks screams as I am hoisted over the railing, my feet dangling in the air. She sprints toward the staircase, but she won't make it in time to help. I glance through the open window, exhaling as I feel the torrent of rainfall at my disposal. It's my turn to teach a lesson.

A wave of water bursts through the opening, freezing into a wall and cutting the rest of my assailants off. It's just me and him. I grab his wrist and kick off from the railing as a stray stream of water gives me a boost. He topples over the guardrail, arms flailing wildly. My fingers catch the bottom rung of the railing and I strain my muscles, trying and failing to pull myself over the gate. God, how much strength did I lose in the past few days?

Sparks is there a second later, reaching down for me. I clasp my hand in hers, and she hauls me over the bar. I fall into her arms. She squeezes me so hard I can't breathe, but I don't mind. I thought I'd never feel her embrace again.

"Stand behind me," Sparks whispers as she brushes my hair from my face. Her eyes frantically scan my face, no doubt concerned with the exhaustion etched onto my face alongside the bruises.

"Marissa is mine," I pant, my fatigue catching up to me.

"We can make that happen." She wraps her pinky around mine.

Together, we stand, shoulder to shoulder. We lock eyes and she nods. Showtime.

I unfreeze my wall of water, pushing it toward the trapped kidnappers. Sparks throws a shard of electricity, and the electrified current washes over them. Sparks strides toward the group, her cold rage wafting off her. She unholsters her knives, throwing one into the neck of a man reaching for his gun. The other she keeps, slicing through flesh as she twirls into the mass. Man, I love watching her work.

I support from the back, trying to stay out of her way. Tendrils of water lash out, snatching guns from the ground before they can be reclaimed by those who dropped them. A shard of metal clints in the light. Someone pulled the knife out of his fallen comrade. He's hugging the grate, crawling to Sparks's blind side. No fucking way, asshole.

I leap through the air, a tendril of water in my hands. The liquid turns solid as I wrap it around his neck. The knife clatters the ground as he tries to wedge his fingers underneath the noose, but his hands only splash the water futilely. His breathing turns to strangled gasps until a knife is driven into his chest. Sparks removes the blade, wiping the steel clean on her leggings. Dang, she looks so hot covered in the blood of other people.

"Thanks," she says casually.

"You're welcome." I look up and find all nine men crumpled on the gangway. Only one person is left, her pantsuit splattered with crimson.

Marissa stands at the end of the passage. Her chin is raised high, a defiant look plastered on her face. She holds a stun gun in her hands, aimed at me.

"Astrid, stop this right now," she commands. "Kneel."

"Oh, Marissa," I mock, remembering her cruel taunts. I walk up to her and run a finger along her jaw. "I don't have to. You're in no position to make any demands."

Marissa panics, lashing out at me. She expects me to scream, to convulse from the current as it connects with my skin. Instead, she falls to the ground as Sparks redirects the charge, forcing her to experience the pain she tried to inflict on me. Sparks strides forward, her eyes glowing from unleashed power. She stops suddenly as I hold out my arm. Her fists clench at her side, but she stands down as I crouch next to Marissa.

"Did that hurt?" I ask, fake concern in my voice. "I wonder what that feels like."

"Are you really going to crawl back to her?" Marissa spits. "She left you here. You can't trust her. How long until she leaves you again?"

I look down at my arms, covered in painful bruises.

"Don't listen to her!" Sparks steps forward, knife glistening with power, but I hold up my hand once again.

Sparks steps back while she angrily clutches her knife, sparks flying from her fingertips. I stare at her, contemplating Marissa's words. *How long until she leaves you again?*

Memories of Sparks flash through my mind. Tackling the man in the forest. Flinging her knife in the alley behind the gala. Reclining on her motorcycle after I was released from prison. Protecting me at Synergy Labs. Stepping off the train as it chugged toward San Francisco. Even when she hated me, she was always beside me.

"I don't know where Sparks has been," I confess. "I don't know why she left. But you see, it doesn't matter either way. Why? Because I trust her. And through everything, she has always come back for me."

Marissa's face pales as I form a perfect marble, rolling the water around my fingers. I've gotten quite good at it over the past week. I flick my fingers, and the orb flies toward her head. I chuckle as Marissa flinches, the orb a hair's breadth away from her forehead.

"I knew you couldn't do it," she cackles. "The vigilante afraid to kill. You don't have it in you."

"Maybe you're right." I shrug as I stand up. "Maybe you're wrong. Maybe I want you to live the rest of your life knowing that despite everything, you could have died tonight."

I turn and extend my hand toward Sparks. Marissa shifts behind me and Sparks screams. I whip around as

Marissa pulls the trigger of her concealed pistol. My face pales. Blood splatters onto her pantsuit. The bullet flies wide as a knife protrudes from her chest.

"Astrid!" Sparks whirls me around to face her, searching for injuries. Seeing none, she pulls me tightly against her chest. "What did I say about bad guys? You have to finish the job!"

"What the heck, Sparks?!" I push her away. "You almost killed me!"

"What?" She blinks rapidly, confused by my outburst. I point to the knife that barely missed my shoulder. "I've been practicing!"

Laughing at her defense, I wrap her in my arms. Sparks burrows her head in my neck, holding me tightly.

"I didn't leave you," she whispers. "I swear, every single day I was trying to get back to you."

"I believe you." Her hair is soft in my fingers. My tears slide down her jacket, dripping through the grates of the floor. "Just promise you'll stay with me, from now until forever."

"I promise," she says breathlessly. "From now until forever."

EPILOGUE
CHARLOTTE

Astrid finally rode a train with me, all the way from North Dakota to Boston. We waited until she got released from the hospital first though. It was hard to explain why she was covered with bruises, and why I was dripping blood that wasn't mine, but eventually the doctors just shook their heads and gave Astrid some much needed pain meds.

I called Derek from the lobby. It took ten minutes for him to stop screaming long enough for me to say anything, and another twenty for him to stop crying. Once he was calm, he wired me the money for the train tickets. A few days and several transfers later, he's screaming at me in person before wrapping me in his arms. Licorice happily licks Astrid's palm. Bitch didn't even notice I was gone, ungrateful cat. She makes it up to me by sitting in my lap the entire cab ride back to the cafe. I move back in with Astrid, content to wake up every morning to the smell of hot chocolate and the loving caress of her hands.

But today is the big day. I take a breath and walk through the doors. Astrid squeezes my hand, giving me a burst of confidence. She looks beautiful in her white dress. I turn to the man standing between us.

"One library card application please." My chest is tight, my palms are sweaty.

"Absolutely." The elderly gentleman smiles as he grabs a form. "Name?" Astrid holds her breath.

"Charlotte Jennings." I say calmly. Boom. Nailed it. He doesn't have to know how long I practiced in the mirror last night. That is, until Astrid starts cheering next to me.

"Yes!" She pumps her fist. "That's my girl!"

I laugh and pull her in for a kiss, her enthusiasm infectious. The man slides the clipboard across the counter, unsure what to make of Astrid's crazy reaction. We fill out the application, and I leave the building holding a brand-new library card.

"Heck yes!" Astrid gives me a high-five.

"Driver's license and a library card." I smile, feeling proud of myself. "What's next on my mission to reenter society?"

"The IRS." Astrid wags her finger at me.

"Fuck no."

"What about getting your GED?" She offers instead, trying not to laugh.

"Yeah." I nod my head. "That sounds great."

Astrid leans toward me, eyes closed. I cup her cheek in my hand and brush my lips against hers, teasing her with a slight electrical charge. She jumps back, startled by the shock. I throw my head back, laughing as she rolls her eyes. I've been laughing a lot lately. So has Astrid.

"Come here, you jerk."

She weaves her fingers in my hair, pulling me into her. I oblige, holding her body flush against mine. My lips meet hers, and this time, a different kind of spark runs through my body. No more running. No more hiding. Just the two of us, wrapped in the arms of the other.

From now until forever.

Looking for your next read?

Stay tuned for
a sneak peek of
LOVE FROM THE
SHADOWS

Coming Summer 2025

LOVE FROM THE SHADOWS

VIVIANNA

My entire life, one thing has been true. The Palazzos protect the Maranos. One statement. One fact. As undeniable as gravity or the moon. Grass is green. Two plus two equals four. Garlic doesn't belong in carbonara. The Palazzos protect the Maranos, and I'm a Palazzo.

It's been this way for generations, far longer than since our families emigrated to the U. S. from Italy. The details of this arrangement have been lost to time. Vague family legends speak of a life debt owed from when a Marano saved a Palazzo centuries ago, but the truth of the story is, the origin doesn't matter. My ancestors created the Ombra, the protective shadow always a step behind, silently standing guard over the one we shield. Grass is green. Two plus two equals four. Garlic doesn't belong in carbonara. My life's purpose is to join the Ombra and protect the Maranos.

Or, it should be. It would be if I was a man. Instead the role falls to my twin, Vincenzo. From a young age, he trained with firearms, blades, fists. Instead of geometry and physics, his education consisted of first aid and defense training. They didn't know what to do with me. My mother tried to entice me with cooking and housekeeping lessons, teaching me to be the perfect wife for a good Italian husband, but it didn't fit. Then, much to my mother's chagrin, my father pulled me into Vinny's lessons.

"Enzo needs a training partner," he said. "Someone his age to push him to improve. Let Anna help him."

She protested with excuse after excuse, wanting to raise me as a proper woman to be wed off, much like her own life. But she married into the Palazzo family. She doesn't understand. The Palazzos protect the Maranos. And I'm not a woman, I'm a machine.

It didn't take long for me to catch up to Vinny, and even less time to surpass him. I excelled, spending all of my free time in the shooting range or the gym, pushing myself harder and harder. Meanwhile, Vinny seemed to withdraw, begrudgingly going through the motions of training. I still don't understand how he doesn't want this, to fulfill the Palazzo legacy and become a member of the Ombra, especially when it comes to Damian Marano.

Dad is responsible for protecting his father, but Damian, he is our duty. No, my brother's duty. Born just a few months apart, Vinny and Damian were sent on playdates since before they could talk. I have always been kept away from Damian, though I sneak glances through the kitchen window to catch glimpses of his black hair, carefully combed out of his face. Our interactions come in small moments. His voice as he says my name. His smile as I deliver biscotti to Vinny's room. His eyes catching mine as someone closes his car door. Then he is gone again, ushered back to the compound of his father's mafia, where he waits until Vinny is old enough to protect him. Turns out, the magic age is sixteen.

My mother has never been more restless in her life — fluffing pillows and picking lint off of Vinny's suit jacket. Dad walks into the living room and wraps his hands around her waist, lightly kissing her neck. She relaxes into him and just for a moment, she smiles. Dad tousles my hair as he moves to sit next to Vinny.

"I'm so proud of you, Enzo." Dad beams, nudging Vinny's shoulder. "Finally joining the Ombra, becoming a man."

"Thanks, Dad." His voice is quiet, submissive. He doesn't lift his eyes from the black material of his suit sleeves, a perfect match to Dad's. Every member of the Marano syndicate wears the same black suit. Vinny got his today. I'll never have one. Maybe that's why today I'm wearing a black dress, trying to pretend in some way that this isn't the day my dreams finally wither and I am left behind, trying to pretend that today I am also pledging my life in service to Damian.

But I'm not.

Instead, I'm summoned to the kitchen to help Mom put the finishing touches on the tiramisu. The doorbell rings and I hear Mr. Marano excitedly greet my father. The two are practically inseparable, both physically and emotionally. Best friends. Companions. Confidantes. The ideal Ombra and protectee.

I take our finest china to the table, meticulously setting each place setting as I try to duck the melancholia floating aside me. Napkin. Fork. Knife. Spoon. Napkin. Fork—

"Hi, Viv."

Only one person calls me by that nickname.

"Damian." I glance up to see him casually standing in the entryway. It seems Damian also got his suit today, crisply pressed and tailored to his frame. A sleek tie is carefully knotted around his neck, setting him apart from Dad and Vinny. The suit makes sense on him, befitting his smooth charm and suave confidence. "I like your suit."

"Thanks," Damian chuckles, smoothing his lapel. He steps into the dining room fully and grabs a few wine glasses from the hutch. "I can set these out for you."

"Oh, this isn't something you need to worry about." I reach out to take the crystal from him, but he takes a step back out of my grasp.

"I'm not worried," he counters, clutching the glasses to his chest defensively. "Let me help."

"Okay," I relent, returning to my napkins and silverware. Damian follows me to each place setting until we fully circle the table.

"What's next?" He asks. His gaze settles back onto me, awaiting instruction.

"Next you go back to the den and get ready." I lean over the table and adjust the centerpiece, spinning the vase so the prettiest flowers face the seat which I know will be Damian's later. We shouldn't be talking. I'm not supposed to interact with him. "My mother and I will finish up here, but my father is probably getting nervous that you're not spending time with Vincenzo before the ceremony."

"I would argue that I'm with the more interesting twin." He says that with such informality, though I'm acutely aware of every move he makes as he leans against the wall. "Besides, I'll see Enzo every day for the rest of my life. He can wait."

Before I can stop it, I frown ever so slightly. Vinny will be his Ombra, not me. I never had a chance. I shove my dismay down somewhere hidden inside and recollect myself, but not fast enough for Damian to miss my reaction. His eyes stare into mine, a slight flicker of concern hidden carefully behind his composed expression.

"Enzo will visit often," Damian promises. "I'm not trying to separate you two."

"I know." I turn away from him, smoothing down the perfectly fine tablecloth.

"It must be hard watching your father and your brother risk their lives for my family." His voice is soft, sympathetic. "But I swear to you, that is not something either my father or I take lightly. I'll do everything I can to keep Enzo safe."

"They'll be fine." My expression is steeled, concealing my dejected thoughts from view. "Palazzos don't go down easily."

"Viv..." His hand brushes my shoulder, and I whip around to face him, startled by the sudden contact. Damian retreats a step, hands in the air nonthreateningly. After a breath, I relax and he cautiously moves closer. His brows furrow as he scrutinizes my obscured emotions, unable to see through my practiced defenses. "Talk to me. What's wrong?"

"Damian!" Mr. Marano calls from the other room. "Where did you run off to?"

"Go," I urge softly, forcing a smile to my face. "I need to check on dinner anyway."

"We're not done," Damian protests weakly, but it's no use. I step around Damian to close the doors of the hutch before I leave the room. As I cross the threshold, I spare one final glance his direction. His head is bowed and his shoulders sag as he fiddles with his cufflinks.

"The suit really does look nice on you." I hesitate as Damian looks up at me, meeting my eyes one final time. "I'll see you at the ceremony."

With that, I leave him. My mother directs me around the kitchen, finishing this and that for dinner. She's acting as though we're cooking for the Queen, and I suppose in a sense, the Maranos are our royal family. Mr. Marano is our king, Damian is our prince, the Ombra is the guard, and I am no one. There's no place for women in the mafia. There's no place for me.

But now's not the time for my self-pity. Now's the time to celebrate Vinny. The families gather in the den. The two sons face each other in the front of the room, with their respective fathers standing proudly behind them. My dad passes a small knife to Vinny, the polished metal reflecting the ceiling light. Vinny slowly kneels before Damian. The blade shakes in his hand until Dad places a reassuring hand on my twin's shoulder. A deep breath in. He closes his eyes and presses the edge into his palm until it draws a thin line of blood. Mr. Marano nudges Damian forward and he extends his hand down to Vinny, looking just as uncomfortable as my brother. Their hands join and Vinny recites the blood oath in Italian, the words stumbling from his mouth nearly incoherent.

Then it's done. Dad bandages Vinny's hand with proud tears in his eyes. Mr. Marano claps his son on the back as Damian stares at the blood smeared on his palm. My mother clenches her hands in her lap, but I just sit there.

Numb.

Vacant.

A forced composure masks any emotion I won't let myself feel as I watch my brother get everything I ever wanted. And I just... sit there.

As the fathers continue celebrating, my mother ushers me into the kitchen. I take trays of food to the dining table. Osso buco, citrus gremolata, polenta, bread. No sooner than the last dish was laid on the tablecloth did the men stride in, glasses of whiskey in hand. Mr. Marano and my father take the head and foot of the table. Vinny and Damian sit on one side, and my mother and I sit on the other.

Mr. Marano doesn't visit often, and when he does, I never get so much as the time of day from him unless I'm doing something useful. He stops by occasionally to watch Vinny train, admonishing him when I win our spars. My successes are always viewed as my twin's failures. Even seated, his intimidating stature seems to swallow me in his shadow. The upside is, I am sitting across from Damian. So there's that.

Food is passed around, and the adults launch into jovial conversation. Vinny pushes his veal around his plate with his fork. Damian's gaze keep drifting to me, and I can see the gears turning in his head, still digesting our earlier conversation. But I was trained better than to let anything show. *Emotions make you vulnerable,* my dad would always say. *Hide them or they will be used against you.* So I don't let Damian see my disappointment. Instead, a fake smile brightens my face as I listen to Mr. Marano tell a story about my father hitting some thug over the head with a table lamp once upon a time. I chuckle absentmindedly at a joke my Dad quips and Damian quietly spreads butter onto a hunk of bread. Our eyes meet once again and linger there, his amber irises trapping me in their depth. It's no wonder I don't see the gunmen until it's too late.

BANG!

I leap over the table without a second thought, tackling Damian to the ground as a second bullet pierces the wall behind where he was sitting a second earlier. With my body shielding his, I turn and see eight pairs of boots storm into view. Who knows if there's more coming? We can't stay here.

"Dad!" Damian screams from below me, reaching for his father's crumpled form. Blood seeps from the wound in his forehead. He's dead. My mother's shrieks cut through the sound of the gunshots. I risk a glance up and see my father firing at the horde of men streaming into the doorway. Vinny is crouched under the table, eyes wide.

"We have to go!" I tug on Damian's arm, urging him to follow me, but instead he crawls to his father, shaking his shoulders as if he was only asleep.

"No, Dad!" Damian's voice cracks in desperation, but we can't stay here. There's no time for compassion as bullets continue to fly.

I yank Damian harder, and he slips in the growing pool, drenching his new suit in ruby blood. My cruelty persists as I drag him to his feet, forcing him to abandon his father's corpse to try and save his life. He staggers behind me still in shock as I lead him to the wine cellar, taking the stairs down two at a time. We sprint toward the back, and I pull on the sconce hiding the false wall, grunting at the exertion of moving the heavy bricks. Damian's hands wrap around mine lending his strength, and the emergency exit is revealed. This was put in ages ago, originally meant for Mr. Marano, but it seems it will only benefit his son now.

"Get in." I wave frantically. "There's a kit at the end of the passage with a burner phone. Call someone you trust."

"You're not coming?" His eyes widen in alarm. "I can't just leave you!"

"They're not here for me." I glance over my shoulder as gunshots echo down the stairs. How much longer can my dad hold them off? "I can buy you time to escape, but you have to go *now*!"

"Viv," he pleads, his hands trembling at his sides. "They'll kill you."

For the first time, I don't see Damian as a god-like figure, as a Marano lifted onto a pedestal. Instead, I see a kid, barely sixteen, covered in the blood of his father. I wonder what he sees when he looks at me. I squeeze his hand in mine, the only reassurance I have to offer.

"Palazzos don't go down easily," I whisper. Footsteps pound down the staircase and Damian's breath catches in his throat. "Go! Now!"

He pulls me into an anguished hug, and for only a second, I allow myself to absorb the slight comfort, but then I push him off into the corridor and close the wall behind him.

Focus, Vivianna. I might not be in the Ombra, but I can still protect Damian, if only for a few more seconds. I steel my nerves as I turn to face the approaching intruders. Run, Damian. Run.

◆　◇　◇　◇　◆

There's a pounding on the door an hour later. Piercing headlights glare through the windows. Help is here. Damian made it out safely. My family is sitting in the den. Silent. Dazed. Lost.

I wince as Vinny dabs my face with a wet cloth, cleaning the blood from my skin. Mom sits on a footstool, her skin pale from shock. Dad is the only one not here. He is alone in the dining room. Well, kind of alone. He refuses to leave Mr. Marano's side, though his corpse has long grown cold.

Another knock at the door. Louder. More insistent. Voices yell. My mother shakily moves to the entryway, peering through the peephole. She steps aside as men in black suits force their way in. I recognize a few of the men, including the one currently barking orders at the rest of the crew. His disgust in us is evident, and I can't blame him. We failed.

A final gunshot rings through from deep within the house. The unit draws their weapons, but Vinny beats us all to the dining room. He gasps as he steps over the threshold, but then immediately turns to block the doorway, pushing my mother and me away. Mom sees though. She falls to the floor wailing as her heart breaks.

"What happened?" I claw at Vinny's arm, trying to get by. "Where's Dad?" Tears well in Vinny's eyes. I push through as I see the gun fall from my dad's fingertips. "No... No, Vinny, help him! No!"

My father is dead.

Two funerals on the same day. My mother covers my face with a veil, trying to pretend that she can still wed me off in a few years to a respectable family. It's not likely. No one will look or stand within ten feet of us. We're social pariahs. The only ones trusted with the lives of the Marano family, and we failed.

Vinny stands behind Damian during the funerals, the perfect shadow, the perfect Ombra. He blends in among the other upper-ranking mafia members with his matching suit, or he would if he were ten or twenty years older. Damian stands at the front of the group, watching his father's casket get lowered into the ground. He is poised, composed, stoic. The scared sixteen-year-old is gone, in his place is the new Don of the Italian mob. I guess he's Mr. Marano now. He flinches as my mother sobs, watching the dirt filling in her husband's grave, but forces himself to keep his head up, shoulders back.

The priest says a final prayer and then dismisses the mourners, and for a moment, I had to admit that I was impressed by Damian. He didn't cry or show any emotion through the entire funeral, he was strong. That is, until he glances at me. Regret. Grief. Remorse. All of those feelings flicker through his face in a millisecond. He takes a step toward me, but Vinny grabs his arm in a vise, firmly whispering in Damian's ear. Damian looks at my brother and then back at me, torn by whatever my twin had to say. He stands there for a moment before mouthing two words.

I'm sorry.

That was the last time I saw Damian for ten years.

ABOUT THE AUTHOR

L. J. Wede has a guiding philosophy – write the book that you want to read. An avid lover of spicy romances, Wede delivers a passionate sequel to *Igniting the Spark,* exploring the parallels between hatred and love.

Born in rural Iowa, Wede has always had a passion for books and for reading. While she originally worked in marketing, she would choose to unwind most nights with a book. It was out of this passion for literature that she began to write her first novel and fell in love with the craft.

Follow her on social media or subscribe to her newsletter at https://ljwede.com/newsletter/ to catch her latest release.

www.ingramcontent.com/pod-product-compliance
Lightning Source LLC
Chambersburg PA
CBHW071345300726
48976CB00006B/1778